PLEASURES OF A NOTORIOUS GENTLEMAN

LORRAINE HEATH

AVON

An Imprint of HarperCollinsPublishers

This is a work of fiction. Names, characters, places, and incidents are products of the author's imagination or are used fictitiously and are not to be construed as real. Any resemblance to actual events, locales, organizations, or persons, living or dead, is entirely coincidental.

AVON BOOKS
An Imprint of HarperCollins*Publishers*
10 East 53rd Street
New York, New York 10022-5299

Copyright © 2010 by Jan Nowasky
ISBN 978-0-06-192295-4
www.avonromance.com

First Avon Books paperback printing: December 2010

Avon Trademark Reg. U.S. Pat. Off. and in Other Countries, Marca Registrada, Hecho en U.S.A.
HarperCollins® is a registered trademark of HarperCollins Publishers.

Printed in the U.S.A.

10 9 8 7 6 5 4 3 2 1

He did not force, but he invited.
She accepted the invitation.

His flavor was rich and powerful, wine and whiskey combined into a darkness that was as intoxicating as the caress of his tongue. He caused every nerve to tingle, every inch of her body to respond as though he slowly stroked her from toe to chin.

She'd dreamed of him sweeping her off her feet a thousand times. But in spite of her imaginings, she'd not been prepared for the compelling nature of his kiss, delivered with such urgency. She returned it in full measure.

She stepped into his embrace and felt as though she'd finally returned home, to the spot where one night with him had shown her she could be.

As his arms came around her, drew her even closer, she knew she was where she was meant to be.

For Patti, Lynn, Pattie, Kathee, Carol, Connie, Linda, Nancy A., Nancy D., and Merrilee

To sleepless slumber parties; walks after midnight with no fears; cruising the quiet streets of Angleton; going dateless to high school dances; pep squad; long afternoons at the beach; football games in the rain; Girls State basketball tournament our senior year; talking on the phone at all hours *for* hours; powder puff football; Bobby Sherman; the Monkees; sharing the thrill of first kisses, first crushes, and first loves; the heartache of breakups; the wonder of truly falling in love; and all our dreams of what would be . . .

To the way we were.

PLEASURES OF A NOTORIOUS GENTLEMAN

Prologue

April 1854

Stephen Lyons loved women. Tall, short, plump, slender. Young and not so young. He loved them all.

He loved most whichever woman was presently keeping him company.

He teasingly referred to her as Fancy, because she was a fancy bit of work. The illegitimate daughter of a duke, she intended to follow in her mother's footsteps and seek out a protector. While she was well aware he would not accommodate her in that regard, she knew his notorious reputation well enough to be assured he would provide her with an education in pleasure that would see her in good stead. The numerous weeks of secret trysts had not been in vain. She now possessed talented hands and a wicked mouth that had kept him pleasantly occupied until dawn.

"I'm going to miss you so frightfully much," she said, fanning her ebony hair out over the pillow, stretching languorously across the rumpled bed in a spartan room of the tavern where she'd joined him the evening before.

"You'll be warming another gent's bed before

nightfall," he said distractedly, standing at the window, buttoning his scarlet jacket.

He thought it should have bothered him that her silence acknowledged the truth: They meant little more to each other than an evening's delightful entertainment. He never promised a woman more than he could deliver, never took one to his bed without her clear understanding that she would never have him beyond the sheets.

He was grateful Fancy wasn't making a fuss, that she was already acknowledging he would no longer be in her life. Change was on the wind and he welcomed its arrival.

Exhilaration thrummed through his veins at the prospect of the escapades awaiting him once he departed this room. From his vantage point two flights up, he could see the crowds lining the street, could hear their raised voices as they sang "The Girl I Left Behind Me" while the regimental band pounded out the tune. With an excitement vibrating on the air as the sun peered over the horizon, the soldiers marched through in an undisciplined style that would be overlooked by their superiors. Who could blame them for their heady anticipation as they made their way to the railway station and the first leg of a journey that would deliver them to the Crimea? Adventure awaited. Honor. And Russian women. Stephen could delay no longer. It was long past time he joined them.

He crossed over to the bed and planted a lingering kiss on Fancy's luscious mouth: plump lips that excelled at bringing a man unbridled pleasure. When he drew back, he gave her a devilish grin. "Thanks, darling, for the lovely farewell."

"Take care of yourself. When you return—"

He touched her lips, silencing a promise that neither of them would be destined to keep. "Your allegiance will be to your protector. With my leaving, our time together is past. But I shall never forget you, Fancy, or the jolly good fun we had."

"I've no doubt you say that to all the ladies."

He didn't deny her accusation. It was the most precious gift he gave each of his paramours: the belief that she was the one he would reminisce about when the devil came to collect him for his sins.

Reaching up, she flattened her hand against his chest. "In my dreams you will continue to do wicked things to me."

He gave her his most dashing grin. "In mine as well."

Then he kissed her again for good measure, before rushing out the door, down the stairs, and into the mass of people who were celebrating as though Great Britain had just claimed victory over the Russians rather than having only recently declared war on the blighters. The regiment had been preparing for their departure for some time now. Far too many new recruits, still fresh-faced and eager, confident that success in this campaign would come swiftly.

"Captain!" a young man shouted at him, grabbing his attention.

"Mathers." With long, confident strides, Stephen fell into step beside him. The onlookers had taken up the tune of another ditty, somehow managing to cheer, clap, and wave at the same time, all with an enthusiasm that instilled confidence and belief in their cause. Boys ran alongside them, dreaming of the day when they could join them. Men clapped their shoulders, reached out to shake their hands. Women blew kisses at them.

Ah, when they returned victorious, doors to many a bedchamber would open for those who arrived to a hero's welcome. Stephen had never had any troubles in that regard, but surely coming back with tales of heroics would add a touch of spice to any flirtation, would open the arms of the shyest of maidens.

"Was afraid you wouldn't make it, Captain," Mathers shouted over the din.

"What? And leave you to give the Russians a sound beating all by yourself? Don't be daft, man."

Mathers's rumbling laughter would match the boom of any cannon fire. He was a big, brawny brute, who had toiled in the fields before setting aside his plow for a rifle. Stephen was grateful that Mathers and others like him would be at his side in the coming months while they faced whatever lay in store for them in the Crimea.

"Stephen!"

The echo of the familiar feminine voice sent desire rippling through him. Leaving Mathers, he worked his way through the cheering crowd to a brown-haired, green-eyed beauty waving her handkerchief at him. Taking her in his arms, he blanketed her delectable mouth with his before pulling her into the shadows between two buildings.

"Lady Gwendolyn, I didn't expect to see you here today."

She was breathing rapidly, as she had many times in his bed. Her flushed cheeks brought forth vivid images of the nights of pleasure they'd shared. "I wanted to give you this. It carries my perfume."

He brought the silk she'd pressed against his palm to his nose, inhaled, and closed his eyes as though in rapture. "I shall always have heaven near."

With a light laugh, she lifted herself onto her toes and kissed him quickly. His time was short. They both knew it. "Please do be careful," she pleaded.

"When I have one such as you awaiting my return, how can I not be?" Kissing her once more, he left her there with tears in her eyes while he shoved his way through the throng to rejoin the marching troops.

They were supposed to be disciplined, fierce; but they smiled as though they were on their way to a party. Not so fearsome at the moment, but it would come. They would prevail, and swiftly.

He heard another feminine voice calling his name. He spotted Katherine—Kat—waving enthusiastically on the far side. He darted in and out between the soldiers, keeping an eye on her as she dashed between the people lining the streets, until he and Kat finally met. Winding his arm around her, he held her steady, protected her from the crush of bodies while he kissed her passionately, knowing that if her father were in the vicinity, he wouldn't approve. She was fun because of her rebellious spirit and her love of adventure. He suspected that, if it were allowed, she'd be marching off with them.

"A lock of my hair is in the locket," she said.

He closed his fingers around her offering, the heart-shaped locket with a gold chain threaded through it. "Then I'll hold you near every night."

"Please return home soon."

"With you waiting, I shall not delay my return a single minute longer than necessary."

He gifted her with a final kiss of farewell before stepping back into the stream of soldiers. He was washed along as though caught in a powerful flood. There was no stopping where it would go, what havoc it would wreak, what misery would remain in its wake. But no one thought of the work ahead. They concentrated only on the rewards they'd receive when it was all over. Accolades for a job well done. Service to a country and a queen they all loved.

Mayhem followed on their heels into the railway station.

"Keep yer pecker up!" someone shouted.

Laughter followed and another man yelled, "Give 'em what fer!"

The support and enthusiasm was incredible. From the beginning, when Victoria ascended to the throne, she'd had her soldiers engaged in small skirmishes somewhere. But this one was different. From the moment war was declared, on March 27, the nation seemed to come together as it hadn't since it had faced down Napoleon. Victory was not questioned. The jubilation had begun. All that remained was for the men being sent off to deliver a sound beating before returning home to warm fires and warmer women.

"Stephen!"

He spun around at the commanding male voice he recognized as belonging to his younger half-brother, the Duke of Ainsley. How was it that at only two and twenty Ainsley could exude such power and authority, so much more than did Stephen? Perhaps because Stephen had always preferred play to responsibility, while Ainsley had determinedly taken up the reins his father had dropped upon his death. He'd always held them with a steady hand and a confidence lacking in most men twice his age.

Stephen had not expected his family to see him off,

but there they were. His mother—the present Duchess of Ainsley, not yet a dower as her youngest still had not taken a wife. Ainsley. His older brother, the Earl of Westcliffe, and his wife, the lovely Claire. Other than his mother, she was the only woman Stephen had ever loved. He'd do anything to assure her happiness. It had taken him a while to accept that the honor belonged to his brother—which was how it should be, when all was said and done—and his feelings had untangled themselves. She was more sister than lover to Stephen. But a corner of his heart would always be reserved for her.

"Surely, you all have something better to do at this ungodly hour of the morning than deal with this maddening crowd," Stephen said flippantly. He'd given them enough worry during his life. He didn't want them to view his departure as anything other than a fun adventure. Even he refused to acknowledge that it could be more difficult than anticipated.

His mother's arms were around him before the last of his words were spoken. "You're going to give me more gray hairs," she chastised lovingly.

She credited him with every one that now peppered her black hair. But at forty-five, she still cut a fine figure. She was sixteen when she'd married her first husband, the seventh Earl of Westcliffe. She'd given him two sons before he died: Morgan, the present earl, and then Stephen. The brothers, however, looked nothing alike. Westcliffe was dark and sinister in appearance, while Stephen was fair and playful, seeming not to give a care about anything. Life was to be embraced, enjoyed, and explored. It was what his family had always expected of him, and if he believed in nothing else, he believed in living up to expectations.

Leaning back, she studied him, her brown eyes searching his of blue. "There's no reason for you to go. I have influence in very high places."

He had no doubt. Her second husband, the eighth Duke of Ainsley, had been a very powerful man. She'd made certain his authority rubbed off on her. Who could blame her? Her first had left her nearly destitute. She'd done everything necessary to ensure she never again found herself in a situation that left her with no control.

"I've been accused of lacking character," he drawled. He didn't blame his family, or anyone else for that matter, for not looking below his surface. It was such an enticing surface, after all. Besides, he took nothing seriously. "What better way to build it than by defeating a few Russians?"

"But Westcliffe has forgiven you for your little prank." She glanced back at her eldest son. "Haven't you?"

The little prank, as his mother referred to it, had involved being caught in bed with Westcliffe's wife. With Claire. His brother gave a brusque nod. Stephen couldn't help but smile.

"I do hope St. Peter offers me forgiveness with a bit more enthusiasm, otherwise I'll never get through those pearly gates."

Westcliffe laughed at that. He saw the humor in things much more often now that he and Claire had reconciled. "You're not getting into heaven any more than I am."

Claire scowled at him and teasingly slapped his arm. It was good to see her so comfortable with her husband now. She'd once been terrified of him. She moved past Westcliffe and embraced Stephen. "Of course he's forgiven you. And you will get into heaven."

He doubted it. He might be on a mission to build character, but he had no plans to stop sinning while doing it. Still, he hugged her tightly. When she finally relinquished her hold on him, he held out his hand to Westcliffe. "No hard feelings."

Westcliffe grabbed his hand and tugged him near, wrapping his other arm around him, clapping him on the back. "Don't get yourself killed."

"Wouldn't dare dream of it."

Then only Ainsley remained. The baby brother who had never accepted his role as the youngest. There were times when he appeared to be even older than Westcliffe. Not in looks, but in behavior. He was far too responsible for his own good. "Take care of yourself, Puppy," Ainsley said.

"Damnation. I hate it when you call me that." It always made him feel as though he were the youngest—which he knew was Ainsley's intent. He was always admonishing Stephen to grow up. It grew quite tedious after a while, especially as Stephen had no plans to change his self-indulgent behavior.

Ainsley nodded to signify it was the very reason he used the term, squeezed Stephen's hand, and slapped him hard on the shoulder. "Get back here as soon as you can."

"This is nothing to worry over. I'll be home in time for pheasant season."

The train whistle sounded, harsh and loud.

"I must be off." He hugged his mother fiercely one last time, before rushing to board the train that would carry him toward his destiny.

Chapter 1

Northamptonshire
November 1855

Mercy Dawson thought she'd prepared herself for the shame she'd endure at this precise moment. She'd been wrong.

It hit her with a force so strong that she almost regretted her decision to return to England. She'd often heard that love was blind and fully capable of transforming even the wise into fools. Apparently, she was no exception. Love—so deep and profound that it had the power to overwhelm and bring her to tears at the most unexpected moments—had driven her here. Well, love and her father's carriage.

In spite of her conviction to the path she traveled upon, she was quite surprised that she was finding it so blasted difficult to hold her head high and meet the gaze of the Duke of Ainsley. With his black hair and sharp features, he looked nothing at all like his half-brother, Stephen Lyons. While Ainsley was the youngest of the three brothers, he wore the mantle of responsibility on his shoulders and wore it well, as though it were a second skin. He understood the influence of his title and gave the impression he wasn't one with whom a person should trifle. Within his dazzling green eyes, she saw evidence of a calculating mind while he studied her as though he'd just pinned her to a board for bugs and, after careful scrutiny, determined her to be little more than a maggot.

Obviously, he doubted the veracity of the incredible tale upon which her father had just expounded.

She was the first to look away, in the pretense of admiring her surroundings. They were in the front parlor of Ainsley's country estate, Grantwood Manor. The room, almost as large as her father's house, had more than one sitting area. White, yellow, and orange dominated the fabrics, giving the room a cheerfulness that would have welcomed her and made her smile if she were here under different circumstances. She imagined that on the coldest day of winter one could find warmth within these walls. She was presently sitting on a sofa nearest to the massive fireplace. Still, the heat from the writhing flames failed to ease the chill in her bones that had settled in while she and her father had traveled here. A chill that had intensified as Ainsley raked his gaze over her.

"Well?" her father bellowed, standing behind her as though he could no longer stomach the sight of her face. She jumped, but Ainsley's steady gaze never left her or faltered. She suspected he'd have been as courageous on the battlefield as his brother. Stephen Lyons had arrived in the Crimea as a captain, but his daring exploits during battle had seen him rise with surprising swiftness to the rank of major. "Your boy got my girl with babe. You'd damned well better do right by her."

The aforementioned babe was presently having his

cheek stroked by Ainsley's mother. The duchess looked up at her son. "He very much reminds me of Stephen at this age."

"All babies look the same, Mother."

"Not to a mother."

The duchess's formidable gaze came to bear on the new mother, and Mercy fought not to wither beneath it. She couldn't imagine possessing the confidence that these people had. She'd been forced to shore up her own courage for this encounter. She'd known it wouldn't be pleasant, but she also knew her only hope for happiness resided here. So she would stand her ground until the final bastion had fallen.

"Or to a grandmother, I suppose," the duchess added.

Mercy's original plan had been to simply leave the child here, within his relatives' safekeeping, but in the end, she'd not been able to give him up. It was astonishing, how much she'd come to love the babe in the three months since his birth. She would do anything at all to protect him, to remain with him. Sell what remained of her soul to the devil if need be.

"What did you name him?" the duchess asked.

"John."

"A strong name."

She nodded. These were good people. She shouldn't have brought her father into the matter. She should have come here first, only she hadn't known where to begin to find this family, and she couldn't very well live on the streets while she'd made inquiries. After all she'd seen and suffered during her months serving as a nurse, she'd thought her father would be as grateful to have her home as she was to have arrived. She'd known him well enough, though, to suspect he'd not look upon a new life as something to be cherished, regardless of how it had come about. Her father had not watched as hundreds of men died. He was landed gentry, and by arriving on his doorstep with a babe in her arms, she'd brought shame to him and his household.

But she didn't regret what she'd done. She couldn't. She wouldn't.

"Your father mentioned that you met Stephen during the time he served in the Crimea," the duchess said, but her voice also held a question. The East was far away, not a place to which a gentle lady should travel.

"Yes, Your Grace. I was serving as a nurse in Scutari." She'd discovered that few people truly understood the geography of the area. Although the duchess may have been an exception. In a corner of the room stood a globe, the portion of the world that had caused so much turmoil and heartache clearly in view. Mercy wondered if the duchess had pressed her hand there in an attempt to feel closer to her son, to somehow bridge the endless miles that separated them. "Many of the soldiers were brought there to be tended."

"Admirable. Then you were one of Miss Nightingale's ladies?"

Miss Nightingale. To the nurses, the doctors, and the patients, she had simply been Miss N. "Yes, ma'am."

"The newspapers paint a rather gruesome portrait of the war. I do not know how anyone could remain there with the deprivations, the cold, and illness. They say more men die of disease than battle."

Mercy nodded, forced a tremulous smile. "John is the only good thing to come out of the war as far as I'm concerned."

The duchess's brown eyes softened. Stephen had not

inherited his eyes from his mother. His were a rich, dark blue. She remembered the concern she'd seen reflected in them just before he'd taken her into his arms. So tenderly. After what she'd endured at the hands of three ruffians, she'd thought she'd be unable to suffer the touch of a man, but he had proved her wrong. How she longed for those powerful arms at this moment. But she would never again know their strength, would never again feel the firm muscles beneath her fingers. He'd been killed in September. Because of the wonder of the telegraph, the names of the fallen were known quickly and reported in the newspapers. She was surprised the duchess wasn't wearing mourning clothes, but instead wore a dress of deep purple.

"Well?" her father bellowed again. "I want to know what you're going to do for my girl."

"I suppose you're looking for some sort of monetary restitution," Ainsley said.

"That would be a start. But she's ruined. No decent man will have her now. She went to do good works and he took advantage."

"Father—"

"Shut up, girl. The last thing I expected was for you to come home with some bastard."

"Don't call John that." She would fight to the death to protect John. How could her father not see beyond the child's illegitimacy to what he meant to Mercy? In a world devoid of joy, he was the only bright spot. "Please, Your Grace, I want only to stay with John. I could serve as his nurse, his nanny. I would require very little."

"That will not do at all," her father said. "The shame that has been brought to my household . . . I demand this be made right. You, sir, Your Grace, you should step in where your brother didn't."

Ainsley's mouth twitched, and he looked as though he might burst into laughter. It was the first sign he'd given that he might not be as blasted serious as she'd assumed. "Are you suggesting I marry your daughter, sir?"

"I am indeed."

"Father, no!"

"She needs a husband," he continued as though she hadn't objected. "I'm washing my hands of her."

Madness was surrounding her. She didn't know how to stop it. "Your Grace, this is not why I brought John to you. You are his family. I expect nothing."

"Miss Dawson, do you swear that the child to whom you gave birth is my brother's son?" Ainsley asked, a kindness in his voice that had been lacking before, as though he was beginning to understand that regardless of the unconscionable position in which she found herself, she placed the child first and that her father only added to the difficulties of her situation. She was grateful that the print of his hand was no longer visible on her face. He'd slapped her for her foolishness, then slapped her for her sins.

"I swear to you, Your Grace, by all that is holy, that John is Stephen's son."

"I do not doubt it," the duchess said succinctly, her opinion obviously carrying a great deal of weight with the duke.

Ainsley nodded slowly, and then in long strides, he crossed the room and opened the door. "Find Major Lyons and inform him that I need to have a word."

Mercy was on her feet before Ainsley had finished

shutting the door. Dizziness assailed her. Her heart pounded with such force that she was certain they all could hear it. Her throat knotted up and it was all she could do to force out the words. "He's here? He can't be. He's dead."

Ainsley seemed quite surprised by her outburst. As was she. She wasn't prone to histrionics, but this turn of events was not at all expected. Relief danced with fear. This changed everything. *Everything*. Her legs weakened, but she forced herself to remain standing. Better to face the devil on her feet.

"Yes, the initial reports were that he'd died," Ainsley said, studying her. Did he have to continually examine every blasted inch of her? What the devil was he searching for, what did he hope to find? Evidence of her deception? "Considering what I've since learned of the carnage that was Sevastopol, I'm not surprised mistakes were made. He *was* gravely wounded and not expected to survive. But those who doubted his will don't know my brother. He is as stubborn as the day is long. He arrived home only a month ago. He's not quite up to snuff, still recovering."

Gladness at the news almost replaced every ounce of her common sense. Once Major Lyons strode through that door, everything would change. He would laugh at her claims, if he even remembered her. Chaos reigned on the battlefields and in the hospitals. Like thieves in the night, soldiers, doctors, nurses had stolen moments of happiness wherever, whenever, they could. Hoarded the memories away for the exhausting, dreary days when there was nothing except the blight of suffering.

Her time with Major Lyons had been brief, all too brief. But her feelings for him had still managed to blossom into an emotion she didn't understand but that frightened her with its intensity.

She jerked her gaze to John, held securely in the duchess's arms. John. Her son. Her joy. She wished she'd never handed him over. She should dart across to where he gurgled, snatch him up, and dash from the room. Only he belonged here. She couldn't whisk him away from where he belonged. He was her one opportunity for redemption, but the thought of losing him was like a knife twisting through her heart. She'd never expected he would become her salvation.

Good Lord, everything would come to light now. Everything. When Major Lyons saw her—

What if his first words revolved around her shame and suffering? But he'd promised, promised to never tell a soul. While he held her—

The door opened, the *click* echoing through the room like a rifle report. Imminent disaster loomed, but still she hungrily took in every beloved facet of him. Only he was a far cry from the man she'd come to admire, the man with whom she'd become ridiculously infatuated.

Shock reverberated through the very core of her being. He limped in, using a walking stick to steady his stride, which was not nearly as long or as confident as it had once been. He was not wearing the scarlet uniform that had made him such a dashing figure. Instead, he was dressed in a white shirt and cravat. Black waistcoat and jacket. Black trousers. As though he were in mourning.

Perhaps he was. How many of his comrades had he watched fall? How many had he held while they died on the field?

He was so thin that he barely resembled the robust

young man who had exhibited such enviable self-assurance when he'd been discharged from the hospital that first month after she'd arrived with Miss Nightingale. Then he still spoke of routing out the enemy, sending them to perdition. He urged those not yet well enough to be released to recover quickly, to get the job done so they could all go home. They were not yet defeated. She overheard him delivering rousing words to so many that he strengthened her own resolve, made her determined to see them all recovered.

But he no longer looked to be a man who believed the declarations he'd once articulated with such conviction.

A ragged, unsightly red scar trailed from just below his temple to his chin, yet it did not diminish his rugged handsomeness. But his eyes—his beautiful blue eyes—had changed the most. They held such an incredible bleakness when he looked at her that she almost wept. His wounds went much deeper than his flesh; they had penetrated his soul.

The only thing about him that remained unchanged was the shade of his hair: a golden brown with streaks of blond woven through it. She'd often wondered how it might look with the sunlight bouncing off it. But she'd met him in winter amidst gray skies. Little sun chased back the dreariness of the hospital.

She wanted to race across the room, take him in her arms, and confess everything before he had a chance to denounce her for the fraud that she was. She should be trying to determine how best to save face, but all she could do was wonder about him. What had transpired during the months since she'd last seen him? Had he even noticed that she'd left Scutari? If he'd had occasion to visit the hospital, had he asked after her? He had been so terribly important to her, but he'd never made any declarations of affection. It wasn't his way, she'd been told, but the knowledge had not stopped her from dreaming that he saw in her something special, something he saw in no other woman.

"Stephen," Ainsley began, a gentleness, a caution in his voice, a tone that one might use when confronting a wild and unpredictable beast, "surely you remember Miss Mercy Dawson. She was a nurse at a military hospital in Scutari, tending to the soldiers who fought in the Crimea."

She wondered why he'd felt the need to categorize her, to label her as though so many Mercy Dawsons filled his brother's life that he would be unable to identify which one she was, precisely. She knew of his reputation with the ladies, knew that he sought pleasure with wild abandon, but surely, he was gentleman enough to recall every woman with whom he'd experienced carnal knowledge.

Tension rippled through the room, as if they were all connected by the wires on a pianoforte, each of them waiting for a chord to be plucked.

Major Lyons studied her for a heartbeat, and then another, but she saw no recognition in his deep blue eyes. None at all. She was but one of many nurses who had garnered his attention. The mortification of this moment, of being relegated to nothingness, to being completely unmemorable in spite of all they'd shared . . . it was almost more than she could bear. She didn't know how she would survive it, but for John's sake she would.

A dilemma reared its ugly head. Should she fight for John's right to be here, to convince them that Major

Lyons was his father, or should she take her son and be done with them, find a way to survive as best she could? She knew her father would not return her to his residence. He was done with her. He was here now only because he thought to gain from the situation, if not a pocketful of coins then a powerful son-in-law. She wondered what his impressions were, but she dared not look back at him. It took little to earn his wrath these days.

"Of course, I remember her."

She blinked in surprise. Relief and dread beat within her breast. Conflicting desires, conflicting troubles. Everything had seemed much simpler when she thought he was dead. Now the truth picked at the lock, and she didn't know if its release would serve her good or ill.

Major Lyons bowed slightly. "Miss Dawson."

"Major. I'm so grateful you're not dead." In spite of the troubles his resurrection might cause her, the words were heartfelt. Grief had nearly done her in when she'd seen his name on the list of casualties. She owed him more than she could ever express, more than she could ever repay.

"No more so than I am, I assure you."

The rough timbre of his voice sent a quiver of longing through her. *What a silly chit you are, Mercy. He speaks that way to every lady. You are not so special after all.* But there had been times when she'd thought, hoped, dared to dream that he gave her attention because he considered her distinctive, because he could distinguish her from the other nurses. After only one telling, he remembered her name. She learned later that she'd given too much significance to that small triumph. He knew every nurse by name. He could even differentiate the twin nuns—Mary and Margaret—from each other when no one else could.

"And her father, Mr. Daws—"

"You ruined my girl," her father bellowed, interrupting Ainsley before the introductions were properly finished.

Mortification swamped her. *Oh, what a tangled web we weave. . .*

Major Lyons's eyes widened slightly at that, and his gaze swung back to her. His brow furrowed, and she could see him concentrating, trying to remember what had passed between them. How could he forget? Had he not seen her clearly in the darkness? Had she only imagined that he'd known who she was? She didn't know if it would be better if he did recognize her as the lady he'd rescued that horrid night. Perhaps there was a mercy in his confusion. She should simply confess everything now, save herself further embarrassment.

But where to begin? How much to reveal? How much to keep hidden? How much would he deduce by whatever she told him? She had sworn an oath. No matter the price, she intended to keep it until she drew her last breath.

"Stephen, darling, do come here," the duchess said, ushering him over to her side.

He walked slowly, as though even in this great room that was surely familiar to him he was lost, searching for his bearings. She'd seen far too many men with the same haunted quality, the same emptiness of soul in their expression. As though they'd left their essence out on the battlefield and only their bodies had returned. The price of war went far beyond the stores of munitions, food, uniforms, and medical supplies.

"This is John," the duchess said softly when he reached her. "Miss Dawson claims he is your son. I can see a resemblance."

"I don't. For one thing I'm considerably taller."

The duchess released a small laugh and tears welled in her eyes, as though she'd caught a glimpse of the teasing young man her son had once been. Reaching out, she squeezed his hand. "Is it possible, do you think? That he's yours?"

He moved around to acquire a better look at John. With his large hand, he cradled the boy's head, the pale wispy curls settling softly against his long, slender fingers. Mercy's heart lurched, swelling with joy and breaking at the same time. How often she had dreamed of him holding his son, but none of her fanciful imaginings had prepared her for the moment of reality, of seeing him touching this precious child. He would recognize himself in the boy. Surely, he would. He would claim John as his, even if he would not offer Mercy the same consideration. For John, she could hold no greater joy than that he be accepted by his father. For herself, she knew it held the potential to have John ripped from her. A bastard child was the responsibility of his mother, but this powerful family could circumvent laws. With the proper amount of blunt slipped into her father's palm, Mercy would be relegated to a pauper, with the one thing she treasured beyond her reach.

"Considering my well-earned reputation with the ladies, of course it's possible," he murmured. He lifted his eyes to hers, and she felt the full force of their impact as he studied her again. What did he see when he looked at her? Did he see her as she was the night he'd come to her rescue? Or did he see her as she was now? Determined to save the child when she'd been unable to save so many?

"You must do right by the girl," his mother said softly. "If indeed, you have no doubt that she has given birth to your son."

He would tell them now, would laugh at the ludicrousness of her claim. That a man such as he would ever desire a woman such as her—

"Of course, I should do right by her."

Mercy's knees shook and turned into jam. She sank into the chair. Had he just agreed to marry her? Surely not. She'd misheard. The Honorable Stephen Lyons, known rake and seducer of women. Major Stephen Lyons, admired soldier who had managed to make every nurse swoon. He couldn't possibly be seriously considering marrying her with as much ease as he might snap his fingers.

"Miss Dawson, will you take a turn about the garden with me?"

"You can't possibly think I'm going to leave her alone in your company," her father barked.

"Walk along behind us if you like," Major Lyons said, before glancing back down at John. "Although I daresay there is little I could do at this point that would ruin her reputation any more than it's already been." Once again, his gaze leaped across the distance separating them to land on her as powerfully as a touch. "Miss Dawson?"

She rose on unsteady legs. "Yes, Major. I would very much like to take a stroll with you."

It was a lie, of course. She dreaded it with every fiber of her being.

* * *

He didn't remember her. That truth disturbed Stephen more than he could voice with words, because if there was anything about the past two years that he should have remembered, it should have been her—or at the very least her eyes. An unusual shade, they reminded him of whiskey. But they were haunted, no doubt by things he couldn't even begin to imagine, but with which he should have been intimately familiar.

War, blood, death.

The scars riddling his body and the still healing wounds served as a testament that he'd experienced the worst man had to offer, but his mind couldn't recall a single detail of what he'd endured. He'd awoken in a regimental hospital on an odorous, thin pallet on a rickety wooden cot, tormented by physical pain that made no sense. Because the very last thing he'd remembered before he became fully conscious was having tea in the garden at Lyons Place with Claire.

The scent of flowers had been replaced by the pungent stench of oozing and rotting flesh. The sweet song of the meadowlark had been replaced by the moans and cries of dying men. So many calling out for their mothers, needing a familiar bosom upon which to take a final rest. The green of England had been replaced by the gray squalor of the Crimea. Even now he could still taste blood at the back of his throat, and he despaired of ever being free of it. An imperceptible red mist, it had been thick on the air, had saturated what remained of his tattered uniform. His blood, the blood of countless others—men he couldn't remember. His inability to draw up memories of them dishonored them, disgraced him.

Lying beside them in the hospital, he'd wallowed in his own filth, his own pain, his own anguish. They would talk to him of battles fought and courage shown. He would pretend that he shared the recollections. They would talk fondly of those who were gone, and he felt he'd betrayed those who had died for his country—who might have died for him. What he didn't know, what he couldn't truly appreciate gnawed at his conscience, day and night. He remembered England, his family, his lovers in precise detail. What he couldn't remember was how he had come to be in that wretched place.

He'd yearned to escape the reality of his surroundings. He'd longed to feel the silky softness of a woman's body. He'd craved the solace her soothing hands and warm voice could offer.

But nothing was as it had been. The joy he'd once taken in women had been replaced by an almost desperate need to rid himself of what he'd become: a man who had lost two years of his life. He had an abbreviated past, had leaped over a chasm of time.

And now here was this woman who had emerged from that gaping, black nothingness that tormented him. He'd known her, bedded her, filled her with his seed. . .

Yet he couldn't remember the flavor of her kiss, how soft her skin might have felt against his caressing fingers.

Perhaps that was the greatest tragedy: that she was obviously a lady of good breeding and she'd willingly given herself to him. It would not have been something she'd have done lightly. The way she constantly averted her gaze alerted him that she harbored guilt over their assignation. Yet for the life of him he remembered nothing at all about her.

He could tell—in spite of the unflattering black dress that might have given an unhandsome woman the appearance of a crow—that she was not easily forgotten. Yet, forget her he had.

She was tall for a woman. He stood over six feet, and if he tucked her against him while they were standing, he'd have to tilt his chin up to get her as close as possible. Her hair, a burnished copper, more orange than red, was pulled back severely and tucked up neatly beneath her bonnet. She was slender, far too slender for a woman who'd recently given birth. He wondered if she'd had a difficult time of it. Guilt plagued him as he considered the hardships he'd brought upon her. Certainly, they went beyond the shame and mortification of having a child out of wedlock. Why had she not abandoned it somewhere? She could have returned to England with no one the wiser, concerning her indiscretions.

He ignored the chill in the air and the sharp ache in his leg as they trudged through his younger brother's gardens. They were bleak now. Not a blossom to be seen, the leaves and stems withered. Still, it was only here, in the quiet and solitude, that he could almost pretend that he was once again normal.

He looked up at the gray sky. So much seemed without color of late—except for her hair—that he wondered if his vision had been damaged as well. His family and the physician who'd treated him knew of his mental affliction, but otherwise he'd not spoken of it to anyone. Pride forced him to hold his silence on the matter, and to beg of his family to do the same. He'd never begged in his life, but here he was—a man he barely knew. Somehow, he had changed, but he didn't know what had transpired to change him.

Sometimes he would have a blink of memory—a bloody arm, an earth-shattering boom, a yell, a scream, the rancid smell of death—but it would flitter away before he could snatch it and hold it close to examine it. Perhaps he was a fool to desperately want to regain such hideous images, but the not knowing, the emptiness of his mind was far worse.

"Are you cold?" he asked, and she staggered to a stop. Obviously, not the first words she'd expected him to utter. Her dark green cloak was thick and heavy. It was probably doing the job it was intended to do; still the damp could eat through to the bones.

"It was much colder in the Crimea," she said. "Although I've heard that England had an exceptionally cold winter at the start of this year. I can't help but wonder if God wanted people to have a taste of what they'd sent their countrymen into."

"And their women."

She averted her eyes and a blush crept into her hollow cheeks as though she were embarrassed by what certainly must have been good works.

He considered for the span of a solitary breath telling her of his affliction, but he couldn't bring himself to do it. He couldn't add insult to the injuries he'd already inflicted upon her, to admit to not knowing who the devil she was or what place she'd held in his life—other than a possible night's entertainment. But it was more than a desire not to embarrass her or cause her grief. It was his own pride, his own shame. And his paralyzing fear.

What did it say of a man's mind when he couldn't tug at a thread of memory?

Those who'd served under him lauded his heroic

efforts. But he couldn't recall a single action worthy of praise. A month after returning home to recover from his grievous wounds, he had no memory of how he'd acquired a single scar—except for the tiny one on his cheek, just below his eye. Westcliffe had given him that one when he'd split his skin with his fist after dragging Stephen from the bed he'd been sharing with the wife Westcliffe had acquired only hours before. In truth the encounter had been quite innocent, involving nothing more than holding and comforting her, but Stephen had wanted Westcliffe to believe otherwise. He'd paid for it with a sound beating, but it was nothing compared with what he'd suffered lately. Or so other scars seemed to indicate. They alone knew what he'd endured. Pity they didn't speak.

He resumed walking. It was better to keep moving, although toward what destination he hadn't a clue.

She hurried to catch up, which wasn't difficult. He suspected her legs were as long as his, although they were no doubt more shapely and appealing. He tried to remember them wrapped around his waist, and he couldn't. Had she cried out his name or whispered it? He would have spoken hers numerous times as he murmured sweet words near her ear. *Mercy, Mercy, Mercy.*

Nothing stirred within him now, nothing at all.

"How old is the babe?" he asked.

He couldn't recall the child's name. His mother had mentioned it, but he'd paid little attention, assuming at first that the babe was of no importance.

Again, he'd surprised her. This time it was the deep furrow in her delicate brow that alerted him. Damnation. What exactly had their relationship been? Had they taken quiet moments to converse? Or had they sought to become lost in frenzied lovemaking to escape the horrors that surrounded them?

While he had no memory of what had come before he awoke in that hospital, he'd witnessed enough while recovering there to know that hell had arrived on earth with a mighty vengeance.

"A little over three months," she finally responded.

He heard the hesitation in her voice, the discomfort over having to reveal what he obviously should have known. Had she told him she was with babe? Or should he have been able to calculate the months since their last tryst? Had he offered to marry her? *Dear God, don't let her realize that I don't remember her.*

It had never been his way to insult or harm women. They had always been his passion, his *raison d'être*. He'd appreciated all they had to offer and had made damn sure they were aware of his admiration for them. He'd never knowingly caused one to regret being with him.

Except possibly for Claire. He'd sought to spare her from his brother, and in so doing, he'd given her years of torment and loneliness, sadness and abject guilt. While he'd gone on to satisfy the ladies of London with his sexual prowess.

But Claire and Westcliffe had reconciled, and Stephen had never known her to be happier. It was a condition he thought the woman walking beside him might never achieve. He could see she was burdened, and he had little doubt that his actions had only added to the weight she carried on her narrow shoulders. Yet he sensed she was made of stern stuff and would not topple. He suspected that more than the shell of her beauty had attracted him, that she was one of those rare creatures who had the ability to appeal to him on a much deeper level. Yet he'd always avoided them, had not wanted to become entangled with a woman from whom he might desire more than physical release. So why had he been unable to resist becoming involved with her?

Surely, if he had told her he loved her, she'd be giddy with delight that he was walking beside her instead of lying beneath six feet of dirt.

"Why did you wait so long to bring him here?" he asked. A safe question because certainly he'd have not known her reasoning.

She seemed to be searching the barren gardens for her answer. He recalled a time when he'd had the ability to charm a lady into revealing *everything*, from her deepest secrets to the dimple just above her rounded bottom. He'd lost more than his memory. He'd lost his wicked ways. He should have had Miss Dawson laughing by now, but he'd forgotten how to laugh as well, couldn't remember the last time he'd made such a wondrous sound. Had even wanted to.

"I wasn't . . . I wasn't quite sure how I was going to handle the matter," she confessed. "You weren't aware that . . ." Her voice trailed off, and a blush deepened the ruddiness of her cheeks where the cold had begun to chafe them.

So she hadn't told him she was with child. Thank God, for that. He'd not abandoned her then, not left her to face it alone. Strange, the comfort he drew from that knowledge. At least the man he'd been in the Crimea had resembled the man he'd been before. While he'd always been cautious, had avoided any by-blows, he'd always wondered how he would respond if faced with the situation. His family had accused him of being a man without character, but he'd hoped it was a façade of his fun-loving youth. Yet he'd never been tested. Until now.

"John was born in Paris," she continued, her voice growing a bit stronger, as though she now traveled on firmer ground. "I'd considered raising him there, but then—"

John. The boy's name was John. It was a good, strong name. He wondered why she'd selected it, if it held any significance for her.

She stopped walking, causing him to do the same. His leg welcomed the reprieve. He seldom gave it any, as though he could punish it for its constant ache, for his inability to remember how it had come to be injured.

"I saw your name on a list of casualties." A mist formed in her eyes, and she blinked them back. He'd meant something to her, something precious. Had she meant anything to him other than a wild romp?

What had he felt for her, damn it! He wanted to know. He wanted to ask her what they had done, where they had gone, how long they had been associated with each other. He wanted to know her secrets, wanted to know if he'd shared his. Had he trusted her? Devil take it! Had he loved her?

"I thought you were dead," she said hesitantly, as though she feared if she spoke the words with assurance she could cause them to come true.

No, only a portion of my mind died out there on that god-forsaken battlefield. A field that he couldn't envision no matter how diligently he tried.

"My family thought so as well," he told her. "It was the news that was initially given to them."

"They must have been devastated."

He had no words for the agony they must have suffered. During the first week after he returned home, his mother had barely let him out of her sight, as though he were once again a child to be constantly watched, so he didn't endanger his existence.

"I can sympathize with how they must have felt. I knew I couldn't keep John to myself then. You must understand. I love him more than my own life, but he is yours and I thought he would bring comfort to your family."

"And shame to yours."

"My father doesn't understand, but then how can he? He's not been through what we have been."

As far as his mind was concerned, neither had he.

"Life is so precious, so very precious. I don't expect you to marry me. I—"

"Why?" he asked, unable to control his curiosity, to prevent the word from being uttered. "Why do you not expect it? I got you with child."

Her eyes widening, her mouth opening slightly, she turned away. He saw the visible tenseness in her shoulders, the way she clutched her hands, as though she were in need of comfort. Was their relationship such that he would have offered it? Should he fold his hand over her shoulder? Should he squeeze it? Should he take her into his arms? Good God, the awkwardness of the moment was almost beyond bearing. He should tell her.

Forgive me, but I don't know who the bloody hell you are. I don't remember what you were to me, what I was to you.

Staring at the withered garden, Mercy prayed she'd turned away quickly enough that he'd not seen the confusion clouding her eyes. This stroll with him was not at all as she'd anticipated. She'd expected accusation, a demand to know the game she played. And yet it seemed he was the one playing games.

I got you with child.

The words had been spoken with conviction, as though he believed them. But how could he? She knew that sometimes a battle could rattle a man's mind, leave him bewildered, befuddled.

But Major Lyons seemed to be in complete control of his faculties . . . and yet, his statement indicated otherwise.

He had confused her with someone else, someone who could have given birth to his child.

Not a woman whom he had merely held and comforted through the night. Not a woman who had fallen in love with him, knowing that she would never possess his heart.

She couldn't help but be disappointed that a night that had changed her forever had apparently meant nothing at all to him. He'd been so solicitous, so kind, so tender that long-ago night. What a fool she was to think he'd held her in any sort of special regard. No other man ever had. And Stephen Lyons was far above every other man in existence. Handsome, charming, devoted to women. Not a single nurse had been immune to his charms.

Mercy had been no exception.

She wanted to be angry that she'd been no more than a momentary diversion, but she was also acutely aware that his not remembering the details of their association could work to her advantage. And why not make the most of it? From the moment John had come into her life, she'd been more duplicitous than she'd ever thought herself capable of being. Her love of Stephen Lyons and subsequently his son had ruined her reputation, had ensured that no other man would have her.

She had so much to gain, and Major Lyons had very little to lose. She'd already proven herself an excellent mother. She would excel at being a wife. Marriage would ensure that John remained in her life and she in his.

Was she truly considering moving forward with this farce?

And what if he did remember? He would loathe her. Dare she risk it?

Mercy had never declared to anyone that she had brought John into the world. That honor had been granted another. But the woman who had birthed him had turned away from him. Had abandoned him because his presence was a threat to the prestigious life she'd always envisioned for herself. So Mercy had sheltered him and found a wet nurse to provide the nourishment she could not. He'd been sickly in the beginning, and Mercy had tended to him with an obsessive need to ensure he lived. She'd been so dreadfully weary of watching men die. She'd refused to allow Death to snatch him away. She'd fought vigilantly until her own health suffered.

But during those difficult and frightening weeks, she'd come to love John as though she *had* given birth to him. She'd become his mother in every sense of the word. She'd made no plans for his future or hers. She'd simply taken each day as it came.

During her time in the Crimea she'd learned that not even the next moment was guaranteed. Then she'd seen Major Lyons's name on the list of the dead, and she'd known that she had to bring John to the duchess. He was all that remained of her son.

But fear that John, whom she could not love more if she had actually birthed him, would be taken from her had caused her to declare herself his mother. She'd known shame and humiliation would accompany her declaration, but they were nothing compared with the heartbreak she would endure if she were not allowed to be part of his life. She could not explain the motherly instincts that rampaged through her. But to lose him would be to break her heart.

She'd known a frisson of fear when she'd learned Major Lyons was alive—because surely he would know that she could not possibly be John's mother. In spite of the night she'd spent with Major Lyons.

But it seemed he did not remember their night together. That he did not truly remember her. Did he not remember her because she was forgettable? Had there been so many women that he had confused her with one he'd bedded?

She should ask him: Who do you think I am? What do you think happened between us? But what would she gain beyond further mortification? What did she risk losing?

John. The only person who mattered in her life, who gave it purpose.

She could not reveal the truth, could not risk losing him. Everything within her shouted that she could not continue on this course. But her heart would not listen. She would compromise. She would not lie. But neither would she reveal the entire truth.

"It was only one night." The words were rough at the edges, as their night together flooded her with memories. She'd endured mortification and shame far worse than being considered the mother of an illegitimate child.

"It's getting dark. We should return to the house before your father comes searching for us, convinced I've yet again had my way with you."

She spun around, her gaze leveling on his. She searched for some understanding, some hint regarding his abrupt dismissal of the situation. "What of John? What are we to do about him?"

"I don't know. We still need to discuss that."

"He's not a *that*. He's a babe, a child, a delight."

"I was referring to *that* topic. You're extremely protective of him."

"He deserves better than he's had so far."

He narrowed his eyes. "Better than his mother?"

Was he trying to trick her? Did he know the truth? Did he suspect—

"I'm not enough. I can give him love, but it will not keep him warm, or his belly full, or protect him from harm."

"Who would harm him?"

She glanced past him. "No one, I'm sure. I meant harm in the general sense."

"You'll stay the night."

He immediately began trudging back toward the house, his limp more pronounced.

"What do you mean I'll stay the night?" she asked as she grabbed his arm.

He jerked beyond reach. He acted as though he couldn't bear her touch, when she knew he'd once been a man who relished any contact with women. What exactly had happened to him after she'd left the hospital?

She wanted to comfort him as he'd once comforted her, but where to even begin?

"We still have much to work out," he said. "We have an ungodly abundance of rooms here. I'm certain you could be hidden away in one and I'd never find you."

With a nod, she began walking, and he strove to catch up.

"Your limp is more pronounced than it was earlier," she said softly, slowing her pace.

"The cold aggravates it."

"What was the injury?"

"A ghastly gash, hip to knee. It's still healing. I don't know if I'll ever walk without the pain. I suppose I should consider myself fortunate to still have possession of my leg. My head constantly aches—" He stopped, sighed deeply. "My apologies. It was not my intention to burden you with my various afflictions."

"No, I . . . I wish I'd been there to tend to your wounds. I'd already left. Miss N had no tolerance for . . . inappropriate behavior."

"It must have been very difficult for you."

"I will do anything for John. Anything at all."

His lips curved up slowly into a semblance of a smile, as though he'd grown unaccustomed to using those muscles. "He's a very lucky fellow."

She could only hope that Major Lyons would always believe that.

Chapter 2

Sitting at the vanity, Mercy met her gaze in the mirror. It was a bit more difficult to do than it had been yesterday. She'd have to be quick on her feet tonight.

She'd been prepared to stay—only because her father wouldn't accept any other outcome regarding this visit. He'd had her trunk packed and loaded on the coach. If she'd not been welcomed here, he'd have left her on the side of the road. Her and John. How could he not love John? An innocent babe caught in a web of deceit.

Mercy fought not to think about it as the abigail the duchess sent her worked to arrange her unruly hair. It behaved much better when it was bound tightly, although she couldn't deny that the maid's skillful hands were hiding its imperfections.

With the duke and his mother vouching for her safety and the return of her good name, her father had taken his leave as though the matter were settled. When it wasn't. Far from it. Still she felt safe here. More important, John was safe here. She'd seen the way the duchess had looked at the babe. Already she loved him. He was incredibly easy to love.

He'd taken that attribute from his father. Although

Mercy couldn't deny that he was very different from the cocky young man she'd first seen at the Barrack Hospital. But then she had changed as well. It was John who had made her feel like herself again. After what she'd experienced, what she'd witnessed, she'd thought never to smile again.

But he made her smile. At first it had been only a small smile, but it had widened with each passing day as she'd watched John grow, as she'd held him near, as she'd seen him marvel at the world surrounding him. Eventually, he would become more adventuresome and she wanted to experience those moments with him. She wanted to teach him to climb a tree, as unladylike as it was. She wanted to watch him master his first horse. She wanted to watch him become a man to be reckoned with. Like his father.

When the maid finished with her hair, Mercy carefully stepped into the pale green gown. She'd worn nothing beyond black in two years. It had seemed somehow important, as though the somber color would reflect the seriousness of her purpose. But tonight, it was far more important that she catch Major Lyons's eye, that she do all in her power to ensure he accept her into his life. For John's sake.

Green had always flattered her, accentuated the red of her hair. The harsh red had made her easy to spot as she'd walked among the wounded men. They'd begun to refer to her as the Red Angel.

To her shame, her reason for going with Miss N had not been entirely altruistic. She'd had no marriage prospects and she'd thought—foolishly hoped—that she might meet someone who would fancy her. She'd even had a romantic notion that she would be wiping the brow of a wounded soldier, and as they gazed into each other's eyes, love would immediately blossom.

But love was far from a man's mind when he was retching, shivering, unable to control the simplest of bodily functions. There was no romance when a man lost a limb and was wallowing in pain. The soft words spoken were all hers, to give comfort when illness reduced a man to a shell of his former self, until he faded away to nothing. She'd forced herself to withhold tears because she'd known the moment they started flowing, she'd have no success at stopping them. She'd loved every man in her ward, but it had not been the emotion written about in romance novels or sonnets.

It had been a love born of gratitude for service to country, a desire to ease the suffering, to grant comfort. She'd begun her journey as an idealistic young woman in search of adventure and the attentions of men. She'd quickly fallen into the routine of serving a greater good, until her needs mattered not at all, until what she'd been had ceased to exist and a woman she barely knew began to inhabit her skin. And then the night when her world tumbled . . .

Once again, she looked in the mirror as the maid adjusted the sleeves of her gown, her petticoats, and her skirts. She should tell Stephen Lyons everything—but by doing so she would risk losing John.

"Thank you. That's all I require at this time," she said to the abigail, dismissing her. Once the girl had left, Mercy walked over to the bassinet that the duchess had somehow managed to secure for her. John lay there, sucking on his tiny balled fist in slumber. She needed to summon the wet nurse she'd hired in Paris and who accompanied her wherever she went with John. Jeanette had traveled with Mercy and her father in the coach. While they'd had their audience with the duke and his mother, Jeanette had been served tea in the kitchen. When it had become apparent that Major Lyons wished that Mercy stay, her hosts had provided the wet nurse with a bed in the servants' quarters. Jeanette had lost her babe and husband to cholera. She'd been only too willing to leave France, and Mercy had welcomed the help she would provide with John. She'd known very little about caring for an infant, but she'd been determined that nothing would separate her from John.

He held her together, kept the nightmares at bay. She knew it wasn't fair to place such a heavy burden on an innocent, but she couldn't bear the thought of never again holding him, looking upon his beloved face, caressing his soft cheek.

If marriage to Stephen Lyons was required to ensure that she remained with John, then she would do all in her power to secure that marriage.

Even if it meant that she'd never reveal the entire truth about John, even if it required that she spend eternity burning in the fires of hell.

Nothing was too great a sacrifice. Nothing.

Stephen felt as though he were perpetually waking up following too much drink the night before. It didn't matter that he was consuming far less alcohol than he ever had. His head was reacting as though he were drinking gallons.

Even now, in early evening, a fogginess clouded his thoughts. Sitting in a stuffed leather chair in his brother's library, he rubbed his temple, grimacing when his fingers skimmed over the scar that began just below it.

He did not fool himself into thinking that even if he remembered the battle, he'd have been focused enough on his own welfare to be aware of each wound that he'd received, but at least they'd have made some sense. As it was, the past two years were nothing more than a gaping hole filled with nothingness.

"Mother is quite relieved that you remember Miss Dawson," Ainsley said as he took the chair across from Stephen and stretched out his long legs. They'd not had a moment alone since he'd informed his mother and brother that they'd have overnight guests. "Surely, if you can remember her, the rest cannot be far behind."

If only it were true.

"Unfortunately, Mother never has been able to tell when I've spoken false words. Why do you think I've managed to stay in her good graces for so long?"

In typical style, Ainsley did not give away his thoughts. If he was surprised, he didn't show it. "I feared that was the case, that you were striving . . ."

"To hide the truth?"

Ainsley blatantly ignored the biting retort. Stephen found his tolerance irritating, but then of late he lost patience with everything. He'd come to his brother's estate to recover, to regain his strength. He thought he was as healed as he would ever be. He was itching to move on—to go to London, lease a house, return to the life he'd known. It would be as though nothing had changed. Yet, somehow, even without his memories, he knew he had—in some fundamental way. He was as much a stranger to himself as Miss Dawson was.

"If you don't remember her, then how can you be certain she's not lying?" Ainsley asked. "Perhaps she's taking advantage of your , situation."

Everyone parried so lightly around his affliction, striving not to call it exactly what it was: evidence of some sort of mental deficiency. He supposed he should be grateful that they'd not locked him away. What if this forgetfulness was only the beginning? What if there was more to come?

With fingers that had once caressed Miss Dawson, he rubbed his brow. "No one knows of it except for my family and the physicians who attended me. I demanded discretion. I must believe it was granted. So she came here fully expecting me to remember her. To lie would have served her no purpose. Her story would have been immediately discredited. Besides, I believe she thought I was dead."

"She did seem taken aback to discover you were alive, but that doesn't prove the child is yours. Perhaps she came here thinking there was no one to disprove her claim."

"What a suspicious gent you are. She doesn't strike me as capable of deception."

"You deduced this after a mere half hour in her company? Did you tell her the truth about your circumstance when you took your turn about the garden?"

He slid his gaze over to his brother. Among his friends and associates, Stephen was the only one to have an older brother who was an earl and a younger one who was a duke. His mother had wasted no time in securing a second husband after her first had perished leaving her with two sons and no means of support. In her way of never putting off what must be done, she'd quickly given her second husband his heir. Ransom Seymour, the Duke of Ainsley, always gave the impression that he was far older than he was. His tendency toward responsibility was sometimes irksome, especially when Stephen preferred to play. Although his desire for games was what had gotten him into this current debacle with Miss Dawson. He wondered if she'd been worth it. He imagined so. He thought that, hovering above her, gazing down into her whiskey eyes, a man could very well take a journey into paradise.

"She gave birth to my child, Ainsley. How do I tell her that I have no memory of her whatsoever? It would only add to the mortification she has already endured."

"It seems going to war made a worthy man of you yet."

"But at what cost?"

He was haunted by his loss of memories. His leg, of late, was becomingly increasingly agonizing and at times he thought it might finish him off as the enemy had been unable to. His head kept him in a haze. He felt a burden to his family. He wanted to be fully recovered so he could get on with his life.

"I should think while you may not remember the horrors of war that you'd not forget a pretty face."

Stephen would have glared at his brother but it would have served to intensify his head pain. Besides, Ainsley had never been one to be intimidated by a good glare. "I didn't forget portions of the past two years; I've forgotten every damned thing associated with it."

"But still . . . to forget a lady—"

"I could have bedded a dozen ladies—in all likelihood I did—but not a single one comes to mind." He couldn't see the face of one woman or man he may have encountered during the past two years. No soldier, no enemy. Shouldn't he at least recall the features of a man he may have killed? Although God knew, the dead were not memories he wished to possess. But he would take them if they were all he could own.

"What are you going to do about her?" Ainsley asked, turning Stephen's attention back to Miss Dawson.

"Haven't the foggiest."

"If the boy is yours—"

"Do you doubt it?"

Ainsley straightened and leaned forward, placing his elbows on his thighs, his glass of port held loosely in his hand. "She wouldn't have been the first woman to . . . select the father based upon her desire to move up in the world."

Stephen ceased his rubbing and pressed his fingers against his temple. "She didn't strike me as promiscuous. She said we shared but one night."

And he had to wonder: Was she like the myriad of women who'd come before her? He'd wooed them into his arms, into his bed with no more care than one might gentle a horse. In London, he'd taken such pride in his sexual exploits, had thought of nothing beyond the pleasure. He'd competed with his older brother in the boudoirs, determined to be known as a far greater lover than his sibling.

Or had Miss Dawson been more? Had their love been so grand that she'd given herself to him fearing that one night might be all they'd have, that on the morrow he'd die?

And now there was this wretched awkwardness between them. If their situation had been the latter, it made matters all the worse for her. Surely, she'd have expected a more emotional reuniting.

Regardless of their circumstances, he was beginning to feel like a swine.

"Which makes it even more unlikely—"

"Or more a certainty if I were the only one."

"Marriage will not restore her reputation, now that the child is born."

"But it will lessen the taint of her sins—to marry the boy's father. Dowagers will find it romantic."

"Marrying her will not legitimize the boy."

"But an act of Parliament would, and how fortunate for me to have two brothers who sit in the House of Lords."

Ainsley studied him with that damned fine mind of his. "Why are you arguing to be shackled when I'm striving to find an argument to prevent it?"

Stephen dropped his head back and contemplated the fresco painting on the ceiling. Woodland nymphs and enticing beauties with bared arms . . . a peacefulness that eluded him. He was tormented by what he could not dredge up from the farthest recesses of his mind. Would the torment increase if he did recall those two years? From everything he'd read, all that he'd heard, it was a blessing not to remember. Amnesia, the physician had called it. *Not unusual to forget unpleasantness.* As though Stephen lacked the backbone to face the horror of what he'd experienced. It gnawed at him to think that he would be so cowardly, that he would welcome the comfort of no memories.

"I don't know why I'm set on this course," he finally responded to his brother. "Marriage is not something that ever appealed to me."

"Which is the very reason I'm confounded by your willingness to accept it as your fate so readily."

"Mother says the child favors me."

"I've seen numerous babes in my life and they all

look the same. Ruddy cheeks and pursed mouths and squinting eyes."

"You're becoming quite the cynic as you grow older."

"Taking after my older brothers."

"So you excel in the bedchamber?" he asked, with a desperate need to divert the conversation away from him before his skull split in two.

Ainsley did little more than give him a sly smile. "You're attempting to change the subject."

"Well, yes, I—"

The door clicked open, and he glanced over his shoulder as his mother and Miss Dawson entered the room. Then he was coming to his feet more swiftly than he should have and the pain shot through his leg, nearly causing him to lose his balance. He caught himself on the back of the chair, hoping to God that Miss Dawson's attention had been turned toward the books or some trivial piece of artwork and not him. If she had seen his pitiful display of rising she gave no sign of it. His mother, on the other hand, looked as though she wanted to weep, but, thankfully, recovered herself quickly enough. She knew he hated to be smothered by motherly concern.

To be smothered by a lusty maiden, however, brought no objections from him.

Although he'd not been with a woman since he woke up in that damnable cesspool that they called a hospital. Of late, he'd had the stirrings again, but what woman would want the scarred creature he'd become?

"I'm fine," he muttered to Ainsley, jerking free of the helpful hand he'd been too preoccupied to notice until that moment. "I'm fine."

Only he wasn't. Mercy Dawson was not what he

would consider beautiful, and yet there was a radiance to her. As though somehow from the moment he'd left her in the parlor after alerting his family that she'd be remaining and this moment when she'd arrived in the library, she'd found a measure of peace and contentment. He wanted what she seemed to possess so damned easily.

"Miss Dawson," Ainsley began, stepping forward and bowing slightly. "Allow me to say that you look lovely. I assume you've found everything to your satisfaction."

"Quite. Yes. Thank you, Your Grace. I'm not sure how your mother managed the miracle of finding a bassinet on such short notice, but John is quite content there. I'm not sure I've ever seen him sleep so well."

John rolled off her tongue like a sweet lullaby, soft and soothing. Stephen wondered how his own name might have sounded on her lips during the height of passion. It would be easy enough to find out later tonight. He'd had the servants place her in a bedchamber in the same wing as his. Scandalous, but then they were all adults, and her reputation was already ruined. Besides, at his brother's estate, who was there to know? His mother's lover, while not flaunted, was not hidden away either. Ainsley certainly wasn't going to castigate Stephen for finding pleasure where he might. The servants knew a bit of gossip would result in their dismissal and that the duke never threatened what he would not carry out.

"You may thank my eldest brother, the Earl of West-cliffe, for that accommodation. He acquired his heir this summer past. The duchess insists that the little urchin be comfortable when he visits. She is quite adept at spoiling him beyond measure."

"And I cannot spoil one grandson without spoiling the other," the duchess said.

Stephen wasn't certain why it hadn't hit him before that if the child was his, his mother had another grandson. The knowledge made him feel remarkably old.

As though the same truth had occurred to Miss Dawson, he watched as her cheeks took on a pinkish hue. No cold wind biting them now. He found he rather liked the high color in her face. She did look lovely. The gown she wore now was a bit more fanciful, with a rounded neck that exposed her throat and shoulders while offering only a hint of cleavage. Had he ever seen her in the dress before? Had he commented on it? Or was it something new, something she'd expect him to remark on? She seemed to be expecting something. Perhaps for him to speak instead of standing there like a dimwit. "Miss Dawson, would you care for some wine before dinner?"

She appeared startled and disappointed. Should he have gone over and kissed the back of her hand? Had he been unable to keep his hands off her? If she were any other woman, he'd not be plagued with these questions. But not knowing a woman he *should* know was fraught with difficulties. Especially as he didn't wish for her to know.

Preposterous. If they'd been close, she'd be understanding. As a nurse, she'd possibly seen others suffer the same fate. But he couldn't bear the thought of seeing pity in those whiskey eyes. He might not remember her, but he knew his pride well enough and was determined not to lose it.

"A bit. Yes. Thank you," she finally responded.

He fought not to favor his right leg as he made

his way to the sidebar. "Will Leo be joining us this evening?"

"Most certainly," the duchess said, and then he heard her explain to Miss Dawson, "He is a remarkable and talented artist I've commissioned to paint portraits of the family. I daresay he shall want to do you in oils."

But it was not his talents with the brush that kept his mother near the younger man, but rather his talents elsewhere. Stephen was glad his mother had a lover who appreciated her, made her feel special. Perhaps it was her own scandalous life that made her so accepting and nonjudgmental of Miss Dawson.

"That may be a bit premature," Miss Dawson stammered. "I'm not yet part of the family."

"Of course you are, dear girl. If not legally, then morally," the duchess assured her. He wondered if Miss Dawson possessed an inkling of knowledge regarding his mother's determination. Defeat had never been in his mother's vocabulary.

His cane seemed to be unusually loud as he hobbled across the room. Miss Dawson met him halfway. She reached for the glass. Their bare fingers touched. Hers sent a shock of warmth through him that settled low in his groin and caused him to tighten with desire. Was that the way it had been with them before? She appeared discomfited but not alarmed, as though the sensations had not taken her off guard. Or perhaps they had.

She took a very unladylike gulp of wine, coughed, and covered her mouth, her eyes watering. "Forgive me."

"You might try sipping it."

"Yes, of course. It's excellent. Thank you."

And they were left to stare at each other as though no

one else was in the room. He noticed that her nose tilted up slightly. She had a miniscule mole at the corner of her mouth. Her lashes were long and he imagined them feathering over his face when they kissed. She had a permanent crease between her eyebrows as though she spent a good deal of time frowning. Caring for wounded soldiers, she no doubt had. He wished he'd known her three years ago, so he could now catalogue the changes in her.

How many might he be responsible for? For the first time in his life he wished he'd kept his damned trousers fastened. But more than that, he wished he remembered every single moment that he'd been nestled inside her.

His musings were interrupted by the arrival of their last dinner guest.

With no fanfare but still managing to draw attention, Leo strolled in. Before Stephen had met him, he'd not known anyone who did everything with as leisurely a purpose as Leo. The man had never revealed his last name. He simply went by Leo.

"Miss Dawson," his mother began, drawing the woman away from Stephen, leaving him to wish she hadn't, "allow me to introduce to you the artist I was telling you about earlier. Leo."

"Mr. Leo."

"It's simply Leo," he drawled as he sauntered forward, took her hand, and lifted it to his lips.

Stephen was aware of the hand not holding his cane balling into a tightened fist. He wanted to snatch Miss Dawson's fingers free from Leo's lips. From where had this possessiveness emerged? He was never jealous of another man's attentions on a woman he favored. He could always easily find another to replace her. He'd had lovers, but never a mistress. He'd never bothered to go to the trouble to set a woman up for his amusements alone, because he grew too easily bored. He preferred variety.

"Your arrival has made the duchess exceedingly happy," Leo murmured, "which in turn pleases me. Thank you for coming."

Ainsley gave Stephen a pointed look. Their mother was happy because she thought Stephen was regaining his senses. He'd have to find a private moment with her to reveal the truth. Yet another time in his life when he'd disappointed her.

"I must admit to being curious. I took a quick peek at the boy before coming down. He is quite the handsome lad," Leo said.

"Thank you. I can take no credit for that. He takes after his father."

"Yes, the resemblance is uncanny."

"Leo is quite skilled at noting the particulars of the human form. The artist in him. If he sees a resemblance, you may rest assured it is there," the duchess said, pride in her voice at her lover's incredible ability—as though with it, he could capture the moon and stars for her.

Beside Stephen, Ainsley issued a low groan and whispered, "That was no doubt for my benefit."

"To quell your doubts regarding the boy's sire?" Stephen asked.

Ainsley shrugged. "Mother will have her way."

"Do you enjoy your work?" Miss Dawson asked of Leo, a sparkle in her eyes that once again had Stephen clenching his fist. Was she flirting with the artist? Why was she so relaxed with him and not with Stephen? What the devil had their relationship entailed?

"Very much so." Leo placed his finger beneath her chin and tilted her head slightly so she was looking toward a distant corner of the ceiling. "I would very much like to paint you, Miss Dawson."

"As long as all you're doing is painting," Stephen grumbled.

"Stephen," his mother chastised.

Leo grinned. "Why would I do anything else? I have a woman I love. Why would I want for more?"

"Oh, Leo." The duchess certainly meant to chastise him as well, but her voice held the satisfaction and teasing of a woman half her age. "Let's go in to dinner, shall we?"

"Yes, by all means," Stephen said. He took Miss Dawson's wineglass, twisted to set it down on a nearby table, and when he straightened, discovered that Ainsley had already wrapped her arm around his and was leading her from the room, murmuring near her ear.

Stephen's stomach tightened. He knew his brother would never reveal a secret that was not his; he'd not tell her the true depth of Stephen's injuries. Still, he didn't like seeing the easy camaraderie between them. Nor did he like being left to walk with his own company. Of late it was sour and displeasing.

He had a feeling that it was going to be a very long dinner indeed.

The seating arrangement determined by the duchess placed Mercy between the duke, who sat at the head of the table, and the artist, who was seated near the duchess at the foot of the table. His fingers constantly sought excuses to brush against the duchess's—not by accident, Mercy was fairly certain. While reaching for their wine at the same moment or signaling a servant. Eventually the pretense that they were less than what they were to each other dissipated and Leo wove his fingers through the duchess's and simply stroked her hand in between servings of the most delicious dishes Mercy had ever eaten.

The bittersweet realization hit her that the duchess was the woman Leo had referred to when he'd said he was in love. She felt silly for not realizing it sooner, but she also longed for the same sort of declaration from Major Lyons.

Not that it was likely to ever come. Even in the Crimea, even when they'd found moments alone to talk, it had been little more than talking. He'd never even attempted to kiss her. She told herself that it was respect for her that held him at bay, when in all likelihood it was her plain features. Or her height that sometimes made men feel awkward. Or the awful shade of her hair. Or perhaps he'd seen that she was dedicated to her service.

At least three nurses had tittered about receiving kisses from him. One had received a good deal more. He'd certainly not been a saint. Not that she could blame him for taking pleasure where he might when any day would again find him in the midst of battle. Her own moral compass had lost its direction. She had hung on his every word, welcomed his attentions, prayed that they would be more than they were.

The Crimea was not England. It was not afternoon tea, ballrooms, and chaperones. It was not innocent ladies. It was putting aside one's sensibilities. Men needed to have their dressings changed, and wounds were not always in the most convenient of places. Men needed to be bathed, and turned, and fed. They were attended to during the day and during the night. They needed the comfort of touch and a gentle word.

She remembered an afternoon when he'd escorted her from the hospital to her sleeping quarters. They were discussing literature, and he'd announced that Jane Austen wrote rubbish. Mercy had come to the woman's defense. She wrote of love and people with frailties.

Mercy had finally demanded to know, "If you think she wrote rubbish, then why on earth do you read her works?"

He'd winked. "Because the ladies enjoy her, so I never lack for a topic of conversation."

Now, directly across from her, he watched her with increasing confusion clouding his eyes, and she wondered if he was beginning to remember the details of their association. It brought the heat to her cheeks to consider that he might be.

She'd thought him incredibly handsome as he'd strutted about in his scarlet uniform, but she had to admit that she preferred him in his evening attire. His shirt and cravat were pristine white, but everything else was black. He'd taken some care to style his hair, she realized, because it partly covered the scar on his face, as though he wished to draw attention away from it. She supposed she couldn't blame him for being self-conscious about it, but she viewed it as a badge of honor, more worthy than any accolade he might be given.

Curling at the ends, his hair was longer than she'd ever seen it. John had inherited his curls from his father—and the light blond of his hair. She wondered if it would darken over the years to match Major Lyons's exactly. She imagined it would. Already his eyes were the blue of his father's. But fortunately, they still contained the innocence that was lost to Major Lyons.

The lit candles on the table caused shadows to flitter over his face, like garden nymphs playing games among the flowers. But her fanciful thoughts didn't do justice to the strong lines and planes of his features. They'd been carved by a master sculptor of flesh, then tempered by the brutality of war. At the corners of his eyes and mouth were deeper crevices that he'd not possessed when last she saw him. They spoke of hardship, endurance, pain. He'd suffered, and she suspected it had not all been physical. Mental anguish had worn at him.

He'd cared about his men. That had been obvious as he'd recovered, walking the wards to check on other soldiers almost as often as Miss Nightingale. Disease had taken far more lives than bullets or swords, and he'd exposed himself over and over to the dangers of illness, as he'd not limited his visiting to only those who had been wounded while serving under him. His voice, his words, had served as a rallying cry to the most disheartened. Their commanders had defeated Napoleon. They would be victorious in the Crimea.

Little wonder that every nurse had fancied herself in love with him. Little wonder that her solitary night with him had meant so much. She'd known him as a man with a heart as large as Russia, had thought his ability to care would span an ocean.

Yet, regardless of what they'd shared, she was fairly certain now that she'd been merely one more woman whom he'd held in his arms, one more lady to whom he'd whispered soft words of tenderness. He looked upon her now as though she were a stranger. In spite of that, she refused to cast what they'd shared into a pit of meaningless encounters. For John's sake. She would continue to believe that the good in this man was deserving of her unfailing and heartfelt regard.

"Did you miss England while you were away, Miss Dawson?" the duke asked, and she cursed herself for flinching at the deep voice that intruded unexpectedly into her thoughts.

"More so than I expected."

"Why ever did you do it, Miss Dawson?" the duchess asked. "Why traipse along in the footsteps of Miss Nightingale?"

"It seemed a noble endeavor and I . . . I had no other interests that I thought would be more worthy." She'd had no suitors. She'd grown disenchanted serving as mistress of her father's house. To her shame now, she had to admit that she'd also longed for adventure. Such a trivial reason, when the need—the war—that had caused the adventure to be available had brought with it so much suffering.

"Tell me. What is it truly like?" the duchess asked.

"Must we follow this path of conversation?" Major Lyons barked before Mercy could even open her mouth to respond. "I'm certain that Miss Dawson is as weary of the talk of war as I am."

"My apologies. Of course you are. I suppose there is no reason to live again what you've already witnessed."

Mercy could have sworn that Major Lyons flinched. His hand was unsteady when he lifted his wine goblet and drained its contents. It seemed an odd reaction, yet she couldn't deny that the horrors he'd experienced were no doubt far worse than anything she'd endured. He'd been in the thick of it, while she'd been only on the outskirts, dealing with the aftermath. It had not been pretty, but at least it had not involved the paralyzing fear of being brutally killed on the battlefield.

"Was John's birth difficult?" the duchess asked.

"Good God, Mother," Major Lyons snapped. "Have you become a barbarian since I left England's shores? That's hardly proper dinner conversation, not proper conversation at all."

"Then what would you suggest we discuss?" the duchess challenged.

Much to Mercy's surprise, she appeared triumphant, and Mercy realized that she'd purposely chosen those subjects to goad her son into doing something other than sit there and brood. She could only conclude that his taciturn mien was not out of the ordinary or brought on by Mercy's sudden appearance in his life. But then how could she—or anyone—expect him to behave as though he weren't haunted by the horrors of war?

Every day was a challenge for her. If not for John, she feared she might not even leave her bed some days. Sometimes walking through the hospital, she'd felt so helpless and ineffectual. John was a constant distraction from such dire journeys into a past she could not change.

What distracted Major Lyons from taking similar phantom walks over battlefields?

As she watched him down yet another full goblet of wine, she thought the answer might reside in the bowl of that glass.

"The weather," he said laconically.

"It's dismal," the duchess responded. "And boring. Select another."

He narrowed his eyes first at his mother, then at Mercy as though she were somehow responsible for the strange mood at the table. No doubt she was.

"Do you play the pianoforte, Miss Dawson?" Leo asked.

She jerked her attention to him, grateful for a simple, normal question, and gave a small laugh. Out of the corner of her eye, she saw Major Lyons take on a more murderous expression. Good Lord, whatever was wrong?

"Years ago, yes, but it's been some time since I've run my fingers over a keyboard." It sounded as though Major Lyons was choking on his wine. "I fear my skills are sadly lacking now."

Leo smiled kindly at her. "I believe you're being unduly modest. Perhaps we should give it a go sometime. I'm very good with duets. I could easily cover any of your missteps."

"Why place her in a position of possible embarrassment?" Major Lyons asked. "I should think she's had enough of that."

Mercy stiffened, grew sick in her belly. The food she'd just enjoyed was fighting to work its way back onto her plate.

"Stephen!" the duchess gasped. "Apologize this instant."

"For speaking the truth?" He came to his feet with such force that his chair wobbled. If not for the fact that it was constructed of such sturdy wood, Mercy was fairly certain that it would have toppled over. "You're all trying to pretend that nothing is amiss. I've done egregious harm to this girl. Her reputation can never be restored. Her only recourse is to marry me, and you're well aware that with that way lies only madness."

Leaving them all stunned, he stormed from the room. She wanted to go after him, she wanted to apologize, she wanted to confess everything. She was also confused. Why did he think the tragedy would be in her marrying him and not him marrying her? Madness? To what was he referring? Did he suffer from injuries that were not visible?

She didn't care. Nothing would dissuade her from being a wife to him if he would have her. The challenge was to convince him to have her.

Ainsley cleared his throat. "Allow me to apologize for my brother. He's not been himself since he returned home."

"With all due respect, Your Grace, I suspect he's being *exactly* himself. He's just simply no longer the person you knew before he left. How could he be? He lived through horrors that I pray you have not the ability to even imagine." Embarrassed by her brutal honesty, she set her napkin aside and rose. The gentlemen immediately did the same. "If you'll be so kind as to excuse me, I must see to John."

She was surprised by how easily the lie rolled off her tongue. She wanted to run from the room, but she forced herself to walk sedately as a lady and not as a hoyden. She needed to make a good impression on these people, but at the moment she cared about only one. Where would she find him?

In the library, standing at the window, gazing out on the night, with a glass in one hand and a decanter on the table near the other. Her heart was hammering and her steps seemed exceptionally loud as she crossed the massive room to join him. His face was a wreath of torment and fury. Studying her as he had at the table, he'd obviously remembered her, knew of her duplicity. He'd take John from her. She should have been honest from the beginning. Perhaps with heartfelt honesty now, she could repair some of the damage and ensure that the precious babe remain in her life.

"Major Lyons—"

"Good God, Mercy, considering the intimacy we've shared, do you not think we should go by our Christian names?"

Relief swamped her with such swiftness and force that her knees almost buckled. He didn't remember the precise circumstances of the night they'd spent together. Another reason had heralded his departure from the table. It was only by force of will that she remained standing.

"I know it's difficult to hear others speak so carelessly of war," she said softly, wanting to fold him into her embrace as he'd once done her. But she didn't have the courage to risk his rebuff. "And for all the correspondents writing so passionately about the intolerable conditions into which we blithely sent our soldiers, words on paper are not the same as blood on hands. Your family was not there. They can't know how you suffered."

"But you were there," he said quietly, staring into the darkness beyond the window. "You know."

She nodded. Physicians, nurses, soldiers—they all concentrated on the physical wounds, those they could touch, knew existed, but Mercy was confident that there were invisible wounds that needed to be administered to. How many men had she cared for who appeared to be well on their way to recovery, only to succumb to death? She'd known of a case where a man had complained of pain in his arm so severe that he'd been unable to hold a rifle. But numerous examinations had found no cause for it. They'd labeled him a liar and a coward, but she'd not been convinced. She'd known of other illnesses that couldn't be diagnosed. The human body was not like a timepiece that could be easily opened in order to learn precisely how it worked. She'd seen men die from wounds that had not appeared severe. She'd seen men survive injuries that had torn them apart. She was convinced there was an element of the soul or the heart or the spirit with immeasurable influence on the ability to flourish after a catastrophic injury.

"I think the constant fear of dying must take a toll," she continued. "I think experiencing the hardships we are willing to inflict upon each other gives us a perspective that nothing else can. It batters us without our realizing it. I've had mornings where, if not for John, I'm certain I would have never left my bed."

Turning slightly, he pressed his back to the corner of the window casing. The sharp edge could not have provided comfort, but he seemed not to notice. Or perhaps he needed the discomfort to keep him focused on the present so he didn't slip into the past horrors. Sometimes she would awaken disoriented and think she was back in Scutari. For all the good she'd done there, it was not a place to which she wished to return, not even in dreams.

She grew uncomfortable under his increasing

scrutiny. What was he searching for? Did he suspect her duplicity?

"Why did you keep him?" he asked. "The babe. Why not find a good family for him?"

"Because he is yours."

"You say that as though you care deeply for me. Do you not think whatever feelings you may have, I may have, were brought on by the circumstances of where we were? That none of it was real."

"It was all real. My God in heaven, I wish it wasn't. The blood, the filth, the men weeping for their mothers, their wives. None of the horrors of that ghastly place discounts what I felt—feel—for you. If anything it only made me realize how very fragile life is, that we have no guarantee of tomorrow, that we must make our decisions based upon what we know at this moment."

He set the glass aside, then reached out and cradled her face, his thumb sweeping along the curve of her cheek to capture a tear she'd not even realized had formed. His action was heartbreakingly familiar. He'd done the same in Scutari, just before he'd drawn her into the circle of his arms and provided her with a safe haven. "What do you know at this moment?"

"That you're the most remarkable man I've ever known."

His thumb stilled. "Do you know that my brothers bought me a commission because they thought me lacking in character? That I preferred women above all things."

"And women prefer you above all men."

His eyes widened slightly.

"I do not think there was a nurse in all of Scutari

who didn't fancy herself in love with you. You have the ability to smile at a woman and make her believe that you have never smiled in quite the same way at any other."

"Was it my smile that charmed you into my bed, then?"

Once again, all hope that she'd been more than simply one of the nurses shattered into sharp shards with the affirmation that she'd been merely one of a dozen. When he touched her, when she was near enough to look into the blue depths of his eyes and absorb the beauty of them, when his attention was focused on her, she could easily forget that she'd meant nothing to him. While she had worshipped him for his strength, his unselfishness, and his willingness to tend to her heart, she'd obviously misread his affections for her, had thought herself more than she was. But what did her place in his heart truly matter when he had so courageously secured a place in hers?

Slowly she shook her head, unable to usher forth the teasing smile that he was no doubt expecting. How could she when her heart was cracking? "No, not your smile."

His other hand came up, as large and strong as the first. His gaze wandered over her face, stopped at her lips. They tingled, parted. In his eyes, she saw interest, curiosity . . . desire. "My kiss then."

Before she could inform him that he'd not enticed her with a kiss, he was doing exactly that, his mouth plying provocatively over hers. She stiffened when he pushed his tongue between her lips and swirled velvet over silk, then relaxed as his skill seduced her. He did not force, but he invited. She accepted the invitation.

His flavor was rich and powerful, wine and whiskey combined into a darkness that was as intoxicating as the caress of his tongue. He ravished without brutality. He caused every nerve to tingle, every inch of her body to respond as though he slowly stroked her from toe to chin.

She'd dreamed of him sweeping her off her feet a thousand times as she'd walked the narrow path between the beds at the Barrack Hospital tending to the needs of other men, as she'd prepared to leave Scutari because of John's impending birth, as she'd traveled the rough seas on a ship, as she'd journeyed via railway to Paris. Major Stephen Lyons had never been far from her thoughts.

But in spite of her various imaginings, she'd not been prepared for the compelling nature of his kiss, delivered with such urgency. She returned it in full measure. Life was short, opportunities few, and she'd yearned for this nearness for too long to be demure now. She stepped into his embrace and felt as though she'd finally returned home, to the spot where one night with him had shown her she could be. As his arms came around her, drew her even closer, she knew she was where she was meant to be. She had looked into his eyes that long-ago night and she'd seen his compassion and kindness. She knew of his bravery, had seen his unselfish devotion to his men.

A man lacking in character? If he'd ever truly been such, she had no doubt he'd left that part of himself on England's shores when he'd boarded the ship that carried him east.

She'd feared that he'd left his memories of her in Scutari, but he kissed her now as though he were intimately familiar with the contours of her mouth. He left no part wanting for attention. His feral groan echoed around them, and he deepened a kiss that she'd thought could go no further. Intense heat swarmed through her. If she didn't know better she'd have thought she'd suddenly taken ill. Her stomach clenched, and between her legs, warmth pooled with the promise of more pleasure and eventual surcease.

He dragged his mouth from hers, his breathing harsh and heavy. She drew in great draughts of air, as his hot, moist lips trailed to the sensitive spot below her ear and nibbled there. She wanted to tell him that his kiss had not enticed her before, but he'd left her without the strength to speak. It was a wonder she still stood. If not for the sturdiness of his arm at her back, she suspected she'd be on the floor now, a silken puddle of heated desire.

Then he returned his mouth to hers with an urgency that matched hers. She wanted this, wanted whatever he would grant. A kiss, a touch, a caress, yes, even more. She'd come too far, taken too many chances, ruined her reputation. She had nothing else to lose and all to gain. She could tell him that she loved him, because she did. The man she'd met on distant shores was worthy of her devotion.

She might not have stood out in his mind as memorable, but he'd never become diminished in hers.

She heard the clatter of pins hitting the parquet floor, felt the strands of her hair falling free to brush along her shoulders. He tunneled his fingers through her hair—

His mouth left hers with an abruptness that startled her. His brow was furrowed with confusion. His breathing was labored as though he'd just run up a hill. Hers was no better. Her pulse thrummed an unsteady beat. She wanted his mouth back on hers. She wanted to be locked in his embrace, the key tossed away.

"Your hair. It's . . . short."

It was considerably longer than it had been, but not nearly as long as it once was. What did that have to do with anything? The words made no sense, lifted her from the sensual well into which she'd fallen. "Vermin. Difficult to keep it free of vermin. With all the wounded . . . so little time. Cropping it was—"

He released her with a suddenness that had her staggering. Why had she gone on and on about her dratted hair? Why hadn't she simply moved forward before the spell was completely broken?

"My God. I forgot myself," he said, his voice rough with needs unfulfilled. "Forgive me."

Before she could assure him there was nothing to forgive, he snatched up his walking stick from where it had been resting against the wall. Without another word, he began trudging toward the door, his limp incredibly pronounced.

Had she caused him pain by forcing him to hold her aloft, by pressing against him? Could he better place her now? Was he toying with her? Surely, he had to know that he'd never before kissed her. Had he finally desired her as she'd always desired him?

She was confused, mortified. Why did he act as though he didn't know her at all? "Stephen?"

"I need to ride."

And then he was gone.

She stood there for the longest, trying to regain her bearings, clutching the short strands of her hair, trying to determine why he would be so bothered by them. They'd been even shorter when she'd tended to him. He acted as though he had absolutely no memory of her at all. Wretched tears burned her eyes. How could she have meant nothing *at all* to him?

She heard a distant door slam. She hurried in the direction of the sound.

"Have you seen Major Lyons?" she asked the first servant with whom she crossed paths.

"Yes, ma'am. He retrieved his greatcoat and left."

By the time she was standing outside the front door, he was already galloping away, his greatcoat billowing behind him. She wanted to be on the horse with him. She wanted him, pitiful creature that she was, content to receive the smallest bit of his attention. He gave it so easily and so completely to other women.

Why not to her?

Chapter 3

All he wanted was to bury himself, bury himself in woman after woman, bury himself and forget . . . that he couldn't remember.

So why the bloody hell didn't he turn his horse in the direction of the nearest village where he'd find a tavern and a willing wench? Why was he riding hell-bent-for-leather into the countryside where he'd find no solace? Because he couldn't bed another woman when the mother of his child smelled so enticing and smiled so sweetly and laughed so softly.

It was the laugh that had done him in. He desperately wanted to remember hearing it before. Had they laughed in bed? Had she been comfortable with the intimacy?

Only one night. He should ask her why.

Had he left her feeling abandoned while he flitted to another flower, or had the roar of cannons torn him from her bed?

He'd sat at that blasted table and studied her features—every movement, every expression, every nuance—searching for the smallest glimmer of familiarity. He wasn't greedy. He'd take crumbs.

He'd watched her fingers dancing over the table,

signaling for bread, lifting a fork, holding a knife, carrying red wine to her lips, and he'd wondered if they'd danced over him, eliciting pleasure. He'd wanted them to skim over him again, to caress and stroke. He wanted to know if he'd had a pet name for her. Red, perhaps, in honor of her hair. Had he teased her about its brightness, or had her eyes always held the majority of his attention?

Had he looked into them before war had torn away her innocence? Or had he always known them as they were now, with the haunted shadows weaving in and out? He'd seen her stiffen at his mother's intrusive questions, and even though he desperately wanted to know the answers as well, he'd put a stop to the inquisition. He might have known her reasons at one time. He might have known her dreams and her hopes.

Why was she not more comfortable with him? Had they parted in anger? Or had he broken her heart?

She certainly hadn't kissed him as though he had. She'd been eager, but there had also been a hint of shyness. Perhaps it was because of the length of time they'd been separated. He'd hoped that the kiss would spark his memory, but more than that, he'd simply wanted to kiss her, to know how it might affect him.

It had very nearly dropped him to his knees. No other woman had ever affected him so, no other had ever made him not want to waltz into lovemaking, but to rush headlong toward pleasure. He'd not wanted to hold back. He'd wanted to sweep her into his arms and carry her up the stairs to his bedchamber. He'd wanted to take her someplace where he knew that they'd not be disturbed. He'd almost forgotten what had brought her to Grantwood Manor.

They'd been intimate before. Would she detect the uncertainty in him? Did they share little jokes? Did she have a preference for a particular position? Was there one she abhorred? Would she deduce by his actions that he was not familiar with her?

What did he know of her? What did she know of him?

The not knowing, after only a few hours, was driving him to madness. He should confront her, tell her everything. She wouldn't be quite so enamored of him then, not when she learned the truth. What did he owe her? Marriage? His name?

The tension shimmering through the dining room had been almost unbearable, everyone waiting for confirmation that he'd been restored to normalcy. His family had struggled to engage both Miss Dawson and himself in conversation. His family, who was so very skilled at walking through social situations unscathed, seemed to stumble tonight. Ainsley had the devil's own tongue. His mother was herself an artist, an artist at deflecting conversation from her faults and scandals when it suited her, luring others into revealing their darkest secrets when she longed to know what they were. During dinner she'd stammered around like a schoolgirl at her first tea party.

All the while, Miss Dawson had squirmed in her chair, obviously wishing to be elsewhere. She'd avoided his direct gaze, studied her place setting as though she'd never encountered china or cutlery and was striving to unravel the mystery of each.

He made her uncomfortable with his intrusive staring, but he'd been unable to direct his eyes away from her.

It didn't help matters that his leg ached unmercifully,

to such an extent that he could barely tolerate his trousers touching it. Riding was excruciating, but he desperately needed to escape. His mother thought he should marry the girl who served as a constant reminder of all he'd lost.

But he couldn't marry her without revealing the truth regarding his affliction—it wouldn't be fair to her not to tell her he was but a partial man—and then she'd look upon him with the same pitying expression that he abhorred. And other doubts would surface. What if his memory loss was not related to the battle but to some deficiency in him, some madness?

Rain began falling, pattering his greatcoat, beating out a steady staccato that added a haunting element to the thud of the horse's hooves as they made light work of rapidly distancing him from Grantwood Manor. He couldn't get far enough away, quickly enough. He knew he'd have to return and face the dilemma before him. Even if they didn't marry, he'd make arrangements to see after the boy's welfare as well as hers. What sort of life would she have then? Men would see her as nothing more than a trollop. No man would ever want her as his wife. Stephen would be condemning her to spinsterhood. She deserved better.

Didn't she? His conclusions were drawn after only a few hours of visiting with her. What did he truly know about her? What if Ainsley read her better? What if he could see her more clearly? Stephen's thoughts had been in a fog ever since he awoke in that damned military hospital.

He urged his horse up the rise. At the top, he drew the gelding to a stop and dismounted. His right leg buckled and his knee hit the ground hard and torturously, shooting pain straight to his hip, before he could catch his balance. He roared out his frustrations, competing in volume with the thunder rumbling across the sky, as the anguish spiked. He tried to rub out the agony, but it only increased with his touch, as though he dug the blade of a knife into it.

He wouldn't mind the scars or the discomfort so much if he knew that he'd given as good as he got.

He'd been making some progress toward letting the mystery of the past two years go. He couldn't reclaim them. Maybe he didn't want to. He wanted nothing more than to heal and then get on with his life. But Miss Dawson—Mercy, *Mercy*—had arrived and suddenly the past two years had become unbearably important. What other mysteries resided within the murky depths? Were there other children, other women he should have remembered? Or had she been the only one?

Only one night with one woman. Unlikely. Not in the span of two years. Not with his sexual appetites. Before he'd awakened on that damned filthy mattress, he'd barely been able to go a night without playing a game of seduction. Would she expect him to give up his nightly carousing?

A forced marriage had certainly never been his goal in life. He doubted it had been hers either. She'd probably dreamed of heartfelt declarations and a bended knee. He'd intended to die a bachelor. He had no title, no property, nothing to leave to a son.

But suddenly he had one. And a woman whose reputation was in shambles because of his actions.

The rain pouring around him couldn't wash away his doubts or his burdens. He had to face them. On the morrow, he'd offer to marry Miss Dawson. It would certainly be no hardship. The kiss in the library had proven there was a spark between them that could be ignited into a roaring blaze with only a bit of kindling. Perhaps once she knew his intentions to do right by her, they would regain whatever comfortableness they'd once shared. Perhaps if he pretended all was well, it would be.

Wearily he battled the pain and shoved himself to his feet. Without his cane, he was fairly crippled when the agony was as great as this. Staggering forward, he fought to keep his balance as he made his way to the horse. It shied away. He cursed. He cooed. He sought to gentle it as he limped toward it. Thunder boomed and it skittered away.

He dropped his head back and allowed the rain to beat unmercifully on his face. With the increasing torment of his leg, he couldn't walk all the way back to Grantwood Manor. He needed the damned horse. Why the bloody hell had he ever dismounted? The throbbing ache he'd experienced in the saddle was nothing compared with what was coursing through him now.

With renewed determination, he took a deep breath, struggled to ignore the shards of pain, and hobbled after his beastly horse.

"What do you think of the girl?" Tessa Seymour, Duchess of Ainsley, asked.

"She'd look lovely on canvas."

Sitting at her vanity, she twisted around and glared at the young blond Adonis with the golden eyes lounging on her bed waiting for her to finish her nightly rituals. All the various creams she applied to her face, throat, and arms were all that kept her from looking all of her forty-seven years. "Leo."

She did not bother to hide her displeasure with his answer. He demanded complete honesty between them. It had terrified her at first, but now she saw the wisdom in it. It was liberating, and she had come to realize that no matter her faults, he would always forgive her.

He shrugged. "You think she could be his salvation."

"I hope she could be, yes. He seems so lost. While they don't say anything, I know Westcliffe and Ainsley harbor much guilt over Stephen's circumstance. After all, they purchased his commission."

"And the queen sent him where she would. They couldn't have known that this bloody situation with Russia was going to erupt into a godforsaken war that would not be over quickly."

True enough. The newspapers had been filled with reports. And the casualties. So many casualties. The telegraph had shrunk the world, given the war an immediacy unlike any before it.

It had nearly killed her when she'd received word that he'd died. A mother was not supposed to have a favorite. But she did. She always had. Stephen. She had adored his father with every fiber of her being. The Earl of Lynnford. He'd been her lover when she was married to the Earl of Westcliffe. She'd never told Stephen the truth of his parentage.

Shame, when she was younger, had stopped her. Fear, as she grew older, trapped the truth within her.

Lynnford had not even known. But since Westcliffe had stopped visiting her bed as soon as she announced she was carrying their first child and never returned, even after his heir was born, she had no doubts regarding Stephen's true father.

She'd gone to Lynnford with the news of Stephen's death. "You must go to the Crimea and fetch his body. I'll not leave him so far from home."

"Tessa, he would want to be buried beside those who fought next to him."

"I don't care what he wants. Call me selfish, but at this moment, I only care what I want."

"This is a fool's errand."

And so she'd told him that which she'd sworn to never reveal. "He's your son."

She'd held him while he cried. She'd given him a son and taken him away in the space of a solitary heartbeat.

He'd admitted that he'd sometimes suspected Stephen was his son. But he had his own family and had been too cowardly to pursue the matter.

But she didn't view him as cowardly. She saw him as a man who wished to bring as little hurt as possible to those he loved. What was to be gained with knowledge?

It was when he'd sent word to the army, alerting them that he would be arriving to bring back the body of Major Stephen Lyons, that they'd learned Stephen was not dead.

It was when he'd returned home that they'd learned he was not the young man who had left.

Her heart had broken all over again. How many times could a mother's heart break? An infinite number. Each time her children were hurt. She'd long ago accepted the pain of it, as well as the stoicism to never let it show. It was a mother's lot in life.

"Are you going to insist that he marry Miss Dawson?"

Leo asked her now, drawing her back to the present moment and her current lover.

"You grant me more power than I possess. When it comes to my sons, they will do as they will. Still, I don't see that he has much of a choice. The one thing he does not relish is disappointing me, so I might have a bit of leverage. I have no doubt that John is his son. I can already see the shape of his smile on his mouth. It would be unconscionable for him not to marry the girl."

"Stephen's father didn't marry you."

Leo, with his artist's eye, had seen what she'd tried so valiantly not to reveal—that Lynnford was Stephen's father. "Because I was married at the time and well you know it. I never should have confessed to you about my indiscretions."

"I'd already guessed them, my love, as well as your feelings for the man. I still long for the day when you look upon me as you do Lynnford whenever he is near."

Her heart nearly shattered. He asked so little of her, only this. Why could she not love him with the intensity that she did the Earl of Lynnford? Especially as it was obvious to one and all that Lynnford adored his wife. He'd not been married when he was Tessa's lover. By the time she was once again without a husband, he'd been spoken for—and loyal beyond measure to his wife.

Leo held out his hand to her. "Come and join me. Allow me to erase the sadness from your eyes."

She could never resist him. Rising gracefully, she glided over to the bed, crawled onto it, nestled against Leo, and caressed his cheek. "I do love you, you know."

"But not as much as you do others."

She opened her mouth to protest and he touched his

finger to her lips. "I do not resent the love you have for your sons and now your grandsons. I would never seek to usurp their places in your heart. I cannot even resent the lover of your youth, because at least through him you knew what it was to be loved. But he is not here now. Tell me you do not think of him when you are in my arms."

"Never does he cross my mind when I am here with you."

"Liar," he whispered softly, and proceeded to ensure the words she'd spoken took on a measure of truth.

Chapter 4

As Stephen headed into his bedchamber—exhausted from chasing down and finally recapturing his idiot horse, then stubbornly galloping back to the manor while every beat of the hooves jarred his leg and sharpened the pain—he heard the baby cry out. Immediately he paused, his hand on the doorknob.

Before this afternoon, Stephen had enjoyed having the entire wing to himself. Then he'd asked that Mercy be given a room near him. He didn't know if she was aware that he was across the hall. In spite of the fact that he'd been wearing a greatcoat, which he'd discarded downstairs, he was wet and chilled. His hair clung to his head, the water dripped onto his shoulders. He was hardly presentable.

The babe's wails rose in crescendo. There could be no doubt he had a good set of lungs. Why was he caterwauling? Why didn't he cease his screaming?

Stephen crossed the hallway and knocked on the door. No one else was in this wing to be disturbed, and sleep never came easily to him. He could ignore the crying, but he was concerned for Mercy. He felt a need to do something to assist her.

Lie to everyone else, you fool, but not to yourself. You

simply welcome the excuse to see her again in spite of your disheveled state.

The crying stopped, but now his curiosity was piqued beyond measure. Even though he was wet, shivering, and in need of a good dose of laudanum, he found himself knocking on the door once again. "Miss Dawson?"

He heard the soft pad of bare feet just before the door clicked and she peered out through the narrow opening. Fear and worry furrowed her brow. That was how she had come to have that little indention. It deepened with her concern, and she'd no doubt spent a great amount of time concerned.

"Is anything amiss?" Stephen asked.

"No. John gets hungry this time of night."

He found himself peering over her shoulder, striving to see the boy. What was with his blasted curiosity?

"I'm sorry if he disturbed you. I thought this was the guest wing, that we were alone."

He saw no need to alarm her by revealing how near she was to his chambers. He would not take advantage. For some inexplicable reason, it calmed him to know that he was available if she had a need. She was in no danger here, but still the notion reverberated through his aching head that he could protect her. It was only natural that he would want to shield her from hurt, but there was more to it that he couldn't explain.

"Is there anything you require?" he asked.

She shook her head briskly. "No. I have a nurse." She blushed to the roots of her hair, which was caught in a stubble of a braid. He imagined it much longer, draped over her shoulder, falling just past her breast. The thought was quickly followed by the realization that he'd cupped that breast, run his tongue over it, drawn the nipple—that even now puckered under his gaze—into his mouth. "John doesn't go hungry."

"You hired a wet nurse?"

The blush deepened, then retreated. She angled her chin with defiance as though quite offended. "A lady of breeding does not . . . she does not handle the task herself."

"It seems a rather odd place to draw the line."

"Whatever do you mean?"

He leaned toward her, bit back his groan as his thigh protested. "A lady of breeding doesn't give birth to a child out of wedlock."

"You were otherwise occupied and not available for marriage."

She did not attempt to excuse her behavior. He liked that about her. It was also obvious that she took exception to his finding fault with her. He didn't blame her. He'd been attempting to distract himself from traveling a path that might have led to a disastrous destination: her again in his bed before anything was resolved between them.

He wanted to take her hand and lead her across the hallway. He wanted to feather his fingers through her hair while kissing her. He wanted her draped over his bed, too sated to move. Then he would curl around her and . . . sleep. What an odd thought.

"My apologies. My words were uncalled for. It seems my sins regarding you know no bounds. I shan't add preventing you from sleeping to the list. Good night." He turned to leave, his leg gave out on him—

She was there in the hallway, supporting him, one hand clutching his elbow, her arm wrapped around his waist, her scent—lavender—wafting up to tease his nostrils, while that damned breast he'd been fantasizing about pressed up against his upper arm.

"You're cold and in pain. What were you doing out and about?" she chastised.

"I needed to ride. Now if you'll release me and return to your room, I'll make my way to my bedchamber."

"I'll assist you. Where is it?"

He nodded toward the door across the hallway and her eyes widened.

"You claimed there are an abundance of rooms."

"There are. I cannot be held accountable if one of them is across from mine."

Her lips twitched.

"Where's the humor in that?"

She shook her head. "I'm just thinking of something you said when we first met."

Damnation. They shared intimacies that went beyond the bedchamber. He couldn't fool her regarding his mental affliction for long. He should just come out with it now, but the pain had ratcheted up to a level so intense that he could barely think.

"You may release your hold on me," he informed her laconically.

Doubt flooded her eyes, but she moved away.

"Good night," he repeated.

She did little more than arch a brow and cross her arms beneath her breasts, a challenge in her eyes. She didn't believe any more than he did that he could make his way to his room without making an embarrassing spectacle of himself. Still, he was determined to try. Clenching his teeth, he stepped forward—

Pain sliced through him, he couldn't swallow back

the groan as his leg buckled, and she was once again supporting him.

"Don't touch it," he growled.

She froze. "What?"

"My leg. I can't stand for it to be touched."

"Why ever not? Is it not yet healed?"

"It's healed. It just hurts like bloody hell."

"May I have a look at it?"

"To what purpose?"

"I don't know, but something isn't right here. Based upon when I saw your name listed among the casualties, you've had ample time to recover. If it's healed, you shouldn't have this pain."

He shook his head. "It's not usually this bad, but tonight—"

"I insist. I need to see it."

Her tone was adamant, her gaze unflinching. Was this how she'd ended up in his bed? He couldn't deny the allure of a determined woman.

"Very well." Having conceded that point, he also acknowledged that he required her assistance to reach his room. He dropped his arm around her shoulders and allowed her to escort him into his bedchamber.

Once inside, she helped him out of his jacket. While she went to drape it over a chair, he stood beside his bed and watched her, mesmerized. The efficiency in her movements appealed to him. Opening a cabinet, she removed a couple of towels and returned to his side. She'd no doubt known where to look because a similar cabinet was in her bedchamber.

He took a towel from her and began rubbing it over his hair, holding her gaze, wondering how long it would take her to realize that in order to see his leg she was going to see a good deal more. He might have been amused by the prospect, if he wasn't shaking so badly from the cold and the agony.

"Let's get you out of the remainder of these wet things," she said. The words were delivered with the flat tone of a dozen nurses who had tended to him, no hint of allure, but still his body jerked with arousal that he steadfastly tamped down. His waistcoat and cravat were quickly dispensed with and found their way to the floor.

His shirt came off more slowly, her fingers tormenting him as they skimmed along his sides after she'd gathered the hem and begun lifting it over his head. She stopped, continued on, stopped again, and he knew she was cataloging the scars that were revealed.

"I suppose my chest looks very different than before," he said quietly, wondering if they'd made love in the light, as was his preference.

His shirt landed on the discarded clothes, then she was looking up at him, her hands hovering within a whisper's breath of his skin. Did she think he would shatter if she touched him? In all likelihood, he might. It was an aphrodisiac to know that he'd been with her before and to wonder what it might have been like. It was also unsettling. Not to know how he'd brought her pleasure, what he might have introduced her to, what still remained to be shared.

She reached past him, her breasts brushing along his shoulder and arm. In spite of his pain, her touch went straight to his groin like lightning striking the earth. He was not going to be in a position to unfasten his trousers. Although having been with him before, she shouldn't be surprised by his arousal.

Straightening, she draped a blanket around his shoulders, overlapping the ends to spare his modesty—of which he possessed not an ounce. She, however, obviously did. In the dark then, he must have taken her in the dark. Why was she so shy, when he was so skilled at introducing a lady to the particulars of a man's body, making her comfortable with it? Although never had that intimacy, or those lessons, resulted in a squalling babe.

"You should remove your trousers," she said, stepping back.

"Why the blush, Mercy?" he asked as he did as she bade. Her name sounded strange on his tongue, as though he'd never before spoken it. But surely he had.

"The hour is late," she said.

Was that her true reason? Or simply her feeble attempt to deflect the question? Tending to the wounded, she surely had been exposed to more naked bodies than his.

Trying to remove his soaked trousers and drawers while holding the blanket proved an impossibility, especially with his leg refusing to support his weight. "Give me a few moments of privacy and then return," he ordered.

With a quick nod, she made a hasty exit. A strange reaction. Perhaps it was simply the intimacy of being in his bedroom, bringing forth reminders of another night when passion had flared between them. With great difficulty, he shed his trousers and drawers, sat on the bed, and wrapped the blanket around him—for her modesty, not his.

"Mercy!"

The door opened a fraction and she peered in,

reminding him of someone fearing a monster. He wanted to laugh, but removing his trousers had brutalized his leg. He should have cut the damned things off rather than subject his leg to the struggle.

She knelt in front of him, and he wondered if she'd knelt for him before. A tremor of desire raked through him, causing him to shudder. What the bloody hell was wrong with him?

He was reacting like a randy schoolboy—in spite of everything. If not for the pain shooting through his leg, he'd already have her on top of the covers, her nightgown a distant memory, her body bared—

"My apologies," she whispered, easing the blanket up over his leg. "I'll be gentle."

Only he didn't want gentle. He wanted rough, fast, passionate. He wanted—

"Oh, my dear God," she whispered in horror.

The pain burst through his leg, sending him off the bed, the blanket fluttering to the floor. "Christ! I told you not to touch it!"

It was only then that he realized he'd grabbed her wrist and jerked her to her feet. Her gaze darted down and then back up to his eyes. Hers were wide and she was trembling as much as he. The pain had diminished his arousal but it didn't mean he wasn't a sight to behold.

"Why the shocked look?" he asked. "Why the blush, the panting? You've seen it before." *Felt it. Welcomed it.*

She swallowed, licked her lips, and in spite of the burgeoning agony, damn it all, he wanted to lean in and taste her. Distraction. He needed a bloody distraction.

"It's . . . it's been . . . some time," she stammered. "I'd forgotten . . ."

He knew he shouldn't be insulted that she'd forgotten his endowments—after all, he'd forgotten her completely. Still it stung, providing him with an inkling of understanding regarding what it meant to be unmemorable. How devastated might she be to know he had no memories of her at all—other than those he'd gathered since her arrival this afternoon?

Then to his utter surprise, she thrust up her chin and took on a mulish expression. "I also know you're attempting to distract me. How long has your leg looked like that?" she demanded.

Swollen, red, hot to the touch.

"A few days now. I've been riding, walking, striving to get it to heal more quickly. It protests. I'm certain if I just rest it—"

"I need to examine it more closely."

"You see what happens when you touch—"

"You endured much worse in Scutari without so much as a by your leave. Sit. Now."

Her commanding voice was not that of an angel. But it intrigued and aroused him. And she'd provided him with a hint of their past. He wanted to mull on it. She'd known him wounded. Perhaps she'd nursed him back to health. When had she arrived at the hospital? Which of his scars did she know the origins of?

He sat and flicked the blanket over his good hip, leaving the other slightly exposed for her perusal. Again she knelt. As her fingers neared, he braced himself.

Her touch was feathery-light but it was still agonizing. It was as though she were taking a dagger—

"I believe there's something in there," she said, sitting back on her heels.

He looked at her in stunned disbelief and then

examined his leg more closely. Tensing in anticipation
of the onslaught of pain, he skimmed his fingers over it,
detecting a hardness—was it possible? Was that why it
had seemed so slow to heal, the reason the pain never
went away? "You might be right."

"You silly man. What were you thinking? You need
a physician."

"I thought I'd simply overworked it."

"With that swelling and redness? I've no doubt it's
infected. You might even have the beginnings of gan-
grene. It's ghastly. You absolutely cannot delay sending
for a physician."

"You could tend to it."

"It requires far more skills than I possess."

Gazing up at him, she looked so earnest, so young.

"You've nothing to fear," she said softly. "I'll watch
over you."

He did not doubt her. Not for a single moment. "Then
we should indeed send for a physician posthaste. Do
not, however, alarm my mother. My brother can see to
the matter."

With a brusque nod, she rushed from the room on
bare feet that barely made a sound. But to his immense
delight, she had left behind her fragrance.

After having the duke roused from slumber, Mercy
explained to him what was needed. He hesitated not
one second before sending for a physician who he assured her would arrive within the hour. Obviously, he
was accustomed to having his way, of being in charge.
She pitied any woman who might fall in love with him.
He would no doubt prove a challenge as a husband. But
then she supposed all men did.

She went to see after John. His late-night feeding complete, he was lost in the world of dreams. Jeanette assisted her in changing into her simple black dress.

"Are you certain you should be in a gentleman's bedchamber at night?" Jeanette asked, her French accent thick. No one would ever doubt her origins.

"He is fairly incapacitated. He can do me no harm."

"A man can always do harm."

"I must tend him." The next few hours would not be pleasant. She dreaded them. For his sake, as well as hers. She did not want memories stirred.

"Your generous heart will get you in trouble," Jeanette murmured.

"It already has."

When she returned to Major Lyons's room, she discovered he was beneath the covers. Thank goodness. Everything neatly tucked away and hidden. She was familiar with the naked form, had bathed men, tended wounds in the most private of areas—but still she'd been unprepared for the sight of him. He'd not been aroused, but the promise of what he offered was quite evident. He'd fairly taken her breath.

His brother was giving him the proper dressing down that she had wanted to.

"What were you thinking?" the duke demanded. "Even I can look at your leg and tell it needs tending."

"I thought"—Stephen shook his head, his jaw clenched—"I thought I might lose it."

"Not facing reality doesn't make it go away."

"Easy enough for you to say when your reality comes with no troubles." He shifted his gaze to her. "Mercy, come sit over here."

The first time she'd heard her name coming from his

lips, a shiver of pleasure had rippled through her. She'd thought the pleasure would diminish the next time, but it only increased. "Major—"

"For God's sake, Mercy, as I said earlier, you've given birth to my son. Formality between us is hypocritical."

"And politeness? Shall we dispense with it as well?"

He sighed heavily. "My apologies. I'm not at my best when my leg is consumed by fire."

"You're an idiot," the duke muttered. "I cannot believe you let it come to this."

"And I cannot believe you harp like an old wife. Leave it be."

To stop the squabbling, Mercy took the chair beside the bed and asked, "How much longer do you think before the physician arrives?"

"Not long," the duke said.

"When my brother barks, the people in this area all jump," Stephen said.

"And you're irascible when you're in pain," Ainsley muttered.

"If you don't like it, leave."

Ainsley crossed his arms over his chest and leaned against the post at the foot of the bed. His dark features were a sharp contrast to his brother's, made him seem more forbidding. "I still think I should alert Mother—"

"No, not until this ordeal is over. She'll only worry and there is naught she can do," Stephen said, his voice tight with pain. Mercy wished there was something she could do to relieve his suffering.

"You simply abhor the thought of Leo traipsing in after her," the duke said.

"That too. He's like a well-trained dog."

"He loves her." Ainsley smiled wryly at Mercy. "You might have noticed that during dinner."

She returned his smile. "I did."

"I like him," Ainsley said. "Stephen doesn't because Leo provides competition for Mother's attention and Stephen has always had the lion's share of it. He's our mother's favorite."

"I don't believe mothers have favorites," she said.

"Trust me. Ours does."

With the physician's arrival, all conversation ceased. He was an elderly gentleman, and while his hands seemed skillful, Mercy could tell that his examination was causing Stephen a great deal of pain, which he was stoically attempting to mask. But his sharp intake of breath and the stiffness of his body revealed the truth of it.

He was in agony.

Sweat beaded his brow and he locked his gaze on hers, much as he had during dinner, and she wondered if he found her to be a distraction from the torment. Against her will, she slid her hand beneath his, and he closed his strong fingers around it. Tiny tremors traveled through him.

"At least you're in a comfortable bed," she said, to divert his attention away from the examination. "And it's quiet here."

He looked at her as though she was prattling nonsense. Perhaps she was, perhaps she needed the diversion as well. "I always thought it a shame that the men could not have private rooms in which to heal. How demoralizing it must have been to see others suffering while you were healing. There was so little we could do sometimes. But things will go much better for you here. You will be cared for."

If he had any comment to offer, it was locked behind his clenched jaw. Taking her handkerchief from her pocket, she reached up and blotted his damp brow.

"Christ!" he suddenly barked.

"Forgive my clumsy fingers, Major," Dr. Roberts said quickly. "I don't see many battle wounds here in the country, but I think you might be right, Miss Dawson. I do believe we have something nasty going on there. Our best recourse will be to go in and get it out."

"How could something have been left in his leg?" the duke asked.

"Depending on the severity of the wound, the amount of blood, the conditions of the hospital"—the doctor shrugged—"I wouldn't think it would be unusual that something is missed. Medicine is not an exact science. But I shall have this matter fixed in no time. And we're in luck, Major." He opened his satchel. "I have ether."

"No."

The resounding word came out with such force as to brook no argument. Still Mercy spoke. "It'll go much easier on you."

"I need to see what he's doing."

He didn't. She knew he didn't. He had to know it as well. It would only add to his torment. He would have to be held down to prevent his natural instincts to fight the surgeon's scalpel. Why was he being so stubborn?

"Please." She placed her hand over his. "I watched too many men suffer when ether was scarce. You should accept this small mercy."

"You're all the mercy I need."

Ainsley scoffed. "You never miss an opportunity for a bit of flirtation, even in a situation such as this."

Her heart that had begun an erratic patter with Stephen's words settled into calm with Ainsley's. Of course, Stephen would use any means to get her to do his bidding. Had he not enticed her into looking the other way when he'd wanted to sneak out of the Barrack Hospital for a short walk—in spite of the physician's orders that he was not to leave his bed? Had he not given her a devilish wink that had caused her to slip him a flask of spirits? She'd have been summarily dismissed if Miss N had discovered her with the contraband. He'd made the simplest of gestures seem more daring.

"She's quite right, Major. I'll be doing a good bit of digging around in there."

"Please," she pleaded again, determined that she would be the one to prevail.

Clutching her hand, Stephen pulled her down, his voice rough and urgent. "Only if you'll ensure that he doesn't cut off my leg. Promise me."

"I don't think it'll come to that, but the physician will know best."

"I'll go bloody well mad if I lose anything else. Promise me."

The desperation in his voice tore at her heart. How many promises had she made and not been able to keep? They drove *her* mad, caused nightmares to visit often when she slept. But he didn't know what he asked of her or he'd have not asked. She was fairly confident of that deduction. They were practically strangers, their time together far too short. So short that he didn't seem to remember the night that they'd spent together. But she'd never forget what she'd seen of the fierceness in him when there was little he could do to prevent harm from being inflicted on another. He was courageous, strong, unyielding in his convictions. She'd witnessed his compassion when he'd reassured more than one dying soldier that he'd not let his brothers in arms down so the man could leave this world in peace.

He'd lied in order to bring comfort. She could do the same. "I promise."

Leaning forward and kissing his brow seemed the most natural thing in the world. Just as protecting his son had been. She couldn't explain the yearning in her heart for this man, but it was there, fervent and powerful. It had driven her to Paris, then to London, and finally to this place at his bedside.

She felt the fevered heat of his skin against her lips, and she prayed they were not too late. That his leg could be saved. That *he* could be saved.

"Will you assist me, Miss Dawson?" the physician asked.

Dread coursed through her. She didn't regret a single moment of tending to the sick and wounded, but it had taken more courage than she'd ever known she possessed to assist with the surgeries. Still, she gathered her resolve around her and straightened. "Yes, of course. I shall need to wash my hands. I must insist you do the same."

He brought himself up like a rooster whose feathers had been ruffled. It wouldn't do for him to be out of sorts when he began hacking away. She needed him focused on his chore, not his pride, and so she explained calmly and quietly, "Miss Nightingale was convinced that cleanliness saved lives. It is next to godliness, after all."

He harrumphed. "Yes, of course. Quite right."

She'd not thrown out the name of her mentor lightly. She was well aware that ever since an engraving of Florence Nightingale holding a lamp had appeared in the *London Illustrated News*, she was considered a saint. Mercy suspected she could tell the doctor that Miss Nightingale advised jumping out a window before surgery and he would proceed to do exactly that.

Ainsley ordered the servants to bring up warm water and cloths. Mercy fought off the images of the wards crowded with men that sought to distract her from her purpose. She'd felt a sense of relief when she'd left Scutari. She knew she'd done good works there, had helped many a soldier, provided comfort. But she'd lost a good deal of her innocence there, because she'd discovered so much she couldn't control. And she'd learned that not all men were good. War brought out the best and the worst. It was not only one's enemies that a person had to fear.

She washed her hands, surprised that the water appeared as clean afterward as it had before. In the hospital it had always been tinged with blood. Exactly as they had in Scutari, her hands trembled slightly, not enough for anyone except her to notice, but bothersome just the same. She forced them into submission, into steadiness. She'd not have John's father, a man who had shown courage on the battlefield, think her cowardly in any way.

Over her head, she slipped an apron she'd asked to borrow from one of the maids. She reached around to tie it—

"Allow me."

Startled, she lifted her gaze to Ainsley. Enough lamps

had been lit to provide a good deal of light. His eyes, an incredible green, held a great deal of compassion.

"You're almost as pale as Stephen is," he said quietly. "Are you certain you're up to this task?"

She nodded jerkily, her mouth absent of any dampness at all. "I've administered ether before."

"You're very brave, Miss Dawson."

"You give me far more credit that I deserve."

His gaze traveled over her face, and she realized she'd misjudged him. He was formidable when it came to managing situations, but he was not a hard man, and she reversed her earlier conclusion. Some woman would be very fortunate to have him.

"I doubt it," he said as though they were conspirators. "I'm a rather good judge of character. Our family will once again be in your debt."

"I wouldn't want John to lose his father." Now that she knew Stephen was alive, that John would have a chance to know him, to grow up within his shadow. "If you'll excuse me?"

"Yes, certainly." His expression communicated faith and trust in her abilities—both a relief and a burden.

She walked swiftly to the head of the bed. It had been little more than an hour since she'd first seen his leg, and during that time he'd diminished. He'd been fooling them all into believing he was strong and well. The moment for pretense was past, and he'd sunk into the pain. His skin, stretched taut across his cheekbones, seemed hotter to the touch. They had not a moment to lose.

She took the glass inhaler with its ether-soaked sponge and placed it carefully over Stephen's nose. "Simply breathe," she said solemnly.

He wrapped his long, slender fingers around her wrist and she wondered if he could feel her thready pulse. "Smile for me," he ordered.

"I can't, not at a time like this. There's no joy in it."

"Don't let the last thing I see be your worried frown."

"You're not going to die. And when you awake, I'll smile to your heart's content."

He shook his head. "Smile."

She should not have been surprised by his insistence. He'd never backed down when she'd known him before. Why would she think he'd changed? He was stubborn, determined to have his way. But she didn't find fault with him. She simply wanted this ordeal finished. Closing her eyes, she thought of the first time that *he* had grinned at her. Such a devilish smile, filled with self-assurance and teasing. He'd seemed to take nothing seriously, and for a few moments, in his company, she'd been able to do the same.

Opening her eyes, she forced her lips to curl upward, her brow to relax, her eyes to sparkle. "Now, Major . . . Stephen," she said, her tone filled with a lightness she didn't feel, "follow my orders and breathe . . . deeply."

She settled the inhaler back into place and watched as his eyelids grew heavy. They fluttered, his eyes opened wide, and then they closed, his thick, dark eyelashes—which matched the blond of his hair not at all—coming to rest on his cheeks.

As far as she was concerned, the moment when he opened those beautiful blue eyes again could not come soon enough.

Chapter 5

Every time the agony in his leg brought him to the surface of wakefulness, she was pouring something thick down his throat and he began the spiraling descent once again into oblivion. The only consolation was that until he succumbed completely to the sweet allure of a painless existence, she caressed his brow with cool fingers, wiped his chest with a damp cloth. For those few moments when awareness hovered, he wondered how much longer the physician would be ripping into his leg. Or was he finished? Was that the reason for liquid instead of ether? Everything was a confusing swirl of pain and nothingness.

When he awoke with no agony, panic set in. He feared his leg was gone. He couldn't feel it. Throwing off the covers, he struggled to find it.

Her hands met his, palm to palm, cool to heat. "No, no, you must let it heal."

"It's gone. I can't feel it. He took it."

"No. It's the laudanum."

She'd give him more. The panic would subside. The ache would settle in. He could feel it then with the panic gone. He wanted to explain why it was so important that he not lose the leg. He'd lost his memory; he couldn't bear the thought of losing something else. He should have told her before. When they'd walked through his brother's garden. He wished there'd been roses to pluck for her. He'd have shaved off the thorns before handing one to her. He wanted to slip a violet behind her ear. He wanted to lie her down on clover, while the sun beat warmth over their skin, and passion unfolded.

Strange. Strange, how when he became lost in his own mind, he felt the allure of her, the tug of her. He wanted to draw her near, kiss her. He wanted to talk with her. Wanted to know her secrets, her dreams. He wanted to make her smile.

Not that pitiful attempt that she'd given him before he'd succumbed to the lure of the ether. It had been more grimace than anything. Forced from her. He wanted to see her real smile, one of joy. He wanted soft laughter to accompany it, teasing laughter, the sort that would erupt as she ran barefoot across a field of daffodils.

She swam in and out of his vision.

"Why did you come to my bed?" He didn't know if he'd thought the words or actually spoke them. No answer came. But the question seemed to reverberate on the air. Her reason a secret. He didn't fancy secrets unless they were his.

Somewhere he thought he heard a baby cry. Then she was gone. He didn't want her to leave. Why? Why was she important? Who was she?

Remember. Remember. Surely here in this swirling vastness he could find answers. But his mind worked no better here. It was worse. It was hot. Perhaps he was in hell. At last. He'd done wicked things, selfish things. He knew he had no hope of heaven.

His leg. He had to find his leg. Now, while she was gone. But when he reached down, her hand was suddenly holding his, and she was whispering words he couldn't understand. He simply wanted to wake up.

To drink in the whiskey of her eyes. To ask for forgiveness. To make matters right.

His fever came with a swiftness that alarmed Mercy. Dr. Roberts had discovered a piece of steel—which looked to be the tip of a sword—embedded in Stephen's leg. He surmised that all of his activity of late, as he'd grown stronger, had forced it to begin working its way to the surface, but it had done some nasty damage on its journey.

Having witnessed the chaos as the wounded were treated following a battle, Mercy was not surprised that a piece of metal could be overlooked. Weary physicians worked swiftly, blood was in abundance, lighting was inadequate. Based on the thick, unsightly scar that ran from Stephen's hip to knee, she could only surmise that it had been a ghastly gash to begin with. He was no doubt fortunate that they hadn't simply lopped off his leg. She'd seen limbs that had looked almost perfect as they were being carried out for disposal. They would all visit in her dreams once she took time for a moment's sleep.

Instead she tended to Stephen's needs as though she alone could save him, leaving his side only for short spans of time to hold John. He was far from being neglected, however. Jeanette saw to his needs for sustenance and cleanliness. The duchess had taken a fancy to him. On more than one occasion Mercy had caught her rocking him or carrying him through the hallways, telling him of his past—even if it didn't truly originate here. Ainsley's father was not Stephen's and yet Stephen had grown up in this house.

Mercy yearned to walk along behind them and hear the tales of Stephen as a child. But it was he as a man who needed her now.

She supposed it was because of John that no one raised an eyebrow at her being alone in the room with Stephen. Or perhaps it was because he was incapacitated, with a raging fever and a leg that must once again go through the process of healing. During the daylight hours she could hear the buzz of activity inside the house and out. But it was with the night closing in, when all grew quiet except for an occasional creak or a moan of things settling in, that she was the most content.

Shadows could hide a great many sins, and she felt less likely to be accused of being the fraud she was. Nor was she likely to be interrupted. For all that the duchess loved her son, she did not sit by his side through the long hours until dawn. That task was reserved for Mercy, and she gladly welcomed it.

Knowing she wouldn't be disturbed, her hands didn't shake when she moved the sheet aside, removed the bandages, and examined Stephen's wound to ensure it wasn't festering. Gingerly, she would apply a salve to help with healing that the physician had left with her. Using clean strips of cloth brought to her by a servant, she would carefully wrap his leg.

Then she would begin the nightly ritual of bathing him. She would start at his feet, wiping the moist cloth over his soles. From there, she would travel upward, wondering at each scar—whether it be small or large— how it had come to be. The amount of puckered flesh told her of many battles fought, many wounds sustained. She'd not been there to treat all of them. He might not have even been brought to Scutari. As the war lingered, so other hospitals were outfitted, closer to the battles. The long journey from field to hospital had cost many a man his life. But what was to be done when the military lacked so much?

Her sojourn stopped at his left arm where a saber had once sliced deep. She skimmed her fingers over the mutilated flesh that she'd first bandaged in November of 1854, shortly after she'd arrived at Scutari, one of more than three dozen nurses accompanying Florence Nightingale. She'd been completely unprepared for the horrors that awaited them. The Battle of Balaclava, immortalized by Lord Tennyson in "The Charge of the Light Brigade," had taken place before they'd arrived, but the wounded were wallowing in the overcrowded Barrack Hospital and on a nearby ship. The army had been ill equipped for the tremendous influx of casualties. Some soldiers had received only cursory treatment. They lay on stuffed sacks or nothing at all.

Even now, the smell of rancid meat made her violently ill. It reminded her too much of putrid flesh and the stench of that hospital when she'd first walked into it.

She'd considered herself fortunate to be selected to accompany Miss Nightingale. In her naïveté, she'd even been excited. Reality had slammed into her with the force of a hand grenade. She'd wanted to run, to return to England's green fields. Instead she'd strengthened her resolve. If these men could fight to survive, the least she could do was help them battle death. So she'd donned her uniform: a hideous black woolen dress, unbleached apron, and white cap. Around her shoulders she wore a scarf with "Scutari Hospital" emblazoned in red thread to identify her—as though someone might mistake her for anything other than what she was: a woman who had come to give comfort.

Although one night, someone had mistaken her for something else. When those thoughts intruded, she shoved them back. She would not journey into that particular hell. Others had needed her, had rescued her from dark thoughts. In saving them, she'd saved herself. In saving Stephen, she had allowed for him to be there to save her.

Life was a strange circle. She tried not to decipher it, but rather to accept it as it came.

It was the third day after she'd arrived in Scutari when she caught her first glimpse of Captain Stephen Lyons, sitting up in a corner, fevered. His arm had become infected, but he'd stubbornly refused any sort of treatment until those around him were tended to. By the time he finally relented, the physicians wanted to amputate. He'd been as determined to keep his arm as he'd been to keep his leg. He'd proven to them that he still retained use of it, convinced them to work to save it.

"I could treat two more men in the time it'll take me to try to save that arm," one doctor had lamented.

"Then treat them," he'd retorted. "And come back to me when you're done. But I swear to you that I'll make saving my arm worth the military's bother."

She'd assisted as another doctor cut away the dying flesh. Stephen had grunted only once, when the doctor had begun his work, and he'd remained stoically silent after that, his jaw clenched so tightly, she was surprised he hadn't pushed his teeth down through his chin.

He was her first close look at bravery. She suspected the seeds for her admiration of him had begun that cold, dark night.

She'd wished that she could devote all her time to him, but far too many men required attention. But as he recovered, she sought him out as often as she could, wiping his brow when he was fevered—as she did now. She had studied his face, memorizing every line and curve, so she recognized now that he sported more creases and deeper furrows. Patting the cloth along his throat, across his chin brought to mind a long-ago night when she'd been doing the same. His eyes had suddenly sprung open, his mouth had curved up slightly.

"Hello, sweetheart."

His voice had been rough, scratchy, but her heart had reacted as though they were at a ball and he'd invited her to dance, beating a steady staccato like that of a drummer pounding the drum before battle.

"Would you care for some water?" she asked breathlessly, embarrassed that she seemed unable to control her reaction to him.

"Love some."

Her hands trembled as she poured water from a nearby pitcher into a glass. With a great deal of care and gentleness, she slipped an arm beneath his shoulders and lifted him slightly, cradling him, and bringing the glass to his parched lips. "Only a bit," she admonished, pulling away after he had a few sips.

He was breathing heavily when she lay him back down, as though he were the one going through all the effort.

"I have . . . my arm." The words were a statement and a question.

"Yes," she reassured him. "I believe it was your threat to murder whoever took it that convinced them."

"I cannot be held accountable for what I may have said under the influence of pain, although I daresay I did want to bloody well murder someone." His words sounded weary, but she had no doubt he meant them.

"It would serve better to murder the enemy, don't you think?"

"What's your name?"

"Mercy."

"Mercy." His eyes began to flutter closed. "Now I have a name for the lady who visits my dreams."

He drifted to sleep, and she sat there far longer than she should have, wiping his brow. When she had finally left his side in the early hours before dawn to retire to her bed, it was *he* who visited *her* dreams.

That evening, as she was returning to the hospital to begin her duties, she spied him leaning against the wall. She knew that to be caught alone with a man outside the hospital was grounds for dismissal, knew she should carry on as though she'd not seen him, but she couldn't seem to help herself. She approached cautiously. "Captain, you should not be out here."

"Miss Mercy." He murmured her name as though it was the gentle refrain of a sonnet. She couldn't deny the pleasure it brought her. One of the other nurses, Miss Whisenhunt, had told her that in London he was known for his charming ways.

"Be careful," she'd warned. "He'll have your skirts raised before you even realize he's tossed you onto your back. Not that any lady objects, if she's fortunate enough to garner his attention . . . from what I hear."

She knew a great deal about him. That his family

was nobility. That he was a second son. That *marriage* was not a word that would ever cross his lips. Still, Mercy could not help but be intrigued by him.

"Captain, please, you must return to the ward," she coaxed.

"Do not deny me a few more moments. I needed to be rid of the foul stench of that place."

No matter how much they cleaned, the air remained heavy and rancid. Was it any wonder so many men worsened, became ill, even as their wounds were healing? "Very well, but do not tarry long." She turned to leave—

"Don't go," he pleaded with a near urgency.

She glanced back at him.

"I could do with a bit of company," he added.

"A moment, perhaps. But then I must see to my duties." In the dim light, she could see that he was wearing his trousers. Someone had laundered them. He also wore a new white shirt. When the ladies were not in hospital, they sewed clothing for the men. They could never hope to clothe them all, but those who would be returning to the front lines needed to do so in uniform. She moved into the shadows so as not to be spotted, although few people were traipsing about that time of night. Those who could find solace in dreams slept. Those who couldn't—stared at the ceiling.

"Why ever did you come here?" he asked.

"To be of service."

"You should be at a dance." He scoffed. "And I should be pheasant hunting. I told my brother I would be home for the season. What naïve fools we were."

"All of England thought this would be over quickly," she reassured him.

"I daresay it will continue on much longer than any of us thought."

She did not want to talk of war or the price they paid for it. "I understand you have two brothers."

He flashed a grin. "The Earl of Westcliffe and the Duke of Ainsley. Not many second sons are bookended by such esteemed fellows."

"Surely, with their influence you could be returned home."

"I've no doubt. Do I strike you as the sort who would ask for such a favor?"

She slowly shook her head. "No, Captain, you don't."

They stood in silence for several long moments before he asked, "Do you miss England?"

"Remarkably so."

"Well, then, I shall make it my personal mission to recover in haste, return to battle the Russian hordes, and bring an end to this war so you are once again dancing in a ballroom."

Silly girl that she was, she imagined dancing with him.

A nightly ritual began. Before he was discharged, she would find him waiting outside the hospital each evening, and they'd converse about the most mundane topics, but they all centered around England. They spoke of parks, gardens, and the wonders they'd seen when visiting the Great Exhibition. They might have even walked past each other, two strangers then, who now were brought together by war. Food was scarce in Scutari, and they reminisced about their favorite dishes. He had a fondness for pork. She preferred poultry. He had a weakness for chocolate. She favored strawberries. He enjoyed reading Dickens, while she preferred

Austen. Two months after he returned to the campaign, she received from a London bookseller a leather-bound copy of *Pride and Prejudice*. The note that accompanied it said simply: *Sent at the behest of Captain Lyons*.

She had given far too much credence to the gift, had assumed he saw her as more than an anonymous nurse. Yet comments made—and more important, words left unsaid—since her arrival at Grantwood Manor indicated that she'd been easily forgotten. Based on his reputation, she shouldn't have been surprised, she supposed. But still, the yearnings of her heart refused to abate.

Lightly she trailed her finger over the scar that ran the length of his ruggedly handsome face. It still looked fresh enough that she assumed he'd acquired it during the final battle in which he'd fought. She remembered how she'd wept in that small room in the boarding-house in Paris when she'd seen his name on the list of dead. John had been in her life a mere fortnight by then. She'd held him near and rocked him. With tears streaming down her face, knowing he was too young to understand any of her ramblings, for her sake as well as his, she'd told him about his father.

The strong, the dashing, the courageous Captain Stephen Lyons, who had kept his promise and returned to battle the Cossacks. The soldier who had saved countless lives. The man whose subsequent rise to major came about not through a paid commission but through endeavor. The man who had stormed to her aid one cold and rainy night outside the Barrack Hospital.

Their night together had been brief, important to her, nothing to him. She combed her fingers through his hair. The man she'd known would not have forgotten. How could she have judged him so poorly?

Did she really desire as a husband a man who could forget her so easily? She feared she did.

It seemed she was once again sleeping in his bed, albeit not as comfortably as he was willing to make it for her. She sat in a chair, bent at the waist, her face resting on the mattress near his hip, one hand tucked up beneath her cheek, the other curled around his wrist as though she sought to keep apprised regarding the continual beating of his pulse.

The shadows filtering through the room, the solitary lit lamp, indicated it was still night. And there was a stillness to the residence that only came when the sun bid farewell to day. How long had he been wandering through the maze of healing?

He remembered experiencing bouts of delirium and the suffocating sense of being wrapped tightly in a shroud. Her voice was always near to calm his erratic heart. Her fingers caressed and cooled his heated flesh. And sometimes, when he was very, very fortunate, she would look at him just right, perfectly, and the lamplight would capture the glow of her eyes in such a way that a memory teased—and he latched on to those eyes with the full knowledge that they alone kept him tethered to this world.

Had she nursed him in the Crimea? She'd not said, and he'd not dared to ask for fear of discovering it was one more thing he should never have forgotten. She'd not been there when he'd last awoken in hospital, but judging from his scars, some still pink as though newly formed, others appearing older, he assumed that he'd been wounded on more than one occasion. It was not something he'd thought to ask before leaving for England. All he'd wanted was to escape as quickly as possible the unknown that haunted him and the horrid place that housed him.

The physician had been sure the answers would all return to him in time, with adequate rest, as though the mind healed in the same manner as the body. "It's just the trauma," he'd said. But his words had lacked confidence, had seemed more a question than an answer.

Perhaps Stephen should seek out a more knowledgeable physician. Quite suddenly, he was very much interested in knowing exactly how Mercy's life intertwined with his.

She'd given birth to his son. But how had they met? He was beginning to understand why he might have been drawn to her. She had a caring nature, and an inner strength that wasn't quite visible at first glance. He wasn't even sure how he'd known it existed. It wasn't as though they'd had much involvement since her arrival. A walk. A dinner. A mortifying midnight visit, when he'd been forced to succumb to the pain and weakness in his leg. Yet, he'd instinctively known that she'd not break any promise she made to him.

Ainsley would have. If he thought anything the physician recommended was to the good, he'd feel honor bound to do what was best—regardless of how Stephen might have preferred to handle the matter. Ainsley had never taken a misstep, had never doubted his course. He studied, he examined, he researched. He never went with his gut.

Stephen had trusted his gut instincts. Of the three other people in the room, at that moment when so much was at stake, he trusted Mercy the most. Pity for her. He expected she'd rather be saddled with a man who went with his heart.

Did she dream? Not the ones that accompanied sleep, but those that were of larger things, that hovered nearby when one was awake? She'd come here expecting to find him dead—not breathing and available for marriage. Her father had demanded it, but she'd spoken not a single word of it. What sort of woman didn't desire marriage? What sort of lady gave all she had to nurse the sick? No, not all. She still managed to make time for someone who was incredibly special to her.

Stephen had awoken once to see her holding her son. He'd only squinted at her, not wanting to alert her to his wakefulness, not wanting to distract her from her purpose. Besides, she'd have poured more laudanum down his throat, and he was sick unto death of it. He knew his leg was still there. It throbbed unmercifully, but the pain was a different sort than he'd had before. Then he'd felt as though demons were slicing through his muscles. Perhaps they had been. Now it was just the weary pain of flesh mending.

Even the pain in his head seemed duller.

It took little movement at all for his fingers to graze her chin. Her eyes fluttered open. "Off with you now," he ordered in a voice raspy from disuse. "Get some proper sleep."

Jerking upright, she immediately reached for his brow. "Your fever's gone."

He tried to nod, but that motion seemed beyond him. Where had he found the strength to touch her? He was exhausted. He had no idea how long he'd been sleeping, but he wanted to roll over and return to slumber. But first—

"Thirsty."

"Yes, of course you are. Hungry, too, I suspect. I've managed to get some water and soup down your throat, but not nearly enough."

So it hadn't all been laudanum as he'd thought. His ability to taste had been playing tricks on him, or perhaps he'd simply been too fevered to know exactly what was going on around him. He thought he remembered his mother. What else had transpired?

Mercy poured water from a pitcher into a glass. Slipping her arm beneath his shoulders, she lifted him slightly and brought the glass to his lips with a measured efficiency. She'd no doubt done this for others. Had she done it for him? He despised the constant ignorance that hounded at him, the questions that plagued him.

The water was cool, and he wondered how something with no flavor could taste so damned good.

He knew she must have bathed recently because she smelled of lavender and carried none of the sickly sweet odor of illness. Her breast rubbed innocently against his arm, but he'd recovered enough that his body reacted with a twitch. He had memories of her wiping a damp cloth over him. The fever had plunged him into hell, and she had lifted him into heaven.

Eventually, she laid him back down and set the glass aside. "Your sheets are damp, from the fever breaking. I'm going to change them, but first I'll give you a quick wash."

"I can manage. Just help me sit up." Words he'd never expected to hear himself utter—to turn down an opportunity to have a woman bathe him? But she was not just a woman. She was the mother of his child. She'd also quite possibly saved his life. After his time at the military hospital, he wasn't certain he'd ever want to deal with physicians again. He'd heard too many men beg that their arm or leg not be taken. Gritted his teeth against the screams and sobs that followed when their wishes were ignored.

His refusal to seek out a physician to examine his leg had been reckless in retrospect, but in his mind it had been the safer course to remaining whole.

Once he was sitting up with the sheet draped over his waist, she brought him a bowl of warm water. She dipped in a cloth, wrenched the excess water out, and handed it to him. He could have sworn she blushed before she turned away.

"Have you a nightshirt?" she asked.

"No. I don't like to be confined in bed." She glanced back at him, and he gave her what he thought might have been his first true smile in months. "Unless it's within the arms of a beautiful woman, of course."

Her mouth twitched. "I see you *are* feeling better."

"Thanks to you. So what was it?"

"A bit of saber, I think." She retrieved a handkerchief and unfolded it to reveal glinting steel that was a couple of inches long. "It could have broken off during the battle . . . or there's so much flying debris, from what I hear . . . I've never actually been on a battlefield."

As far as his memory was concerned, neither had he.

"I don't know how they missed it, but I've seen it happen before," she assured him. "You're very fortunate that Dr. Roberts was able to save your leg."

"I don't remember a good deal about the past . . . how many days was it?"

"Three."

After he finished washing up, he moved to the chair. She managed to change the sheets with a quickness and efficiency that had him back in bed before he could break a sweat from his previous efforts.

"Shall I fetch you some soup now?" she asked.

"No. Not hungry."

"You need to eat."

"I will in the morning." He sounded impatient, irascible. She merely nodded and glanced down at her clenched hands, hands that had comforted him. "I'm sorry."

She lifted her gaze. "No, don't apologize. You've been through an ordeal."

"No more so than you. I know I'm not the best of patients. Why didn't you have a servant tend me?"

She tugged on the blanket, bringing it closer to his chin, as though she needed to occupy her hands. "Caring for those who suffer from infirmity is what I was trained to do."

"But now you have a son who needs your attention."

"I see him often. Jeanette is very skilled at caring for him. She's been with us almost since the beginning." She touched his knee. "And I kept my promise. You have your leg."

"So I noticed. Thank you for that."

She shook her head. "I don't think Dr. Roberts had any plans to amputate it. Not like they had planned with your arm."

Good God! They'd tried to take his arm? How bad had it been? Instinctively, he touched the large thick scar. He'd wondered how it had come to be.

"I'm sorry," she said. "I've upset you. You probably don't like to think about that time. I know I don't."

He took a risk—"You tended to me then, when my arm was wounded."

"Yes. At least this time you didn't call out the names of at least a dozen other ladies."

He gave her an ironic grin. "Is that what I did before?"

She nodded, a light twinkle in her eyes. "When your fever was at its worst. You had quite the harem."

"I suppose a lot of secrets are spilled in delirium." Perhaps memories as well.

"They are all safe with me."

He did not doubt her words. "War is harsh. A lady shouldn't be exposed to it. Why were you there?"

She sank onto the chair, as though her legs could no longer support her, and folded her hands in her lap. "My life seemed without . . . purpose. There were dances and visiting. But it all seemed so trivial. I wanted to do something to help those who were in need. I had a younger sister. She became very ill. Mother had passed, and it was left to me to take care of Maryanne. She died. I often thought if I'd only known more that I could have prevented her passing somehow."

His gut clenched with the knowledge that she carried that burden. "It was not your responsibility to cure her. Your father should have sent for a physician—"

"He did. And I know in my head there was nothing I could do, but my heart wonders. I was quite inconsolable after Maryanne's passing, so Father indulged my whim to learn nursing. I had only just completed my four months of training when I learned of Miss Nightingale's pleas for nurses to accompany her to the Crimea. The articles in the newspapers were depicting such madness there. Our soldiers didn't have supplies.

There were no adequate hospitals." She released a self-conscious laugh. "I'm not telling you anything you don't know."

Only she was. He'd been so focused on what had happened to him and what he'd lost, that he'd not given any thought to discovering what might have happened to others beyond him. Even his family—he'd assumed they'd gone through nothing of consequence other than the birth of Westcliffe's son.

"Since you weren't here," she continued, "you might not realize there was a public outcry that something be done. It called to me. Not in the way that God called to Joan of Arc, of course, but I knew I had to do something more than gather linens for bandages. So I arranged an interview with Miss Nightingale and I was selected to go with her."

He heard the passion in her words, and it shamed him that his had not been the same. His brothers had already bought him a commission by the time he had tea with Claire, the last afternoon he remembered. His mother's influence had kept him safe at home, away from any of Victoria's little wars. He'd picked a hell of a time to let go of his mother's skirts. But after listening to Mercy's story, he couldn't confess any of that. It made him feel petty and small. It made him feel as though he'd truly been lacking in character, as his family had claimed.

"It gave your life purpose, then?" he asked her instead.

"It gave me John."

Chapter 6

Now that he was on his way to recovery, he was left to his own company more often than he'd have preferred. Mercy was no longer constantly at his bedside. If not for the occasional squalling of the babe, he would have thought she'd left the residence entirely. But in the short time he'd come to know her, he knew she'd never leave without the child. Where the child goeth, so went she.

"Your wound is healing nicely," Dr. Roberts said as he examined the wound. "How does it feel?"

"Not nearly as painful as it was." He could touch it now without flinching. As a matter of fact, the pain was so diminished that he had hope that he'd eventually walk without the blasted limp.

"I should think it would be good for you to start moving about. Nothing too strenuous. No riding as of yet, but a short walk might do you some good."

After Dr. Roberts had left, Stephen took his advice, drew on his trousers along with a loosely fitting linen shirt, left his bed, and using his walking stick, hobbled to a chair by the window. The vast sky was gray, the clouds dark, yet he watched as sunshine—*Mercy*—strolled through the garden, holding her son, his son.

He'd barely given any notice of him after that first viewing. She cradled him now, and in spite of the distance separating them, the love etched in her face as she gazed down on the child backed the breath up painfully in his chest. It was pure adoration, without resentment of any sort. An angel gazing down on wonder.

The child had turned her world upside down, had forced her to leave her mission of mercy, had caused her shame, had ruined her reputation, had led her here. Her future was uncertain, yet still she held on to him as though he were the only thing of any importance.

He wondered if she'd ever feel that way about the child's father.

Because of the way they were facing, of the boy, he couldn't see much more than the light blond curls. Like Stephen's, they'd no doubt darken as the lad grew older. He tried to recall the color of his eyes. Blue, he thought. Like his.

He wanted to join them. If he took it slowly, perhaps he could at least get nearer, close enough to watch her holding the child, to see the joy in her eyes. How much courage it must have taken for her to face her father and then to deal with Stephen's family. Strangers. She'd had no way of knowing how they might react. She could have taken the secret of being with Stephen to her grave, but she'd ruined her chances of a good match with a decent fellow when she'd chosen to keep the child. What an extraordinary decision for a lady of quality. She could have found someone to take the child in and no one would have been the wiser.

She was a remarkable woman of determination and courage. She was not the sort he usually took to his bed. She was so damned serious and responsible. She placed others' needs above her own pleasures. She didn't have a flighty bone in her body.

She'd have not become intimate with him on a whim. Yet, for the life of him, he couldn't see himself going to the trouble it would have required to seduce her—not when there were always willing women who required far less effort. Had he simply been bored? Had he considered her a challenge? Could he have—by God, could he have possibly fallen in love with her?

It would have been a first for him. He squeezed his eyes shut, trying to see beyond the black haze. It suddenly seemed vital to remember her. But no memories of her surfaced, not even a shadow of one.

A brisk knock sounded, one he instantly recognized as belonging to his mother. He welcomed the distraction. "Come in."

She walked in with her usual poise and grace. He didn't remember a time when she hadn't been formidable, although he was fairly certain that Westcliffe did. He was five years Stephen's senior, remembered a father that Stephen didn't. Their contradictory memories had never bothered him before. The recent gaping hole in his life made him view everything differently. Now he longed for memories he'd discarded carelessly. Strange to realize that they needed to be nurtured, thought of often, or like the bloom of a rose, they simply withered away. Once gone they could not be regained.

He chided himself for the morose thoughts. He'd been too young to have memories of his father. It was as simple as that. But memories of Mercy, those perhaps he could regain with a bit more exertion.

"I just had a word with Dr. Roberts," his mother said sublimely. "He's most pleased with your progress."

"Well, then, I consider myself a success." Stephen glanced back out the window, aware of his mother coming to stand beside the chair where he sat.

"What has your interest so?" she asked, peering over his head. "Ah, I see."

He didn't like the implication that he was at the window *because* of Mercy, like an unschooled lad experiencing his first infatuation. "I didn't know she was there when I came to have a look. I merely wanted to gaze at something besides the canopy over my bed."

"Of course, dearest. I thought nothing else. Although I will concur that she is of far more interest than a canopy."

In silence, they watched Mercy for several minutes. She held the boy aloft, smiled brightly at him, then brought him in close to the warmth of her body, layering her cloak over him.

"It's dashed cold out there, but she says the boy needs the briskness of fresh air," the duchess said. "She is a strange one, wanting her window open at all hours. She bathes daily. Constantly washes her hands."

"No doubt trying to rid herself of the filth of the military hospital."

She jerked her gaze around. "You remember it?"

"I know something of the conditions of the place from when I woke up there recently."

"Yes, of course. Silly of me to think you meant your memories went farther back than that. Far enough back to include her."

"We spoke at length, she and I, while she was tending me. I am left with the impression the situation in the hospital was much more unpleasant for her."

"You talked, so then she knows of your . . ."

He could see her struggling to find the correct word that wouldn't cause him any embarrassment. "Affliction, Mother. I have an affliction. And no, I didn't tell her of it. It's bad enough she saw me trembling like a leaf in the wind in the hallway when my blasted leg gave out on me."

"It was not your fault that you took a fever or that some imbecile physician didn't do his job properly. It's a wonder you didn't die."

"Because of the efforts of a man who in his eagerness to save me overlooked a bit of metal. I wouldn't be so quick to find fault. You don't know the conditions under which he worked."

Silence greeted him. He was not usually so understanding of shoddy workmanship, but he felt an exception might be in order. He'd returned home. Many hadn't.

"What are you going to do about her?" his mother finally asked. Not exactly a smooth change of topic, but then his mother had never been one to mince words.

He shifted his gaze up to her. "Have you no doubt the boy is mine?"

"None whatsoever."

Well, then, he'd best get on with what needed to be done. "Will you have the servants prepare a warm bath for me?"

"What of your wound?"

"I can bathe without getting it wet. Send in my valet as well."

It was a painstaking endeavor to properly prepare himself. In the tub, he'd required assistance from his valet. Then the man had begun to shave away several days' worth of bearded growth on his face.

Stephen wasn't quite certain why he bothered to make himself presentable. Mercy had seen him at his worst. The night he'd trampled through the rain, when he'd finally given into the pain, given into the haven of her arms. He'd taken advantage of her once, in a foreign land. He had no intention of doing it on English soil.

Yet she drew him like the nectar of a blossom drew a bee. With her, he could almost forget that he didn't remember—

Until she began to talk of her time away from England's shore. They shared memories, they shared experiences. They shared horrors and filth and wretchedness. He cursed himself for entertaining her in a place such as that—and then he would wonder if they'd both needed the escape. Certainly, he would have done all in his power to take her to heaven even if beyond them hell had reigned.

He'd been sixteen when he'd learned the wonders of a woman's body. Westcliffe, bless him. They'd never been close, but in that one regard he'd been an exceptional brother. He'd taken Stephen to his first brothel, introduced him to a woman with impeccable talent and patience. As a callow youth, Stephen had disappeared behind a red door. When he'd emerged the next morning, he'd been determined that in this one area of his life he'd best his brothers. They were titled. They had respect. Westcliffe had already acquired a reputation as an unprecedented lover. Stephen had decided he would surpass him, his would be the name whispered about London's wicked circles.

No lady had been safe from his amorous attentions.

The thought of him taking advantage of Mercy sickened him. But he couldn't imagine that he'd held any true affection for her. They couldn't have known each other long. Their time together had been brief. And yet he'd managed to do with her what he'd done with no other woman. He'd brought her harm. He'd ruined her reputation. He'd saddled her with a child.

And what had she done as retribution? She loved and cared for his son. She might very well have saved Stephen's life. She asked nothing of him except that she be allowed to remain in the boy's life. Her father was the one insisting upon marriage, and while Stephen had not initially been impressed with the man, he couldn't deny that if he found his own daughter in the same state, he'd insist the man do right by her—only he'd do it with a pistol at the offending man's back.

None of this leaving her with the man, expecting the right thing to be done. By God, he'd ensure it or the blackguard would answer to him.

The sharp pain nipped at his chin. "Dammit, man!"

"I'm sorry, Major," his valet said. "I didn't realize you were going to clench your jaw so suddenly. My fault entirely."

"Hardly. Let's just be quick about this, shall we?"

His hair needed trimming, his nails clipping. He couldn't recall the last time he'd truly cared about his appearance. He'd dressed appropriately and with some style each morning only because he'd not wanted to disappoint his mother. But the particulars that he'd cared about when it came to women—he'd given little thought to.

When he was finally dressed to disarm, he tossed his greatcoat over his shoulders, snatched up his cane, and went in search of Mercy.

She was returning to the residence, the boy snuggled

in her arms, hidden beneath her heavy woolen cloak. A smile wreathed her face as he approached and he felt it like a kick to his gut.

"You're barely limping," she said, as though he'd made a major accomplishment, when in truth he had absolutely nothing to do with the healing. "Jolly good for you. Has the pain diminished?"

"Yes, somewhat. I feel confident that I'm well on my way to recovery. No little thanks to your efforts."

She blushed, but her eyes sparkled. "I did nothing really."

He nodded toward the bundle in her arms. "Should he be out here?"

"The air does him good, I think. But we've been walking about long enough. I was going to take him in now."

He was astounded by his disappointment. The cold was bracing, and rain scented the air. Still he wanted to linger in her company, take a turn about the garden with her at his side. "Dr. Roberts said I should not overdo. As this is my first venture out, I should probably be content I made it this far without stumbling and head back in myself. Would you be kind enough to join me in The Duchess's Sitting Room?"

"Will your mother mind?"

He found himself smiling as he hadn't in a long while, and he couldn't for the life of him explain why he was amused. "It's not my mother's room per se. I believe it is where the first duchess preferred to spend her afternoons with her ladies, and it has been named The Duchess's Sitting Room ever since."

"If we're not imposing on anyone, then yes."

He waited until she fell into step beside him. He

wanted to offer her his arm but hers were full. "That is where we differ, you and I," he said solemnly. "If I wanted something, I'd not care one whit if someone was imposed upon."

"I know that's not true. I witnessed your stubbornness and refusal to be tended until every wounded man around you had first been seen."

He stumbled at her words, nearly tripped. Dammit. *Clod.* She reached out with one hand to steady him and he reached out with the other to ensure she didn't drop the child. He stared into her eyes, trying to absorb more information without words. Had this happened when he was in danger of losing his arm? He'd insisted others go before him? Had he lost his mind? That sounded not at all like him. To put others ahead of himself? Had she confused him with someone else? Or during the war had he become a man who would be unrecognizable to him? It hardly signified.

"You've gone pale again. You should get off the leg," she said.

She assumed it was pain that drained his face of blood. It was discomfiture, yes, not of the body, but of the soul. He nodded quickly. "Yes, of course."

They shared not a single word as they made their way into the house. He, because he could think of nothing to say that wouldn't make him sound like an idiot. She? No doubt because she was worried he'd lost the ability to converse while walking, and therefore risked causing himself further injury with any sort of distraction.

Once inside, they left her cloak and his greatcoat with a servant. He ordered that tea and biscuits be brought to The Duchess's Sitting Room. Then he led

Mercy through the warren of hallways to the small room.

"How deliciously quaint," she exclaimed softly with a thread of joy woven through her voice as they entered.

He realized he'd selected this particular room because he'd somehow known that it would please her. The beige walls were lined with portraits. A fire was already crackling in the hearth. A settee was before it, chairs on either side of it. But it was the bay window that he'd anticipated would draw her. The matching stuffed velvet armchairs were arranged so one could enjoy the room as well as the gardens. The draperies had been pulled back, providing light that the unlit crystal chandelier could not.

"I can quite understand why the first duchess appreciated this room," she said as she wandered to the window and sat, tucking the boy into the crook of her arm. She glanced up at Stephen. "Is it a favorite of yours as well?"

"It is now." He joined her.

Laughing lightly, she shook her head, then gazed around the room with obvious curiosity. "Are any of your ancestors in the portraits on these walls?"

"No. Mine are all at Lyons Place, which is West-cliffe's estate. He and I share the same father. Ainsley and I don't."

"I'm not particularly intimate with the circles of the aristocracy, but I should think it is rare for one man to have two titled brothers."

"My mother has always been one not to be outdone. Quite honestly, after Ainsley's father died, I'm surprised she didn't marry again and try for a third titled son.

She was still young enough to have accomplished it."

"Do you think she'll marry Leo?"

"He may have . . . talents that she appreciates, but he is a commoner. I very much doubt she would settle for him."

"Even if she loves him beyond all measure?"

He wasn't certain his mother was capable of loving anyone other than her sons. "Do you believe someone should marry for love or gain?"

"I don't believe one excludes the other," she said.

"But if you could have only one?"

She turned her attention to the gardens. He wondered if she'd be here to see them in the spring.

"I think one must do what one must do to be happy," she said finally.

"Can one be happy without love?"

"I think one can be happy without a good many things. If my time at the military hospital taught me anything at all, it was that."

And what, he bloody well wondered, had his time in the Crimea taught him?

The gray sky chose that moment to lighten; the sun that had been hidden behind heavy clouds for most of the day broke free and sunlight poured in through the three windows to focus on her. If he were a religious man, he might have thought it was a sign. She possessed a calmness that appealed. Even at his worst, even when he'd forced her to give him a vow regarding his leg, she'd never wavered, never panicked. The light landed upon her cheeks, glowed in her eyes. Not for the first time, he thought it must have been her eyes that had drawn him to her. A man would be a fool not to notice them, not to wonder at the secrets they held.

"You're doing it again," she said softly, and he watched as pink tinged her cheeks.

"Whatever are you on about?"

"What you did that first night during dinner. Stare at me as though you were counting my freckles."

"Have you freckles?" He'd been so distracted by her eyes that he'd not noticed.

"I've not spent much time in the sun of late, so they've faded. But they're quite unbecoming when they have their way."

"I can't imagine anything about you being unbecoming."

Her mouth quirked, the start of a smile, the beginning of a laugh. He knew not which. A time had existed when he'd been able to read women so easily. Was he simply out of practice, or was she unlike any woman he'd ever known?

The babe mewled, squirmed, then pressed his tiny balled fist to his mouth and began to suckle. Stephen had forgotten the lad was there. How could he not notice the child when he noticed everything about the mother? He had little interest in the boy. If he was indeed his son, shouldn't he give a bloody damn? But still—

"Why John?" he heard himself ask.

She looked at him, her eyes wide, her brow furrowed as though he'd confounded her with his query.

"The boy. Why did you name him John? Why not Stephen or Lyons or something to brand him as mine?"

"Because he is to be his own person. I didn't want him to feel he had to live up to his namesake—a war hero."

"I'm hardly a hero."

He'd surprised her with his words. It was written on her face in the widening of her eyes, and the parting of her lips, lips he desperately wanted to kiss again. Perhaps that was the reason he'd selected this room in a distant corner of the residence. It was seldom visited. He could flirt, seduce—

The boy's sucking grew louder. Stephen had failed to take into account that they would have a miniature chaperone.

"I'd not expected you to be overly modest," she said softly. "I heard tales of your exploits even in Paris."

"I don't want to discuss the war or my role in it," he said more harshly than he'd intended. That too surprised her, but she recovered quickly enough.

"Yes, no, of course not. John. I named him John because . . ." He could see the desperation, the fear, as though he'd find fault with her reasons. "I don't know. It seemed to suit. I simply looked at him and thought . . . John. His name is John."

He tried to make up for his earlier blunder, his harsh tone. He forced a lightness into his voice. "A mother's instinct perhaps."

"Yes, quite."

She'd forgiven him so easily. He saw it in her winsome smile. He'd been wrong. It hadn't been her eyes that had drawn him to her. It had been her smile. When it was freely and joyfully given, it eclipsed everything else about her. He thought he might give his last breath to see her smile.

"You've hardly gotten to know John. Would you care to hold him?"

Again, the reminder of the boy. He shook his head. "What do I know of babes?"

"But he's your son. At least come nearer." Her invitation was accompanied by another smile that he scarcely could resist.

He wiped his hand across his suddenly dry mouth. Where was the bloody servant with the damned tea? He darted a quick glance toward the door.

"Searching for an escape or a rescuer?" she asked, and he heard the amusement in her voice. He glared at her. "How can you be afraid of a child?"

"I'm not afraid of him," he said, with an annoyance that belied his claim. "I simply have no interest in children. Whatsoever. At all."

This time his words hurt her. He saw it in the darkening of her eyes, the unnatural blush in her cheeks. She'd given up so much—everything—to bring that child into the world and to keep him near. He acted as though he couldn't be bothered.

Her gaze averted, she rose. "He's getting hungry. I should find Jeanette."

As she made to walk past him, he wrapped his fingers around her arm. "Don't leave."

She didn't look at him. It was astounding how much that small act hurt.

"You don't want him." Her voice was thick with tears. "If you will please arrange for a carriage, I shall pack our things and we shall be gone from here."

"Your father will not welcome you back unmarried."

Angling her chin, she met his gaze and he saw determination that put him to shame. "I'm well aware of that. I'll be off to London. I'm certain to find employment as a nurse. I can make my way. It was never my intent to bother you. I thought you were dead. I thought your family . . . that they would appreciate knowing you had a son, that a small part of you lived on. But John is too innocent, too precious to be made to feel unwanted. I will not abide it. Not from you. Not from anyone."

For her sake and the boy's, he should pry his fingers from her arm and let them leave. What did he truly have to offer her? He was no good to the army. Acceptable positions for second sons were limited to the military and the clergy. What sort of success could a non-religious man hope to find in a parish?

He should release her. Instead, his fingers closed ever so slightly, staking a claim. "You're right. He terrifies me. I know nothing at all of children. The responsibility . . . I don't know how you manage it. But I would very much like to be introduced to him again."

Her smile came with hesitation, her eyes wary. Still, she nodded. "With your bad leg it would be best if you sat. Shall we move to the sofa?"

"Yes, of course." He'd managed to sound interested, when in truth he saw it as a chore. He wanted more time with her, wanted to experience *her*. But he could not have her without the child. He couldn't understand his sudden obsession with her, why he was willing to do anything to keep her near. But he wanted her, wanted her to cross the hallway to his bedchamber. He wanted to gaze down into whiskey eyes. He wanted to see them across a room. Obviously, he'd lost more than memories. He'd lost his mind.

Limping, he allowed her to precede him.

The settee, with its bright yellow brocade, was small, with room enough for only two. And the child. He couldn't forget the child. She wouldn't let him.

She held the babe toward him, not for him to take,

but as a means to display him. "This is John. Your son."

Her soft voice held conviction, no doubt. And more love than he thought it was possible for one person to possess. Her expression was earnest, her eyes pleading with him to recognize the miracle she held in her arms. He wanted only her. To be here with only her. But the child would intrude. Soon, he was fairly certain the babe would start to cry. And she would leave.

He didn't want her to leave upset. Not after all she'd done for him . . . and for his son.

Lowering his gaze, he looked, truly looked, at his son for the first time. He had chubby cheeks that puckered as he sucked on his fist. He had no chin to speak of. His nose was more a dollop, with no real indication of the shape it might one day take as he grew into manhood. His eyebrows, as light as his curls, almost touched where his brow puckered in concentration. His long, dark lashes dominated his face. Stephen had never understood, as fair as he was, why his eyelashes had always been so dark. A bit of inherited rebelliousness, he supposed. But then most of him had rebelled. He'd taken very little from his father.

This boy, however, had taken almost everything.

As though acutely aware that he was being watched, he suddenly opened his eyes, and Stephen found himself staring into a sea of blue. Intelligence lurked there and inquisitiveness. Who would explain to this boy the joys—and more important, the pitfalls—of women?

"I wish he had your eyes," he heard himself say.

"Sometimes a baby's eyes change over time, but I suspect his color is here to stay. They are too much like yours. You can touch him, you know. He doesn't bite."

"His father does."

Mercy turned scarlet, and he wondered if he'd nipped at her shoulder, her ear, her backside. Had he nibbled? Had she done the same to him? What had it been like with her? He couldn't imagine that it had been anything other than wondrous. So why only one night?

The question hung desperately on his tongue.

Cautiously she wrapped her hand around his, threaded their fingers together. Doubt clouded her eyes. She brought his hand to her lips, kissed each finger. "Trust me?" she whispered.

With my life.

But he held the words. They were too powerful, too soon. In her world, they'd known each other for a good deal longer than they had in his. He should tell her, should bare his shortcomings, his failures, his affliction. But all the *shoulds* escaped his mind as she nudged their intertwined fingers against the boy's hand. Four tiny fingers and one small thumb wrapped themselves securely and tightly around his forefinger. He felt a hard, painful tug in his chest, and he thought perhaps his heart had stopped. But it beat, rapid and strong, his blood pulsing through him.

His blood pulsing through John. John. *John.* His son.

"He's damned strong," he said, barely recognizing the strangled sound as coming from him.

"He's amazing, isn't he?"

"Was it a hard birth?"

She lowered her eyes from his to John's. "It was worth it."

"Were you alone?"

"No, a friend, another nurse was with me."

"Were you afraid?"

She lifted her gaze back to his, and he saw the wonder of the child in her smile. "No."

So much was said with that one word, her expression. She'd wanted this child. Had she not proven that with her actions? She deserved so much more from him than he'd given.

"I'd like to hold him now," he said quietly.

Exquisite joy lit her face. Once again, he realized he'd been wrong. It wasn't her eyes or smile that had drawn him. It was something more, something deep, that on rare occasion rose to the surface. Her inner beauty was breathtaking and he thought he'd have done anything to ensure that he saw it often.

She transferred the child to Stephen's waiting arms. Not once did John release his firm grip on Stephen's finger. His throat knotted, Stephen forced out the words. "Hello, John. You and I are going to have quite the time of it, aren't we?"

The boy blinked up at him, a question in eyes of blue, a shade that mirrored Stephen's. *Who the devil are you?*

I'm your father.

Chapter 7

Mercy wondered if it was possible to die from too much happiness and love. Watching Stephen with John . . . her heart had swelled to such an extent that she feared it might burst through her chest. The resemblance was so strong. She knew no one could doubt that the child was his. She didn't want life to pass swiftly, but she could hardly wait to see John as a man. With his father's influence, he would no doubt resemble him in manner.

He would gain his devilish smile. He would tilt his head just so when he studied something of importance. He would issue orders expecting to be obeyed. He would have a confidence to his stride that even a limp could not diminish.

By the time the serving girl, Anna, finally brought in the tea, John had begun to fidget. It was long past his time to nurse. Mercy asked Anna to take John to Jeanette for his feeding. When she turned from the doorway, Stephen was standing at the window, gazing out. Twilight was descending, red and orange hues streaking across a darkening blue sky.

She watched him for a moment, just watched. All she'd endured had been worth the decision she'd made to claim John as her own. Observing as the bond developed between Stephen and his son had been the most rewarding moments she'd ever experienced. The seed of love for Stephen that had been planted so long ago at Scutari blossomed into a full bloom. She'd never known such contentment. Or such desire.

She wanted him to hold her, to kiss her. She wanted his embrace, the nearness of his body. She'd come here not for marriage, not expecting it in spite of her father's blustering, but suddenly she wanted it with a desperation that astounded her. She wanted more than John in her life forever. She wanted this man.

He had never given her cause to think that anything other than friendship would exist between them, yet still her heart had yearned. They had lived in a place where everything moved so quickly. Everything was more intense. Death was faced daily, life was celebrated with abandon. Emotions were always deeply felt—whether it was fear, hatred, or love. They skirted the edge of danger, and it gave a deeper appreciation to each moment. It was as though they rushed headlong toward every experience, never blanching, never stepping back, never taking a second to catch their breath.

It was difficult now to walk through this placid life where she had time to think, to ponder, to wonder. The doubts surfaced if she slowed at all, and she didn't want to experience the doubts. She had claimed John as her son, because she knew of no other way to keep him near her. She had wanted him because she had admired his father. She couldn't stand the thought of Stephen's son being orphaned, of taking a chance that he might be taken in by a family who could not love him as she did.

She was barely aware of her footsteps clicking over the wood flooring as she went to stand beside Stephen. *Turn to me now,* she thought. *Turn to me and look upon me with the love you did John. Take me in your arms. Take me in your heart.*

"I don't remember you," he said quietly.

She barely had time to brace herself for the devastation that slammed into her with the confirmation of her earlier suspicions. What a fool she'd been. Then and now, to think she could garner the attentions of man such as Major Stephen Lyons. She was a little brown wren hopping along among graceful swans. She didn't know how to be flirtatious. The smile he'd bestowed on other nurses had been wider than those he gave her. He'd spoken with others. He'd made them giggle like silly ninnies.

They'd all been infatuated with him. They'd all garnered his attention. The quiet moments she had spent with him outside the hospital had not made her special.

But it didn't matter. Acknowledging all of that, it didn't matter. What mattered was John. She loved him so terribly much. She couldn't bear the thought of losing him. She would go down on her knees; she would beg; she would plead. She would somehow make Stephen understand why she'd done what she had.

Four words. He'd spoken but four words, you silly chit, and you've concocted an entire epistle. He doesn't remember you. It doesn't mean he's questioning that you're John's mother. He no doubt took many women to his bed. He can't possibly have remembered them all. That's all he means. He simply doesn't remember you. Play along. Be vague. Do not give him cause to doubt you.

The panic swirling through her heart subsided only

slightly, but it didn't leak into her voice. Inner strength that had been forged in Scutari served her well now. "I fear I suspected as much. I can hardly blame you for not remembering me. I'm hardly worth—"

"No. No. God, no." He plowed his hand through his hair, his gaze hard and focused on something in the distance. She'd seen enough vacant stares on the wounded to know that sometimes, when gazing out, a man was gazing in. "I don't remember *anything*."

She studied him. The sharp cut of his jaw. The quick tic of the scar that ran down his face as a muscle jumped in his cheek. She'd almost forgotten it was there, because when she looked at him, she didn't see it. She saw only the devilishly handsome features that had caused nurses to swoon, that had caused her to hold him near in her dreams. Even when he was filthy and his uniform tattered, he'd still managed to charm them. A couple of the Catholic nurses had held prayer vigils for him. All the nurses had welcomed any excuse to work in the area of the hospital where he was recovering. It shamed her now to know they'd placed him above others. Not that they'd neglected anyone in their duties, but he had been the one they cared about most.

"I fear I don't quite understand what you're saying," she said quietly.

He still wasn't looking at her. His penetrating blue eyes were focused on something that she couldn't see. "I have no memories of the time I was in the Crimea. Not a single bloody one." The last words were shoved out between clenched teeth.

Astounded, she fought to wrap her mind around the implications. "But you were there—"

"For a damned year and a half." He turned to face

her then, pressing his back against one wall of windows. He gave her an ironic twist of his lips. "Yes, I know. I've been *told*."

This was monstrous. She could hardly fathom it. Not to remember *anything*. "How could this have happened?"

"I don't know." He viciously rubbed the scar that began at his temple as though he wanted to erase its existence. "I awoke in a regimental hospital in Balaclava. In immense pain that made no sense. I'd been having tea with my sister-by-marriage. Claire. I learned later that it had been two years prior. From the moment I set down my teacup until I awoke on an uncomfortable sack of rags, I remember not one incident I experienced, not one person I encountered. I don't recall the journey I took to get there. I don't know what it feels like to rush headlong into battle. I don't remember the men who fought beside me or the ones I killed. I don't remember the women . . . I might have known."

Her hands were shaking, the delicate china beating out a soft clinking tattoo that irritated the devil out of him, as she poured them tea. The English answer to everything. A nice cuppa tea.

He and Mercy were sitting in the chairs by the window. He took the cup she offered him, then set it on the table between them. He knew she'd needed something to occupy her while she considered all he'd said, so he'd accepted her offer for tea. In truth, it didn't appeal to him in the least. He was tempted to stalk to his brother's library and snatch a bottle of whiskey. *That* had been his answer to everything since he returned home. Create a fog within the fog.

The sun had nearly disappeared beyond the horizon. They would have to join the others for supper soon. Or perhaps he'd have it delivered here. Having admitted his deficiencies, he wasn't certain he was up to presenting a polite façade. God knew his family had been forced to endure his irascible temperament since he'd returned home. Mercy's arrival had granted them a bit of a reprieve. But now she knew the truth and he no longer had a reason to pretend nothing was amiss.

He studied her delicate profile as she blew softly on her tea. He noticed the freckles now, where the sun had kissed her cheeks, her nose, her chin. Often, from the looks of it. He wanted to do the same: to kiss her briefly, softly. To kiss her deeply and lingeringly. "For what it is worth, if there was anything from that time that I should remember, it would be you."

Finally, she looked at him. She gave him the soft smile that he'd come to adore, but compassion and pity in her eyes accompanied it. Compassion—he knew she could no more withhold it than the darkness could hold back the sun. But the pity angered him. He didn't want it. It was the very reason he'd hesitated to tell her.

"I can't comprehend . . . the magnitude of this. You recall nothing?"

"Nothing. No battles, no hospitals. The men I fought beside are complete strangers to me."

"I remember one occasion when a soldier awoke, terribly confused, seemingly lost, and remembered nothing of the battle in which he was injured, but not to remember anything that occurred during two years . . . it's inconceivable. How could it have happened?"

"That is a question for the ages. The physicians

speculated that I'd taken a powerful blow to the head that knocked me senseless—literally. Apparently, I was comatose for several days. I had other wounds. Severe wounds. I have scars and no earthly clue what caused them. It's not only the war and my service that I don't remember. I remember *nothing*. I was, apparently, told of my nephew's birth, but I was stunned to discover I had a nephew when Westcliffe and his family came to visit me here. I don't think it was until that moment that the full extent of my affliction hit my family. Anything they had told me in letters might as well have never been written."

"Why didn't you tell me that first afternoon when we were in the garden? Or later? After my father left. Or—"

"I was ashamed, Mercy. I *am* ashamed. Good God, what sort of man am I to forget something that was so significant in my life? I went off to a bloody war!" He shoved himself out of the chair, took three painful steps to the window, and raised his hand to the cold glass. At least his leg could support him somewhat now. In time, it might support him completely. "I have only a gaping, black hole, filled with nothingness, that is two years of my life. I do not know if I was a man of honor. I do not know if I stood my ground on the battlefield or if I showed the enemy my back. I don't know how many men I may have killed or what they looked like. Did I feel remorse upon killing or did I celebrate? Did I become the man of character that my family wished I would be? I haven't a clue regarding what sort of soldier I was. What sort of man. Was I a man to be revered or one to be reviled?"

"I can't even imagine the horror of all that, of not

remembering, but I can assure you that you were not reviled. Those who spoke of you spoke highly. You were an accomplished soldier."

Spinning around, he captured her gaze. "You and I were intimate. I got you with child, for God's sake. But I have no memory of ever having kissed you before I did so in the library. I thought it would help me remember—the taste of you, your scent, the texture of your skin, the echo of your sigh . . . but there was nothing. You accuse me of staring at you. I'm searching for an inkling of recognition. I can't remember what you look like beneath your clothes. God forgive me if I gave you no more care than a rutting stallion."

"No!" She came up out of the chair with a force that propelled her into his arms. She touched his cheek, searched his eyes. "No, you mustn't torment yourself with what you can't remember of me. The one night we shared . . . it was the most remarkable night of my life." She caressed his cheek, his chin, and trailed her fingers over the dead flesh of his scar. He knew she touched him there only because the tips of her fingers teased the living skin around it. Why couldn't she tease the dead memories? Why couldn't she somehow resurrect them?

"I fell in love with you that night," she said quietly. "That's the reason I kept John. That I subjected myself to shame and mortification. Because he is yours, part of you, and you are part of him. I could not abandon him. I could not let go of the one person who could still connect me to you."

But had Stephen loved her? Or had she simply been one of many? What were his feelings where she was concerned? Even after having confessed his affliction, he couldn't ask her that, he couldn't humiliate her further by confirming that he hadn't a clue regarding what she might have meant to him.

"It's all right," she said, as though reading his mind. "I understand that you don't know what I may have meant to you. But that doesn't mean that we can't begin anew, does it?"

He'd expected her to be horrified by him, and instead she was horrified *for* him. He'd expected her to rebuff him. Instead she accepted him. He'd thought she'd be frightened by what he'd become—a man uncertain of his past. Instead she embraced him.

If he'd not loved her, he thought, he damned well should have.

Chapter 8

"Oh, John, I am a wicked, wicked girl," Mercy lamented hours later as she rocked John to sleep following his feeding. Where the duchess had procured a rocker, she didn't know. Truly didn't care. She was grateful to have it but more pressing matters were on her mind.

She and Stephen had enjoyed a private dinner. They'd spoken of nothing of consequence. Their childhoods, hers in Shrewsbury, his here at Grantwood Manor. They'd talked of London. Theaters and pleasure gardens. Their favorite parks. He told her of his older brother, the Earl of Westcliffe. How they'd never been close, yet he'd finally come to appreciate him. His younger brother, Ainsley, who had always made him feel like a child.

"I think I saw my time as a military man as a chance to prove something to them. I don't know if I did."

It was the only time he mentioned the recent past. She didn't pursue it further.

They had quiet moments, filled only with the scraping of silver over china, or the constant ticking of the clock on the mantel. He studied her during those times, with an intensity that might have been unsettling if she didn't know that he recalled nothing at all about her. Still he had to be wondering what it was about her that had attracted him. She thought more than once about telling him of their time together in Scutari.

But she sensed that he didn't want to journey there. Not tonight. Tonight was more about coming to know each other as though the past two years had never been.

She was grateful for the reprieve, because when he did ask—and she was fairly certain that at some point he would want to know how they had met, what exactly they'd done together—she wasn't entirely certain what story she would tell.

"I've never truly lied," she whispered to John, watching as his eyelids grew heavier and heavier. This was her favorite time, after he was bathed and before bed. He smelled of sweet milk. He was always at his most content. "I am your mother for all intents and purposes even if I did not give birth to you."

That honor had been granted to Sarah Whisenhunt. A striking woman with a mane of glorious black hair, which she'd refused to shorten in spite of the health benefits, and a voluptuous figure that Mercy was fairly certain had been responsible for Miss Nightingale selecting the horrid plain black dresses as their uniforms. Many considered a nurse little more than a prostitute putting on airs. Miss N was determined to alter that perception.

Mercy had never quite understood why Sarah had interviewed for the challenging position of being one of Miss N's nurses. She complained of the boredom and the backbreaking work of scrubbing floors and mopping up the blood in the hospital. But she was exceedingly kind to the men, and she could not be faulted for her devotion to the soldiers. In particular Captain Lyons. Mercy had often seen her reading to the captain when she was finished with her duties.

In spite of it all, she was a likable girl and Mercy had befriended her.

And, of course, Sarah had quickly fallen under the spell of Stephen Lyons. Six months later, when Sarah could no longer hide her condition, Miss N had summarily dismissed her. Amidst her tears and shame, Sarah had begged Mercy not to abandon her as well. She couldn't return to England in such a state. Fearing the girl might do something dangerously drastic, Mercy had left with her to provide moral support and aid as best she could. She'd always intended to return to Miss N after the babe was born.

"But I couldn't leave you, my little one," she said now.

Sarah had planned to deliver him to a foundling home, but Mercy had fallen in love with him moments after he was born. One morning when she'd gone out to get pastries for breakfast, she'd purchased a newspaper. As was her daily habit, she scoured the list of French and British casualties. That particular morning the paper had listed Major Stephen Lyons as one of the fallen. Her first idle thought was that he'd been promoted. And then the devastating news sunk deep. John was all that remained of the charming young man who had captivated hearts.

She and Sarah had argued heatedly. Mercy had wanted to take John to Stephen's family. Sarah had wanted to be rid of him.

"His death does not obliterate my shameful behavior. If it is learned I had a bastard child, I will lose all prospects for a good marriage. I will be ostracized. It was a mistake, one night of sinful passion, and you expect me to pay for it forever. I would be relieved if it died."

Mercy had awoken the next morning to find Sarah gone and John ill. His little body burned with fever. She'd found a permanent wet nurse for him. Jeanette. Mercy had bathed him, cooled his skin, held him, rocked him, sung lullabies to him, and pleaded with him to live. When his fever finally broke, they were both exhausted. So she'd decided to take just one day for them to regain their strength. It turned into two, then three, then a fortnight, then a month. With each passing day, he wormed his way into her life, into her heart, into her soul. She had every intention of giving him up freely, but by the time she arrived on her father's doorstep, she had well and truly become John's mother.

Her greatest fear now was that he would be torn from her life. If Stephen remembered their night together, what had happened to her, why he'd stayed with her until dawn, he'd be disgusted with the knowledge. To tell it was not the same as to experience it. She could not recreate the horror of what she'd endured or the comfort she'd taken in his arms. That night he'd saved her in ways that he would never be able to fully comprehend. He'd given her a reason to live . . . when all she'd wanted to do was die.

Stephen awoke to a scream that damned near shattered his eardrums. He scrambled out of bed, drew on his trousers, and rushed across the hall, throwing open the door just as another scream sounded.

Mercy was thrashing about on the bed. Jeanette was attempting to subdue her, taking a fist to her cheek for her efforts. John was caterwauling—what a fine set of lungs his son had. Stephen was surprised the family sleeping in the other wing wasn't disturbed by this madness.

Jeanette looked up him, frantic. "She's locked in a nightmare."

"See to the boy. I'll tend to Mercy."

Without objection, Jeanette rushed to the bassinet and lifted John into her arms, but the lad was not consoled. God, he was like his sire. When he wanted something, he wanted it at that moment.

"Take him to my bedchamber," he ordered.

Jeanette rushed across the room.

"Shut the door on your way out," he shouted after her, certain the boy's screeching wasn't helping matters.

Stephen sat on the edge of the bed and leaned over her. "Mercy."

"No, no, no. Please, dear God, no."

"Mercy." He tried to gently shake her and received a fist to the eye. Damn, but she had a powerful punch. "Mercy."

She cried out, swung again—

He grabbed her wrists, secured them in one hand, and stretched her arms over her head. "Mercy. Sweetheart, darling. It's all right. You're safe."

She gasped. Her eyes flew open. The horror and fear he saw in the whiskey depths raked painfully through his heart. She was shivering, her skin clammy and cold. Her gown damp with sweat. He realized the moment recognition dawned, and the nightmare faded into oblivion.

"Stephen?"

"I'm here."

She jerked her gaze to the bassinet. "John?"

"Jeanette took him to my bedchamber. He's fine." He couldn't hear any crying in the distance and had to assume Jeanette had managed to calm the boy. He released Mercy's wrists. She raised herself to a sitting position, pressing back against the pillows as though she thought she could escape through them.

Tears welled in her eyes and rolled over onto her cheeks. "So many dead. So many dying. I could do nothing for them. I was powerless. They just kept dying. Hundreds of them. The massive numbers were frightening. The Cossacks weren't doing us in, disease was." She swiped angrily at her cheeks. "They lay there on the floor and on stuffed sacks and filthy beds, holding out their hands as we walked by. 'Sister. Sister. Mercy.' And there was none to be given. I knew they weren't calling for me particularly, but *mercy* echoed up and down the wards. And there were times when I thought I would go mad with it."

He had no words with which to comfort her. He'd been there. He'd been in that hospital. He should have known what she'd suffered. He should have known what she'd given of herself. But the only images he could see were the ones she painted.

She buried her face in her hands. "I'm sorry. I try not to sleep for long periods. I try not to give myself time to get to the place of nightmares. But I was so tired tonight. And I so enjoyed our dinner. I drank too much wine. I'm so sorry. I'm so sorry I disturbed your rest."

"For God's sake, Mercy, do you truly believe that I give a damn about my sleep?" He pulled her hands down, grabbed her chin with his thumb and forefinger, and held her in place so he could lock his eyes on to hers. "Tell me what I can do for you. Tell me what you need."

"I need to forget it all. Ironic, is it not? That you wish desperately to remember what I would give my soul to forget?"

She made another rough swipe at her cheeks. He stayed her actions by slipping his hands beneath hers and gently capturing the droplets that had grown cold. He fought to keep his gaze raised and not lower it to her thin linen nightdress, where her dark nipples pressed, puckered, against the flimsy sweat-saturated cloth. A shiver coursed through her, and he didn't fool himself into thinking it was because of his touch.

Although God help him, he wished for it to be. He wanted to ease her suffering, bring her solace and comfort, and the only way he knew to do that was with his body. But he wouldn't risk subjecting her to further shame. In spite of whatever precautions he might have taken, one night was all she'd required to get with babe. She deserved more consideration from him. Until he knew if he was going to offer marriage, he had to keep his damned hands to himself.

"I wish I still had the memories from those two years, so I would know better what to do for you."

She gave him a heartrending smile. "I have enough memories for us both."

Stephen had offered to have a servant prepare a bath for her. Sweaty and sticky, Mercy appreciated the opportunity to wash the salt from her skin and slip on a clean nightdress.

Between her bedchamber and the next was a changing room. It was there that the copper tub was filled with warm water. She was grateful to remove the clinging cloth from her body and sink down into the comforting scented bath. She'd expected the serving girl to stay with her, but instead she left. Mercy welcomed the solitude. She leaned her head back, partially lowered her eyelids, and watched the candle flames chasing the shadows around the room.

She knew the nightmares hovered nearby like thieves, keeping watch, waiting for the right moment to strike. She'd gotten into the habit of sleeping in short bursts—several moments here, a few more there. John's night schedule in the beginning of waking every couple of hours for a feeding had helped. But he was settling into sleeping for longer periods of time. She was usually able to rouse herself before the dreams took hold. But as she'd told Stephen, tonight the wine had taken her under, to a place where her demons reigned. They were a strange mixture of her time in the hospital and what had happened the night Stephen had saved her from the abuse of three men. They'd become interwoven somehow, but she wouldn't tell him about her attackers. Didn't want him to remember their ugliness, their debauchery.

Besides, they were nothing beyond pitiful specimens of men. The good men dying haunted her the most. Husbands who would never return to their wives, young men who may not yet have had the opportunity to marry. Perhaps they'd had sweethearts to whom they'd not returned. All she'd been able to do was comfort them and then weep for them. And so they haunted her, because she'd failed them.

She wondered if she'd ever again be able to sleep peacefully through the entire night.

The door clicked. The maid no doubt returning to assist her. "I'm sorry, I'm not yet ready to get out," she said, reaching for the soap.

"That's all right," Stephen said. "I'm in no hurry."

She jerked around, the water splashing around her and over the lip of the tub. She grabbed onto it, ducked down as far as she was able to and still see him. He'd put on a billowy shirt but had bothered to do up only half the buttons. She'd seen his chest before. Washed it. Trailed her fingers over the scars. Still, only partially revealed seemed so much more intimate. Wicked even, as though he were taunting, teasing her.

"What are you doing in here?" She'd planned for the words to come out forcefully, demanding. Instead, to her utter mortification, she was breathless. She couldn't deny that she'd often imagined him attempting to seduce her while she attempted to resist, until eventually she succumbed to all the naughtiness he offered.

"I've warmed some brandy for you."

It was only then that she managed to drag her gaze from the enticing view of his chest to the snifter he held in his hand. She watched with increasing alarm as he dragged a small stool over, sat on it, and extended the snifter toward her. "What in God's name do you think you're doing?" she hissed in alarm.

"Distracting you."

She knew her eyes popped. This was ludicrous. "Are you mad?"

He leaned forward, causing her to shrink back, only to realize she was no doubt giving him a clearer view, then return to the side so she was at least partially covered. How best to hide from him? He had her at a disadvantage. It was infuriating.

"Why the modesty, Mercy? We've been together."

"It's been over a year. And it was only one night."

"Take the brandy."

If it would make him leave—

She snatched it from him. He did little more than appear amused.

"Drink it," he said. "You'll feel better."

"I doubt it." Still, she did take a gulp. It burned the back of her throat and her nostrils. It stung her eyes.

"I can't see into it, you know," he said lazily.

"Pardon?"

He nodded toward the tub. "From this angle, I can't see into it. You're well hidden. So relax, enjoy your bath."

"Do you intend to remain?"

"What were you thinking about before I arrived?"

"Can you not give a straight answer to one of my questions?"

"Yes, I can. Yes, I intend to remain. Now you answer mine."

She took another taste of the brandy, savored it a bit longer. "The nightmare."

"Which is what I suspected. Which is why I'm here. Damsels in distress are my forte."

She couldn't deny the truth of that. It was what had prompted their night together. "Why don't you leave and go sit on the couch in there? I'll wash up quickly and join you."

"I'd rather watch you bathe."

"You're a pervert."

He laughed, a deep baritone richness echoing

through the room. She wasn't certain she'd ever heard a laugh such as that coming from him—not even in Scutari.

"Hardly," he finally said, catching his breath, grinning with enjoyment. "I appreciate the nakedness of a—"

"I thought you couldn't see me."

"I can't, but I can imagine."

"You're infuriating."

"Distracting."

She started to set the snifter aside when it dawned on her—"You came in here without your cane."

"And to your bedside without it as well." He rubbed his hand down the length of his thigh, and she imagined it running along hers. Silly girl. He'd barely noticed her in Scutari. Why would he desire her now? "I heard you scream and rushed out without thought. Perhaps I've not needed it since that fragment was removed, but it was familiar and so I clung to it."

"You're healing well then."

"My flesh yes, my mind . . ." He gave her a sardonic grin. "Let's not go there, shall we?"

Nodding, she set the snifter aside and searched for the soap that had plopped into the water with his arrival. At last she located it, and using a cloth, began to wash. He didn't speak, simply watched her. To his credit, he never dipped his gaze below her chin. To her discredit, she was sorely disappointed that he was not more curious.

"Do you ride?" he asked.

She peered over at him. "Once. It's been a while."

"Perhaps we'll give it a go in a few more days. It's my second-favorite pleasure." His eyes dared her to ask what the first was. But she knew. Based on the flush suddenly warming her skin, she suspected he knew she knew.

"Gambling is next," he continued. "Then drink. What is your favorite pleasure?"

"As you didn't tell me your favorite, but merely your second, third, and forth—" She saw in his eyes that she shouldn't have taunted him as she had, so she answered quickly, "Reading, attending concerts, and strawberries."

He gave her a decidedly wicked grin. "I know your first pleasure."

Kissing you, being held by you, inhaling your spicy scent, touching your—

"John," he said.

"Yes, of course. You're quite right. How very clever you are." She scrubbed harder, hoping to cover her blush. John was a pleasure, but so much more that he didn't signify in this conversation. She would never rank him because he would always be above everything.

His dark chuckle reverberated around her. "Truly, Mercy, you prefer strawberries to a kiss? How many others have kissed you?"

Her body grew so hot that she was surprised the water didn't begin to boil. "Only you."

The words came out on a whisper of shame. Why was he doing this? Tormenting her? To distract her? He was doing that easily enough by just sitting there. He didn't need to make her think about his mouth moving over hers.

"Obviously, I did not give you my best, for if I had, surely it would have fallen between reading and concerts."

"You mock me."

"And you lie."

"No, I've never lied to you." She held his gaze with a steadfastness that ensured he would know she spoke the truth. It was important to her that he understood that. She had never lied; she'd omitted information, and if he ever discovered it, it was imperative that she not be seen as deceiving him.

He studied her solemnly, quietly. "Then I was wrong," he said after a time. "I guessed incorrectly your favorite pleasure."

She neither confirmed nor denied, but concentrated on dragging the cloth over skin that had suddenly become unbearably sensitive under his perusal.

When she was ready to get out, he grabbed the towel and held it up for her. "Set it down and leave," she ordered.

"Come along. I'm just going to wrap it around you."

His eyes held a challenge that she couldn't not accept. She rose, the water sluicing off her body. She stepped out of the tub and stood with her back to him, waiting, waiting . . . and then the towel folded around her, covering her from neck to knee. Before she could move away or protest, he turned her around to face him. She clutched the opening of the towel, keeping it closed. His hands were just above hers, knotted around the towel, keeping it secure as well. Then he tugged gently, brought her nearer, until she almost fell against him, lost in the blue of his gaze.

"Why does panic show in your eyes whenever I'm studying you?" he asked. "What is it that you don't want me to see? What is it that you think I'll see? Your freckles, perhaps? You have eighteen of them, you know."

"I don't. Not that many. Half a dozen at the most."

"I suspect I look more closely at you than you look at yourself in the mirror. There are eighteen."

With that he released her and strode from the room. She sank onto the edge of the tub, wondering what other surprises the night might bring.

Chapter 9

Bloody damned hell. Why was he tormenting himself?

It wasn't her eyes, or her smile, or her spirit. It was her body. Lithe and supple with legs that stretched all the way up to her neck. He'd wanted them wrapped tightly around his waist. He wanted them now.

He'd lied. He'd had a damned good view. He'd never known such sweet torture.

It had taken every ounce of strength he possessed to sit there without revealing that he was aching with need, that his own body was rebelling. He'd wanted to snatch her out of that blasted water—water that was teasing her skin the way he wanted to—and carry her to the bed. If she hadn't just experienced a horrific nightmare, he damned well might have.

He rubbed the scar along the side of his face. He was just vain enough to wonder if she was repulsed by it, if she'd be nauseated by the others that marred his body. He'd been aware enough during his own recent ordeal to know that she'd touched them, wiped a damp cloth over them. At one point she'd leaned forward and kissed some of them. His manhood had reacted as best it could under the circumstances, with a swift stirring. If not for the laudanum, he'd have been as hard as stone. But it had kept him subdued. Maybe that was the reason she'd poured so much down his throat.

She was wary of him, too wary. Women usually were eager to have him make love to them again, soon and often. Had he suffered injuries that made him clumsy in bed? Had she not experienced the full pleasure he offered all women?

This hole of memories was a curse. He had no idea how he might have treated her, what they might have done. And he certainly wasn't going to ask her.

Stepping out of the changing room, she approached, watching him warily like a virgin on her wedding night. It made no sense. She *knew* what he was fully capable of delivering.

"Why does being with me frighten you?" he asked.

She darted a quick glance to the bed, then angled her chin defiantly. "It doesn't."

"Then come sit over here"—he slid his hand over the cushion beside him—"and have some more brandy."

"It's frightfully late."

"It usually is when one awakens with a nightmare." From the moment he'd met her, he'd failed to question the heavy circles beneath her eyes, the weariness that shadowed her face. He'd simply assumed she was one of those women who always appeared tired, as though life were a burden too heavy to bear. But what he now knew of her character—she was not one to be weighted down. He suspected she would frolic through green fields with the first hint of spring. "When was the last time you slept for any substantial length of time?"

"I sleep in snatches. John. John does not yet sleep through the night."

He gave her a pointed look. "Jeanette could relieve you of that duty."

"But he's my son. He needs me."

"Once in a while, you *need* to sleep through the night."

"I can't. If it's anything other than a quick nap"— she shook her head forcefully—"*they* come. All those I could not save."

The reminder of what had initially brought him to her bedchamber curbed his desire. He patted the cushion. "Join me. I won't ravish you."

"I never thought you would."

He wasn't quite certain what to make of her tone. Was it disappointment or determination? And why would she ever think she was safe with him? Women weren't. Oh, he never forced them, but he was damned skilled at persuading them. Why did she not think he would take advantage?

The sofa dipped slightly beneath her weight. She brought her feet up, the gown creating a tent over her legs. She wrapped her arms around them, rested her chin on her knees, and stared into the fire. She reminded him of a petulant child. But the gown was thin and shadows teased him. No child there.

With one long swallow to refortify himself, he emptied the brandy from his snifter. After refilling it, he offered it to her since she'd left hers in the bathing room. He supposed he could have retrieved it, but he didn't want to upset the balance that had settled in between them.

She sipped gingerly, her focus on the fire in the hearth so great that he wondered if she even remembered he was in the room.

"Nineteen," she said mulishly, her mouth drawn.

"Pardon?"

"There are nineteen freckles. You must have missed one."

"Then I shall have to recount them."

"Don't bother," she stated flatly. "Take my word for it."

He didn't answer. He would count them again. Before the night was over if he had his way.

For a heartbeat, she looked almost disappointed that he didn't argue further. He could barely contain the relief that went through him. She might pretend otherwise, but she wanted him near, perhaps as much as he wanted to be close enough to enjoy her fragrance.

She grabbed her stub of a braid, dragged her hand down it, and reached empty air far too quickly. He wondered if she'd forgotten that her hair was shorter. "How long was it?" he asked.

Twisting her head, she pressed her cheek to her knees and stared at him.

"Your hair," he said to her unasked question.

"Past my waist."

Reaching out cautiously, the way he might approach a skittish filly, he unraveled her braid, holding her gaze the entire time, challenging her not to stop him. She didn't. She sat frozen. He wasn't even certain she breathed. He combed his fingers through the short strands that curled around her chin, curtained the length of her neck, toyed at her shoulders.

"Was it difficult to cut it?"

"Not terribly. The scissors I used were quite sharp."

He flashed a smile, before narrowing his eyes at her caustic statement. He suspected she could be a good deal of fun when her burdens were light. He wanted to be with her when they were, wanted to be around when her hair once again cascaded down her back.

"I meant—and I know you know what I meant—if it was hard to give up what many consider a woman's crowning glory."

"It was hardly glorious with vermin crawling through it." She feathered her fingers over it. "It's only been a few months since I last cut it. I don't know if I'll ever bother to have it as long as it once was. It's much easier to care for short."

"I rather fancy it, but I would also like to see it long." He arched a brow. "So I can compare. As we've already discovered, you don't study yourself with as much effort as I study you."

She released a short burst of laughter, straightened, and finished off the brandy. He wrapped his fingers around the bowl of the snifter to take it from her. She stilled his actions by laying her hand over his. Then she trailed her fingers over a jagged scar that ran across two knuckles and nearly touched a third.

"You said you didn't know how you came to have all your scars." She lifted her whiskey gaze to his and his gut clenched. Had any woman ever looked at him with such unbridled yearning? Was it the brandy? Had it relaxed her enough that she was able to cast inhibitions and proper behavior aside? "I know how this one came to be."

"Do you?" He shouldn't have been surprised by his strangled voice. Everything within him urged him to hold more than the damned snifter.

"You acquired it the night you saved me."

"Saved you? From what?"

She took the snifter from him, set it aside. She held

his hand with one of hers and with the other trailed her fingers over the scar, as though reading a tale. "It was late. Dark. Only a sliver of a moon in the sky. I should have been in my room in the northwest tower, but sleep eluded me. Which was odd, as I was exhausted from my turn at scrubbing the floors. Miss N could not tolerate the filth. Neither could I. A man should have a clean place in which to die."

Tightening her hold on his hand, she shook her head quickly, as though her story had taken a turn she didn't wish it to take, and she needed to get it out of her mind. She once again began dancing her fingers over his damaged skin. "It was dark, late. I was walking."

She was repeating herself and he suspected she was delaying getting to the meat of the story, perhaps even regretting that she'd ever begun it.

"There were other buildings. Few people were about because of the lateness of the hour. I felt safe. The Cossacks were a danger, but they weren't near us. I never thought I need fear those I'd come to help."

His entire body stiffened, his hand closed over hers. He shifted nearer and with his free hand, he cradled her cheek and spotted the freckle he'd missed before. It was ludicrous to notice something so trivial at a moment like this, but he recognized the distraction for what it was. He dreaded hearing the rest because he was fairly certain he knew where the story was going and it took everything within him to act disaffected, not to display the driving need he had to get up and smash something.

She shivered, and her golden brown eyes took on a faraway, haunted look. "There were three men. One a big, brutish fellow. Another slightly shorter and reed thin. The other an even smaller chap. I don't know why, but when they emerged from the shadows I immediately thought of a tale about three bears that my childhood nursemaid had told me." He could feel the slightest of tremors in her hands, the one he held and the one that continued to stroke him. He wanted to beg her not to carry on with the story, but he sensed that she needed to unburden herself. So for her sake, he held his tongue. If she had borne the reality of it, he could bear the retelling. But he was haunted with the realization that if he'd not lost his memories, she'd not have to tell him. He would have known. He could have spared her this torment.

"They were well into their cups," she continued, her voice faint. "They grabbed me, dragged me between two buildings—"

His healing thigh began to ache unbearably from the tension pouring into it.

"I tried to dissuade them from their purpose but they were of a mind like so many others that a woman willing to tend to men, who didn't shy away from bathing them and assisting them with their personal needs, was of low moral character. That she was a trollop.

"I screamed and fought, all the while knowing there was no hope for it. I could not fend them off. I would be ruined."

His heart was hammering as though he stood in that alleyway with her. The hairs on the back of his neck rose.

She lifted her gaze to his. "And then I heard the voice of my salvation. 'See here, lads, that's not the way to go about charming a lady into lifting her skirts.'

" 'She arn't no lady,' the brute said.

" 'You'll feel a sight differently when it's your blood

spilling on the floor that she's mopping. Leave her be.'

"You swaggered toward us, so calm, so poised. I knew who you were, of course. I'd changed the bandages on your arm." She touched it now, the place where the scars were so thick that he'd often wondered if he'd come close to losing it. Only through her did he know now that he had. "Wiped your brow. Brought you soup. You'd been discharged that afternoon. I thought you were on your way back to the regiment. But there you were, so strong, so cocky. They'd have none of it, though. It didn't matter that you were their superior in rank. They were like animals. They mistook you for a gentleman playing at soldiering." She turned her attention back to his scarred knuckles. She kissed them softly, and he shuddered with the stark need to find those men and beat them into bloody pulps. "You hit the brute who was holding me with such quickness that he had no time to react and with such force that I heard the sickening crack of his jawbone. He landed with a hard thud. He didn't get up. The others ran off. You lifted me into your arms and carried me to a distant corner, crouched in the snow, and held me in your lap, soothing me while I wept." Her eyes rose to meet and hold his. "You were with me until dawn."

Sometime during the telling of her tale, she'd shifted so her knees were no longer raised, but were resting between them on the cushion. She lowered his hand to her lap, but didn't let go.

He still cradled her cheek. He skimmed his thumb over the curve of it. "I take it that eventually I did more than hold you."

A deep red blush instantly flushed her face.

"Do you feel I took advantage?"

"No, like every other nurse, I fancied myself in love with you."

He'd always had a talent for making the women fall in love with him. He'd taken immense pride in it. Of a sudden, he was feeling rather nauseous. He wanted to believe that he'd have been gallant enough to withhold his lust if the situation warranted. But his needs when it came to women had always been powerful.

"I'm sorry I don't remember that night of gallantry. I'm afraid I can't share your conviction that I didn't take advantage."

"The time I spent with you was the most wondrous of my life. You erased the memories of their vileness. I'm not sure, without your comfort, if I would have ever been able to stand to have another man touch me. Everything that happened there was so intense. It was as though each moment encompassed a lifetime. In the months that followed, when despair struck me over the deplorable conditions under which we were striving to save lives, those memories of the time I was with you saw me through, gave me hope—to know there was something better."

"Then why are you so wary of me?"

"Because you don't remember me, and it is as though we are beginning anew. And so much has transpired in my life that I'm not certain I'm the same girl that I was. Or that you're the same man."

All he knew was that he wasn't the same man who'd shared tea with Claire. He'd changed in many ways but not in all ways. Of that he was certain.

He worked his hand free of her hold, slipped his arms beneath her—

"What are you doing?"

"You trusted me that night. In spite of the fact that what happened with those brutes should have made it difficult for you to trust any man. You trusted me. We were together until dawn. Trust me again, Mercy. Tonight. I will hold the nightmares at bay. I will give you a sleep so deep—"

"No, I will not risk getting with child. It is so unfair—"

"That night, did I use my mouth?"

"You kissed me, yes."

"Did I kiss you"—he dipped his gaze to her lap, then held her eyes steadily. "Did I kiss you everywhere?"

Her lips slightly parted, she barely shook her head.

"Then let me give you this gift. It is all that will relieve the guilt and worry that perhaps I did take advantage and you were either too innocent or too upset to know it."

"It's wrong," she whispered.

"It's not wrong to receive pleasure. I can give it to you without removing my clothes, without unfastening a single button."

"And my buttons?"

"I would like to unfasten them, but if you're feeling shy the nightdress can remain."

"Why do you want to do this?"

"Because you've been treated poorly by me . . . and others. I want to apologize and words will not suffice."

"You are the only man I have been with through the night. I can't imagine what you might have in mind that does not involve passion."

"Oh, there will be passion. There will be passion aplenty. You will have the power to stop me at any moment."

"How?"

"Simply say 'no more.'"

She watched him for the longest, her breathing uneven. He couldn't deny that his invitation was prompted by a hope that seeing her in the throes of passion would help him to find one of his lost memories. And if it did not, well, there would still be pleasure in it for him. He enjoyed giving a woman pleasure as much as he appreciated receiving it.

"Trust me, Mercy, and I shall give you a sleep-filled night such as you've never known."

She didn't remember nodding her consent. She knew she'd not been able to form the words to give it. But somehow, he must have read her acquiescence because he lifted her into his arms and carried her to the bed.

Feeling his uneven gait, realizing that his leg was not as healed as he claimed, she protested his carting her, but he'd have none of it. He was determined to give her all his attention.

He laid her on the bed with a gentleness that almost made her weep. He brushed his lips over hers, so sweetly. She lifted up for more, only to be greeted by his soft chuckle as he turned away from her and began to go through the room, dimming lamps, extinguishing candles.

She wondered how he'd known that the request had been hovering on the tip of her tongue. She'd never been truly intimate with a man. In truth, she didn't know if she could be. The brutes had hurt her, and while Stephen had consoled and comforted her, he'd not bedded her.

He'd been a perfect gentleman. He'd shown her gentleness.

Her greatest fear was that if he did take her to wife, she'd be unable to carry out her wifely duties. Even for him.

And while she fought not to reveal it, she was quite literally terrified.

Not of him, but of the act itself.

By the time he returned to her side, her hands were aching from how tightly she'd interlaced her fingers over her stomach. He placed his hand over hers, and she quivered.

"I cannot have given you the pleasure you deserved for you to be dreading it so now," he said quietly.

"One night—"

"I know. One night, more than a year ago. Still, it should have been such that you would desire it again."

"I do not wish to be with child again before I am wed."

"If that is your fear, then relax, Mercy. Nothing I do tonight will get you with child."

She furrowed her brow. "Is the possibility not required for pleasure?"

"If that is what I left you to believe, then I was a dog."

"No . . . I . . . no, you were wonderful." She didn't want him to doubt his ability, nor to realize that they'd not shared their bodies. She was floundering in a well of deception, but to reveal everything now might cause her to lose John. How would he ever trust her?

He took her hands, separated them, and placed them on the pillow, one on each side of her head.

The only light in the room came from the fire. She found solace in the near darkness. His face was ensconced in shadows, yet she could still see the rough planes that emerged into the light with his movements.

Shadows had provided comfort as well that long-ago night, and she'd welcomed them, hidden in them.

"I want to touch you everywhere," he said quietly, and her body tightened with the raspy promise in his voice. "The nightdress will be a hindrance. I'll leave it if you wish, but your enjoyment will be greater if you'll wear only the darkness."

"It's not completely dark."

"Dark enough."

She licked her lips, nodded. "Very well. As you wish."

"No, sweetheart. It's what you wish."

She nodded again. He reached for her button. She grabbed his wrist, tightening her fingers around it. "I trust you not to hurt me."

"Did I hurt you before?"

"No, but . . . I feel more vulnerable now."

"Because I don't remember you?"

"Because I've withstood humiliation."

"What passes here tonight will go no further." The bed dipped as he stretched out beside her. "Let me pleasure you, Mercy."

He wasn't asking permission, as she'd already granted it. He was simply reaffirming his intent. Before she could say a word, he was kissing her. All her doubts, all her worries were absorbed by the sweep of his tongue through her mouth. Her fingers found their way to his hair and she was glad he'd unclamped them earlier, set them free so they could go where they would.

She felt his fingers combing through her hair, and she imagined it longer, wished it longer. For him, she would grow it to her waist, past her waist.

His mouth left hers to rain light kisses over her face, so many that she wished she counted, because she suspected he was kissing each freckle. Only how could he see them in the dark—unless he'd memorized their location? Perhaps he had. He'd studied her often enough, intensely enough.

Just as she'd studied him in Scutari. In spite of his fair hair, his skin had been bronzed. It was not quite as dark now, no doubt because he was not outside as much. But she suspected with his leg healed, he would be riding over the hills. The sun would again paint a golden glow over him, so much more attractive than the freckles it bestowed on her.

He trailed his mouth along her chin, her throat, igniting sparks of pleasure wherever it touched. His hand left her hair to skim along her arm, up and down, up and down. She could feel the warmth through the cloth.

What would it hurt, she wondered, to simply ease out of the sleeve so she might have skin upon skin?

As though he'd read her mind, she suddenly found her arm free of the confining nightdress and his rough palm was sending delicious sensations over her skin, her shoulder, her collarbone, her breast—

Her eyes flew open to be greeted by the deep shadows of the night. She could barely make out the silhouette of his lowered head, so how was it that he was able to so unerringly touch her, never clumsy, each movement as smooth as though he'd practiced a thousand times?

She didn't want to think of the other women he'd known. They'd taught him well or perhaps it was truly as they said: Practice makes perfect. She could not find fault with his past when it ensured now that she found such enjoyment.

She felt the air brush against her skin, her nipples

puckering with the gentle teasing. She realized he had somehow managed, without her noticing, to work her nightdress down to her waist. It would be completely lowered before too long.

What was the point in fighting the inevitable? He was correct. The night was the only clothing she needed.

"Remove it," she rasped, surprised by her rapid breathing, the hoarseness of her voice, as though she'd screamed out his name a thousand times.

Before she drew in her next breath, her nightdress was gone, discarded. She heard it whispering as it settled on the floor. Gathering her own courage, she tugged on his shirtsleeve. "And this."

His dark chuckle, chafing with desire, echoed his satisfaction. She felt the brush of the cloth over her skin as he pulled the shirt over his head and it joined her nightdress.

It increased her pleasure to be able to touch him so, to feel the fiery silkiness of his skin beneath her fingers. She dared go no further than his waist. She knew to do so would be to invite an even greater intimacy. She was not certain she was prepared for that.

Although she couldn't deny that she was enjoying immensely the way her body thrummed, strained, and begged for whatever release he might offer her.

Every nerve ending seemed so alive. Her heart pumped furiously, energy crackled around her. She could not fathom when all was said and done that she would do as he promised—sleep soundly. She suspected she'd don her clothes and go racing through the gardens.

He cradled her breast and all thoughts of gardens skittered away. Her body reacted forcefully, curling toward him, wanting him near. She felt as though she had no say in the matter. It wanted what it wanted, and it wanted whatever he would give her.

Tension stretched from her head to her toes. He flicked his thumb over the tightened nipple. She felt heated dew gather between her legs. His tongue replaced his thumb, swirling slowly, provocatively . . .

She moaned low, a sound that she knew came from her only because she felt the vibration in her throat. He closed his mouth over her nipple, suckled . . . and she sighed.

Stars danced before her eyes as though he'd opened the windows and allowed in the night sky. His hands moved over her, doing deliciously wicked things to her flesh. A bounty of sensations flooded her, and she didn't know how she could possibly contain them all.

She was aware of his shifting, wedging himself between her thighs. His heated breath caused moisture to form on her stomach. He licked at her, his tongue circled her navel. Dipped inside. Tickled. Not the sort to make her laugh, but the kind that made her entire body smile.

Rapture hovered, whispered delicious promises. She wished she'd ordered him to leave candles burning so she could see him more clearly, but perhaps it was the darkness that added to the allure, that allowed her to relax enough to enjoy what he was doing to her. With light, not only would she see him, but he would see her: every blush that she was certain rolled into her face as he eased farther down.

He blew against the soft curls that hid her womanhood. She jerked, dug her fingers into his scalp. "Stephen?"

"Shh. Sweetheart. The best is yet to come."

"This is decadent."

"Of course it is. Did you expect anything less from me?"

He didn't wait for her to respond, but returned to his wicked endeavors. He lightly kissed the juncture where hip met thigh. First one side and then the other. Passion swirled through her with unrelenting heat.

He slipped his hands beneath her bottom and lifted. "Bend your knees, sweetheart, put your heels on my back."

It would open her up to him more . . . She didn't know if she could, if she dared—

"Mercy, do you want me to stop?"

Her body was strung as tight as a bow. It wanted a release she didn't understand. It begged, yearned for more. If she said yes, he would leave her with this unquenched desire.

"No."

"Then do as I ask."

His voice was rough, as though he suffered for what he could not have. Was it painful for him to give and not receive?

"Do you hurt?"

"Don't worry about me, love. Tonight is for you."

Love. Did he mean it? *Sweetheart.* Was it a word he used with all his ladies? She wanted to ask him, but wasn't certain she wanted the answer. What did it matter? He used them with her now.

She did as he bade, then held her breath in anticipation. The first stroke of his tongue caused her breath to heave out in a rush. Squeezing her thighs against his shoulders, she released a low moan. Never had she felt anything quite so exquisite.

But he was not nearly done. He continued to stroke, to suckle, to kiss, to delve deeply, to use his tongue in ways she'd not even considered a tongue could be used. The sensations mounted with each touch, each velvety caress.

One of his hands left her bottom and reached up to toy with her breast. The sensations intensified. She squirmed and his low laughter added to the sensations, carrying her even higher.

She'd never felt anything like this, had not known it was possible. Surely, she would expire before he was done. Perhaps that was his intent. To kill her with his attentions. She'd certainly sleep well then—for all eternity.

Her back arched high and her hands were pressed to his head, holding him near. It was as though she no longer had control of her own body. He was the master of it, enticing it to do his bidding.

She wanted to scream. Perhaps she should. Then everything building within her might find its release.

She wanted to hold on to the sensations. To never let them go. Because he'd given them to her. She wanted to treasure them forever.

She wanted to tell him to remove his trousers, to give her the freedom to touch him as he touched her.

Desire surged through her. Passion rose to exalted heights. Pleasure erupted—

She cried out, thrashed about as though she were captured by another nightmare.

"Oh, God, oh, God!" Her body tightened, unfurled, and catapulted her into a realm of exquisite bliss.

When she returned, it was to find herself gasping and Stephen hovering over her. Even though he was outlined in shadows, his satisfaction was evident.

"Did I not give you that before?"

Why had he asked? She would not lie to him. He hadn't but only because they'd done nothing of this magnitude. But if he realized that he'd never made love to her, he'd realize that she'd not given birth to John. He'd have no reason to marry her, and she'd have no guarantee of remaining in John's life.

So she said nothing at all.

"Shame on me," he finally muttered, before lying down beside her and taking her in the circle of his arms, guiding her face into the nook of his shoulder. "Sleep now, Mercy. Sleep to your heart's content. I'll guard you against all nightmares."

And she believed him.

Chapter 10

Mercy awoke feeling both lethargic and rejuvenated. It was a confusing combination. How could she be both at the same time? But she was. She felt as though she'd slept for a century.

Slowly, she realized that she wasn't alone. Her head rested half on a strong, sturdy arm and half on a pillow. Her hair was being gently tucked behind one ear, over and over, the touch as light as fairies dancing over petals. One of her legs was nestled between both of his, her sole rubbing his trouser-covered calf without any thought from her prompting it. She halfway wished she'd given him leave to remove all his clothes, wished she hadn't slipped on her nightdress.

Warily, she lifted her eyes to find him watching her with a mixture of amusement and—dare she believe it?—yearning. Memories of the late hours of the night and all he'd done to her came rushing back with a vengeance. Heat scorched her like molten metal. Her nerve endings tingled with want.

She'd been more decadent—he'd been more decadent—than she'd ever thought two people could possibly be. She felt a surge of guilt that all the pleasure experienced had been hers, but he'd seemed content

with it. And she'd learned that she could, in fact, tolerate such intimacy. When it came from him at least.

"Hello, there." His voice was rough from sleep, and
to her shame and relief, it sent desire sweeping through
her. Shame because she wanted again what he'd delivered, relief because she wanted it again. What a con-
glomeration of emotions. She would not risk pregnancy
without a husband.

"What time is it?" she asked.

Lifting up slightly, he looked back at the clock on the
mantel. "Looks to be half past two."

She could see sunlight peering through at the edges
of the draperies. Stunned, she asked, "In the afternoon?"

Grinning, he leaned down and kissed the tip of her
nose. "I told you I had the power to hold the nightmares
at bay."

"I've never slept this long. It must have been more
than twelve hours."

"Well, you needed it." He started to skim his hand
down her side and she latched on to his wrist to still
his actions. His eyes challenged her.

"We can't continue—" She eased up slightly for a
better view. "What happened to your eye?"

A bruise, dark blue at the corner of his eye, that
lightened as it spread down to his cheek, appeared
painful.

"You struck me." He apparently awoke in good humor,
finding everything funny, as his mouth curled up.

"What? No?" She remembered thrashing about
during the throes of passion, but—

"During your nightmare," he continued, and once
again combed her hair back as though he was fascinated with it.

"God, I'm so sorry. It seems I'm forever apologizing to you."

"And Jeanette, too."

Groaning, she hoped Jeanette was as understanding as he. "To think you risked further injury by staying with me."

"It was no hardship."

Not for him or for her. But still it had been a deplorable bit of behavior, when she was a guest. "If your family learns of our . . . indiscretions . . . it will no doubt lower their opinion of me."

"With their history, I doubt it."

"My opinion of me is lowered. I should have had the strength to resist."

"You did. I wanted much more. You must have known that."

"And next time you may very well have it. Is that the sort of woman you want as a mother for your son?"

"Would you want a husband who can't remember the past two years of his life?"

"If he is you? Yes."

Stephen headed to his brother's library after dressing himself for the day. He'd been reluctant to leave Mercy. He'd been wrong, yet once again. It wasn't her eyes, her smile, her spirit, or her body that had so enticed him. It had been her passion. He had little doubt that comforting her in Scutari had ignited it and he'd been helpless to extinguish the blaze. It had needed to run its own course. And while it appeared that running its course had been a disservice to her—he'd never placed his *own* pleasure before a woman's—it had resulted in her giving birth to his child. He couldn't deny that any longer. Or what he owed her.

This afternoon, he'd wanted to stay in bed with her and have an opportunity to explore her passions further and discover—or rediscover—all the pleasures she had to offer. But he had other more urgent matters that required his immediate attention. Again, another first for him because always before, nothing had been more important than pleasure.

He'd sought it out, he'd nurtured it, he'd ensured that it encompassed a great deal of his life. What was the point in breathing if pleasure was not available? The quest for pleasure had always dominated his life. Yet, here he was casting it aside for something that seemed more worthwhile. Who was this man striding through the hallways? He wondered if he even knew himself any longer.

Entering the library, he was surprised to see Dr. Roberts sitting in a chair near Ainsley's desk. The man came to his feet swiftly, his face flushed. "Major Lyons. Good to see you moving about so freely."

"Without my cane, no less. I didn't remember having an appointment with you today."

"He's here to see me," Ainsley said, standing now, discreetly opening a drawer and sliding a piece of paper into it before quietly closing it. It was not like Ainsley to be secretive. Although maybe it was, and Stephen had been too consumed with himself to notice.

"What was that?" Stephen asked, stepping nearer.

"Nothing of importance." Ainsley squinted. "What in God's name happened to your eye?"

Stephen glanced between the two men. He recognized guilt when he saw it, but he knew Ainsley well enough to know hammering at the truth wasn't the way to gain it. "I had a bit of a mishap last night. Ran into a door."

Ainsley scoffed. "No doubt one of the serving girls rebuffed your amorous advances. I've told you to leave them alone. I don't tolerate that sort of behavior toward my staff."

Stephen held his tongue. *Let him think what he will.*

"You needed something?" Ainsley prodded.

"Yes, but it's a private matter. I didn't realize you had company. I'll return later."

"No need," Dr. Roberts said. "I'm quite done here. Your Grace, a pleasure as always. Major, if you have any other ill effects, do call on me, otherwise, good day to you, sir."

Stephen watched as the man made a hasty exit, then turned his attention and his glare on his brother. "Want to tell me what the hell that was about?"

"Private matter."

He gave his brother a once over. "Concerning your health?"

"Let it go, Puppy."

"You've not called me that since I returned."

"Apologies. I shouldn't have done so now. Old habit. You earned my admiration with your actions in the Crimea."

"Actions I don't even recall."

"But worthy nonetheless. Some were reported in the *Times* and in the *Illustrated London News*. Other accounts I received from the War Office. They're here if you ever want to read them."

"At some point, perhaps." He ambled over to the sidebar and splashed some whiskey in a glass. "Join me?"

"Bit early in the day, isn't it? Even for you."

"It's never too early to indulge in pleasures. If West-cliffe and I taught you nothing else, we should have taught you that. Otherwise, what good were we as brothers?"

"Something's up," Ainsley said. "You've not been this amiable toward me since you were twelve."

Damn Ainsley's clever mind. Stephen poured whis-key into another glass. Holding both aloft, he strode back to the desk wearing his most innocent smile. "I nearly died. Surely that warrants my taking a kinder regard toward you."

Ainsley took the glass from him and sat in his chair, leaning back. "Perhaps, but I don't trust—"

Stephen opened the drawer, snatched the sheaf of paper he'd seen Ainsley slip into it earlier, and darted away before Ainsley could stop him. "The distrust is reciprocated."

"Damn it!" Ainsley shouted, coming to his feet. "Hand that over."

Stephen moved to the window where the light was better. It was a list of names. All women. "What is this? Your latest list of conquests?" His gaze fell on a familiar name. "Good God. Mercy's name is on here." He spun around and glared at his brother. "What is this?"

Ainsley sat on the edge of his desk and tossed back his whiskey. "You're not going to like it."

"I don't like it now."

"It's a list of the women who were selected to serve with Miss Nightingale."

"Why would you have it?"

"I was attempting to verify her story. That she was indeed a nurse, that your paths might have crossed."

"You doubt her?"

"I just wanted to be sure."

"It's not your place."

"You don't remember a bloody thing about the past two years. You don't even know if you ever bedded her."

"I did."

Ainsley jerked his head back with surprise. "You remember?"

"No." He balled up the paper. "But I know." If he were a romantic, he might have pressed a fist to his heart for emphasis. "The boy is mine. And Mercy will be as well. I came here to ask you to help me secure a special license."

"What if you're wrong?"

"Then it will be my mistake to live with." He took a step toward his brother. "Ainsley, you're three years my junior, yet you've always treated me as though I were the younger. I'm not your responsibility."

"If I'd not purchased you a commission—"

"You and Westcliffe. I don't remember the time I was in the Crimea, but I remember all the years before. I needed to be prodded into putting away childish things. I needed something to give my life purpose." Just as Mercy had. He had no idea if he'd found the purpose satisfying, but he did know that he'd acquired a purpose now which he had no intention of casting aside.

"Do you care for the girl, then?" Ainsley asked.

"As much as I'm able, yes, I believe I do. Which I know seems ludicrous considering that to my present mind she's only been in my life a few days. But there you are."

Ainsley jumped on that argument like a flea on a dog to sway Stephen from the course he'd set. But

Stephen would not be dissuaded from doing what he'd determined he must do.

Next he went to see his mother. He found her in the north drawing room, curled up in a chair near the window, looking up with a serene expression on her face as though she were gazing into heaven. It startled him to see her so. She'd always been strong, formidable, a woman with a reputation for doing as she pleased. In that particular pose, she gave the appearance of being a much younger woman, and he realized for all that she'd seen two husbands put in the ground and raised three rambunctious lads to adulthood, and was now the grandmother of two, she had not yet seen half a century.

Leo was standing off to the side, palette in hand, easel before him. It seemed the duchess was his favorite subject. Stephen had seen countless works he'd completed and she was in the center of most of them.

Leo paused, the brush hovering near the canvas. "Major."

"Leo. May I have a private word with my mother?"

She swung her head around, her lips pursed. "You've asked the girl to marry you."

"You disapprove?"

"Hardly. It is the proper thing to do for the mother of your child. She could have tossed John in the Seine and we'd all been none the wiser. But I expected to have to coerce you. Leo wagered you'd do it on your own. Now I will have to pay up."

Leo put his brush away, sauntered over to the duchess, bent down, and kissed her cheek. "I shall leave you to visit with your son, while I scurry off to fantasize about receiving the payment you owe me."

"Stay away from that young parlor maid. You know the one of which I speak. I don't like the way she looks at you."

"I'd noticed nothing amiss, but then I have eyes for only you."

"Oh, posh," she said, laughing. "Go on with you, then."

As Leo strode from the room, she never turned her gaze away from him. "He has always had too romantic a bent."

Stephen sat in the chair opposite hers and stretched out his legs. Without the sun catching her just so, she didn't look quite so young, but she was still a handsome woman. "What did you wager?"

She blushed. "That is between Leo and me." Sighing deeply, she studied him. "So you will marry her then."

"If she'll have me. I haven't yet asked." He'd hinted, tested the waters, but until she'd arrived here, apparently he'd not given her the best of himself. He intended to make up for that shortcoming.

"But you want the ring?" The ring Westcliffe's father had given her had gone to Westcliffe's wife. The ring Ainsley's father had given her, she would give to Ainsley's wife. The ring her father had given to her mother— it would go to Mercy.

"Yes."

A mist quickly covered her eyes, and she blinked it away. "You have always loved women. So I thought you'd be the last to wed, if you wed at all."

"Women, Mother. I have always loved women. Never *a* woman. Other than you, of course."

Her lips twitched. "Cheeky devil." The amusement faded away. "You don't love her then?"

"For all practical purposes, I've known her for less than a week. How could I?"

Nodding, she gazed out the window. "Do not, I beg of you, be unfaithful to her."

"Just as the conditions of your wager are between you and Leo, so my fidelity is between Mercy and me."

"An unfaithful husband can shatter a woman's heart, destroy her pride, leave her bitter, make—"

"Mother, ours is a forced marriage and will be one of convenience. I do not think either of us expects more," he said sternly.

"I raised my sons to be strong, stubborn men with a good deal too much pride. You will follow your own course, I'm well aware of that. But I pray it will be your heart that serves as your compass."

Stephen had considered inviting Mercy to accompany him on a walk through the garden, but the winds had picked up and it was bitter cold out. The rain arrived at dusk and slashed at the windows. If it were spring, he'd take her on a picnic beside one of the rivers that cut through his brother's land or one of the ponds where they'd sometimes fished as young lads. His chest tightened with the thought that one day he would take John fishing there.

He'd always known the possibility existed that he'd one day have children, but he'd always expected to ease into the role of father. Instead it had been thrust upon him with no preparation. He couldn't bemoan the fact when the same situation had been thrust upon Mercy. He wouldn't complain, resent, or wish matters were different. He would accept his duties as a father and a husband and make the best of them. He never wanted his son to regret that Stephen was his father. More, he never wanted Mercy to regret that Stephen was her husband.

He would begin their arrangement as he intended to continue it: with a great deal of thought and with her desires in mind.

He'd wanted someplace where they would have little chance of being disturbed. Someplace where his meddlesome mother couldn't lurk in hiding and listen to what he intended to say. Finally, he'd decided on the portrait gallery. On the first floor the windows provided an exceptional view of his brother's estate. He'd asked Mercy to join him there an hour before dinner was to be served.

He was standing at a window, rehearsing his words, when he heard her quiet footfalls. A burst of lightning lit up the black night sky and illuminated the countryside. The display was majestic and powerful. An appropriate setting, he finally decided, for a woman who had proven she was made of firmer stuff than he. As nature's light faded, leaving only the lamps burning to provide a barrier against the shadows, he saw her reflection in the glass, standing near his. She was wearing the green gown she'd worn the first night. Only now he knew the treasures it hid.

As they would be going straight to dinner, she'd not bothered with gloves. Neither had he. The way her hair was arranged disguised its shortness. A pearl comb drew the eye. He wondered how old he would be by the time her hair once again reached her waist.

They stared at each other's reflection. They stared at the night. They watched the storm have its way, wind lashing at nearby trees, the rain slashing at the windows. The corridor was long, the entire span of the house. He'd planned to walk the length of it with her. He'd even brought his walking stick so he could mask his remaining limp, barely noticeable as it had become. But in the end, he simply indicated a chair in front of the window. "Please sit."

She did as he bade, folded her hands in her lap, and looked up at him with expectation. He wondered if she knew why he'd asked her to come here.

Placing his hands behind his back, he returned to staring out the window, but he could see her reflection clearly. He was drawn to her. He couldn't deny the truth of that. Nor could he deny that he was responsible for her current situation. He could take the babe, allow the duchess to raise him, set Mercy free. But he'd witnessed her deep love for the child. It would be cruel to separate her from John.

He could take John and delegate Mercy to nursemaid or governess. If she never again claimed him, in time, those who knew of her transgression would forget. She might meet someone, fall in love, and marry. Have her own life. Leave John behind. But that was not fair to John.

If he was honest with himself, he didn't want her to leave. But he did not love her, and again, that was not fair to her. He could think of no perfect solution. So he had to settle on the one he thought would be the best, in spite of its imperfections. She was the sort who would make the best of an unfortunate situation, and he was the sort who would do all in his power to ensure she was forever happy. A woman should know no sorrow, as far as he was concerned, at least none delivered by him. They entertained, they amused, they brought a man pleasure. They were a gift. As such, he had always treasured them.

Taking a deep breath, he held on to her reflection. "I do not know if I am the man you knew in Scutari. I do not know what that man felt for you or what his intentions toward you were. I am not even certain I know the man I am now. All I know is the man I was two years ago. Quite honestly, I'm not certain I held him in very high esteem." He turned to face her. "For what comfort it might bring you, I can tell you that the man I was two years ago never took to his bed a woman for whom he held no affection whatsoever."

She nodded and swallowed, her delicate throat drawing his eye, before he returned his gaze to hers. "You should know that there has never been any man other than you," she said quietly.

He released a light laugh. "That was rather obvious last night. If I didn't know better, I'd have sworn you were a virgin."

"Have you known many?"

He arched a brow. "Virgins?"

She nodded in obvious embarrassment, her cheeks flaming red.

"No, but discussing my past exploits—in detail—is not the reason I asked you to join me here. This morning you indicated you were not opposed to marrying a man who had lost a part of his mind."

"You've not lost your mind. You've lost only your memories."

"And what if this . . . *affliction* is not limited to the time I was in the Crimea? What if it visits me again and I forget you again? Forget you and John?"

"I do not believe in borrowing trouble."

But she had borrowed it, with a vengeance, when she'd made the decision to keep his son. Stephen couldn't continue to allow her to carry that burden alone. Regardless of the man he might have been in the Crimea, he knew the man he'd been before it. That had not changed. Always when he'd bedded a woman, he'd done it with the full knowledge that he would never abandon her in a difficult situation.

"You are the mother of my child, and in my head, I know that would not have occurred if I did not have some care for you. I cannot say that I loved you. Even now, I cannot . . . but just as you did not abandon my son, I will not abandon you." He dropped to his knee, his healing leg protesting as he bent it to accommodate his position.

She gasped. Her eyes widened. He took her hand, pressed it to his lips, drank in her whiskey eyes. "Miss Dawson—Mercy—will you marry me?"

Chapter 11

Mercy continued to feel the weight of his words as they joined the others in the library.

The duchess came out of her chair in a rustle of silk. "Well?"

"She's consented to marry me," Stephen said, his voice strong with the conviction that he'd expected no other response from her.

Yes was the only answer she could have given and ensure her place in John's life. Any other course would put her at risk of one day losing him. She loved him too much to take that chance. And she cared deeply for his father. The stirrings of love. No, he wasn't exactly the man she'd known in Scutari, but then neither was she the woman he'd held through the night.

She knew this was a forced marriage, even if her father was not standing behind Stephen holding a gun against the small of his back. It was his honor as a gentleman that had prodded him to ask her. But that didn't mean that things between them couldn't be good. She could foresee a few complications, but she would find a way to deal with them. For John's sake. And hers. And Stephen's.

"Lovely!" the duchess said now. She swept across the

room and took Mercy into her arms. "Oh, my dear girl. I could not be more pleased to have you in the family."

The duchess stepped away with a no-nonsense gleam in her eyes. "The ceremony will take place here in the estate chapel. The village vicar will do the honors. I think under the circumstances, a small, select number of guests. Family, close friends."

"I have no family to speak of," Mercy told her, "and a letter to my father announcing the marriage should suffice. He's washed his hands of me." Heat burned her cheeks. "If not for Stephen's generous offer, John and I would be living on the streets, I'm sure."

"Nonsense. I would have handled matters if Stephen hadn't. But I'm terribly pleased that he did. It shows he's a man of character."

"Mother, I'm quite famished. Could we possibly discuss the details after dinner?" Stephen asked.

"We can discuss them on the way in to dinner and during dinner." To Mercy's startlement, the duchess wrapped her arm around Mercy's like a clinging vine. "Westcliffe and his family shall attend, of course. I believe you'll enjoy Claire's company. And their son is quite a delight. But I shall show no favoritism amongst my grandchildren. I made that mistake with my sons. We shall also invite Lynnford and his family. The earl served as guardian to my boys after my husband, the duke, passed. One or two others perhaps, but I see no reason for a big elaborate affair unless it's what you wish."

"No, I prefer small." The smaller the better. Tiny even. Simply her and Stephen. She glanced back at him over her shoulder and was rewarded with an apologetic smile.

The duchess had apparently decided she was on a mission and was not about to be deterred. During dinner she spoke of little besides the upcoming nuptials—they would send for her London seamstress posthaste to attend to the gown that Mercy would wear. Flowers could prove a problem this time of year, but if Mercy had no objection to orchids, the duchess knew someone who cultivated them. The wedding breakfast was discussed.

By the time dinner ended, the magnitude to what Mercy had agreed overwhelmed her. She was dizzy with the thoughts of it all, how her life would change.

Later that night, she sat in her bed, her legs drawn up, her arms wrapped tightly around them. "We should elope," Stephen had whispered in her ear as he'd pulled out her chair following dinner.

The thought didn't half appeal, but there was something sordid about an elopement and the time for taking so drastic a measure to protect her reputation was long past. Certainly, if they were to marry, she didn't want to delay it too much longer. Stephen might very well change his mind. Until they were joined by the law, she would not rest easy.

Events were moving at an amazing clip.

The nightmares increased in frequency and intensity. No matter how valiantly Mercy fought to sleep lightly, to not slip into the realm where dreams resided, the horrific images came. After two nights of having his sleep disturbed, Stephen began to join her in bed. He did little more than hold her. But it was enough. With his arms around her, she could sleep without fears. The weariness that had been a constant companion since her days in Scutari began to ebb. The heaviness that had shadowed her movements was no longer there. Her step regained its lightness. She began to put on some weight, so her clothing was fitting her as it had in the days before she'd left England.

But her worries over her wedding night did not abate. It didn't help matters at all that the duchess had given her a white gossamer nightdress that scandalously revealed the shadows of her body.

"I hope you won't be offended," the duchess had said as she'd watched Mercy unwrap her gift. "I've never been one to be demure when it comes to what passes between a man and a woman—or elsewhere. Depending upon one's adventuresome spirit and daring, it can be a glorious thing."

Mercy had little doubt, based upon what Stephen had shared so far.

In three days, she would marry. It was difficult to believe how quickly everything had come to pass. As she rocked John in her bedchamber, he was busy blowing bubbles between his lips. The depth with which she loved him astounded her sometimes. It was almost painful. It terrified her and brought her joy. It was satisfying. All that mattered was that he was happy and well cared for. And that Mercy had the privilege of being his mother.

The knock sounded on her door. She knew it wasn't Stephen. She recognized the rap of his knuckles. She bid entry and discovered it was one of the young maids.

She bobbed a curtsy. "Sorry to disturb you, m'um, but Her Grace sent me to fetch you. Lord and Lady Westcliffe have arrived. They be in the front parlor, waiting to make your acquaintance."

"Thank you. Tell them I'll be there as soon as I've tidied up." Her and John. She wanted to make a good impression. She knew she hadn't quite won Ainsley over yet, and she wanted to have more luck with Westcliffe.

When she stepped into the hallway, she came up short at the sight of Stephen. As always, her spirits lifted at the sight of him, but her arms reflexively closed more securely around John, as though her heart and mind were in conflict. One part of her recognizing the immense feelings she harbored for this man, the other understanding that he had the power to take her son from her if he ever learned the truth, that she had not given birth to his son.

"You're so pale, Mercy. Surely you didn't think I'd allow you to walk into the lion's den unescorted."

Stephen Lyons, lion's den. She wondered if he'd meant the play on the name. She released a nervous laugh. "Should I be fearful of meeting your older brother?"

He offered her his arm. "Not to worry. He only looks as though he bites."

He did at that. Dark hair and darker eyes. His expression fearsome, his features appeared to have been carved from hard rock. He was taller and broader than either of his brothers. A man she could see wielding a broadsword. She saw none of Stephen in him, none at all.

"Condolences on being forced to wed my brother," he said evenly.

"Westcliffe!" The woman beside him had moon-shaded hair, a luster Mercy had always envied. Her eyes were a softer blue than Stephen's, and gentler. "Pay him no heed. He's teasing you, of course. Stephen is an excellent catch. I'm Claire." She glided forward and hugged Mercy. "Welcome to the family."

She leaned back and studied the baby. "And this must be John." With tears in her eyes, she looked up at Stephen. "He does favor you."

"I don't see it."

"Because you're a man." She gave her attention back to Mercy. "They can be so troublesome sometimes. Would you care to meet Lord Waverly, our son?"

Mercy liked Lady Westcliffe immediately. She was welcoming and kind, and she saw no censure in her eyes. "Yes, very much, Lady Westcliffe."

"You absolutely must call me Claire. We'll be sisters after all."

She led the way to where the boy was sitting up on the duchess's lap. He was a miniature of his father. Stephen had already told her that his courtesy title was that of viscount. One day he would inherit his father's title and all he possessed.

But what struck her the most was not the boy but his parents and the obvious love they held for each other, mirrored in their eyes whenever their gazes met. It hurt to know she'd never possess what they held dear.

In spite of all of Stephen's tender regard, he did not love her. He'd accepted her as his duty. For John, she would weather it.

"So what exactly are your plans?" Westcliffe asked.

Stephen and his brothers were in the library. The ladies had gone off to do whatever it was they did when they gave each other sly smiles. He wasn't too concerned that Claire would make Mercy feel as though she were in the midst of an inquisition. Claire and he had been dear friends since childhood. It was that strong bond that had caused trouble when she married Westcliffe. But all was well between them now, and he knew that Claire would make Mercy feel welcomed in a way that few could. He wished he'd thought to have his mother send for her sooner.

With his arm raised, his wrist pressed to the mantel, he studied the way the fire writhed and danced. With the thought of being shackled by bonds of matrimony, he felt his own need to writhe. "Be a good husband I suppose."

"How do you intend to provide for your family?"

He pressed his thumb to his scar and slid it down the mottled skin. "I'm of little use to the military with no memory of all I learned while at war. I'd be no better than a fresh recruit. I'd make a deplorable clergyman. I suppose I could seek to get elected into Parliament."

"I've been giving your situation some thought," Ainsley said.

Stephen wasn't surprised. There was very little that Ainsley didn't put his mind to. When he was younger, Stephen resented that Ainsley always seemed in a position to effectively handle whatever challenge or crisis came his way. Now he appreciated it. He peered questioningly over at his younger brother.

"I was thinking you might manage Roseglenn Manor for me." It was one of his smaller estates in Hertfordshire. "I've been so busy managing other things that I fear I've neglected it somewhat."

"You don't know how to neglect anything."

"True enough. But it would reduce my burdens if I had someone I trusted to look after it. To offer incentive, a portion of the yearly income would go to you. Increase the income, increase your portion."

Knowing he'd never inherit one unless Westcliffe died, Stephen had paid little enough attention to how one went about managing an estate. But his pride wouldn't allow him to admit yet another shortcoming, even to his brothers. He wanted to do right by Mercy, provide well for her and John. God knew he owed her that much at least. "I accept your offer."

Ainsley's green eyes widened. "I'd not expected you to capitulate so easily. I had a whole host of arguments lined up to deliver."

Now that he'd regained most of his strength, he was beginning to feel the walls of his family closing in on him. As the wedding date neared, so, too, was he beginning to doubt himself. He wasn't certain he was cut out to be a husband or a father. What did he have to offer other than passion? It had occurred to him to simply leave Mercy and John here after the ceremony, to go his own way. Marriage wouldn't restore her reputation, but it would make her status not quite so ruined. And surely, with the public outcry of support for the military, all would understand how a man and woman in love might use poor judgment on the eve of battle.

She could twist the tale and make herself out to be a heroine.

But he recognized that any sort of deception was not her way. Besides, while he had little to offer her, broken as he was, he recognized that she had much to offer him. So, be an attentive husband to her he would.

As a young girl Mercy had dreamed often of the day she would marry. While she knew that in most cases people did not marry for love, she'd not wanted it to be the case when it came to her marriage. She'd fully intended to be madly in love with the man and for him to absolutely adore her. As it was, her love for him and his son propelled her toward the altar, where he waited because of obligation.

It was bittersweet knowledge to reflect upon as they repeated vows. And she made silent ones to make certain he never regretted taking her to wife.

She wore a simple beige gown. She thought she would forever remember how handsome Stephen appeared standing there, in his dark blue jacket and black trousers. When he removed her glove and the simple gold band he placed on her finger fit perfectly, she wanted to believe that fate approved, that destiny had somehow brought them together.

Following the ceremony, they retired to the residence, where a late breakfast awaited them. Mercy had never seen so much food in her life as had been set on the sideboard. Succulent aromas wafted through the residence. Her mouth watered. Guiltily, she thought of how little food had been available for the men in the hospital, and it seemed wrong to have such abundance here.

"Is something amiss?"

She looked up at Stephen. Until that moment, she hadn't truly understood exactly what his loss of memory meant. He didn't remember being hungry or cold. She'd been so focused on the fact that he didn't remember her that she hadn't considered that without his memories a great deal of what they had in common was gone as well. Like smoke blown away in the dark.

"Not at all. It's just so overwhelming that it's difficult

to believe it's really happened." She touched the ring. "I don't know why it surprised me that you had a ring."

"It's rather plain, but it was my grandmother's."

"I don't require anything fancy, and it has great sentimental value. Thank you for entrusting it to me."

He lifted her hand and pressed a kiss on her knuckles, just below the ring. "I entrusted my son to you. What is a bit of jewelry?"

He held her gaze as she'd imagined a hundred times that he would, the blue of his eyes darkening like a storm on the horizon. She shivered with the realization that while it was only late morning, he was already contemplating the evening. When she'd truly become his wife.

"Come along, you two, you'll want to eat before you begin your journey," Claire said, touching Stephen's cheek with a familiarity that caused a sharp pang in Mercy's chest. She wondered if they'd once been intimate. Surely not.

It didn't help the spark of jealousy to realize that Claire knew something that Mercy didn't. "What journey?"

Stephen gave her a crooked grin. "It was to be my surprise. Ainsley has some property he's been neglecting. He's offered to let us live there, as long as we'll care for it. Roseglenn Manor. I think you'll like it."

"I'm sure I will." Because he would be there.

Chapter 12

They arrived at Roseglenn Manor when it was too dark to get a good look at anything. Still, Mercy squinted, attempting to see what she could of things. This would be her new home, the beginning of a new life.

The journey had been long and wearisome, and to her consternation, incredibly silent. Stephen sat across from her, while Jeanette sat beside her. For the most part, Mercy held John, knowing he would be relegated to Jeanette's care for the night once they arrived at the manor. They stopped when John required a feeding, so Stephen could leap out of the carriage and give them all privacy.

She would watch as he paced along the side of the road. His limp was barely noticeable. His leg had recovered well. She wondered if his mind might. She knew it bothered him greatly not to have those memories. But if he regained them, how might things for her change?

She shoved the doubts aside. She would be a loving and exemplary wife. He would come to care for her deeply, and then none of the falsehoods that had brought them to this moment would matter.

Flickering torches appeared and just beyond was the manor.

"It's not as large as Grantwood," Stephen said, and she flinched. It was the first time he'd spoken in hours. She'd seldom felt his gaze leave her. She wondered what he'd been thinking during this entire journey. No doubt his mind had been on tonight.

"It's perfect," she said softly.

"You haven't seen it clearly yet."

"Doesn't matter. We'll be a family. That's far more important."

"Were you this easy to please in Scutari?"

"Witnessing all that I did gave me a different perspective on things, I suppose."

His gaze darted to Jeanette, and he merely nodded. She suspected had Jeanette not been in the carriage he'd have said that his perspective might be different as well if he remembered anything. The experiences that had brought them together, that they'd shared, now served to keep a distance between them. How did she convince him that it didn't matter?

It was over, it was done, it was time to live in the present.

The carriage rolled to a stop. He was the first to disembark, opening the door himself, as though he couldn't stand the confinement any longer. Then he was reaching back for her. Holding John close in one arm, she placed her other hand in Stephen's, felt the strength in his fingers as they closed around hers and he lifted her down.

For a heartbeat they simply stood there, gazing at each other, their breaths visible in the cold night air.

The momentousness of this moment was not lost on her. They were connected, the three of them, in different ways. Love and blood. Desire and obligation. Truth and deception.

"Welcome to Roseglenn, Mrs. Lyons," he said finally, his voice rough, as though he'd had difficulty forcing out the words but had been determined to do so for her benefit.

Mrs. Lyons.

Lord, she thought her knees might buckle. Those two words delivered from his lips hit her with a force she'd not anticipated. The world reeled around her. The momentousness of exactly what had transpired today, the irrevocableness of it, slammed into her with the intensity of cannon fodder.

What the hell had she done?

Oddly, her worries increased as they entered the residence. It was gorgeous. Paintings and decorations artfully arranged. Everything was clean and tidy. The wooden floor was polished to such a sheen that she could almost see her reflection. It was fully staffed; all of the servants were gathered in the entry hallway to greet the new lord and lady of the manor, even if they weren't a true lord and lady.

The butler stepped forward and bowed. "Major. Madam. I'm Spencer. The duke sent word that you would be taking up residence here. The servants shall gladly see to all your needs. A light repast has been prepared and will be served in the small dining room unless you would prefer it served elsewhere."

"The small dining room will suffice," Stephen said. "Then I'd like baths prepared for my wife and myself."

"I shall see to it immediately."

"Very good." Stephen turned to her. "Is that satisfactory for you?"

"Yes, of course." They seemed more awkward strangers now than ever and she realized the consummation of their marriage loomed over them both. "I'd like to settle John into the nursery."

One of the younger serving girls escorted them upstairs to the room that would serve as the nursery. It had everything that was needed: a small crib, a rocking chair, even a rocking horse. One area was prepared for the nurse, with a bed, dresser, and chair.

"I see my brother has not lost his flair for attending to details."

She glanced over at Stephen, who was leaning against the wall, his arms folded over his chest. By his stance, she could see he was favoring his injured leg, and she realized the journey had been hard on it. "You think this room was prepared especially for our arrival?"

"As he has no children of his own, I cannot believe otherwise."

"Perhaps he is simply anticipating their arrival."

"I think what he anticipated was that I'd accept his offer. He probably began planning this the moment you arrived at Grantwood."

"But he couldn't have known that we'd wed."

"Mercy, my family would have accepted no less of me. And if I'd not seen to my responsibilities, Ainsley would have. He always does. I expect he planned to offer you sanctuary here."

"You say that as though you resent it."

He rubbed the scar on his face. "I want what's best

for you, Mercy. If accepting my brother's generosity provides it, so be it. I'll be waiting for you in the small dining room."

No sooner had he left than Jeanette ambled into the room. She'd no doubt been waiting in the hallway, not wishing to intrude on Mercy and her husband.

"It's a very fine residence," Jeanette said, wandering around the room. "I think we shall be very happy here."

"I do hope so."

Standing at the window in the small dining room, Stephen downed his second glass of wine while he awaited Mercy's arrival. Obviously, Stephen and Ainsley had a differing opinion regarding the meaning of the term *neglected*. For his wife's sake, he was grateful. For the sake of his pride, however, he would have liked to have seen some evidence that *something* required his attention.

He shouldn't allow his brother's machinations to put him in a foul mood. Not when he would once again know what it was like to lie completely and absolutely with Mercy, to be surrounded by her heat, to match the rhythm of his body to hers.

He couldn't recall ever having anticipated the bedding of a woman so much. If they hadn't been sharing the carriage with the nursemaid and John, he suspected Mercy's marriage bed would have been the bench upon which she'd been sitting. It had been the longest journey he'd ever taken in such a short span of time. Or at least the longest he recalled.

He poured more wine and drank it as though it could wash away all his doubts. The past made a man, and he was missing two years of his. He had to let it go. He wasn't going to regain it. He had a wife, a son, responsibilities. He'd done the right thing by Mercy. Marrying her. He would tend his brother's estate that needed no tending, while he determined how to best provide for his family in his own way.

He turned at the soft footfalls. She appeared nervous, her hands clasped in front of her. It bothered him immensely that she seemed so uncomfortable with what was to come, as though she'd never truly experienced it. Had he been so in need of release that he'd taken her swiftly, without thought to her pleasure? It had never been his way before. Surely, when it came to women, he'd not changed so very much while at war.

He was certain other aspects of his character might have shifted, hopefully for the better. But where women were concerned, as arrogant as it was, he knew he had little room for improvement.

Because he knew it would please her, he asked, "Did John get settled in all right?"

She smiled. Mentioning their son always had the ability to bring a smile to her face, to put her at ease. "Based upon how rapidly his greedy little mouth worked, I would say yes."

"Good. Shall we?" He indicated the cloth-covered round table, where candles flickered and their food awaited their appetite.

Blushing, she nodded and walked over to a chair. He pulled it out for her. Once she was seated, he bent and pressed a kiss to her nape. "Relax, Mercy. It's not as though we've not done this before."

"But it was so long ago."

"And apparently, I was not at my best. If I didn't make it pleasantly memorable for you, then I owe you an apology. I assure you that won't be the case tonight." He heard her sharp intake of breath, watched as her blood rose to the surface, a blush that spread far beyond her face. Taking his chair, he tried to read the answer in her eyes. Was before less than she'd expected?

Reaching over, he poured wine into her glass. "I instructed the servants to leave us in peace. It seems I've hardly had a moment with my own thoughts during the past week."

"If you wish solitude, I could leave."

"On the contrary, being alone with you is all I want." He tapped his glass to hers. "To my wife. May you never regret being forced into this arrangement."

The glass trembled as she carried it to her lips. "I would never regret it. I hope the same can be said of you."

If he'd had his druthers, he'd have never married. A bachelor was forgiven indiscretions much more easily. He was even expected to have them. But a husband—as such, he would have to curtail his sinful exploits. It was a dilemma he would consider when faced with it.

For tonight, he could truly say there was no other woman he wished to be with more.

Her bath had been quick, because she'd continually expected Stephen to saunter in as he had that first night when he'd witnessed her nightmares. She slipped on the nightdress the duchess had given her, then ruined its allure by wrapping a blanket around herself and curling up on a corner of the sofa in front of the fireplace.

She knew she had nothing to fear from him. But tonight she would know the full measure of his coupling. As much as she desired it, she couldn't help but fear she'd be fumbling and disappoint him. He expected her to know what he liked, to know how to receive him.

God help her. She was going to make a mess of this.

Her virginity had been brutally taken from her. It had hurt and it had been quick.

Stephen had shown her passion, he had shown her the wondrous sensations that a woman should find with a man. But when it was time for him to push inside her—

She didn't know if she would be able to bear it. Nor could she bear to tell him why. If he knew she'd been with another man, he might doubt John. Even if he didn't, surely he would look upon her with disgust. It was better if he thought he were the only one.

Her heart leaped in her chest when she heard the door that joined her bedchamber to his opening. She stared intently at the flames. What if he was naked? What if he was already fully aroused?

Would he expect her to leap on him? To be demure? Even if he didn't remember their night together, he must have expectations.

His hands came to rest heavily on her shoulders. Such large hands. So strong.

"You're trembling," he said quietly.

"A bride's nerves. I didn't think I'd have them, considering . . . but here they are." She dared to glance back at him. He'd bathed as well. He smelled clean and spicy. His hair was curling more than usual, as though he'd left it to do as it would. The ends that were still damp were darker. He wore trousers and a deep blue velvet dressing gown.

Lowering his head, he took her mouth, slowly, luxuriously, as though they had all night. Which she supposed they did. His hand came up to cradle her face, his thumb stroking her cheek. He was like a fine liqueur, pouring through her veins, warming her limbs. So simple an action, so great a response. She could hardly believe it as she found herself wanting to melt against him. Why did he not move around so they could press their bodies together?

Drawing back, he smiled at her. "You see? Nothing to be nervous about."

He did move around then, to a corner table where wine waited. His movements were unhurried, relaxed. Confident. He might not remember two years of his life, but he remembered all that had come before, and if legends were in fact based on truth, he'd conquered half the boudoirs in London. Sarah had certainly known tales of his exploits, which may have been the reason she'd sought him out as soon as he began regaining his strength. One of the nurses had pursed her lips and called him "notorious." Then she'd refused to go anywhere near him, as though she would catch something from him.

But like Mercy, most of the nurses had been mesmerized by his easy charms.

She watched as he wrapped a hand around a bottle of wine, a hand he would soon wrap around her. After pouring the dark red liquid into two stemmed glasses, he ambled back over, offered her one, and sat on the other end of the sofa. He stretched out his trouser-clad legs and lazily extended his arm along the curved back until his fingers could toy with the ends of her hair.

"What was it like between us the first time?" he asked, and she nearly choked on her wine.

She set the glass in her lap and ran her finger around the rim. "What does it matter?"

"For me, tonight, it will be like having you for the first time. I'm not sure what you expect."

She dared to peer over at him. "I'm not expecting anything. Besides, it's not always the same, is it?"

"I like variety, so seldom is it ever the same. Still, I feel at a disadvantage." He skimmed his finger along her cheek. "Was there anything you didn't particularly like?"

"No, not as I recall."

A mocking smile twisted his lips. "And here I was arrogant enough to believe every moment spent with me was unforgettable."

Drat it! Here he was, a man she'd dreamed of and fantasized about. Her husband. To take her to bed. Perhaps to even get *her* with child, and she was slashing at his pride.

She scooted toward him until her knees touched his hip and his hand slid around to the back of her head. "The night we were together, I mostly remember the wonderful sensation of you holding me near. Your comfort and your strength. You always send the monsters to perdition. Why don't we simply pretend that it's our first time together—for both of us? I can lock the memories of our previous encounter away, and not even think about them tonight."

"Can you?"

"Yes." With ease. With relief. Let him think her upcoming clumsiness was her pretense not to remember.

Let him not wonder why she had no idea how to touch him to bring him pleasure.

Jeanette had provided her with some information, some suggestions for what she might do, how she might touch him, but she couldn't see herself kissing anything beyond his lips. His neck maybe. Perhaps his chest. But what his trousers hid? Touching it with her tongue? Tasting it? No. And he'd not require that of her, she was certain

But had he not done something similar for her before? Had he not used his mouth to bring her to un-heralded heights of pleasure? Was Jeanette's suggestion so very different?

"If you love him, there is nothing you will not do for him," she'd said with her French accent. But her husband had loved her. What did Stephen feel for Mercy?

But did it truly matter? What she felt for him was enough.

He downed what remained of his wine and finished off hers as well. Setting both goblets aside, he turned to her and pulled loose the blanket surrounding her until it fell to her hips. She felt a strange urge to cover herself, even knowing he'd seen her the night of night-mares But she'd been in the dark then, protected by shadows. He skimmed his knuckles over the cloth behind which her nipples puckered and strained. His eyes darkened as he leaned forward and took one in his mouth. The cloth served as no shield against the heat as his tongue swirled and dampened it. His lips closed securely around it, tugged. She moaned as the molten heat flowed lower, to settle between her thighs.

"Did I touch you like this before?" he asked.

This time she groaned. "Please don't talk of the past.

Please." She cupped his strong jaw, held his gaze as though her life depended on it. "I don't care that you don't remember it. I see no need for you to remember. We shall make love so many times in the coming years that surely we will not remember them all."

A wicked glint entered the stormy blue. "How many times, do you think?"

"A hundred. A thousand. I don't know. More than we can possibly count."

He grinned. "I like the possibility of that. You're right. No more harping on the past. And no more wearing of a nightdress."

"Or a dressing gown," she said, laughing as he pulled her to her feet.

His velvet hit the floor only a few seconds before her silk. He drew her near, kissing her deeply, while his hands roamed over her body.

"Do you have any idea how beautiful you are?" he asked.

She'd never considered herself as such. She'd never thought herself hideous, but beautiful was reserved for women like Sarah or Jeanette. Women men noticed immediately.

"Especially your legs," he said, lifting her into his arms. "I want them wrapped tightly around my waist."

"Right now?"

He laughed. "No. When I'm buried deeply inside you."

She pressed her blushing face into the curve of his neck so he wouldn't see how his frank remarks brought her blood to the surface. She had to appear as though she was accustomed to him speaking so bluntly about lovemaking, when in truth it shocked but titillated her.

He laid her on the bed as one might a gift that was being presented. Then slowly, tauntingly, standing there, his gaze daring hers, he began to unfasten his trousers. She'd never seen him fully, completely aroused, but what she had seen was enough to let her know that he was larger than many men she'd tended to. Her mouth went dry with the thought and it took every ounce of strength she possessed not to lower her lashes.

"No need for worries," he said. "Westcliffe told me that after having a babe, you're likely to be as tight as a virgin. He's had some experience in that regard."

His words brought her a measure of relief. As far as she was concerned, even though she no longer was in possession of her maidenhead, she was a virgin.

"But you'll be ready for me by the time we get to that part."

He lowered his trousers . . . and doubts assailed her. He was not as most men. She wasn't certain how she'd ever be ready. But he thought she'd once been, so by God, she couldn't let her insecurities show.

The bed dipped as he stretched out beside her. He skimmed his hand from her shoulder to just below her knee, as far as he could reach, as though branding all that belonged to him.

"How the devil I ever forgot this—"

She slapped her hand over his mouth, cutting off the ravaged words. "No more talk of the past."

Rising up with a courage that had accompanied her to Scutari, she rolled into him, kissed him, took her turn at skimming her hand along his side. Uneven flesh greeted her perusal, and she had to force herself to follow her own command—she wouldn't think about how each scar had come to be, how he might have suffered. He'd gained several since she'd treated his wounds at the Barrack Hospital. But that was the past. They were in a peaceful area. No gunfire would roar in the distance. No cannons would shake the earth. No men would cry for mercy.

His manhood, hard velvet, burned against her belly. Guilt surged through her because she'd not had the courage to tell him the truth, that she'd feared losing him, losing John . . . and in a way she'd led him to believe she'd been more to him than she had been.

Silly girl, as long as he never regains his memory, he'll always live in blissful ignorance. Could she wish that on him? Based on the horrors of her own memories, it was a mercy for him not to recall a single moment of what surely must have been a hell far worse than hers.

She kissed his neck, his chest. Flicked her tongue over his turgid nipple, felt him jerk against her. She understood Jeanette's urgings now, her promises. She could see herself easing lower. In the heat of passion, nothing was forbidden.

Suddenly she was on her back, and he was again in control. Oh, the things he did with his hands, his mouth, his teeth. A stroke here, a lick there, a nip. He was young, and in spite of all he'd suffered, in fine shape. He moved over her with a powerful grace, leaving nothing untouched, nothing wanting. Passion burned hotter than any flame.

She adored this man, wanted to give him everything. Her heart, her body, her soul. He'd been the light in a dismal world. He'd been her knight. War could bring out the worst and the best in men. For the first time, she regretted that he didn't know, deep in his soul, that he had been the best.

He could be told. Over and over. But the broken linchpin of memory could not allow him to *know* it, to feel it. Yet, she knew. She had experienced it, witnessed it. She would hold the knowledge dear for him. It would be enough. It had to be.

"I love your breasts," he rasped near her ear. "They fit my palm perfectly." Bending his head, he suckled one nipple, this time with no cloth to separate her flesh from his questing tongue, and she turned her body into him, needing to ease the awful ache between her thighs.

His hand traveled a circuitous path over her body, finally reaching its destination, settling with surety and purpose between her thighs. She gasped with the first intimate touch, the sharp spark of pleasure, the slow stroke of his thumb over her nubbin.

"You're like tinder," he whispered provocatively, "so easy to burn. You can't believe how badly I want you."

"Then why do you not take me?"

"Because when I do, it'll be over all too soon. Touch me, Mercy."

She placed her hand on his shoulder. His eyes, smoldering with desire, lightened with silent laughter, as he took her hand and guided it down until she was able to wrap her fingers around him. His groan was low, guttural. She might have thought she'd hurt him if not for the triumph that sparked his eyes.

He taught her movements that she feared he might later question her not already knowing, but she was fascinated by the feel of him, steel encased in silk. Smooth and not. Hard. She felt the dampness, the first spill of his seed. She didn't want to lose any of it. She wanted his child to grow in her womb. She wanted to give him another son, a daughter, two daughters. She wanted to be irrevocably connected to him.

Just as she'd once feared losing John, now she feared losing Stephen.

When had she become such a worrier, such a fearful soul? After watching so much taken away from so many others.

But she was safe here, safe in his arms, safe in his bed. Just as she'd been that night outside the Barrack Hospital. He was still the courageous, determined man she'd known then. What were memories when the core of who he was remained intact?

She grew bolder with her strokes, and he growled, low in his throat, a rumble in his chest that tickled the breast flattened against him.

He slid his finger into her. "My God, but you're wet and hot . . . and tight. How can you be so damnably tight after giving birth?"

She almost said because the babe was so small, but she'd never lied to him. Not one false word. She'd simply not told him everything. She'd never said she'd given birth to John. Only that she was his mother, and in her heart she was.

"I might hurt you yet," he rasped, and she saw the torment on his face with the thought. "Is that why you're as shy as a virgin? Because there was pain before?"

It was not his way to hurt women. She'd learned that much about him in the short time she knew him. But, yes, with her fingers wrapped around him, she thought he very well might hurt her.

"The memory of pain dwindles with time," she reassured him. "I only remember how much it meant to me to be with you. I want you."

"Then you shall have me."

With a smooth movement, he was suddenly wedged between her thighs, his body pressed to hers as he kissed her deeply. The musky scent of sex wafted between them. She ran her hands up into his thick curling hair. She skimmed her thumb along his scar. He was a man of such confidence that a physical imperfection bothered him not at all. But losing two years of his life was another sort of imperfection altogether. She wanted to relieve him of all doubts.

She opened herself up to him—heart, body, and soul.

He rose above her, his face a mask of dark pleasures, as he guided himself into her. Yes, she was tight. Yes, there was discomfort. But she fought to ignore it, fought instead to relax, to make the way easier for him.

He pushed. Coated her throat in kisses. Pushed again.

"Wrap your legs around my waist." His voice was strained, his arms taut as he held himself aloft.

She did as he wanted, and he slid farther, farther, until he filled her completely.

"God, I've dreamed of this," he murmured. "Of you. Of those lovely long legs."

I've dreamed of you, too.

Where he found the strength to speak, she hadn't a clue. With all these wonderful sensations dancing through her, she could barely think. All she could do was feel. The press of his mouth, the caress of his hands. His slow withdrawal, his determined thrust. Her hips lifted to meet him, her body curled, desire peaked.

His tongue played havoc with her breasts while he again retreated, only to return with more force, more pressure. She whimpered. Whatever discomfort she'd initially experienced was gone, replaced by this need to have him closer, nearer.

He was whispering things, tawdry things about her breasts, her throat, her stomach, the haven where his body joined hers. She thought she should have been shocked. Instead she become more aroused, her pleasure increased.

He began rocking against her, faster, deeper, stronger. Sensations built. They spiraled, they soared. As her back arched, she pressed her head into the pillow and his hot mouth was immediately nibbling at her throat. Her fingers scored his back, and then she was crying out as stars burst forth inside her. Lightning flashed, sunlight poured in. It was a storm of pleasure that took her under and lifted her up, left her trembling on the shore of passion.

His grunt echoed·around her as he tensed, his body pumping into her, fast and furious—

"God, Mercy!" Other sounds of gratification and satisfaction echoed around her as he stilled and slowly lowered himself to press a kiss to her lips. "There is no way in hell I should have forgotten that."

Chapter 13

Stephen stared at the canopy, while Mercy dozed, snuggled against his side. All blood had drained from her face with his words, and he regretted them the moment he'd spoken, bringing his loss to a place where she didn't want it to be.

But it was true. How could he have forgotten what they had together?

He remembered every detail of every woman with whom he'd been intimate until the moment he had tea with Claire that long-ago day. He remembered every encounter, every cry, every spark of pleasure. And he knew—*knew*—every one paled when compared with what he'd experienced with Mercy. None were as tight or as hot. None held onto him as though she'd die if she released her hold. None carried him to a realm of sensations where everything else had ceased to exist except for the two of them.

She was perfection, she was radiance, she was his wife.

For the first time, he was convinced he'd not made a mistake in marrying her. There was so much about her that he admired, that he enjoyed.

He'd been wrong. He'd tried to identify exactly what

it was about her that drew him in . . . and it was everything. Everything. The last he'd discovered tonight quite simply topped it all off nicely.

And he'd forgotten her, forgotten that they might have had a night like this. What the bloody hell else had he forgotten? What else that was as important as she was?

While one arm held her securely against him, with the hand of the other he pressed the scar on his face. He'd thought he'd forgotten only battles and blood and men dying. Then he discovered that he'd forgotten a nurse whom he'd left with child. But now he realized it was so much more. He'd lost moments of joy, moments of laughter, moments of pleasure that far exceeded anything he'd ever experienced.

It wasn't fair. He wanted those moments back. He wanted to know what had happened during those two years of his life. He needed to know. He wanted to regain what he'd lost.

Twisting his head, he glanced down on her sleeping form. Her coppery hair stuck up at odd angles, much as his did first thing in the morning. Her auburn lashes rested gently on her cheeks. She breathed softly. Her balled fist rested on the hollow of his stomach. Neither of them had bothered to put on their clothes. Their flesh warmed the other.

It had been cold in the Crimea—from what he'd experienced after waking without his memories. She and he would have created a fire that would have burned through the night and quite possibly longer. He'd always been angry about what he'd lost, but never so much as now, when he realized exactly what had been taken from him.

Moments with her. Words spoken, passion shared.

He wanted to know what the first smile she bestowed upon him had looked like. Had she flirted with him or had he pursued her?

He would have pursued her. He was certain of it. And she would have resisted. She was too good. She'd left England behind, to return with nightmares. Her motives had been altruistic. She came from a good home, had resisted his attentions at Grantwood Manor. Yes, she'd have been hesitant to accept what he'd offered. But he'd worn her down, somehow. The night the men attacked her.

Bastards. If he ever laid eyes on them again, he'd give them what for.

Only he damned well didn't remember what they looked like.

Her life was tangled with his. It was a blessing and a curse. He shuddered to think what would have happened if he hadn't gotten her with child. He'd have never seen her again. And if he had . . . he'd have not known who she was, not known what they'd shared.

There was the true tragedy of his affliction. On the street, he might run into someone who had saved his life—and Stephen would ignore him because he wouldn't recognize him. He should buy him a drink. Hell, he should buy him a woman. And instead, he'd casually stroll by as though the man were nothing.

The not knowing ate at him. More so now than ever before.

He needed to know everything that had transpired during those two lost years.

Although she was sore in places that had been stretched and contorted during their lovemaking, she awoke feeling marvelous. She opened her eyes to find Stephen staring down on her. Sunlight eased in through a part in the draperies to glint over his hair, to mark the sharp planes of his beloved face.

All her fears were gone. She had survived the night. Their relationship had survived. No more worries that he'd realize she'd not given birth to his son.

Everything would be all right now. They'd live happily ever after.

Smiling warmly, he trailed his finger between her breasts. "I do so love waking up next to you in the morning."

"I do so love having you wake up next to me in the morning."

"No nightmares last night?"

"Nary a one."

"Good." Gently, tenderly he kissed her lips. "I was thinking of having breakfast delivered to us in bed."

"I do appreciate the way you think."

"Are you sore this morning?"

She felt the heat blush her cheeks with the reminder of all that had transpired between them last night. "A little. To be expected, I suppose."

"We'll rest today then."

"I'm not an invalid."

He tilted his head. "All right then. Perhaps we'll take a ride over the estate. Check things out."

"That would be lovely."

"Very good."

For several minutes he simply drew patterns over her flesh with his finger, creating languorous sensations. She could feel the passion simmering just below the surface. Perhaps she shouldn't have admitted to being sore.

"What were the first words I ever said to you?" he asked.

"Pardon?"

"The first words I ever said to you. What were they?"

She licked her lips, trying not to let on that his answer bothered her. "Water. I need some water."

"I was in the hospital."

Everything within her stilled as a frisson of fear went through her. "Yes. Are you remembering, then?"

Had the cataclysm of their lovemaking shaken the memories loose?

"No, but I'm thinking that maybe I can rebuild the memories. If I know what happened, what was said, then perhaps I could envision it."

"What does it matter? We have now. That's what's important."

"I have so many memories that are gone. Moments with you."

"But if you spend your time looking back, you'll miss making memories now. So you'll have fewer of them."

His brow furrowed. "If I didn't know better, I'd think you didn't want me to remember."

"Now you're being silly. Of course I'd be delighted if you remember." Her first true lie to him. "But the memories should come of their own accord. You shouldn't take up precious time trying to recreate them. If you do, you might not have time for this . . ."

With a boldness that surprised her, she straddled his hips.

"I thought you were sore."

"Tender . . . but willing."

"I don't wish to hurt you."

"Then live with me now in the present." Before he could respond, she latched her mouth on to his with near desperation. She wanted him to stop interrogating her about their time together in Scutari. For her, it was a place of horrific memories, except for the night she'd been with him. But even it had begun badly.

Three men. Drunk. Filled with lust.

She bit Stephen's shoulder, not hard enough to draw blood, but with enough force to make him curse and grab her head, cradling her face between his large palms.

"What the devil—"

"I don't want to think about it," she said. "Don't you understand? I want to be like you. I want to forget every moment that I was there. Please." She kissed where she'd nipped him. An apology. "Please."

He cupped the back of her head, his eyes earnest. "It's what I've lost with you that I can't stand not having."

"We'll make new memories. The ones worth having were only a few hours of one night. Everything else is rubbish. Please, let us just have now."

He levered up to his elbows, bent her head toward him, and took her mouth with an urgency that gave her hope that he would leave the past behind. She didn't want him to remember it. She would do nothing to help him remember.

She felt his arousal tapping against her backside.

As he dropped back down, she pressed kisses to his chest. To each scar. She wished he didn't have them. But they were safe, because she didn't know how they'd come to be. They didn't detract from his beauty.

He was all sinewy muscle, in spite of the fact that he'd been recovering. She felt his muscles rippling as he caressed her.

Then he lifted her up, guided her down, and she welcomed the fullness of him.

Here, here, here was where she could forget.

She rode him fast and hard. She watched his face. Watched the pleasure darken his eyes. His jaw was tight. His nostrils flared. His teeth clenched.

He drove into her over and over. The pleasure mounted. Cascaded through her, to her fingertips, to her toes.

And then beyond.

She cried out with the force of it, heard his guttural grunt, felt his final driving thrust. They had peaked at the same time, completely and absolutely as one.

Falling forward, she wrapped her arms around his shoulders. "That is a far better memory than anything that happened in Scutari."

His response was to kiss the top of her head and drift off to sleep. She could only hope that she'd convinced him.

Chapter 14

With some reluctance, Stephen left the bed. He'd awakened to discover that Mercy had fallen asleep. He was tempted to stay until she awoke, have another rousing session of lovemaking, but if his brother was entrusting the care of this estate to him, then he intended to be responsible, and that meant finding out exactly what he needed to do.

Returning to his bedchamber, he prepared himself for the day. This notion of two bedchambers struck him as silly. He had no intention of ever sleeping in a bed without his wife in it.

The thought brought him up short and he sank into the nearest chair. It wasn't only that he didn't plan to sleep in here alone. He had no desire to visit another's bed. He wanted no other woman. He wanted only Mercy.

Surely, this was a temporary condition. He'd always been adept at juggling women, never giving only one his attentions. He always made each woman feel as though she was the only one, but in truth, another was always waiting for him. He'd never yearned for one woman exclusively.

But at that precise moment he couldn't envision

going to another's bed after leaving Mercy. All he wanted, with an almost ridiculous desperation, was to return to her.

It was the novelty of her. The newness.

But that's never mattered before.

It was the shackles of marriage vows, spoken before his family, vowed before God.

Only it doesn't feel like manacles and chains.

Maybe it was because he wasn't quite up to snuff, was still healing.

Only I feel stronger, more myself than I have in months.

The thought that he couldn't see himself slipping into bed with another woman, because Mercy mattered so much more than any other, scared the devil out of him. It wasn't possible. He cared for all women equally. Even if he enjoyed one woman more than another, his feelings for her were no deeper, no shallower, no different.

But Mercy *was* different.

She was courageous and strong and so incredibly compassionate. She brought sunshine into a room. She'd sacrificed her good name, mothered his child. She was a wicked wanton in bed.

He smiled at the memory of her seduction this morning, as though he'd needed any sort of enticement to once again possess her. Every fragrance, every touch, every moan and sigh, every undulating movement of her lithe body was indelibly branded in his mind.

His hands balled into tightened fists on his thighs. He'd had it all once before, and he'd lost it, lost so much more than he'd ever realized. He'd lost her.

He could not, would not, let that happen again, even as he realized that it was beyond his control.

"You're going in circles, old boy," he whispered to himself. "There is no reason you'd ever lose any of this."

But his words brought him no comfort.

A distant sound disturbed his disquieting ruminations. He tilted his head to better hear it. Was that crying? Yes, John. No doubt with an empty stomach. They'd had to make several stops on the journey here. The boy had one hell of an appetite. Took after his father in that regard.

So why was he still crying? Where was the damned nurse?

Stephen shoved himself to his feet, stalked to the door, flung it open, and stepped into the hallway. No servants were about and the wail was rising in crescendo. He stormed into the nursery, crossed over to the crib, and glared into it. "You're a Lyons. A Lyons does not cry."

John immediately stopped his caterwauling. With water-filled deep blue eyes, he blinked up unhappily at Stephen. His puckered mouth trembled. A little bubble burst from one nostril.

"Disgusting," Stephen muttered as he took his handkerchief and cleaned the boy's face. "There. Better. I'm sure your nurse will be here soon with what you require. You're going to discover that you'll spend a good deal of your life waiting for women, so you might as well get accustomed to it early. You wait patiently like a gentleman."

John's mouth quivered and he began taking in quick breaths. Distressed, obviously. Damnation, where was the blasted nurse?

Stephen leaned in. "I've got no breasts, lad. I can't help you."

The lips quivered faster. The boy pleated his brow into what looked to be quite painful. A new tear leaked out from the corner of his eye.

"Oh, very well, if you insist." Reaching in, he lifted the boy into his arms. John's brow relaxed. His mouth spread into a contented smile. Ah, yes, he was quite the charmer. He was heavier than he'd been before. His limbs longer. He seemed so much stronger. "You're growing rather fast, aren't you, you little bugger? You look like me, you know. Have they told you that?"

The blue eyes blinked slowly. The urchin made a mewling sound that was obviously supposed to be some sort of answer.

"No? Want to see how handsome you'll be when you grow up? You'll have all the ladies begging for a bit of your time," Stephen told him as he walked to a cheval mirror in the portion of the room designated for the nurse. He held John up so their faces were side by side: one chubby and round with huge blue eyes, the other a sharp contrast of defining edges.

"There. What do you think?"

The babe seemed remarkably unimpressed. Stephen wondered if perhaps children's eyesight was limited until they got older. He moved in closer and suddenly John erupted with peals of laughter that shook his tiny body.

"What the deuce?" Stephen stepped back and the merry cackle abruptly subsided. "You can laugh. For some reason, I'd not expected that. What did you think was so funny? Certainly not me."

He leaned toward the reflection and the boy chortled again. Stephen couldn't help himself. He laughed right alongside his son.

When he retreated, silence again swept in. He swayed toward the mirror . . . a series of guffaws that once again had him joining in. Stepping back, he tossed his son up and peals of delight echoed around him. He'd never given much notice to children, but damned if they couldn't be jolly good fun.

Or at least *his* son was.

He turned back toward the mirror and that was when he saw they had an audience. Mercy was captured in the reflection, her smile so bright as to compete with the sun.

He spun around. "Did you hear him?"

Laughing lightly, she nodded. "I did indeed."

"My son is going to be quite the ladies' man, I have no doubt."

With a small gasp, she pressed her hand to her lips as tears filled her eyes.

Holding the child close, he stepped toward her. "Mercy, what the devil is wrong?"

"You've never called him that before. Your son." Lifting up on her toes, she pressed a hard kiss to his cheek as she wrapped her arms around them both. "It makes it all worth it. Every moment of doubt and despair."

He wound his arm around her and pulled her in even closer. Bending his head, he whispered, "Thank you, Mercy. Thank you for the gift of my son."

She wept even harder, and John, not to be outdone, joined in. When Jeanette finally arrived with effusive apologies for slipping away for a solitary morning cup of tea, Stephen was more than relieved to turn John over to her and carry Mercy back to bed, where he could thank her properly.

Chapter 15

S heep. Smelly creatures," Stephen muttered.

"My nose is so cold that I can't smell anything," Mercy said with a laugh.

Reaching over, Stephen squeezed her gloved hand where it rested on the pommel. "Forgive me. I shouldn't have brought you out in this weather."

"Nonsense. I wanted to see the estate."

The weather was bracing, not ideal for riding, but when Stephen had suggested an outing, she'd not been able to resist. She wanted to do everything with him, explore their new home.

"I think it'll be lovely come spring," she added.

Placing his hand behind her head, he held her steady while he leaned in and kissed her. "You're lovely now."

She felt the warmth suffuse her face. His remarks, delivered with such ease, always made her heart flutter madly. She wished she could return them, could tell him that he was remarkably handsome, because he was, but the words, which when spoken to her brought such joy, somehow seemed silly when said to a man.

Straightening, he looked out over the rolling land.

"If you don't like the sheep," she began, "perhaps

you can convince your brother to allow you to raise something else."

"The sheep belong to the tenants, who lease the land from him. Besides, it irks to ask my brother to *allow* me to do something."

She felt a spark of guilt. He'd been forced into this because of his marriage to her.

"If you could do anything at all, what would it be?" she asked.

Shifting in his saddle, calming his horse as it side-stepped, he glanced around, studying the land, and she could see that he was giving a good deal of thought to her words.

"I would spend all day in bed with my wife—every day."

She laughed. "Is that all?"

"And feed her strawberries."

She shook her head at his silliness. "That's not very ambitious."

"It's not, is it?" He gazed into the distance. "I gave my future so little thought. Until you came into it, I was content to take each day as it came. I made no plans. I was a gentleman, my brother gave me an allowance, and I was content. I can hardly fathom now that I settled for so little, so easily."

"You were a very young man." He still was. "And then you joined a regiment and that was not so little or so easy."

"Yes, the military life. Of which I remember so very little." He narrowed his eyes, clenched his jaw. "Horses, I think."

"Pardon?"

"Horses. I'd like to raise horses."

"For racing?"

"For the regiments."

"Why don't you then?"

Shifting his gaze over to her, he smiled. "You don't see anything as impossible, do you?"

"Not if you truly want it. How badly do you want it?"

"I'm not sure I gave it much thought until recently. But smelling these sheep, I'll want it more with each passing day. I'll be selling my commission. That'll bring in some funds. I have the salary the regiment paid me. I hardly spent any of it." He shrugged. "It could be a start."

"I think you should give it a go."

She could see the wonder in his eyes. "I don't know if I've ever had anyone have such faith in me before."

"How can I not? I know you. I know your courage and your determination. You have a strong heart. I regret that in losing your memories you lost sight of the remarkable man you are, but I have no doubt you can accomplish anything you set your mind to. Anything."

"You humble me, Mercy. Damn, but you do." He pulled on the reins, turning his horse about. "Come along, let's get home so I can warm you."

He warmed her in the bed, then he warmed her in the bathtub, the heated water lapping at her skin. She was nestled between his legs, her back to his chest, his hands gliding languorously over her.

"Do you think we shall ever grow tired of each other?" she asked.

"God, I hope not."

She felt pleasure that had nothing to do with physical sensations spiral through her. "I fear you will grow bored with me."

He trailed his finger along her neck, across her shoulder, down her arm. "I won't."

His words were spoken with conviction today, but what of tomorrow? Would he speak them as assuredly tomorrow? Or next week? Or next month? He'd been kind to her in Scutari but taken another to his bed. Had he told that woman that he'd never grow bored with her?

"What is the longest you've ever been faithful to a woman?" she asked.

"Do you really want to talk about all my conquests?"

She twisted around, the water splashing over the side of the tub. "Yes. Were there many?"

"Too many to count."

"What was the longest—"

He touched his finger to her lips. "I've told you. I was a cad. There was never one woman who held my attention to the exclusion of all others."

"You saw more than one woman at a time?"

He shrugged. "I made certain they understood . . . I had no desire to be limited to one woman."

Her stomach dipped. She couldn't bear the thought of him wandering. What sort of woman would want him desperately enough to take him on any terms? Oh, God, a woman such as she, who would lie to have him. "Then you must be frightfully bored with me already."

He tucked her damp hair behind her ear. "On the contrary, I've never been quite so . . . enthralled. Each moment with you is a discovery. And this is truly odd . . . something I can't quite fathom."

His brow was deeply furrowed, his eyes so incredibly serious as almost to frighten her. "What? What is so odd?"

"I enjoy talking with you, just being with you almost as much as I enjoy making love to you."

Releasing a light laugh, she buried her face against his neck.

"You find it humorous?" he asked.

"I find it remarkable." She cradled his jaw, rubbed her finger over the abrasive stubble that he would no doubt shave before coming to bed for the night. It was darker than his hair, gave him a rugged, dangerous air. "I want a marriage like Claire and Westcliffe have. You've given me hope that we might eventually achieve that."

"Claire and Westcliffe? You do not want a marriage such as theirs."

"But I do. When they look at each other—it is so obvious they adore each other."

"He married her for her dowry."

"And you married me because of your son." She shook her head briskly. "You're correct. I should not have taken the conversation down this path."

She settled back against him. He pressed his lips to the nape of her neck. "We're to visit them at Christmas," he said quietly. "Unless you'd rather stay here."

She would. She was content here, safe. She never wanted to leave. But they could not hide away forever.

"We should be with your family. It'll be nice to have a proper Christmas."

He folded his arms around her, hugged her tightly. "Ah, Mercy, forgive me. I forget. I suppose we were both in the Crimea last Christmas."

Nodding, she ran her hand along his thigh, feeling the scar beneath her palm, grateful that she could touch it now and it caused him no pain.

"What was it like?" he asked quietly.

"Cold, miserable. We were working in the hospital twelve to fifteen hours a day. I was so exhausted. It was late. I was changing a bandage when I realized it was Christmas, and I began to sing *Silent Night*. Then everyone in the ward was singing it. I could not hold back the tears."

"Was I gone by then?"

"Yes, you'd returned to your regiment. I thought of you, though. Wished you well." She scoffed. "As I recall, I think I wished us both home by the next Christmas. I suppose I should be a bit more careful in what I wish for."

"What would you like for this Christmas?"

Twisting around, she straddled his hips. "One to remember."

"Knowing my family, that should not be difficult to grant you."

It was a two-day journey by carriage to Lyons Place. Stephen had planned the journey so they would arrive in the late afternoon of Christmas Eve.

"So this was your father's estate," Mercy said, occasionally peering out the window, anxious for her first glimpse.

"I barely remember it," Stephen said. "I had occasion to visit two years ago. I had tea with Claire on the terrace there."

It was where his memories had stopped. Her stomach tightened. She wondered if returning would cause his memories to return. If he would look at something there and the intervening two years would flutter through his mind like the pages of a book riffled through in order to more quickly find a particular passage.

He sat across from her and Jeanette. John was sleeping on the bench beside his father, Stephen's hand resting on his back, holding him in place. How John slept was beyond Mercy, but sleep he did for a good bit of the journey.

"I consider Ainsley's estate more my home than this place," he continued.

"Do you remember your father at all?"

"No." He rubbed his jaw. "Seems to be a habit of mine, not to remember things."

The statement was innocent enough that Mercy knew Jeanette didn't understand the message beneath the words. From time to time, he would ask her a question about the Crimea—he would just toss it out as though it was truly insignificant, but she knew he was hoping to spark some memory. While she continually stressed that what he didn't remember didn't matter, he still seemed to search for the memories that eluded him.

"I suppose Ainsley will be here," she said, to turn the topic from memories.

"No doubt. Mother. Leo. Possibly Lynnford and his family. Ainsley sent a message that they'd returned from the South of France."

"I look forward to meeting him. He no doubt helped to shape you. Was he a good guardian?"

"We seldom got along. I don't think I could have disappointed him more if I were his own son."

"Surely, whatever disappointments he might have experienced are overshadowed by your heroics in the Crimea."

"I wasn't a hero, Mercy."

"But you were."

He gave her a hard glare. "Were you on the battlefield?"

"No, but I heard your name mentioned among many of the men we treated." She issued a soft curse beneath her breath. "I keep vowing not to speak of war, and yet I do."

"It is hard to overlook it. However, regarding Lynnford, you'll no doubt find him very charming. His entire family is very charming."

The carriage turned off the main road, and her stomach knotted. "We're almost there, are we?"

"Almost."

Leaning across, she squeezed his hand. "I'm glad we're going to spend Christmas with your family."

"And what of yours?"

She sat back. "It's only Father, and he made his choice to be done with me."

"His loss."

She smiled. "I like to think so. Oh, look!" She pointed. "There it is. I didn't expect it to look so . . . dark."

"Foreboding, no doubt." He glanced out the window. "It suits Westcliffe's temperament."

But inside could not have been more warm or welcoming. Candles were flickering amidst greenery. The spicy fragrance of the outdoors and the warm scent of cinnamon wafted on the air.

"You've arrived at last!" Claire exclaimed as she swept into the room, leading the others into the entry hallway, and took Mercy in her arms. "It's such a dreadfully long journey. I was beginning to despair that you'd met trouble on the way."

"Only a hungry lad who needs to be fed far too often," Stephen said, but Mercy heard the pride in his voice, and it touched a special place in her heart.

Westcliffe took his brother's hand and clapped him on the shoulder. "I don't think you've been here for Christmas since you were a lad."

"It wasn't Mother's favorite place, as I recall," Stephen said.

"But that has changed," the duchess said, taking John from Jeanette. "Oh, look at you, my darling boy," she crooned. "You have grown, haven't you? Leo, don't you think he's doubled in size?"

"Not quite, my love," he said, his voice warm with affection.

"Lynnford, come meet my newest grandson." She turned to a tall, blond man.

Mercy couldn't help but stare as he bent over the blond-haired child. Lynnford was Stephen's guardian, but surely he was related in some manner as well. Although no one had mentioned a relationship, she could see an uncanny resemblance between him and Stephen. Surely, it was that side of the family that Stephen had inherited his light features from when everyone else was so incredibly dark.

"He's quite the charmer," Lynnford said, an odd expression on his face as though he were holding back his true emotions. He looked up at Stephen, and Mercy realized his eyes were a remarkable blue. "Takes after his father in that regard. It's good to have you home, lad."

"Thank you, m'lord." Stephen's tone contained a

stiltedness, and she remembered that he'd mentioned the difficulty he'd had in pleasing Lynnford. "Allow me the honor of introducing you to my wife, Mercy."

Lynnford bowed, then as though deciding it was not enough, he moved forward, took her hand, and placed a kiss against her knuckles. "Mercy, it is an honor to make your acquaintance. I never thought to see this one settled."

"I consider myself most fortunate. He was quite remarkable in the Crimea."

"So I've heard."

"Come," the duchess said. "You must meet Lynnford's family. They're waiting in the parlor."

The duchess grabbed her arm and was steering her toward another room before she had a chance to object. Glancing over her shoulder, she saw Lynnford approach Stephen, say something to him. Based on Stephen's expression, she could only deduce that he was very touched by the words.

In the parlor, a tree sat on a table. Lit candles adorned the branches. Small gifts rested at the base of the tree. Garland was draped over the mantel. This Christmas was going to be celebrated a bit differently from what Mercy was accustomed to. She'd seen an etching in the *Illustrated London News* showing the royal family with their Christmas tree. She'd assumed Stephen's family would embrace the new tradition. Thank goodness she and Stephen brought presents to put under it.

Two young men who very much favored Lynnford approached. The duchess introduced them as Lynnford's eldest son, Viscount Mallard, and his other son, Charles. Mercy then met his daughters: Emily, Joan, and Charlotte. The girls favored their mother, Lady

Lynnford. She was a small woman with brown hair. Mercy recognized right away by the pallor of her skin that she was not well.

"A malignancy of the bone," the duchess said quietly, before Mercy could ask, as though she recognized that Mercy's training would alert her to the woman's health. "I shall miss her. She is a dear, dear friend."

Mercy squeezed her hand. "I'm so very sorry."

"My dear girl, it is life. We must not let it dim the festivities. Angela would never forgive us."

"May I hold your son?" the countess asked.

"Of course." Mercy bent down and placed John in the woman's arms. He stared up at her with his large, blinking eyes.

"Oh, what a lovely lad. I can see the family resemblance. He looks so much like his father."

"Yes, he does, doesn't he?" the duchess asked.

"Tessa, you must be beside yourself with two grandsons already."

"They are an absolute joy." John began to fuss. "And when they cry, they can go back to their mother or the nursemaid."

"I would so like to have grandchildren," the countess lamented.

"You will, darling," the duchess said.

John released a wail that startled the countess and had Mercy reaching for him, taking him, and quieting him in one smooth movement. "I think he's simply hungry after the long journey."

Mercy felt a familiar hand come to rest on the small of her back. "If you'll excuse us," Stephen said, "we're going to retire to our chambers and freshen up before dinner."

"Of course. Absolutely," the duchess said. "We shall dine within the hour."

"I'll show you to your rooms," Claire said. Once they were back in the entry hallway, she wrapped her arm affectionately around Stephen's. "I've put you at the far end of the west wing. You shan't be disturbed there."

"I barely remember this place from my youth," Stephen said, "but I recognize your influence now."

"Westcliffe's fault entirely, since he left me to wallow here while he gallivanted around London."

"Which was my fault." Stephen stopped, held her arms so she faced him directly, and he could study her eyes. "But you're happy now, Claire, aren't you?"

"Frightfully happy. It means the world to Westcliffe that you're here. He always felt as though the family abandoned this place when your mother married Ainsley."

"I daresay we did."

Claire looked around Stephen to Mercy. "It is no secret that the duchess did not fancy her first husband. He was not a kind man."

"She's happy now though," Mercy said.

"Remarkably so. Leo is good for her. Tomorrow he plans to begin a portrait of Lynnford and his family. They're going to stay here until he's finished it." She moved until she stood between Mercy and Stephen. "We must have him do a portrait of your family."

"I would like that very much," Mercy said.

Claire led them down a long, broad hallway. A portrait gallery. Mercy slowed to study one portrait after another. "These are your ancestors," she said quietly.

"Yes, I suppose they are. I've never seen portraits of them. Never really cared, quite honestly."

"They're all so dark."

"I can see Westcliffe in them," Claire said. "It's uncanny really."

"I must have taken from Mother's side of the family," Stephen said. "Never gave it much thought."

Although Mercy wasn't as sure. Even the duchess had dark hair and brown eyes.

Leaving the portraits behind, they ascended a wide sweep of stairs. At the end of the hallway, Claire escorted them into their suite of chambers. "We've assigned servants to see to your needs, so don't hesitate to ring for them." Leaning up, she kissed Stephen briefly on the cheek. "I'm so grateful you're here."

With that, she slipped out, closing the door behind her.

"You two are very close," Mercy said.

"We grew up together; I was always tugging on her braids," Stephen said as he walked over to the window and glanced out. "You've no cause to be jealous."

"I'm not." Strangely, she realized she wasn't. "It's obvious she adores Westcliffe and looks upon you as a brother. I'm going to take John to Jeanette."

Merely nodding, he continued to gaze out. When she returned, he was still standing at the window. She crossed over to him and laid a hand on his back. "Are you all right?"

"Lynnford said something rather odd. Said my father would be proud of my accomplishments. Then he added, 'I could not be more proud if you were my own son.'" Stephen shook his head. "I don't remember my father. Couldn't tell you if his portrait is in that gallery. I barely remember Ainsley's father. But Lynnford . . . he's been harping on me for as long as I can remember."

"Your mother was a young widow—twice."

A corner of his mouth curved up. "Very young. I didn't make things easy for her."

She eased around him, nestled against him until he was forced to turn from the window and place his arms around her. "That's all in the past." Easing up she nipped his chin, which caused him to give her his first genuine smile since they arrived. "We're going to have a jolly lovely Christmas here."

Dipping his head, he began to ravish her neck. "Perhaps we'll be late to dinner."

"It would be rude."

"My family's known me to be rude before."

He nibbled on the sensitive spot below her ear. He could control her so easily.

"Not too late," she murmured.

"Not too late."

Laughing with triumph, he lifted her into his arms and carried her to the bed.

Drawing her cloak more closely around her, Tessa stepped out onto the terrace. "Lynnford, whatever are you doing out here? It's freezing."

He didn't speak, just continued to stare at the winter gardens. Even in December, Claire managed to see that they retained some beauty.

Tessa stepped nearer to the earl. She had been a young girl when she'd fallen in love with Lynnford. He'd brought joy into an otherwise miserable life. "I've never liked this estate, but I come here because it's important to Westcliffe. It's his inheritance. Claire has somehow managed to erase the coldness of it."

"My memories are a bit fonder. It was here that I met

you. I'd come for a fox hunting weekend with my father. He and your husband were friends."

"That was so long ago."

"I was a fool, Tess. How could I have not seen the resemblance all those years? Stephen favors me a great deal."

"You had no reason to look closely. What do you think of . . . our grandson? He's remarkable, isn't he?"

"I can hardly fathom it. It took everything within me not to ask to hold him."

"You should have. No one would have thought anything of it."

He shook his head. "Will you ever tell him?"

"Stephen?"

He nodded.

"I don't know. I don't know what good would come of it. And there is your family to think of."

He nodded again, and finally his gaze came to land on her. She remembered a time when she had lived for the moments when he would look at her.

"Your young painter is in love with you," Lynnford said softly.

"Yes, I know. But it is not a love that will last. He will meet someone younger, prettier, and I will be relegated to pleasant memories."

"I would not be so sure if I were you. When a young man falls in love with you, it is very difficult for him to fall out of love with you."

"It has been many years since you've spoken to me of love."

"I do not do so now, Tessa. I speak to you only of young men, of which I am no longer one."

"Oh, yes, you are so terribly old."

"A grandfather. Christ."

"Do you want Stephen to know?"

"I don't know. I have not yet wrapped my head around all the implications. I have no desire to cause hurt to my family, especially to Angela."

"Then our secret it shall remain."

"Is that fair to you?"

"My dear Lynnford, I have long had the strength to weather unfairness. We shall be dining soon. Don't stay out too long."

She stepped into the house and came up short at the sight of Leo lounging against the wall. "How long have you been standing there?" she demanded.

"Long enough to know he still doesn't put you first."

"Don't start, Leo."

Reaching out, he took her hand and tugged her into his embrace. "Let's forego dinner. My appetite leans more toward carnal delicacies."

"I shall satisfy that appetite after dinner."

"Then I shall dine quickly."

She laughed as he led her from the room. She wasn't certain how she would survive when he did grow bored with her. But surely, he would.

Stephen and Mercy were indeed late to dinner, but as he'd anticipated, it hardly mattered. It was an extremely informal affair. Several conversations were going on at once, and no one was being particularly quiet or discreet. It was as though they were all caught up in the festivities and thought their voices should compete with the church bells that would be ringing on the morrow.

Stephen became acutely aware of Mercy growing

anxious as she sat beside him, hardly touching the food on her plate. As for himself, he was downing the wine as though it were the main course. He didn't know why he was feeling tense. He usually enjoyed the camaraderie and was as loud as the rest of them. Leaning over, he asked Mercy, "Are you all right?"

She nodded, but he could see in her eyes that she wasn't. When had he come to read her so well? In the Crimea? Was there a part of him that while he didn't remember her, still knew her?

Or was it simply the closeness that had developed over the past few weeks?

He knew the nights when bad dreams stirred within her, and he calmed them by holding her near and whispering reassurances in her ear before she ever awakened. He knew how much she ate when she was happy, and how little when she was distracted with worries.

He suddenly felt as though he had nothing in common with these people. He didn't know the people about whom they spoke. Emily would have her first Season come summer and she was rattling off the names of the girls who would be joining her on the marriage market. He'd never heard of any of them. Or if he had, he didn't remember them. When the deuce had the girl grown up?

He'd not seen Lynnford's family since his return, and he'd been so distracted watching for Mercy's reaction upon their arrival that he'd paid little attention to the other guests. But now he could see that they were all considerably older. Two years, he supposed. What a difference it could make. Once again he was hit with all he'd somehow lost.

But then he glanced over at Mercy and realized all

that he'd gained. He'd known her such a short while, but he couldn't envision his life without her smiles and laughter. Without her conversations.

Still, he was grateful that the meal was fairly brief. The ladies went off to finish preparing the boxes of clothing they would deliver to the poor the day after Christmas. Stephen found himself joining the men in the billiards room for a spot of brandy. He didn't know why he was surprised that Lynnford's sons joined them. Two years. The boys were men now.

"I'm thinking of joining a regiment," Charles suddenly blurted, his gaze falling on Stephen as though he were seeking praise or perhaps confirmation that it was a wise move.

Standing by the fireplace, his arm on the mantel, Stephen didn't glance around the room, but he could feel other eyes come to bear on him—Lynnford's especially. As well as Ainsley's. "You might want to wait until this bit in the Crimea is over," he finally said quietly.

"Austria has stepped in to help negotiate a peace," Mallard said. "They expect it to all be resolved by spring."

"There will no doubt be another battle to be fought somewhere," Lynnford said laconically to his son.

"You're not in favor of his joining up?" Ainsley asked Lynnford.

"I think his mother needs him near right now."

Charles sat back with a grumble, and Stephen nearly laughed. It seemed he wasn't the only one who took issue with Lynnford's controlling ways. He swirled the brandy in his snifter, wondering if he would ever again feel as though he belonged with these people. He had a strong urge to find Mercy. It seemed as though it had been hours since dinner, since he'd had her at his side, but when he glanced at the clock, he saw that it had not been even half an hour.

Ainsley ambled over. "Would you care to join me in a game of billiards?"

"I need to speak with you about Roseglenn."

He seemed taken aback. "Did you find something amiss?"

"No. Which is my point. You didn't neglect it."

"I believe I said I hardly have time for it. Only you would complain because it is in working order."

"I want to feel useful, Ainsley."

"You are. It takes a weight off my shoulders to know it is in your hands."

Stephen scoffed. "It practically manages itself."

"Then spend the time you're not looking after it with your wife."

Speaking of his wife—the ladies chose that moment to rejoin them. Mercy appeared more relaxed. No doubt doing something that would help others had appealed to her giving nature. Stephen downed his brandy, set the snifter aside, and walked over to his wife, taking her hand, feeling a calmness settle over him as her fingers intertwined with his.

"You enjoyed your visit with the ladies."

She smiled up at him. "I did. I like Claire a good deal."

"She has always managed to charm."

They soon found themselves in the grand salon, where Charlotte entertained them on the pianoforte. Stephen sat on the arm of a chair, his arm around Mercy's shoulders. For the occasion she'd donned a dark green gown that brought out her best features, her eyes, her hair, the tilt of her nose. Even her freckles seemed to have emerged for the holidays, although he suspected she'd not be pleased to hear that. He had a strong urge to remove the pins and the pearl clasp that held the strands of her hair in place.

Then Charlotte began to sing *Silent Night*, and he saw the sorrow sweep over Mercy's features. He tucked his finger beneath her chin and turned her toward him. Without words, with merely a nod of his head toward the doorway, he indicated they should quit the room. Quietly, she followed him out. He waited until they reached another gallery. The walls were home to paintings by the masters. No family portraits here. He wasn't certain why, but he preferred this gallery.

"They predict the war will be over come spring," he said quietly.

Her fingers flinched where they rested on his arm. "I indeed hope so."

"Is it difficult for you to be here?"

She peered up at him. "I simply have little in common with these people."

"I feel the same way—which is odd since I can't remember what makes me so different."

"I thought returning here might . . . cause you to remember."

He led her over to the window. "There is the terrace where I had tea with Claire. I remember the taste of the tea: Earl Grey. I remember the fragrance of the fall blooms." It was visible because torches lined the garden path, as though someone might wish to stroll about in the brisk night air. "She was already married to Westcliffe. She'd had a . . . mishap. We thought she was going to die. He thought she wanted me, but she loved him. I remember telling her that I would be leaving England. But I don't remember leaving here. I still find it all remarkably strange, that my mind refuses to cooperate. I was quite shocked to see that Lynnford's brood had aged. His daughter will have a Season come spring. Did you have a Season?"

"No, my father is not so well off as that."

"Do you miss him?"

A sadness touched her eyes. She moved in closer to him. "I don't think about it. Just as I try not to think about those who are in the Crimea. Do you truly believe there will be peace soon?"

"I hope so."

"As do I."

Chapter 16

Mercy awoke from an uneasy sleep. As much as she was glad to be visiting with Stephen's family, appreciated how they welcomed her, she missed Roseglenn. She'd begun to think of it as her residence, her home.

Although her back was to Stephen's chest, and her bottom was nestled in the curve of his hips, she knew he was awake because he was feathering his fingers lightly over her arm—as though he thought that faint action wouldn't disturb her. She loved waking up to find herself cradled by his body.

"Mmm," she murmured. "What time will they be expecting us?"

"Mother said something about opening gifts after breakfast, but I thought"—he slid an oblong package wrapped in white up her pillow in front of her nose—"*before* we eat."

Releasing a small squeal, she snatched it and sat up. Leaning down, she kissed him.

"You don't know what it is yet. It might not be worthy of a kiss."

"Doesn't matter. You're worthy of a kiss." She gave him another one, this time lingering, as his hand slid up her calf, up her thigh. Then he was pulling her beneath him. "No, wait!" She laughed. "I want to see what it is."

Scooting back, she leaned against the pillow and slowly removed the paper, savoring the moment. Looking past the gift, she saw Stephen raised on an elbow, smiling as she'd never seen him, a warmth in his eyes. Joyous. She didn't know if she'd ever seen him look quite so relaxed and happy. At that moment, she didn't know if she'd ever been happier.

The paper fell away to reveal a finely grained leather box. Cautiously she opened it to reveal a strand of pearls. "Oh, my goodness. They're beautiful. You shouldn't have. They must have cost a fortune."

Chuckling low, he slipped his hand beneath the pearls and removed them from the box. "Lean forward, so I can put them on you."

Twisting around, she lifted her hair, wishing it was once again to her waist, for him. She would never cut it again. She heard the clasp *snick* into place and quickly scooted off the bed.

"Hold on there, where are you going?" he demanded.

"I want to see." She rushed around the bed to the vanity and peered into the mirror. Enough light was coming around the edges of the draperies that she could see. She touched the pearls gently. "They're perfect."

"Not quite."

She jerked around. He was lying against the pillows, his hands tucked behind his head, satisfaction in every line of his lithe body. Even with the scars he was magnificent.

"What is lacking?" she asked.

"More skin." He nodded toward her. "Remove your nightdress."

"You're insatiable." They'd made love before they went to sleep last night.

"Where you're concerned, yes."

She eased the nightdress off her shoulders, felt it slithering down her body as she began walking toward the bed. She stepped out of it in a fluid motion as it hit the floor, saw the heat immediately fill his eyes, and his body's swift reaction which only served to warm her further.

"Come here," he ordered, holding out his hand. "I want to make love to you wearing nothing but the pearls."

"You want to wear the pearls?"

"You vixen," he snarled, grabbing her, and pulling her onto the bed.

Because it took Mercy longer to get ready for the day than it did Stephen, he'd left her and gone on to breakfast. When she was finally ready, in an emerald green gown for the holidays, she slipped down the stairs quietly. It had taken her so long, she wondered if he was in the parlor. He'd told her that he'd meet her there if he finished with breakfast before she joined him.

Peering into the room, she saw him partially bent over, examining something beneath the decorated tree. No doubt getting into mischief, searching for a gift for himself.

As quietly as a mouse, she tiptoed in, and when she was near enough, reached out and pinched his bum. "What are you"—he spun around and she gasped, pressing her hand to her mouth—"oh, my dear Lord!"

She found herself staring into the face of Lord Lynnford. She curtsied. "My lord, please forgive me. I mistook you . . . oh." For my husband. No, she couldn't say that.

He laughed. "It's quite all right, my dear. The blond locks, I'm sure, confused you. Although from the front, I do have some gray showing up."

The blond hair, the height, and the form. The way he stood, the way he moved. She shook her head. It made sense that Stephen would mimic the only man who had been in his life for any length of time. Because to consider anything else . . . that this man and the duchess . . . it was not possible.

"Again, my apologies."

He bowed. "And again, no need to apologize. I'm glad to see that things are so . . . well between you and your husband."

He gave her a knowing look and she felt the heat swarming her cheeks.

"I'm sorry we weren't able to attend your wedding," he said.

"No, that's quite all right. We all understood. And it came about rather quickly and unexpectedly."

"But you're happy."

"Extremely so. Yes."

"And you knew Stephen in the Crimea." He rubbed his jaw. "I heard Stephen was a remarkable soldier."

"He was very courageous, yes. I did not know him on the battlefield, of course, only in hospital, but he always put the other men first."

"I sometimes doubted he would ever grow up."

"It must be very difficult to raise another man's sons."

He touched one of the presents, shifting it into another position. "Yes, it is."

Yet she was raising another woman's child. "But I could see where it would be easy to forget that they were not yours, and to love them as though they were."

He smiled. "Indeed."

"Ah, Lynnie, I see you got caught," the duchess said as she waltzed into the room. "He has a habit of shaking the gifts. Most impatient, this man." She patted his arm with a familiarity that spoke of doing so a thousand times. "Don't you look lovely, my dear."

Mercy curtsied. "Thank you, Your Grace. I should probably find Stephen."

"He finished with his breakfast and went for a walk with Westcliffe. You can probably catch sight of them from the terrace."

"Thank you." She nodded toward Lynnford. "My lord."

"Mercy, it's a pleasure to have you in the family."

"I'm very happy to be here."

Then she was bustling out before she said something else to get her in trouble. She made her way down the hallway to the door that opened on to the terrace and had just opened it when Stephen rounded the corner with Westcliffe. She didn't know if she'd ever seen two brothers who looked so different. The thought running through her head, that the brothers did not in fact have the same father, was preposterous.

"Hello, sweetheart," Stephen said, smiling at her. "It's too cold for you to be out here without a wrap."

"I just . . . I just wanted to see you."

Opening the door, he drew her back inside. "Missed me, did you?"

Westcliffe stepped in after them. She felt a little self-conscious saying, "Very much so."

He furrowed his brow. "Is everything all right?"

"Yes, I just . . . had an embarrassing encounter. I mistook Lynnford for you. I pinched him."

Both brothers laughed, which served to only humiliate her further. She was grateful she'd not revealed exactly where she pinched him.

Finally, after their laughter died down, Stephen smiled broadly at her and said, "No need to be embarrassed, sweetheart. I suspect he jolly well enjoyed the attention." He squeezed her hand. "Don't worry about it."

"If you'll excuse me, I need to find Claire," Westcliffe said. "Lynnford is no doubt opening presents already."

Mercy watched as Westcliffe strode down the hallway.

"What were you and Westcliffe doing?" she asked.

"Just looking over the grounds, reminiscing about childhood. Strange to find myself enjoying talking with him when we had so little in common growing up."

"You seem close."

"Not particularly, but we tolerate each other better." He skimmed his finger along her chin. "Something is bothering you. What is it?"

"No, I . . . Lynnford and your mother seem to have quite an affection for each other."

"He's always been there for her."

"Were they ever . . . lovers, do you think?"

"God, no, Lynnford is devoted to his countess."

"Oh. That is unusual among the aristocracy, isn't it?"

"The royal family is setting new expectations. They frown on promiscuity." He narrowed his eyes. "Are you striving to determine if I'll be devoted to you?"

"No, I . . . I want your devotion, but ours is a forced

marriage. Still, I am hopeful that you will come to care for me."

He skimmed his fingers along her hair. "Well, then—"

"Stephen!" Emily cried. "Come along. Everyone is waiting to open presents."

"Ah, then, we must not keep the family waiting," Stephen said with an elaborate bow. He wrapped his arm around hers, and began escorting her to the parlor. "And what did you get me, wife?"

"You shall just have to wait and see," she said teasingly.

It was a gold timepiece and chain.

"I noticed you didn't have one," Mercy said. "It seemed like the thing to pass down to your son."

It was also a reminder, Stephen thought as he sat in a chair by the window and gazed out on the drive, that minutes ticked forward and not back, and that he needed to concentrate on the moments to come, not those that he couldn't remember. She must have spent every farthing she possessed to purchase this for him.

"Now for my sons," his mother said, handing small packages to him and his brothers.

In the chair beside him, Mercy looked on. His mother had given her a lovely lacy shawl, which she now wore draped over her shoulders. She still wore the pearl necklace, and he was half tempted to lead her back to bed, wearing it alone.

"Open it," she demanded with impatience.

He did so and discovered a miniature of his mother, a perfect likeness. Leo was skilled with the brush. He handed it to Mercy that she might see it.

"Oh, he did a wonderful job," she mused. She was

holding John, who was gripping a wooden rattle that Ainsley had given him. He seemed quite fascinated by it, blinking in wonder each time it made a sound when he waved it around.

Stephen understood his son's wonder. He was still amazed to find himself with a family. He glanced back out the window.

"What do you keep looking for?" she asked.

Grinning, he shook his head. "Oh, nothing."

"You're simply bored with opening presents?"

But he wasn't going to tell her. He was waiting for another surprise to arrive.

"Leo, please fetch my gifts for my grandsons," the duchess ordered.

Instantly he left, and returned pushing two contraptions that looked like boxes on wheels.

"What the deuce . . . ?" Stephen murmured.

"They're perambulators," his mother said. "So you can push the babies through the park. They've become quite popular of late."

Claire, Mercy, and the other ladies went to inspect them.

"I've been thinking of getting one," Claire said.

And Stephen wondered if Mercy had wanted one as well. He'd had no idea there was such a thing. He glanced over at Westcliffe, who seemed as baffled as he. Ainsley, standing by the fireplace, appeared bored. And he discovered Lynnford was watching him, although his gaze shifted away quickly enough.

Stephen glanced back out the window and saw the approach of the coach before he heard the horses and wheels bringing it nearer. Rising, he walked over to his wife and placed his hand on her waist. Smiling brightly, she looked up at him with such joy in her eyes.

"Isn't this wonderful? I'll be able to continue to take John outside, even as he gets heavier."

"Marvelous, but I have another surprise for you. Come along."

He passed John off to his grandmother, who eagerly welcomed the boy, then Stephen guided Mercy through the parlor, entryway, and front door, until they were standing at the top of the steps leading up to the house.

"Whatever is it?" she asked as the coach came to a halt.

He placed his arm around her to shield her from the cold and to protect her from hurt if need be. A footman opened the coach door and a man stepped out. Mercy gasped.

"My father. Whatever is he doing here?"

"I invited him."

She jerked her head around to stare at him. "Why?"

"I thought you might like to see him. If he doesn't behave, he'll be back in the coach and on his way home."

Mercy was torn between joy and trepidation as she watched her father slowly walk toward them. When had he aged so much, and what did his presence signify? Had he forgiven her?

Breaking free of Stephen's hold, she rushed down the steps, halting on the cobblestones near enough to her father that she could smell his familiar tobacco scent. She was aware of Stephen suddenly standing behind her, and she realized that he was just as wary as she regarding how this encounter might go.

"Father."

He looked so stern and forbidding. He nodded, suddenly not looking quite so bold. "I was told I'd be welcomed."

"You are," she assured him.

"I see he did right by you."

"He married me, yes."

"You didn't invite me to the wedding."

"I didn't think you'd want to come . . . and it all happened very quickly."

"As it should have."

"Would you like to come inside, sir?" Stephen asked, and there was an undercurrent in his voice that issued a warning along with the welcome.

"No, I won't be staying. I just wanted to see that you were well. And I wanted you to have this." He removed a brown parcel from his pocket.

She opened it to discover a silk handkerchief that smelled of roses.

"It's your mother's. It's all I have of her."

"Then you should keep it."

"She'd want you to have it."

She crushed it to her bosom. "I'll treasure it. Would you like to see John?"

"No, I must be going."

Her heart nearly broke. He turned away. Reaching out, she grabbed his arm, felt Stephen's hand fold around her shoulder—to stop her or offer strength, she wasn't certain until she felt him squeeze gently. Strength, then, as though he knew what she wanted. "Please stay."

He glanced back. "You've always been far too compassionate for your own good. I treated you shabbily, daughter."

"I disappointed you. I do not regret the decisions I made regarding John. It would be a shame, however, if he did not have an opportunity to know his grandfather."

"Well, then," he grumbled, "perhaps I could stay for a bit."

Mercy was not surprised that everyone welcomed her father. As she watched him holding John on his lap, she leaned against Stephen, fighting back the tears in her eyes.

"I never thought to see that," she whispered. "It is a far greater gift than the pearls."

She felt the press of his lips against her hair. "I have learned of late the value of reconciling with one's family. It's not always easy, but it's worth it to make the effort."

"But you did nothing as egregious as bringing your father shame."

"Oh, I think Westcliffe would disagree."

She peered up at him, and he gave her a wry grin. "It is a tale I will not tell. Suffice it to say, it is also one I'd not mind forgetting."

"I would not think you'd want to forget anything else."

"A pity we cannot pick and choose what we remember."

"You've had no success recalling anything that you've forgotten?"

"No."

"I thought being here might rekindle—"

"No such luck. I spent an hour sipping tea on the terrace in the cold this morning. Nothing stirs. Westcliffe found me there, invited me for a walk. We spoke of the past, all that happened when last I was here . . . but nothing."

She hated it for him, but was relieved for herself. Did it make her a horrid wife to wish that her husband never acquired what he so desperately desired?

The remainder of the day was filled with silly parlor games that Stephen refused to be drawn into. He used to participate with vigor, but now he felt remarkably old. Mercy found one excuse after another not to be involved as well. She spent a good deal of time visiting with her father.

"Hmm," Stephen's mother muttered at one point, coming to stand beside him. "I'd never expected to see her father again, especially in such a forgiving temperament. Whatever did you say to him?"

"I may have mentioned that certain family members with access to the queen's ear might not take it kindly if he continued to ignore his daughter."

"Considering how much you always resented that they had a title and you did not, I never thought you'd use your brothers' titles in such a dastardly manner."

"I was referring to you."

"Of course you were, darling. Marriage becomes you."

"She's not like anyone I've ever known." He grimaced. "And yet I have known her, haven't I?"

"It bothers you that you don't remember her."

"I can see forgetting battles, blood, and death . . . but her? She is nothing at all like any of the other women I . . ." He let his voice trail off.

"Entertained?" his mother asked pointedly.

He shook his head. "You are unlike any mother—"

"I've earned the right to do as I please and say what I will. People act as though what happens between a man and a woman is something of which to be ashamed, something to be hidden, not spoken of. In truth, it can be the most beautiful part of our lives. I see no reason to pretend otherwise."

"Obviously you've had some influence on my wife. She asked me this morning if you and Lynnford had been involved in an affair."

"Did she?" his mother asked quietly, in such an unnaturally reserved tone that Stephen shifted his gaze away from his wife and studied his mother. "What did you tell her?"

"I laughed."

"Good for you."

She left it at that, walking away, leaving him with his thoughts.

Dinner was served promptly at four. The seating arrangement was once again informal, people sitting where they pleased. Stephen sat on one side of Mercy, her father on the other. His mother sat beside him, with Westcliffe and Ainsley at opposite ends of the table.

Westcliffe stood and raised his wineglass. "Before we begin, I'd like to make a toast. Last year was the first year, in large part due to the efforts of my wonderful wife, the family celebrated Christmas here since the death of Stephen's and my father. I recall making a toast last year that this year would find Stephen here with us. Brother, I don't imagine the journey to get here was one you would have wished for and certainly your being wounded was not what I had in mind when I made my toast—still we're ever so grateful that you're with us."

"Hear! Hear!" chorused through the room as glasses were lifted and sips taken.

Westcliffe again raised his glass. "Mercy, I don't know how you manage to put up with him"—Stephen heard Ainsley laugh, and beneath the table, Mercy's hand came to rest on his thigh. He wrapped his fingers around it, astounded to realize the rightness of it, unable to imagine how his life would be now if she weren't in it—"but bless you for doing so. We're—all of us here—delighted and honored to have you and John in the family."

More cheers followed. Stephen caught his brother's eye and lifted his glass in a silent salute and an acknowledgment of appreciation. He knew the words had been spoken for the benefit of Mercy's father, so he might understand how much she was valued within his family.

Stephen had never cherished his family as much as he did at that moment.

The conversation at the table was a bit more subdued, no doubt in deference to their guest. Ainsley was given the honor of carving the goose, which he did with considerable aplomb.

"I daresay, Ainsley," Mallard said, "if you ever lose your title, you'd make a fine servant."

"Pox on you, Mallard."

Everyone was giddy from too much wine and fine company by the time the plum pudding was served. As fate would have it, Ainsley was the one who spooned out the ring that had been cooked within it.

"Oh, Ainsley, you'll be married by next Christmas," Emily crowed.

"I will not. I'm all of three-and-twenty. Far too young for such a drastic measure."

"Come on, brother," Stephen cajoled. "With your responsible attitude, you might find it to your liking."

"And then I might not. Emily?"

She glanced up at him. "What?"

He tossed her the ring, which she caught, nearly knocking over her wineglass. "You're having your coming out. You're more likely to get married than me."

"Getting rid of it won't change your fate, Ainsley."

"I'm not getting married."

"Methinks thou doth protest too much, Ainsley," Westcliffe said. "Is there someone you've not told us about?"

"No one."

"I think there is," Mercy whispered to Stephen.

He loved the sparkle in her eyes, the radiance of her smile, the joy that emanated from her. "I think you're right."

It was sometime later—after dinner, after Mercy's father left, when they'd all retired once again to the grand room and Charlotte was playing the piano-forte—that Stephen looked over at his wife and he had a flash of memory.

It was dark. He was in the military hospital, in pain, feeling despair, when an angel stopped by his bed and smiled at him. Mercy.

Perhaps the memory was only his imagination, trying to fill in the empty spaces.

But what he did know was that one of her smiles would have been enough to keep him alive. Just so he could see it again.

He wondered if it was possible that he'd fallen in love with her there as easily as he was beginning to fall in love with her here.

Chapter 17

The new year brought with it snow. Standing at the bedchamber window, watching the huge, fat flakes fall softly, Mercy was reminded of her time in the East, where the winters could get bitter. It was much worse for the soldiers in the field, who were ofttimes brought to the hospital with frostbite. She shook off the thought, not wanting to dwell on unpleasantness. It had been some time since she'd been bothered by a nightmare.

It helped that Stephen held her close every night. She drifted off to sleep with his arms wound around her and awoke to the same. It also helped that he was no longer asking her to recount their time together in Scutari.

During the day she managed the household while he managed the estate. He seemed content. He no longer spoke of what he couldn't remember, never brought up that time at all. For that she was eternally grateful. They were both moving on with their lives. In so doing, she felt confident that John would grow up happy. She could see Stephen falling more in love with his son each day.

She'd never known such contentment, such joy.

Leaving the bedchamber, she walked aimlessly through the house. John was napping. She'd finished with her meetings with the servants. Every task was being handled splendidly. Ainsley could find no fault with her managing of his residence.

It was surprising that of Stephen's two brothers, Ainsley was the one she felt most uncomfortable around. He was always studying her as though she were a wooden puzzle he was attempting to take apart so he could examine each individual piece and determine exactly how it contributed to the whole. He was so at ease with his surroundings, so apparently unbothered by things, but she could sense that below his surface lurked a dangerous combination of suspicion and the ability to decipher the most confounding of mysteries. He quite literally terrified her, an honor that should have gone to Westcliffe, with his darkly brooding mien. But he was too occupied with his wife to care about Mercy.

Perhaps she should see about finding a wife for Ainsley, something to distract him from his unsettling purpose—whatever it was.

Stephen had assured her that she had nothing to worry over. But he didn't know the things she knew, the secrets she wished to keep locked away.

She needed him to distract her from these awful musings. Surely, she could lure him away from his own duties for a while. It would be a challenge—a fun one, even if she didn't succeed. With that thought in mind, she went searching for him.

As she wandered the hallways, she couldn't help but realize how much she'd come to love the house, to think of herself as its mistress. She wondered if Stephen would have difficulty relegating the responsibilities to Ainsley when he came to visit.

She wished she'd come with a dowry. She wondered if he resented that she hadn't. With a dowry, he might not have been dependent upon the kindness of his brother. She'd wanted so badly to have him, to secure John in her life, that she'd given little thought to what Stephen might have yearned for in his own dreams.

But she couldn't imagine that another woman would have loved him as deeply as she did. When she saw him with John, her heart swelled to the point of aching. When Stephen gazed at her with a hint of wickedness in his eyes, she melted. When they talked and shared the moments of their day, she knew unheralded contentment. When they pleasured each other, she was lost in a world of sublime ecstasy.

Her life contained a richness she'd never before experienced. She would do anything to hold on to it.

She located Stephen where she'd expected to find him: in the library, working diligently at his desk. An assortment of papers was spread over the mahogany wood. His furrowed brow revealed his deep concentration—as did the fact that he hadn't heard her enter the room. Usually he was attuned to her presence, turning to greet her the moment she spied him, as though he felt the touch of her gaze.

But not so now. She wondered what had captured his attention so intently as to block out the world around him.

"It's snowing," she said softly.

He jerked his gaze up to her, then shifted it over to the window. "What am I to do about that?"

He'd never sounded so curt, so irritated with her.

She couldn't deny the prick of pain that his tartness caused, then castigated herself for placing too much importance on his annoyance. She had disturbed him, after all. "I thought we might take John out to experience it."

"I have matters that are far more important than a snowflake landing on an eyelash." He turned his attention back to the document he'd been reading.

His dismissal hurt. She wasn't accustomed to their being out of sorts with each other. Since Christmas, they'd experienced an amazing accord, as though their marriage had come to reflect something special for both of them. They had settled in to this arrangement and found it pleasing. "What are you doing?"

"Reading some reports on the war that Ainsley was able to procure, as well as some letters from those who served under my command."

Thinking he'd given up his quest for his memories had been a misconception. He still searched. He'd simply stopped bringing the subject up to her. "Why do you torment yourself?"

"Because I want to bloody well remember!" He held up a piece of paper, clutching it until it crackled. "I've just received word that I'm to be knighted. For services rendered to the Crown. Services that in here"—he slapped the side of his head—"never occurred. Imagine it, Mercy. Imagine walking out into the garden and suddenly a child appears. He runs toward you. You don't know who he is, then you're told he's your son. You brought him into the world two years ago. You don't remember the pain of his birth, the sound of his first cry, watching him take his first step. Everything that should mean something to you doesn't exist for you."

She clutched her hands, squeezing her fingers until they ached. She couldn't imagine it, couldn't imagine the devastation of not having memories of John during the past five months, much less two years. The unfairness of it rattled her to her core. "It's not the same," she insisted. "The memories you've lost were ones of horror, pain, death, and gore."

"Was it horrible when I was with you?"

She felt all her blood draining down her toes. Her mouth went as dry as sand. Yes, it had been horrible, but it had also been remarkable. But if she helped him remember it, he might also remember other things, question her claim that she was John's mother.

"I know you don't understand my obsession, Mercy. I know you think I should be content with what I have now. And I am. But there is a part of me that cannot escape what happened during those two years. I will be knighted for it. People will ask me questions about my actions, my bravery . . . my damned service to country. And what the devil do I say? Do I admit that I have this affliction? That part of my mind is gone? Memories washed away as though carried to a distant shore where I can no longer reach them?"

"Why did you not come to me? Why did you not explain it to me like this before?"

"And burden you? Ask you to resurrect what gives you nightmares?" He shook his head. "I couldn't subject you to that torment."

"So you pretended not to care about the past any longer?"

"I didn't pretend. I simply ceased to discuss it. I acquired a list of names of men in my regiment. I wrote them. Told them I was writing a book about our adventures and that I required some details to confirm our exploits. It seems a good many of the men who served with me are dead. It's a betrayal not to remember them."

She'd failed to understand how much he suffered with what he couldn't recall. But what if those letters spread over his desk contained more than stories of bravery and action against the enemy? What if they mentioned his time in Scutari and the nurses there? What if they mentioned one in particular and a name sparked a single memory, and a bit of that memory sparked another? Had her own selfishness brought him to this moment of grief?

"No matter how many accounts you read, you will never *feel* what you experienced on that battlefield. You will not know if you trembled upon your horse. If you dropped to your knees and cast up your accounts afterward. You cannot experience bravery or righteousness or fear when the moment is long past. You cannot recreate what you went through there. I think you are foolish to try."

"You think me foolish," he stated, each word enunciated with the bite of anger.

"I think you must accept that the queen has determined that you are worthy of this honor and therefore you are worthy."

He laughed harshly. "You've not listened to a damned word I've said." He came out of his chair, his eyes blistering with anger. "You can't possibly understand. You think it trivial. You think me obsessed. Perhaps you even think me mad. And perhaps I am, because I would give my left arm to have the ability to reminisce about those missing two years of my life."

She angled her chin. "You are correct. You do not know the man you were in the Crimea. Because that man did every damned thing possible not to lose his left arm. He defied physicians. He threatened bodily harm to anyone who sawed it off. He proved to them with actions that it still worked, that it could be saved. And do you know why he did that?" She took a step nearer. "Because he refused to let his men return to the battlefield without him. When they wanted to give up and die, he urged them to live to fight again. And those for whom there would never be another fight, he stayed by their side as they surrendered to death and he made them feel victorious with their last breath. That is the man I fell in love with. That is the man whose son I held to my breast and swore I would never abandon. You do not need his memories to be him. Because he is *you*."

She made him feel small, petty, and ashamed. In the midst of his stunned silence, she'd stalked from the library, taking her magnificent fury with her. He'd wanted to rush after her, drag her back into this room, shove all this unimportant garbage off his desk, and lay the most important person of all upon it and have his way with her.

Let her have her way with him.

Instead, he'd dropped down into his chair and, with a shaking hand, he'd snatched up a letter and read words that no longer had any meaning, because hers had rendered them all into insignificance. Why, why could he not let it go? And every time he thought he had, it returned with a vengeance, demanding that he seek answers.

He didn't know how long he stared at the scrawl of

ink on parchment. She was right. He found no answers there. They were inside him, locked away, possibly forever. All the dangers had been in the Crimea. What he couldn't remember could do him no harm here—unless his obsession with not knowing drove his wife from his side.

That would be tragic. That would be unbearable. That would be a hell worse than the empty pit in a distant part of his mind.

He caught a movement out of the corner of his eye, something moving past the window. Shoving the chair back, he rose and strode over to the sitting area that looked out on the garden.

He couldn't prevent his mouth from slanting upward ever so slightly at the sight of Mercy, holding John close. Her heavy red cape swirled around her ankles as she twirled in the descending snow. His son's gleeful laughter filled the air and caused a painful knot to form in Stephen's chest. What a turn of events his life had taken.

John's father would be Sir Stephen. There was honor in that. For Stephen and his son. He'd never before given much thought to how his actions fell on those around him. He'd always only cared about playing. Now he had a chance to play with his son, and he was ensconced in his library reading letters in an effort to reassure himself that the Queen had not made a mistake, that he was worthy of this honor.

Who was he to decide?

Surely, Mercy was right. They'd not confer it upon him if he didn't deserve it. He wished he'd known the man he'd been in the East. He wondered if it was

possible he'd not lost him completely, that remnants of
what he'd done, who he'd been, remained, even if he
didn't recognize them. Surely, the life he'd led for two
years influenced him to some degree.

Mercy moved beyond his sight. He wondered what
else she would share with their son. They would discuss it during dinner, if she was talking to Stephen
by then. Her temper had been royally pricked. The
thought of having her in bed with that fire blazing. . .

That wasn't going to happen, not when he'd disappointed her once again. Strange, how it had never bothered him to disappoint his family. Well, except for his
mother. He'd always gotten angry with himself when
he'd let her down, but he'd continued to disappoint her
just the same. His needs, wants, desires had always
come first.

What a selfish bastard he'd been.

But when it came to Mercy, she was all that mattered.

He had a footman fetch his coat, hat, and gloves,
and before he realized what he'd fully intended, he was
scouring through the winter gardens searching for his
wife and son. He found them on a bench covered with
a light dusting of snow. She appeared serene. No evidence remained of the firebrand that had been in his
library.

"You have quite the temper, Mrs. Lyons. Had I my
memories, would I have known that?"

She glanced over at him, her mouth twitching as
though she fought back a smile. She couldn't stay angry
with him for long. He took comfort in that knowledge,
because he had years left in which to prick her anger.

"A spinster is agreeable in all things with the hope

that she will not chase a prospective suitor away. I don't recall if I ever put my temper on display for you before. I rather doubt it."

He sat beside her and stretched his arm along the back of the bench. "Well, if you had, I can tell you I'd have thought twice before marrying you."

She smirked. "You thought twice anyway."

"I thought about it a great many more times than that." He touched her cheek. "I'm sorry, Mercy, sorry for everything I said in the library."

"I'm sorry, too, sorry that I can't comprehend your situation. You're correct, though. If I lost the memory of a single moment with John, I would be devastated."

Sitting on her lap with his back to her chest and her arms holding him upright, the child was completely ignoring his parents, making nonsensical noises, and becoming fast friends with the snowflakes.

"I think he took your temperament more than mine," Stephen said.

"I'm not so sure."

An oddness marked her tone, as though she were embarrassed by the thought. She curled her gloved hand around Stephen's arm. "I'm not even sure if I should congratulate you for receiving the honor, but I am proud and I know it is deserved."

"I shall take your word for it."

"I would never lie to you. You must believe that."

Such earnestness in the whiskey of her eyes. God, he could drink from them all day and all night. He never wanted to be denied the pleasure of gazing into them.

"There are times when I think that the details of what happened in the Crimea must reside deeply within me, must somehow still have some influence. The man I was before would have laughed at the absurdity of a knighthood, and then he'd have snatched it with both hands and not given a damn as to the reasons that he was being knighted. In here . . ." He touched his fist to his chest. "There are times, Mercy, when I swear to God I do not know the man I have become. I am a stranger to myself."

"You are no stranger to me." She leaned in and kissed him, sweetly, softly. A brief touch of their lips that promised more later. She'd forgiven him. Now if he could only forgive himself.

If only he could come to accept that a stranger did not live inside his skin.

Chapter 18

The grand room of Westcliffe's London residence was overflowing with guests. Claire had insisted that a celebration be held to honor Stephen and his accomplishment. As Mercy watched Stephen wending his way among the crush of people, she was struck by his confident swagger and the ease with which he smiled—even if she suspected much of it was for show. While he accepted the tribute with grace and dignity, she knew he still questioned his deserving it.

Parliament was not yet in session. People had come to London specifically for this affair. While they'd not all attended the ceremony that afternoon, they were all chatting about it, seeking out what details they could find. It was not every day that someone was knighted.

The ceremony had taken place in the ballroom of Buckingham Palace. Mercy's throat had clogged with tears that she'd refused to allow to reach her eyes—she wouldn't embarrass Stephen for the world—as she'd watched him in his scarlet uniform kneel before the Queen. Seeing him in it again made her realize that he'd aged more than the time that had passed since she'd first fallen in love with him. War and wounds had taken a toll. He looked older than his twenty-six years.

So much older. But then she looked a great deal older as well. She wouldn't change a minute of the hardship that had shaped them both.

In a ritual dating back hundreds of years, Queen Victoria touched a sword to one of his shoulders and then the other, spoke words that Mercy barely heard with the thundering rush of blood in her ears. Then it was done. And Sir Stephen rose.

He had looked magnificent.

His family had been there. They were not strangers to the Queen and she'd greeted them warmly. In a ceremony earlier in the day, Mercy had been formally presented to Her Majesty. But her honor was nothing compared with Stephen's.

He'd traded his uniform for a black swallow-tailed coat, white shirt, silver waistcoat, and pristine white cravat. He moved about the ballroom with such grace, no evidence of a limp. All his physical injuries healed. She wished she could be as certain of his emotional wounds.

When the party ended, a little after midnight, they would return to their residence. It was not so far away. An hour at the most. She couldn't wait to be absolutely and completely alone with him. She was even thinking that the carriage might suffice for a bed. Her love for him was so grand, her passion immeasurable. She wanted his hands on her and hers on him. She would tease him about the fact that she'd never taken a knight to her bed before.

Sir Stephen. Lady Lyons.

Her father was certain to be impressed. Since Christmas, she'd received a letter from him, inviting her to visit. She still felt some awkwardness around him, but in time, perhaps it would lessen until it no longer existed. She could hardly fathom how wonderful—

"Mercy?"

The familiar voice turned the blood pumping through her veins into ice. A chill went through her. She straightened her shoulders and her spine. If she'd learned nothing else from tending to soldiers, she'd learned defeat came after the battle and not before. Turning slowly, she smiled as brightly as possible. "Miss Whisenhunt."

The black hair she'd refused to cut while they were in the east was captured into an elaborate style decorated with loops of pearls. Her blue gaze roamed over Mercy as though she was searching for something, and unfortunately, Mercy had a good idea of what it might be.

The woman smiled warmly. "Mercy, after all we've been through, surely there is no cause for such formality between us. But please, tell me. How is my son? How is John?"

Mercy felt as though she were standing in a foggy haze, the ballroom fading away until she was once again in Scutari, sharing a sparsely furnished room in the north tower with a dozen other nurses. Her bed had been next to Sarah's.

One night Mercy heard her crying softly. Fearing Sarah had encountered ruffians as she had, she crept out of bed and knelt on the cold floor beside her bed. "Sarah, whatever's wrong?"

"Oh, Mercy, I've been a naughty girl. I'm in trouble."

"What sort of trouble?"

"The sort that . . . ruins reputations. Captain Lyons and I . . ."

Mercy felt the sharp pain that the man who had been so kind to her had chosen Sarah, had been intimate with her. "We should talk about this in the morning, somewhere private."

Sarah nodded, and Mercy returned to her bed, where she wept her own silent tears. How silly she had been to think that she'd meant something special to the captain. He had saved her and comforted her simply because that was what soldiers did. They protected.

She'd thought something special existed between them, but it was simply her longings, her desires. He was in love with someone else.

But the following morning, as they walked near the waterfront, Sarah confessed, "I believe I shall go to Paris, have the babe, and leave it secretly at a foundling home."

Mercy was appalled. "Surely Captain Lyons will marry you."

"If he knew of my condition, possibly."

"You can send word."

"I do not wish to marry him."

Mercy stared in stunned silence, trying to wrap her mind around this woman not wanting what Mercy desperately longed to have. Finally, she stammered, "Why ever not?"

"I have no desire to be a military wife. Coming here was a lark. And Stephen is the second son. He will inherit nothing. He is not a man of independent means, except for what the regiment gives to him, and that is pitiful. I would have to do without so much, and as I have learned since coming here, doing without does not suit me at all. No, I will not tell him of the babe. No one must ever know, Mercy. I wish to find a man who will provide for me as I wish to be provided for. Knowledge of my indiscretion would hamper my becoming well situated."

"I'm sorry, Sarah. I don't understand what you're talking about. But to give his child away—"

"I do not wish to have children, ever. This was a mistake. If I did not fear that ridding myself of it now might bring me death, I would do so this minute."

"I cannot believe—"

"No, you probably can't. You no doubt believe in love."

"Don't you?"

"No, I believe in being well taken care of." She squeezed Mercy's hand. "I don't suppose you'd consider coming with me, because quite honestly, I'm terrified."

Mercy thought of Captain Lyons—how he had rescued her and comforted her. She thought of how wonderful it had felt to be held in his arms, to inhale his masculine scent, to feel the warmth of his body penetrating his clothes and hers. She thought of his child, given away to someone who might not have a care for it. "Yes, I'll go with you."

Two weeks after the child was born, she'd placed him in Mercy's arms. "Do something with him. I care not what." The next day she'd disappeared, and Mercy had not seen her since. She'd taken John as her own, making a silent promise to Captain Lyons that his son would never be unloved, would never come to harm.

In Westcliffe's ballroom, she stared at the one person who had the power to shatter her promise.

Mercy opened her mouth to assure her that John was well and that he would remain so as long as Sarah remembered that she'd willingly given him up, when

Stephen's familiar hand landing on the small of her back stopped her.

"I've been looking everywhere for you, sweetheart. What say we . . . Sarah?"

Everything within Mercy—every hope, every dream, every desire—died. Stephen remembered nothing at all about her.

But apparently he *did* remember the woman who'd given birth to his son.

Mercy wanted to die right on the spot. The sight of Sarah had been enough to cause his memories to come flooding back. She despaired looking at him, at seeing the disgust and knowledge in his eyes. But when she did dare look, he was gazing on Sarah with fondness. It was as though a thousand swords were slashing into her heart, her soul.

"Sir Stephen," Sarah said, a delicate pleat beginning to form between her brows as her gaze darted between Stephen and Mercy. "Congratulations on your knighthood. Your mother must be delighted to have three titled sons."

"My mother is delighted about a good many things, Sarah."

"Modesty does not become you, Sir Stephen. And please, you must call me by the pet name you gave me." She looked at Mercy. "Fancy. It was a little joke between us, but I've begun to use it with some regularity. It suits better, don't you think, Sir Stephen?"

"It does indeed. I see you've met my wife."

All the blood drained from Sarah's—Fancy's—face, and her mouth opened slightly. "You're married."

"Not a word I ever expected to associate with myself, but yes. Mercy and I met in Scutari. She was one of Miss Nightingale's nurses."

"Yes, I know. That's where she and I met."

"In Scutari?" Stephen barely whispered. His fingers, still on Mercy's waist, spasmed, and she saw the devastating combination of panic and despair in his eyes.

He didn't remember Fancy! He had to have known her before. Of course. Fancy had mentioned his scandalous reputation, but Mercy had thought she spoke of gossip, not knowledge. The joy spiraling through her was unforgivable.

She could not leave him to flounder, to risk Fancy discovering the affliction that still embarrassed him.

"Stephen and I seldom talk of that time. Such harsh memories," Mercy said. "Do you remember how crammed together we were in the nurses' quarters?"

"Yes, of course," she said, but Mercy could see the wheels spinning in her mind as she tried to make sense of things. "Married," she repeated. "More congratulations are in order, it seems. When did this happen?"

"Not soon enough," Stephen said. He seemed to hesitate, then said, "We have a son."

"Do you?" Fancy asked, as though all breath had been pounded from her body. "It seems there is no end to the good fortune that has befallen you."

Mercy wished she could have a moment alone with Fancy to explain . . . before disaster had a chance to strike.

"And what of you, Fancy?" Stephen asked. "Who did you choose, for you wear too much jewelry not to have landed with someone?"

Mercy had no idea what he was on about, but Fancy

apparently did, because a fine blush crept up her cheeks. "Lord Dearbourne."

"He's a damned lucky man," Stephen said, "and he has the means to keep you in style."

"Yes, I am most fortunate that he has favored me."

The strains of a waltz filled the room. "If you'll excuse us, Fancy, my wife was saving this dance for me."

"Yes, it was so lovely to see you again."

"And you." Stephen took her gloved hand and pressed a kiss to her knuckles. "Take care of yourself, Fancy."

"Oh, yes." She seemed to struggling to speak past a clog of tears. "I will."

Mercy didn't think Stephen could guide her away quickly enough. She'd been holding her breath, fearful that Fancy might say something about John, might reveal that she'd given birth to him.

When he swept her onto the dance floor, he said in a low hiss, "God help me. She was in Scutari?"

She realized he'd been as tense as she, fearful that he'd give away his affliction. Perhaps tonight would be the only time that Fancy—why ever had he called her that?—would make an appearance in their lives and they could carry on as they'd been. Happy and content. Joyful.

"Yes," Mercy said, "but you seem to know her from sometime before. Were you friends?"

"In a manner of speaking. She was . . . one of the ladies who contributed to my notorious reputation."

"You were lovers." Even before Scutari.

He gave a brusque nod, and silence stretched taut between them.

"It seems a long time ago," he finally said.

"Did you love her?" Her heart cramped up waiting for his answer.

His gaze traveled over her face and finally settled on her eyes. "I didn't love any of them, Mercy. I was a cad. I cared only about pleasure, mine and theirs. No promises were ever made, none to be kept."

They dipped and swirled, and she realized his leg was truly healed now. It could support him, give him mobility. She wanted to remain in his arms forever, but the fine hairs on the nape of her neck rose . . . and she saw Fancy standing off to the side studying them speculatively, and Mercy feared her wish would not last.

"I don't understand how she could have been a nurse," he said finally. "She was not studying for it when I knew her."

"I don't know. There was an application process, an interview. She must have wanted very badly to go."

"Was she a good nurse?"

She laughed, trying to make light of things. "The men liked her, but I'm not certain it was her nursing skills that impressed them. She had the ability to make even our ugly black dresses look becoming."

"What might she ask that I should know?" he asked, and she detected the concern in his voice that he'd be unable to keep his affliction from her. "What might come up in conversation?"

"It's impossible to know. Perhaps it would be best if I am always near when you speak to her so I can fill in any emptiness between you." And could strive to steer all conversation away from John.

He angled his head thoughtfully, and all the worry that had been marring his features disappeared. "Is that a bit of jealousy I'm detecting?"

"No, of course not. I just . . . I know you prefer that people not know the full extent of your injuries. That's all."

"You're lying."

"I've never lied to you."

He arched a brow.

"Oh, all right. Perhaps I'm a little jealous."

"Good."

"Why good?"

"Because sometimes you're a bit too much of a saint. And I like it much better when you're wicked."

She gave him a saucy smile. "Well, then, tonight when we arrive home, I shall do all in my power to be wicked."

"You'll be too tired after all this celebrating and dancing."

"Oh, no, I am too curious."

"Curious? About what?"

"What it is like to have a knight in my bed."

His boisterous laughter echoed around them, made a few people stop to stare and smile. "My dear wife, I shall be only too glad to show you."

Tessa Seymour glided through the ballroom, her head held high, radiant joy making her feel much younger than her forty-seven years. One son possessed an earldom, another a dukedom, and now Stephen had gained a knighthood. Few mothers had sons as accomplished as she. For a terrified girl whose journey into adulthood had begun with a forced marriage to a man far older than she, she had not done too poorly for herself and her boys. Their welfare had always come first, at any cost. She suspected that was the reason she felt such an affinity for Mercy. She could not be faulted as a mother.

Nor as a wife either, Tessa suspected. Stephen was happier than she'd seen him in ages. Two years of ghosts he couldn't remember were no longer haunting his eyes. He walked with confidence again, no limp remaining as evidence of the wound in his thigh that had nearly taken him from her a second time.

She caught sight of Lynnford standing tall in a corner, observing the festivities. He'd come out of duty, as guardian to her sons, but she knew he would be leaving soon. A higher duty called. She'd once resented that he placed his family above hers. She'd been a silly girl then, full of childish dreams. Sometimes she missed that young girl.

Once she reached Lynnford, she wrapped her gloved fingers around his arm and leaned up to kiss his cheek, his scent filling her nostrils, still enticingly familiar after all these years. "I'm so glad you were able to share this day with us."

"I would not have missed it. I'm sorry Angela was too weary to attend."

"She and I must do the waters again. She seemed much stronger after our last visit there."

"Yes, I believe she was. You're a dear friend to her."

"And to you, I hope. You must know I am always here for anything you might require."

He gave a brusque nod and turned his attention to the gathering. When she looked at him, she saw Stephen. When she looked at Stephen, she saw Lynnford. It was a wonder others didn't comment on the similarities of their appearance.

"I thought the knighting was a nice ceremony," she said softly. "Brought tears to my eyes."

"You, who never cries."

"I cry. Just not where others can see."

He studied her for a moment before saying, "I apologize if I ever made you cry."

She tilted up her chin. "You did, but it was long ago, and I've since forgiven you."

They stood in silence for a long while. She could see Stephen waltzing with Mercy. They made such a lovely couple. As she'd thought earlier, Stephen appeared content. Mercy not so much. She seemed unnaturally pale in spite of the dancing, which had brought a rush of color to her cheeks. Tessa wondered what was going on there.

"He has surprised me," Lynnford said quietly, his gaze following in the same direction as hers. "I doubted he would ever become a man a father could be proud to call son. But he has achieved that end remarkably well."

She pursed her lips and gave him the hard glare she had on numerous occasions when it came to his handling of Stephen. "You were always more harsh with him than you were with the others."

"Perhaps instinctively I always knew he is my son. Why did you never say anything before you thought he was dead?"

"It was so long ago, Lynnie. We were young, and I was not as wise as I am now. Still you'd only just gotten married. Had declared your devotion to your countess. What would I have gained except to make you miserable? You were a man of honor—"

"Who bedded a married woman—"

"After her husband abandoned her bed. Westcliffe cared nothing for me. He had his heir, he had his mistress, who apparently was willing to do disgusting things I was not. You were a joy in my life. And your son was my greatest joy." She held up her hand. "Yes, I know, a mother should not have favorites, but God help me, I do."

He grinned. "You never apologize for yourself, do you?"

"I see no point in it. It is a frivolous use of time." She sobered. She wanted to tell him that she loved him, that she always had, she always would. But they were not words he'd welcome. From the moment he'd taken Angela to wife, he'd made it clear to Tessa that his loyalties would not be divided. His determination had only made her love him more. "I feel as though there is an ocean of things I should say to you about Stephen."

"As I said, I'm proud of him." He touched her cheek. "And I've always been proud of you. You hold a piece of my heart."

But only a piece. While Angela held the whole.

"Duchess."

Spinning around, she smiled brightly. "Leo. Lynnford and I were just discussing how proud we are of Stephen."

"As well you should be." Taking her hand, he brought her fingers to his lips, and she felt the heat of his mouth offering promises for later. She loved about him that he had no qualms whatsoever when it came to displaying where his affections lay. Any other man would have latched a challenging gaze on Lynnford as he staked his ownership, but Leo was not that sort. He gave all his attention to her, treated Lynnford as though he was nothing more than a bit of lint to be brushed away. "I was hoping I could entice you into a dance."

"I would be delighted." She turned back to Lynnford. "If you will be good enough to excuse me?"

"Of course. I must be off myself. Angela is no doubt waiting to hear news of the day." He, too, took her hand and pressed a kiss to her fingers. She hoped Leo didn't feel the shiver of longing that traveled through her. What surprised her was that it was not quite as strong as it had once been. Age, she supposed, and the passage of time.

"Do give her my best," she ordered.

"I will."

"And tell her that I shall be over to discuss with her when we may next do the waters."

"I know she'll look forward to seeing you." He nodded toward the man holding her other hand. "Leo, do take care with her."

"I always do." There was a possessiveness, a challenge to his tone that was not normally there.

After Lynnford strode away, she leaned in to Leo, welcomed the curling of his arm around her. The display was inappropriate, but then she had a reputation for the inappropriate. Now was not the time to worry about it overmuch. "He's proud of Stephen."

It was all she needed to say for Leo to understand what she meant, the undercurrent of her words: he was proud of his son. "Of course he is, sweetheart."

She tilted her head back to study him. "Do you think Stephen should know the truth about his father?"

Leaning down, he brushed a kiss over her brow. "Are you thinking of telling him?"

She closed her eyes. "I don't know. What if it should cause him to hate me?"

"Then he is not deserving of you as a mother."

She smiled at him. "You always know the right things to say."

"Then may I have that dance now?"

She gave him leave to escort her onto the dance area. He always managed to lighten the weight she carried on her shoulders, but this one remained, nonetheless. She would have to determine how best to unburden herself. But not tonight. She wanted nothing at all to ruin the night for Stephen.

After she and Stephen finished their dance, Mercy went in search of Fancy. She had to find her, talk with her, here, now. She spotted her quickly, standing near some fronds. Her nerves knotting, Mercy approached her. "I wondered if you might like to step out on the terrace for a bit of brisk air."

"I would. Thank you."

Once outside, they moved quietly to a corner where they would not be seen or heard.

"Your husband seems quite smitten with you," the woman who'd given birth to John said.

"I love him, Sarah."

"Fancy. I left Sarah in Paris."

Mercy nodded. "You left John as well. And me. With no word. For the longest I didn't know what to do, or if you were planning to return."

"I've never been very good at ciphering," Fancy said, "but I stood there watching you dance, striving to determine how it was that you *and* Stephen could have a son when it has been but six months since I last saw you. I was also considering the conversation that Stephen and I had and what was not said. Does Stephen know you are not the boy's mother?"

"I am John's mother. In my heart. From the moment you placed him in my keeping—"

"Oh, that's rich. I go through the pain and humiliation of bearing an illegitimate child and you reap the rewards by marrying his father, a knight of the realm."

"He wasn't a knight when I married him. You had no desire to marry him. You said so in Scutari. Besides, you are betrothed now, to a marquess—"

Fancy laughed harshly, an unhappy sound reverberating from her throat. "Betrothed? Wherever did you get that notion?"

"You said you were with him."

"As his mistress. He is my benefactor."

Mercy hardly knew what to say. Why would a woman choose being one man's mistress over being Stephen's wife?

"Don't look so shocked," Fancy said. "I'm the illegitimate daughter of a duke. No man with the means to provide for me as I wish to be provided for is going to want to take me to wife. And no man would take me as mistress if I came with the baggage of a child. A man needs to be reassured that a lady in my position knows what she's about and would not litter the world with his bastards."

Mercy couldn't believe the cold, calculating attitude. "But surely you cared for Stephen."

"He was fun. No more than that." She laughed lightly. "I can see you still don't understand. Darling, you wear a string of pearls. I am draped in diamonds."

But I have Stephen, Mercy thought. And he was worth

far more than baubles and frippery. And she had John.

Fancy turned away from her and gazed out on the lighted garden. "How does my son fare?"

"John is well."

"Give him a kiss for me tonight, would you?"

"Yes, of course."

"Well, I'd best get back to Dearbourne," Fancy said, spinning back around.

Mercy thought she saw a glistening in Fancy's eyes, but Fancy blinked them back so quickly, she couldn't be sure.

"Really, my dear, you shouldn't wear your heart on your sleeve. Even in Scutari, I knew where your affections lay."

"Why were you there?"

"For Stephen, of course. I'd known him in London, but I was not yet ready to give him up. I wasn't exactly honest about my experience and training, but I was still able to impress Miss Nightingale. Imagine my surprise, though, when I discovered the hospital where we would work was so far away from where the soldiers were fighting. As happy as Stephen was to have me near, once he returned to the regiment, there was no hope for it. I could not see him. It grew wearisome. Then, of course, I had to leave." She touched her white gloved hand to Mercy's face. "I think you are the only friend I ever had. I knew if you knew the child I carried was Stephen's that you'd go to Paris with me. Still, I misjudged you. I didn't think you'd use the child to land the father."

"It was not my intent," Mercy confessed earnestly. "I thought he was dead. I was returning John to his family."

"But you told them *you* were his mother. Why would you tarnish your reputation so?"

Mercy nodded with the weight of the shame of it. "I had fallen in love with John by then. I was afraid I'd not be able to remain in his life if they thought he was not mine. You won't tell Stephen . . . the truth, will you?"

"What sort of friend would I be if I did?"

She glided away, her movements so smooth and sensuous that it was as though her feet didn't even touch the ground. Now it was Mercy who turned and stared out at the garden. Why was she not calmed by Fancy's reassurance? Why did she feel that she was standing on a precipice and that one false step would send her spiraling over the edge, snatching from her both John and Stephen?

Chapter 19

Mercy awoke screaming his name.

Stephen had been lost in his own torment, visited by what he could not remember, which was no visitation at all really, just a bleak emptiness, so he was still awake, drawing comfort by feathering his fingers over her hair, when her shriek rent the night. She was already in his arms, having nestled there after a passionate session of lovemaking once they'd returned from London. The late hour hadn't mattered. They'd teased and taunted each other in the carriage on the journey back. It was a wonder they'd not ripped off their clothes in the entry hallway as soon as they'd closed the door behind them.

Now she struggled to free herself of his embrace. He only held her nearer.

"Mercy. Mercy. Sweetheart." He cooed, he whispered, he tenderly stroked her back, but she'd have none of it. She thrashed about, lost to the demons that tormented her. It had been weeks since they'd invaded her dreams. He'd begun to think that she'd conquered them. She was so strong, so determined that she put him to shame when it came to battling the irrefutable horrors of the past.

He had no doubt that he was responsible for her anguish tonight. His damned knighthood had reawakened all her dormant memories. The reason behind the accolades, his actions that were heralded as bravery. They all served as reminders of where she'd once been. It probably hadn't helped at all that he'd asked so many questions of Mercy concerning Fancy. He'd been stunned to see her at the ball Claire had arranged in his honor. Even more shocked to discover she'd been in the East, one of Miss Nightingale's angels. He'd have never thought she had the inclination to help others. He'd enjoyed her company immensely but he'd always known that she placed herself above all others. He could not reconcile the woman he'd known with the woman Mercy had told him about. And pestering her for information had no doubt served to bring to her mind all that *she*'d done, all *she*'d seen. All the men who had died while she looked on. How powerless she'd been. How little she'd been able to alter.

But she'd done so much good. He was certain of that. He'd read the accounts about Florence Nightingale. Mercy had been at her side. She'd done many of the same deeds. She'd walked through the wards carrying a lamp, tending to the sick and injured. Had tended to him.

He had no memory of it, but he could see her so clearly in his mind. She'd been wrong with her insistence that he couldn't re-create the memories. Perhaps they were not as vivid or as precise or as true as what he'd experienced. But still, he could envision her bending over his uncomfortable bed, wiping his sweating brow, giving him words of comfort. Compassion filled her. He didn't know how to grant her the same relief.

He would return his knighthood that second if it would release her from the bondage of this nightmare.

He trailed kisses over her face, repeated her name. Suddenly she was clutching him, her fingers digging into his sides, and he knew he'd be bruised come morning. But it didn't matter. His discomfort was nothing if it brought her peace.

"Take me," she gasped. "Please take me. Make me forget. Make me forget it all."

He kissed her as though he would die if he didn't. She responded as she had earlier, with fire and passion. She pushed on him, rolled him over onto his back, and straddled him. She rained kisses over his chest, did to him what he wished to do to her. He wanted to carry her to new heights, wanted to cast her demons into perdition.

It was not fair that one such as she should be so tormented.

He threaded his fingers through her coppery hair. Longer now than it had once been, not as long as it would one day be. He wanted to see it spread out over his chest, his groin. When she was over him like this, he wanted her hair to provide a curtain that closed out the world.

Even as the thoughts scurried through his mind, he knew he would be content if she were bald. Nothing was more precious than this moment. The past, the future, what did they matter, when every nerve was centered on what she was doing? The caress of her fingers, the swirl of her tongue. The heat of her mouth enveloped him.

"Christ!"

He nearly came off the bed. His back arched, his eyes

squeezed shut, his fingers dug into her shoulders, and he forced them to loosen their hold. He didn't want to bruise her, but he needed to touch her. He opened his eyes to the sight of his angel eagerly ravishing him. Sweet Lord. Fiery molten lava pumped through his veins. Each deep breath into his lungs brought the musky scent of sex: his and hers. She was aroused by what she was doing as much as he was. He wondered if he might die of the sensations. His heart beat so forcefully that he was certain she had to feel the pounding through his body. She was driving him to madness.

"Enough! Enough, Mercy." Reaching down he lifted her. "I need to feel you around me." His voice was hoarse, his throat felt raw.

Grabbing her hips, he impaled her. She was hot, so unbelievably hot. Scalding. She cried out, not in pain, but in ecstasy. Tangling her fingers in her own hair, she arched back and rode him. He pumped ferociously. He cradled her breasts, relishing the weight in his palms. She ran her hands over his chest. Then she cupped the back of his head and kissed him, deeply, thoroughly, in near desperation.

It occurred to him that perhaps she was still locked in the throes of the nightmare. Never had she been so wild, so bold, so . . . imaginative.

Their grunts and moans echoed around them. Everything within him tautened, demanded release—

She arched back, calling out his name, her body closing in around him with the force of a vise. Unbearable pleasure ripped through him. He jerked, pumped, shattered.

Spasms shook him as he fell back from somewhere he'd never been before, a height he'd never before attained. He swallowed hard, his breathing harsh and heavy.

She flopped down on top of him, and he felt warm liquid running in rivulets along his chest. Her rasping sobs tore at his heart.

"Mercy, are you crying? Sweetheart, did I hurt you?" He'd rather lose the left arm she'd told him he'd fought so hard to keep, or his leg, before hurting her.

"I'm going to lose you," she whimpered. "I know it. You're going to leave me."

Working his hands beneath her, he cradled her face, forcing her to look at him. Tears filled her whiskey eyes, eyes he wanted to gaze into when he took his last breath.

"Mercy, sweetheart. You're not going to lose me. And I'll never leave you. I've fallen in love with you."

They were words he'd never spoken to another woman. Tensing, he waited for thunder to boom and lightning to strike, for surely the angels were laughing at his downfall. He, who had always been so damned careful not to involve his heart, was holding his breath, waiting for her to—

"Say something."

She opened her mouth, closed it. Her eyes misted. Her delicate throat worked as she swallowed. A bright smile formed. Joy turned the whiskey to gold. She released a light laugh. "I love you, too."

He grinned and threaded his fingers through her hair. "I know. You told me when you were so very angry at me that day in the library. Terrified me, you know. Saying the words to you now. They seem inadequate somehow. They should be larger, bigger to encompass all that I feel for you."

"They're perfect." She laughed again, buried her face in the curve of his neck. "I want to run through a field, climb a mountain, swim an ocean. You have filled me with such joy."

"Give me a few more moments and I shall fill you with something else entirely yet again."

She jerked upright, her cheeks burning a bright red that almost matched her hair. "Were you shocked by what I did? I don't know what possessed me."

"Feel free to *shock* me anytime."

Her laughter touched him once more, as soft as the tinkling of glass bells. "I rather enjoyed it."

"As did I."

She gnawed on her lower lip. "Jeanette tried to tell me . . . but I didn't believe her. But I know now that I would do anything at all for you. Anything. I thought I loved you in Scutari, but what I have come to feel for you since we married . . . it knows no bounds. It's terrifying and yet, and yet it makes me feel so remarkably safe."

He studied her beloved face. "Then why the nightmare? Did all the talk today of my supposed exploits bring it all rushing back to the surface?"

"It doesn't matter. I think I've banished them for good. You're mine now. And I know nothing will ever change that."

Chapter 20

L ady Lyons?"

Mercy thought she'd never grow accustomed to the new name. She was sitting on the floor playing with John in the nursery at Roseglenn, playing as much as she could with someone who was more interested in his hands and his feet than anything she could wave before his eyes. She glanced up at the serving girl. "Yes, Winnie."

"You've a visitor. A Miss Whisenhunt. She says it's most important that she speak with you."

Icy dread slithered down Mercy's spine. Stephen had gone to London to see to some matter. She wanted Fancy gone before he returned. She scrambled to her feet with such urgency that she nearly lost her balance. "Where is she?"

"In the front parlor, my lady."

Mercy rushed out of the nursery and down the stairs. It didn't matter why Fancy was here. Stephen loved Mercy. He had told her so. He had *shown* her so. They were a family, the three of them. Nothing would break them apart.

She came to a halt in the hallway near the front

parlor. She patted her hair into place, wishing for the first time that she'd not cut it, that it was still as long and glorious as it had once been. It had outshone Fancy's. She pinched her cheeks to ensure she had color. She straightened her spine. She felt as though she was preparing to face an army of Cossacks. She was prepared to win.

With a confidence she didn't exactly feel, she strode into the parlor. Fancy was standing near a glass case, studying the various figurines that adorned it. Turning, she smiled, one that didn't reach her eyes.

"I hope you will forgive me for intruding, *my lady*, but I have an urgent matter with which I'm certain you can help me."

Mercy didn't quite trust that smile. "I assisted you once before, Fancy, in Paris. I'm not certain I have anything else to offer you."

She tilted her head slightly. "Not even tea?"

Mercy felt everything within her tauten. Why the deuce was Fancy truly here? She had the power to tear asunder everything that Mercy had built. As calmly as possible, determined not to give any hint as to her trepidation, she wandered over to the wall and yanked on the bellpull. When the serving girl appeared, she said, "Tea please."

"And biscuits," Fancy said. She held up her hand, showing a small amount of space between thumb and forefinger. "As well as little cakes if you have them." When the maid left, she looked at Mercy. "I do so enjoy sweet things."

"What precisely is it that you want?"

Ignoring Mercy, Fancy lifted a small clock from the mantel, studied it, and set it back down. "You do have a ery nice residence. I'd have not thought Stephen would so well for himself."

"It's Ainsley's. He allows us to live here through his good graces. He can take it away at a moment's notice."

"But he won't. He's the good brother. The one who watched out for the other two, even though he's the youngest. Stephen resented his brothers. Their titles, their power, Ainsley's wealth. That's the reason he worked so hard to excel in the bedchamber. He wanted to outshine his brothers in some regard, so why not pleasure? Has he shared all this with you?"

"What has this to do with anything?" she asked impatiently.

"Ah, our tea."

Mercy thought she was going to crawl out of her skin after she had poured the tea and was forced to watch Fancy prepare it. How could a spoon that moved that slowly stir up anything at all? She knew Fancy was being deliberately difficult. If she didn't have so much to risk losing, she'd tell her to go to the devil.

Finally, at last, Fancy sat back and took a sip of tea. "Delightful." She licked her lips. "I've been thinking about our situation."

The words sent a frisson of unease through Mercy. "What situation?"

Fancy smiled benignly. "You have something that belongs to me."

"John does not belong to you. You walked away from him."

"But I was distraught after learning that his father had died. It broke my heart to look upon John and to see his father and to know he would never again be in my life."

Somehow, Mercy prevented her eyes from rolling. "You think that tale will gain you sympathy?"

"More so than yours. You lied, deceived, and used a babe for your own gain."

"No. You guessed right last night. I did wear my heart on my sleeve, and I loved Stephen then, and I love him now. We're happy. The three of us. John, Stephen, and I. Why would you take that from us?"

"Is it fair to say that you've discovered that a night in Stephen's bed is worth any *price*?"

"Is that the reason you're here, that you're making all these innuendoes and claims? For payment?"

"Oh, Mercy, you must understand my position."

Fancy picked up a tiny cake and popped it into her mouth. Mercy prayed she would choke on it. She'd thought her beautiful when she first met her. How looks could deceive.

Fancy swallowed the cake, sipped her tea . . . continued to breathe. Pity.

"I never expected Stephen to do so well for himself, but he was fun. I had no desire to marry him. I wanted someone who could offer me . . . more. When I realized I was with child, sentiment and fear prevented me from ridding myself of it before it was born. Ambition prevented me from keeping it."

"Him," Mercy snapped. "He is a him. Not an *it*."

"Spoken like a true mother. You do know that a marriage built on a foundation of secrets will surely crumble."

"What the devil do you want?" Mercy demanded.

"My plan had always been to serve as some lord's paramour, to be pampered and cared for, to warm his bed. Hence, Lord Dearbourne. Unfortunately, I failed

to take into account that not all men are as talented in
the bedchamber as your husband. Most are bumbling
oafs."

"Then leave Dearbourne and find another."

"He is my third since my return from Paris. I am
weary of the hunt, and I'm sure you are weary of waiting to learn why I am here." Setting her cup aside, she
leaned forward, determination and a hard glint in her
eyes. "I've given a good deal of thought to our little
secret, and I'm certain you wish it to remain between
us. I want to live in luxury without requiring a man.
Four thousand pounds a year should do it."

Mercy dared not understand what she was hearing. The consequences were too dire. She fought to
hold on to her confidence, not to give any hint that
she suspected where this was leading, for surely, even
this hoyden would not go there. "Why are you telling
me this?"

"Why, my dear girl, you are naïve. I expect you to
give it to me."

"We were friends. I wiped your brow when you were
nauseous. I helped to deliver . . ."

"My babe?" Fancy asked with an arched eyebrow.

How had she so badly misjudged this woman? She
was a nurse. She'd gone to the Crimea. She'd attended
the wounded and sick. Stephen had cared for her. How
could he have cared for someone as vile as this? How
could Mercy have befriended her?

"I don't have that sort of money," she said, her mouth
suddenly so dry that she could barely form the words.
"I had no dowry. My weekly allowance is a pittance."
It sufficed for her, she wished for no more. Her needs
were few. But this request was beyond the pale.

"Surely you have a household allowance. Steal from that. Sell the silver. Pawn your jewelry. I don't give a damn how you manage it, just make it happen." She came to her feet in a rustle of silk and satin. "I don't expect it all at once. You may make weekly payments. But make no mistake. I want it. I want it all. Or your husband will learn who the true mother of his son is."

"I am the true mother of his son!"

The rebuttal had lodged in Mercy's throat, to go unspoken.

She walked briskly through the garden, searching for answers. It was a gray day, which mirrored her mood. The dark clouds blocked out the sun. It somehow seemed significant, as though the light would no longer shine in her life.

What the devil was she to do? Four thousand a year. She was given fifteen pounds each week for her own pleasures and enjoyments. She could ask for twenty. She doubted Stephen would deny her. But she would still be far short of what Fancy demanded. Where was she to get it?

She supposed she could find bits of silver here and there in rooms seldom used. Knickknacks that wouldn't be missed. She felt as though she was betraying Stephen, who had admitted that he loved her.

She'd never expected to truly own his heart, to hear those sweet words pass through his lips. His words, so earnestly spoken, had pushed away the last cobwebs of her nightmare. In it, she'd been crawling over a battlefield littered with dismembered limbs. John had been on the other side. She'd needed to get to him, to save him. Then Stephen had swept him up and begun to carry him away. She'd called after them. But they'd ignored her. Both of them. And she'd known once they disappeared into the blackness that hovered at the edge of the field, she'd never see them again.

Now she feared if she confessed the hell she'd plummeted into that Stephen would leave her in truth. And it would be far more painful than in a dream world. And he would take John with him. His son.

"Ah, there you are."

She spun around to marvel at her husband striding toward her. The bleakness of the day could not dim her joy at seeing him. The wind tousled his hair. He must have left his hat inside. He looked young and carefree. Happy.

"How was your business in London?" she asked.

"Incredibly boring. Ainsley wanted to go over some accounts." He snaked an arm around her and drew her up against him. "And all I wanted was to be in bed with my wife."

He kissed her soundly. Passion immediately sparked. She loved the feel of her body pressed against his. She did not want to lose this. She did not want to lose him.

When he drew back, his blue eyes were sparkling brighter than any jewel. "And as I was in Town . . ." Reaching into his pocket, he withdrew a small black box and held it toward her.

She hesitated.

"Come along. Open it. I certainly have no use for it."

Taking it carefully, as though it were as delicate as an egg shell, she again hesitated. Slowly, she opened it to reveal a locket in the shape of a heart. On the back was inscribed, *With love, Stephen and John.*

Tears welled and a sob broke free.

"I had hoped it would please you," he said, his voice laced with amusement, and she knew he took satisfaction in her reaction. That he had meant to touch her deeply, knew he had accomplished his goal.

"I am pleased. So pleased." She wound her arms around his neck, held him close. "Nothing could have been more perfect."

She would do anything to retain this perfection, this idyllic life that she'd sacrificed so much to obtain. This residence contained so many small *things*. Surely, surely, no one would miss a few tiny, insignificant items.

Chapter 21

Sir Stephen."

Stephen glanced up to see Spencer standing there. The doors in this residence were so well oiled that he seldom heard them opening and closing. Spencer seemed to be able to glide around the manor without his feet ever touching the floor. His quietness was unnatural. "Spencer."

"I hate to disturb you, sir—"

"Then don't." He was weary of seeing sheep in the fields. He wanted horses. Good, strong horses for the regiments. Talks were under way to end this damned slaughter going on in the East but there would always be wars, and soldiers needed dependable mounts. He and Ainsley had argued about it. "No need to change from what works," Ainsley had said.

No need to have your brother sitting on his arse all day looking over ledgers.

Stephen wanted to map out a strategy that would show that his plan could work. He'd sold his commission. He had a good portion of the salary the army had paid him. It was a start, but he would still need to borrow some money in order to purchase his own land, his own place, his own horses. Make a go of it.

He remembered what the military had taught him until that afternoon he had tea with Claire. But what had he learned in battle? What had he learned during the campaign? If only he had that knowledge, then maybe he could be of some use, could remain a military man. But it was gone.

Horses, though, he'd always known horses. He could do something with those.

He glanced back up. Spencer was still there. "So although you hate to disturb me, you're going to do it all the same. What the devil is it?"

"The silver, sir. Some of it has gone missing."

"That's a household matter. Discuss it with Lady Lyons."

"I have, sir. She is of the opinion that information I have catalogued in ledgers is incorrect or that items have simply been misplaced."

"If that is her opinion, then it must be so." He returned to scrawling out his ideas. Horses, workers, trainers. With impatience, he looked at Spencer.

The man, slender as a reed, with a face dominated by a large, blade-like nose, was staring at a spot somewhere over Stephen's head. His lips were pursed, his posture so stiff that he may as well be laid out in a coffin.

"Spit it out, Spencer."

"With all due respect, Sir Stephen, I believe Lady Lyons is the culprit."

Everything within Stephen stilled and a rash of fury shot through him. "You are accusing my wife of thievery?"

"I fear so, sir, yes."

"She cannot steal what belongs to her."

"With all due respect, sir, it belongs to the . . . duke."

"Think very carefully before you speak. Why do you think it is her?"

"I can vouch for all the servants. Their loyalty. Their honesty. The newest member of the staff has still been here for three years. Nothing has gone missing until . . . very recently."

Stephen leaned back, seething with anger that he wasn't quite sure where to place. Through a hole in the wall perhaps. With his fist. Or perhaps against Spencer's nose. "Perhaps the nurse, Jeanette, is the culprit."

Spencer cleared his throat, blushed, studied the rug beneath his feet. Finally, he looked up and drew back his shoulders. "I know Miss Jeanette extremely well— *extremely well* if you catch my meaning—and I know it is not she."

"And I know my wife extremely well, and it is not her. Even hint at so ludicrous a claim again and you'll be sacked."

"Yes, sir. Understood. What shall I do about the missing silver?"

"Find it. Replace it. I don't care."

"Very good, sir."

He retreated on those damned silent, irritating feet. Stephen tossed his pen aside, pushed the papers beyond reach. It was not Mercy. He knew that, but his brother had entrusted all of his damned possessions to Stephen. Shoving his chair back, he stood and went in search of his wife. All of Ainsley's ancestors glared down on him. Perhaps he should ask Westcliffe to loan him a portrait of their father. Something to make the residence a little more his. He supposed he could get one of his mother from Leo. The man had painted an ungodly number. Stephen was surprised how different each one looked, as though the artist saw a different facet to the duchess each time he painted her.

Taking the steps two at a time, Stephen went upstairs to the nursery. Mercy was sitting on the floor. Not the ideal place for a lady, but it seemed to suit the part of her that was a mother. She moved a wooden block beyond John's reach. The boy crawled to it on his belly and just as he reached for it, she placed it a bit further beyond his grasp.

"Are you tormenting my son?" he asked.

Looking up, she smiled. "He's learning to crawl. I'm simply encouraging him to try harder."

The nurse was sitting in a chair busy with a bit of needlework. "Jeanette, perhaps you should go have a spot of tea."

"Yes, sir." She popped up and hastily rushed out.

Mercy studied him questioningly. "Is something amiss?"

Stephen sat on the floor, snatched up the block, and placed it within John's reach. The boy closed his pudgy fingers around it, then rolled over, and began to gnaw on it.

"Is he hungry?"

"No, he just likes to chew on things," she told him, but her voice was laced with wariness.

"Did you know that Jeanette and Spencer . . . ?" He rubbed behind his ear.

She studied him for a moment and then her eyes widened. "No. Is he courting her?"

"I don't know how much courting is involved, but I suspect there's a great deal of mischief."

"Is that allowed between servants?"

"Probably not, but who are we to point fingers?"

Her cheeks flushed red. "Quite right."

He took her hand, turned it over, and trailed his fingers over the rough spots that still remained, no doubt from all the scrubbing she'd done in the Crimea. "Spencer thought I should know that some silver is missing."

She pursed her lips. "I told him not to bother you with it. I've never seen the pieces he is concerned about. They may have been gone forever. This house has so many useless items, it's like a little shop of trinkets. So something went missing—"

"Something silver."

"Do you think it important?"

"I think Ainsley will not be pleased to know things have gone missing."

"What are we to do if they were gone before we even arrived?"

"Keep a closer watch on the servants, will you?"

"Yes, of course. Do you think everything in this house is catalogued?"

"Knowing Ainsley, probably. Although I'm sure there are a few things here and there that were overlooked. You are correct. There is an inordinate number of things to collect dust. He could probably let half his servants go if he'd get rid of some of this stuff."

The block suddenly landed on his chin. "Oh, aren't you a strong fellow! Wanting some attention, are you?"

He lifted him up, held him high, studying the features that he thought resembled him not at all. Although he did have his father's smile. "I think his eyes are changing their shade."

"No, I'm certain it's just the way the light is coming in through the windows."

"Perhaps. I'm thinking of getting him a horse."

"Now?"

"Soon. A small one. A pony. When do you think he'll be ready to ride?"

She laughed. He so enjoyed her laughter. "Not for a good long while yet."

"What of his mother? Will she go for a ride with me?"

Her answer came with an impish smile and a promise for flirtation once they were away from the residence. It amazed him that as much as they were together, he still anticipated each moment of being alone with her.

It was two weeks later when Ainsley came to call. Stephen had never seen his brother look so somber.

"What's troubling you? Is it Mother?" he asked as he got up from his desk and poured his brother a glass of whiskey.

"No." He downed the drink. "Best pour yourself one. You're not going to like what I have to say."

And he knew, damn it. He knew. "Spencer notified you of the missing silver."

"I am the one who pays for his services."

"I'll have him gone by morning."

"I suggest you wait until I've had my say."

The coach wheels whirred through the moonless night as Stephen and Ainsley traveled to London. Stephen had told Mercy that Ainsley had a problem with which he needed assistance. Her eyes held a combination of suspicion and curiosity. Without words he'd told her that all would be well.

He could only hope it would be so as the streetlamps of London came into view.

"Today it was two silver candlesticks, an urn, and an assortment of smaller items. From one of the seldom-used guestrooms. How your wife learned where to fence my property is beyond me."

"What is beyond me is why you have me managing your estate when you don't trust me with it. You have damned servants spying on us."

"Spencer reported to Mercy that the silver went a-missing and she had no interest in pursuing the matter. He went to you, and you also failed to understand the implications. So, of course, he wrote me with his concerns."

"And then you had my wife followed?"

"Be grateful that is all I did. I could have had her arrested."

"For stealing candlesticks?"

"They have hung men for less."

Stephen was seething. He should have simply confronted Mercy with his brother's accusation at the residence. He was certain there was a logical explanation. If she needed more money, why did she not simply tell him? He would have arranged it. It might have galled to go to either of his brothers, but they were both wealthy men. They could have accommodated a request.

"After she gets her blunt," Ainsley continued, "she meets Fancy in Cremorne Gardens and passes the money on to her."

"I think you see trouble where there is none,"

Stephen said, trying to keep his voice even, to give the appearance that he wasn't bothered. But he was. It was shortly after he was knighted that Mercy had begun going into London every Tuesday to shop. Once he'd offered to join her, but she'd insisted that she needed a little time alone.

His first instinct had been that she was seeing a gentleman—but when would she have met him to arrange the assignation? Besides, it was a ludicrous thought. Mercy didn't have a deceiving bone in her body.

"She and Fancy were together in the East—at Scutari," Stephen continued. "Mercy sometimes has nightmares. I'm certain she is merely trying to talk it out. Perhaps they are commiserating together. There are a thousand explanations. We should have just asked her."

"My man estimates that Mercy is selling enough silver and other items that she is able to give Fancy seventy pounds each week. That's almost four thousand a year."

"Maybe Fancy is in some sort of debt, and Mercy is assisting her."

"With Dearbourne as her benefactor? The man is almost as wealthy as I am. He would grant her anything she damned well wanted to keep her satisfied and writhing in his bed."

"I don't like this skulking about behind Mercy's back. I should have just asked her." The words repeated a familiar refrain that he'd been singing ever since he reluctantly climbed into the coach with Ainsley.

They'd not drawn the curtains. Ainsley sat in the corner opposite him, a scepter in the darkness, staring out the window. The light from the streetlamps they passed darted in and out, briefly outlining the sharp planes of his brother's face, the set of his strong jaw, his determination. While Ainsley had always acted older, he'd still held the physical appearance of youth. When had that wandered away?

He possessed a mysteriousness now, as though the shadows welcomed him as lord. It was an odd thought, a strange realization. Stephen thought he knew Ainsley well. He was beginning to suspect he didn't know him at all.

"So who is this fellow you hired to spy on my wife?"

"Someone who does the occasional odd job for me."

"And you trust him?"

"With my life."

"Just as I trust my wife."

"If you did, you'd not be in this coach." Ainsley's gaze came to bear hard on him, and it was Stephen who now glared out the window.

The scar on the side of his face throbbed. It had been ages since he'd felt it at all. Even his leg had begun to ache, as though whatever miracle had settled in to lessen his hurts was turning into mist and drifting away. He should order the damned coach turned about.

Instead he stayed as he was, rigid and stiff, his mind wandering over the past six months, and wishing to God the memories recently created were enough to fill in the emptiness left by those he'd lost.

The coach rolled to a stop in front of a terraced house with an elegant façade. The rent would have been a pretty penny, but as Ainsley had pointed out, Dearbourne had an abundance of pretty pennies to shower on his mistress.

Ainsley disembarked and stared back at Stephen.

"The reports I've read of your exploits indicate you weren't a coward."

Stephen studied the exterior of the building. It suddenly seemed foreboding. A bad idea to enter it. "Why are you insisting upon this?"

"Because I believe you need to know the truth."

"And you already know it?"

"No. Not everything."

"What is it you suspect?"

Ainsley sighed deeply and spoke as somberly as one might at a funeral. "You've been swindled."

"Of what, for God's sake? I have little enough—"

"Your heart."

Standing in the grand entryway, at that moment, Stephen despised his brother. He'd always resented him, welcomed the opportunity to best him at everything possible, but he'd never loathed him with a passion that had him trembling. Every muscle tensed in order not to reveal his reaction. His leg ached, and he wished he'd brought his walking stick. He was not going to limp into this preposterous interview, or whatever the devil it was that Ainsley had arranged.

He heard the quiet footfalls on the stairs and glanced up to see Fancy, packaged in red silk, gliding down them. Her ebony hair, still abundantly thick, was pinned up in an elegant style that revealed the sensual slope of her neck. She was designed to attract a man's attention and clasp it close until she tired of him. The blue of her eyes was so deep and rich as to appear violet. He'd never seen eyes her shade before he'd met her. They were exotic, enticing. They promised a man heart-thundering, bone-melting passion.

She'd become a courtesan of the highest regard. Each sensual movement of her body confirmed it. He'd taught her well. He could see Ainsley struggling to remain immune. Oddly, Stephen found himself occupied by a rather strange thought: Why the devil hadn't she shorn her hair while she was in the East?

"Your Grace," she said softly, with a curtsy. "Sir Stephen. What a surprise and a pleasure that you've come to call. My benefactor will be arriving shortly, so I have not much time to visit. How may I be of service?"

Stephen glared at Ainsley. "This was your bloody idea."

Fancy's eyes widened slightly, and she indicated another room. "Please make yourselves comfortable in the parlor. I'll ring for tea."

"This isn't exactly a social call," Ainsley said. "But it would be a good idea to go into the parlor and close the doors."

Stephen couldn't recall ever seeing Fancy disconcerted, but she gave a good show of appearing nonplussed as she escorted them into the parlor. As soon as the doors were closed, Ainsley's gentlemanly façade slipped away and he attacked.

"We're aware that you're meeting Lady Lyons every Tuesday afternoon at Cremorne Gardens. We're also aware that the purpose of the encounter is so that she may pay you a handsome sum. What silence is she paying you to keep?"

Fancy visibly paled, her hands shook, and her eyes misted over as she looked at Stephen. "I'm so sorry." Her voice broke. "I should have stood up to her, but she threatened to destroy me if I told you the truth."

"And what truth is that?" Stephen asked, already weary of the theatrics.

"I gave birth to a son in Paris. It was a difficult birth. Your wife stole him from me when I was too weak to stop her. The boy she claims is hers, your son . . . he is mine."

Chapter 22

Stephen stood beside the crib, staring down at his son. It was long past midnight. He'd awoken the nurse and told her to find comfort elsewhere. He was just drunk enough after stopping at the club with Ainsley to not give a damn about his rudeness.

His mind was foggy from too much drink and the red haze of betrayal. So much made sense. Her encouraging him not to remember the past. Had they been involved at all? Had he ever taken her to his bed? Not according to Fancy.

So little made sense. Fancy had told them that she'd been taking the money Mercy offered because she feared if she didn't Mercy wouldn't believe her claims that she'd not reveal that she was John's mother. Mercy was checking on her, had hired someone to keep watch on her activities. In addition, she took the money because she was terrified that Mercy would turn on her, would destroy her as she threatened.

"I must prepare for a rainy day because when it comes it will be a raging storm."

She'd wept when she'd recounted how she'd awoken

one morning to find the babe gone. "I should have known she'd taken it to use to her advantage."

He'd almost retorted that John wasn't an "it" —something Mercy would have no doubt jumped on like a bird on a bug.

The boy awoke with wide eyes and a wail—just as his mother had on numerous nights. Horrors from the war, she'd claimed. Or had it been guilt that had prodded her restless nights?

Stephen touched his finger to John's cheek. "Shhh, now. All will be right soon."

The child quieted.

"You know my voice, don't you? You know who I am. Do you know your mother, I wonder? Your true mother."

"I didn't know you were home."

His body, traitor that it was, reacted instantly to the sleepy rasp of her voice. His heart felt like a painful block of ice. He didn't turn. He couldn't. Every nerve ending he possessed might be calling out for him to take her in his arms, but he wouldn't. He never would again.

"What are you doing?" she asked softly, coming up behind him, flattening her palm to his back. He stiffened at the familiar touch that had the power to send him beyond the edge of desire.

"Studying my son's eyes."

"I think they're exactly like yours."

"I think they favor his mother's more. A subtle difference in blue. Almost violet."

Her fingers jerked against his back, right before her hand fell away. He turned to face her then. She appeared drained of blood, almost as white as the silk of her nightdress.

"I know everything, Mercy, *everything*."

* * *

His voice was as frigid as the winters in the Crimea. It froze the blood in her veins. The hatred and disgust in his eyes shattered her heart. He couldn't know, he couldn't possibly.

"You remember?" she whispered.

He released a harsh laugh. "I only just realized that there is always a frisson of fear accompanying those words whenever you voice them. Now I know why. No, my little cunning wife, I do not remember my time in the Crimea. I do not remember you."

She forced out the words. "She told you."

"In spite of your threat to destroy her. Try to carry through on it, and it is I who will destroy you."

He made no sense. "I don't understand. What are you talking about?"

"I know, Mercy, I know that you stole the babe—"

"What? No, she abandoned John, left him with me one morning never to return. She wanted nothing to do with him."

She thought she detected a dimming in his anger and hope flared like a newly lit flame.

"Then why didn't you tell me this in the beginning?" he demanded, his voice still harsh, hurt.

She wanted to touch him, to comfort him, to soothe him. But he was not touchable. Everything in his stance yelled for her to retreat, to steer clear of him. But she could not. For John's sake, for her love of him, she would face down Lucifer himself.

"Because I was afraid you'd take him from me, and I love him so very, very much. I could not love him more if I had, in fact, given birth to him."

"You lied, Mercy. Our whole marriage is based on lies."

"No!" She reached out to touch him, jerked back her hand, curled her fingers until her nails bit into her palms. John began crying. The child had to be sensing the tension shimmering between her and Stephen. It was thick enough to pierce with a bayonet. "I never lied to you. Not once. I never claimed to have given birth to John. I only said I was his mother. In my heart, the words were true."

"Lies. Dress them up as you will, deny it if you want, but no honesty exists between us. You forced me to marry you."

Frantically, she shook her head. "I never demanded that you marry me."

"But you ensured that I would ask. With your innocence and your constant nearness. Were the nightmares even real, or just a means to get me into your bed?"

John was wailing now, his screams for attention making it difficult to think, to determine how best to convince him that she'd not come to him with ulterior motives.

"How can you doubt me so? How can you think so poorly of me?"

"You never wanted me to remember. You did nothing to help me remember!" He hit his balled fist on the side of the crib.

John shrieked. Mercy had enough. She shoved Stephen aside and lifted John into her arms, cuddling him close.

"Answer me this, did I ever make love to you in Scutari?" he asked.

Knowing what it would cost her, the dear price she would pay, still she could not lie to him. So she said nothing.

He barked out harsh laughter. "That's the reason you didn't want me to remember. Because then I would know that you were not his mother, that this wondrous night you spoke of was nothing but fiction."

"It was real. It happened. You stayed with me, you comforted me. We just didn't—" She shook her head. "It was all innocent."

"Damn you, damn you to hell for giving me a false memory. You have a week to say good-bye to him, and then I want you gone," Stephen commanded, his voice seething with barely controlled rage.

Mercy went numb with disbelief. "You're banishing me?"

"From my life and his. Fancy is his mother. By God, she shall have him back."

"And you? You are what she wants. Now that you are knighted, now that she may be a lady. She cares not one whit for this child."

"She claims differently. And she will help me remember. She will tell me everything of our time in the East. Memories will spark. I will regain what I have lost."

"Why do you believe her and not me?"

"Because I knew her before I left for the Crimea. I knew her well. You, madam, I know not at all."

He spun on his heel and charged from the room as though the Russians waited in the hallway to engage him in battle. She wanted to call after him, rush after him, grab him—

But her battered pride kept her rooted to the spot. With tears pouring down her face, she crushed John to her. Stephen had ripped out her heart. And in a week, it would be irrevocably lost to her when her dear, sweet child was taken from her arms.

Chapter 23

Stephen left orders with three footmen and two housemaids that one of them was to be watching Mercy at all times, and under no circumstances was John to leave the residence. He didn't trust her any farther than he could throw her.

He didn't trust himself either. Not to crawl back to her, not to curl around her and apologize, not to forgive her. So he'd taken himself to London, to Ainsley's residence, where he could indulge in fine liquor and brood to his heart's content. He knew he'd been rash in giving her a full week to say good-bye. He should have given her a day. An hour. Half that.

Damnation, he wanted her gone because she preyed on his mind. How could he have come to love such a deceitful wench?

"This residence does have other rooms, you know," Ainsley said as he strode across the library and dropped into the chair across from Stephen.

Stephen hoisted his glass, downed its contents, and refilled it. "This room suits."

"You've been here for three days. You're starting to reek."

Leaning forward, elbows on his knees, Stephen studied the whiskey, the color of her eyes. He would always think of her when he indulged in his favorite drink. "Irony. I finally have something that I wish to forget, and I don't think I'll be able to."

"Mercy?"

He lifted his gaze to his brother's before returning it to study the glass. "Her eyes are this color, you know. When I hold it up to the light"—he demonstrated—"I can see her happy. And when I bring it back to the shadows, I can see the pain that I inflicted on her with our final parting."

"You're not going to see her again?"

He shook his head. "I left instructions with Spencer. He's to give her a thousand pounds, put her in a carriage, deliver her to London, and let her make her own way."

"What of Fancy?"

"I shall move her into Roseglenn."

"Without benefit of marriage?"

"A divorce is not easily obtained."

"Is that what you desire?"

"I want to be rid of her."

Ainsley scraped the edge of his thumb over the arm of the chair, creating an irritating rasping that Stephen fought to ignore. "What if . . . she was telling the truth?"

"About?"

"About Fancy leaving the boy with her."

"It would be impossible to prove. So it is one woman's word against another's."

"You choose to believe Fancy?"

"She may be a bit o'muslin, but she's always been honest. Mercy lied about her relationship to the child;

she led me to believe we had a night together, which we did not. She deceived me into marrying her."

"I don't think it would be impossible to find out what really happened in Paris. I could send a man over, have him make inquiries. Jeanette might know where they resided."

"It's been months. Who would remember her?"

"A woman with hair the unusual shade of hers? She may not be a great beauty, but she is hardly forgettable."

"And yet I forgot her."

"You forgot everything."

Stephen narrowed his eyes, studied his brother, who had once again taken to scratching at the chair. He'd never known Ainsley to be uncomfortable. Nervous. It didn't signify. "Damn it. You've already sent a man."

"I didn't see the harm."

"Why are you trying to prove her right? You've mistrusted her from the beginning."

"From the beginning I sensed that something was off. I couldn't put my finger on what it was. So yes, I distrusted her. Yes, I was searching for proof that my instincts were right. But to steal the babe in order to force you into marriage? She thought you were dead. I saw her face when she learned you were alive. She was truly shocked and . . . immensely relieved."

"Fancy is right. She stole the babe for gain. She came to you wanting money."

"Her father wanted money. All she asked was to be allowed to remain as the child's nanny."

The same thoughts that had been swirling through his mind with the whiskey. He'd been so angry, felt so betrayed . . . dishonesty marred her actions.

"She said she loved John, didn't tell me the truth

because she thought she could only assure that she remained in his life if we thought she was his mother,"
Stephen muttered.

"Perhaps we should not have been so quick to draw
conclusions."

"Have you talked with Mother about this situation?"

"She's off enjoying the waters with Lady Lynnford."

"That does not mean you've not told her."

"You are a suspicious soul."

"Because those around me are continually conniv-
ing and plotting." He tossed back his whiskey. "Let me
know the moment your man returns."

He refilled his glass and moved it from shadow to
light, light to shadow. Sadness to joy. Laughter to tears.
Despair to hope. Love to emptiness.

As Mercy packed the last of her belongings into
the trunk, she admitted that seven days had not been
nearly enough time, but she had crammed a lifetime of
memories into them. She sang lullabies to John and allowed him to sleep in the bed with her. With footmen
dogging her footsteps, she strolled with him through
the garden and showed him a newly forming bud.
He could not have cared less, but he gurgled anyway.
Spring would soon be upon them. Jeanette would be
staying on, and she promised to send reports. It was
even possible that their paths might cross in a park
or two.

She considered fighting for her right to stay, trying
again to convince Stephen that she had not deceived
him. But she couldn't remain here as his wife. He, who
had promised on a cold night a lifetime ago to never
harm her, had effectively and with harsh words broken

that promise. She considered telling him, but she had no desire to add to the memory of that night that she'd already given him.

It no longer mattered which of their behaviors was the most egregious. They had both wronged each other. Their pasts—what she remembered, what he did not—made matters all the worse. She could see no hope for reconciliation. And so she saw no reason to stay.

She would not allow John to grow up in a household where his father despised his mother. He would not lack for love. He would receive plenty from Jeanette in that regard. And Fancy would no doubt ignore him for the most part. Which in all likelihood was for the best.

It cut her deeply to think of Fancy warming Stephen's bed, and so she shoved it from her mind as she had cast out other painful memories. They would no doubt visit when she slept, and she'd not have Stephen to make them retreat. But she would find a way to deal with it.

Adversity had strengthened her. She would survive.

A rap sounded and the door opened. The maid curtsied. "M'lady, the carriage is waiting. James is here to take your trunk down."

"He may have it." She walked from the room and down the hallway to the nursery.

Jeanette stopped bouncing John on her lap. "This is not fair."

"Fair is what we make it." She lifted John into her arms and swayed back and forth. "Oh, my precious boy, I shall miss you. Your father is a good man, even if he is amazingly stupid. Know I shall always be with you."

She kissed his brow, then hugged Jeanette, wanting John close to her for as long possible. She considered taking him down the stairs, but she was on the verge of tears. Nothing would be gained by delaying the inevitable. She returned him to Jeanette's waiting arms.

"Take good care of my precious child. Love him as though he were your own."

With tears clouding her eyes, Jeanette nodded. Mercy straightened her spine, the better to bear the weight of her burden, and strode from the room.

She was halfway down the stairs when she saw Stephen standing in the entry hallway. Sunlight poured in through the windows and created a halo around his handsome form, making him appear to be some sort of angel. One night he had been her avenging angel.

But she could tell by the set of his jaw, the hardness in his eyes, that he'd not be saving her today. She came to a stop before him. She wanted to hate him with every fiber of her being, but she couldn't. She owed him too much. And somewhere buried within the shards of her heart was one remnant that still beat for him and him alone.

They stared at each other for a moment that seemed to stretch into years.

Finally, he removed an envelope from his jacket pocket. "A thousand pounds to help you get settled somewhere."

"Keep it. Use it to pay for the silver I stole."

"Mercy, you can't leave here with nothing."

"I leave with my pride." She swept around him and marched out the door, down the steps, a steady refrain pounding with each landing of her shoes that took her farther from her child.

I will not cry, I will not cry, I will not cry.

With her head held high, she approached the waiting carriage.

"Mercy?"

Taking in a shuddering breath, she shored up her resolve, her strength to once again face him. She spun around.

For a heartbeat, he seemed uncertain standing there. "Why did you keep John?"

"I've already told you. Because he was part of you."

"And if I'd not married you?"

"I find it a trivial waste of time to speculate on what might have been or might not have been."

He wasn't happy with her answer. He'd wanted more. She no longer cared what he wanted.

"When you are settled, please send word where you are," he said. "It will make things easier if I know how my solicitor may get in touch as we seek to separate our lives."

A divorce then. He was going to divorce her. More shame and humiliation. She'd borne much worse.

She angled her chin. "I have a wish for you, dear husband. I pray you never remember what happened in Scutari. For if you do, you will never forgive yourself."

She swiftly turned and, with the help of the footman, climbed into the carriage. She didn't glance out the window as the carriage rolled by. She didn't want her last image to be of Stephen standing forlorn in the drive or of Jeanette standing at an upstairs window holding John close.

But with each clop of the horses' hooves that took her away, she felt her strength seeping out of her. By the time they turned onto the main road, she was sobbing inconsolably. She'd never felt such pain, and she'd suffered greatly in the past. But this was worse than anything she'd ever experienced. She didn't know how she'd survive it.

Suddenly there was a shout. "Halt! Hold up there!"

The carriage came to a thundering stop. Was it highwaymen?

Oh, dear God, not brutes, not again. The door swung open, she screamed at the top of her lungs, and lunged toward the shadowy figure.

"Hey! Here now," he said, grabbing her wrists, pulling her close, stilling her actions. "Lady Lyons. It's me, Leo."

Recognizing the voice now, she sagged against him. "I'm sorry. You must think me a ninny." She looked up into his kind face. He grinned.

"I suspect you've had a very upsetting day." He handed her his handkerchief. "Come along with me, the duchess wishes to see you."

"I have no desire for further chastisement."

"My dear girl, she intends to provide you with sanctuary."

Chapter 24

I go to take the waters and return to find that my son has suffered a complete loss of his senses."

Sprawled in a chair in his library, Stephen was not in the mood for company this evening. It didn't help matters that his mother arrived with Lynnford in tow.

Mercy's parting words had been eating at him all day. He'd banged his head against the wall for a good five minutes striving to shake some memories free. Or perhaps he was simply striving to punish himself.

She'd manipulated him into marrying her. Only he'd wanted to marry her. She'd not held his feet to the fire. She hadn't expected him to marry her. She'd said that. A lie. To give him a small sense of freedom, to make him think the idea was his.

She was not that scheming.

"Now is not a good time, Mother."

"When would be? When you've finished off another bottle?"

"Another two, more like."

"Oh, Stephen." In a rustle of silk, she took the chair across from him. "You were happy with her. Why did you send her away?"

Rather than respond, he watched the way Lynnford

stood behind the chair and folded his hand over the duchess's shoulder. How many times over the years had he taken up that exact pose, offering her strength when she had to deal with her unruly and ofttimes rebellious sons?

"Isn't he stepping in where Leo should be?" he asked, nodding toward Lynnford. He'd hardly been able to tolerate the wait of reaching his majority, because it had meant no longer having to answer to the man who had been stern and implacable when it came to raising him.

"He is your . . . guardian. It is his place to be here."

"I reached my majority long ago. I'm past the age of needing a guardian."

"A friend, then," Lynnford said, his gaze razor-sharp as it homed in on Stephen.

They'd never been close. Stephen had been a constant disappointment to the man who had served as the replacement of a father. After Stephen's father had died, Ainsley's father had taken on the role. In his will, he'd named Lynnford as guardian of his son by birth and his sons by marriage. In his youth, Stephen had felt as though there was no permanence. Men came and went. Then, of course, there were his mother's numerous lovers.

Was it any wonder that he'd never even entertained the notion of settling for one woman? Had never had a desire to marry? Until Mercy. The thought of being with another woman had not even crossed his mind while Mercy had warmed his bed.

Getting a divorce was a complicated process that involved courts and Parliament. If he managed to secure one, he could marry Fancy. Unfortunately, he had no desire whatsoever to take her to wife. Stephen had vivid memories of bedding her, several times. She was delightful. He'd enjoyed her. She was John's mother.

But he could not envision her as his lady.

Perhaps it was only because Mercy still preyed on his mind.

"I understand that Leo held up my carriage this afternoon. Stole its cargo."

His mother smiled. "He does enjoy the dramatic. We feared if she got to London, we might never find her, so he sought to catch her before she'd gone too far."

"Is she in your residence then?"

His mother gave a brusque nod. As much as he wanted to know how Mercy fared, he refrained from asking. Why torment himself further? He did not want to know if she was still weeping. He'd seen her struggling to hold back the tears. God help him, he'd almost begged her to stay.

"She deceived me. She is not John's mother."

"She may not have given birth to him, but make no mistake, she is his mother. She will do anything to protect him, to provide him with a safe harbor. Trust me. I know of what I speak."

"I suppose you're about to tell me that you did *not* give birth to me."

She hesitated and his gut tightened. He wished he'd not been drinking ever since Mercy left. Surely, surely, his mother was not here to tell him—

"I most assuredly gave birth to you," she finally said. "Had a devil of a time of it, if you are even remotely interested in knowing the truth. You were always a difficult child. Two days of hell you put me through, and then you were born . . . and I've lost count of all the days of hell you've put me through since."

His mouth twitched. With her acerbic tone, she could always make him smile. He stroked the silky ridge of his damned scar. "Is Mercy all right?"

"Of course she's not all right. What sort of idiot question is that?"

"Has she at least stopped crying?"

"Probably not."

"You're here to torment me."

"No. Well, it may seem that way when I am done. You think she has deceived you because she didn't tell you everything. Sometimes we hold secrets to protect those we love."

"And you no doubt know of what you speak because you have secrets."

His mothered gnawed on her lower lip. "I do. I have one. I have held it close, because revealing it could hurt so many people. I am torn, because telling it will place a burden on you, and I would spare you the weight of that if I could."

"I have no interest in your secrets. They are yours."

"How I wish that was true. But this particular one, while I have kept it, it is not mine, it is yours. But I must have your word that you will not tell a soul, because it can cause great suffering. And I will not have that."

"You and Leo are well matched. You both love the dramatic."

"Your word."

"I prefer that you not tell me, but if you insist . . . you have my word."

"I would prefer not to tell you as well, but I think you should know so you may better understand Mercy."

Stephen sat up, remembering Mercy's parting shot. "You know something about my time in the Crimea?"

"No, darling. I know something about your birth." She took a deep breath, released it. "The Earl of West-cliffe is not your father."

Stephen felt as though she'd punched him in the gut. "Then who the devil is my father?"

"I have that honor," the Earl of Lynnford said.

Stephen felt like an utter and complete idiot. How could he have not seen it?

He stared at the man who had ridden him hard his entire life . . . He shook his head and came out of the chair. "No. No. You always hated Westcliffe, Mother. You just didn't want me to be his son."

"He and I ceased having relations once we knew I was carrying our first child. Since I delivered Morgan, his heir, we never recommenced. He was satisfied with his lover and I . . . I took one of my own."

Suddenly chilled, Stephen moved nearer to the fire and stood with his forearm pressed to the mantel. "Why not tell me?"

"Several reasons. I was married to Westcliffe when you were born, so on paper, he is your father. I saw nothing to gain for you except to make you feel an out-cast. The only thing you and Morgan seemed to have in common is sharing a father. Then, of course, there is Lynnford's family. I thought it would be very hard on them if they knew that he had fathered you."

"That he was unfaith—"

"No! He was not married during the time we were lovers. Once he married his countess, everything was over between us."

Stephen glared at the man who stood stoically behind his mother. "Did you know?"

"Not for some years. Eventually I . . . began to wonder. Then when we thought you were dead, your mother told me."

She was the next recipient of his hard look. "And you didn't think he needed to know?"

"What was to be gained? He had a family."

He wanted to lash out at her, lash out at Lynnford, lash out at the world. At himself. He did not want to ponder the consequences of this news. "What has all this to do with Mercy?"

"She told you she was John's mother because she loved him. I did not tell Lynnford you were his son because I knew it would bring him pain and place him in a difficult position. To claim you would hurt his countess. And knowing he was your father wouldn't change your lot in life at all."

"You should have told me. I had a right to know."

"Yes, I quite agree. But my point, Stephen, is that we will do anything to protect those we love. Anything."

Stephen stood at the window in his bedchamber, drinking brandy and gazing out at the distant fog-shrouded torches that lined the drive. He couldn't quite bring himself to climb into bed yet. The bed he'd shared with Mercy.

He'd barely slept while at his brother's residence. Here, at his own residence, it would be near impossible. There were other beds. He could seek out one of them. But he was determined to be rid of her in his mind and that required conquering every aspect that reminded him of her.

And there was a damned devil of a lot that reminded him of her.

It didn't help matters that once his mother and Lynnford—his deuced father—had left, Stephen wanted desperately to talk with Mercy. To sit with her on a sofa, to have her caress his hair with her slender fingers. To have her hold his gaze and reassure him that nothing had changed with this sudden news.

But matters had changed. He had five half-siblings, for Christ sake. He'd always enjoyed their company, but he'd be looking at them differently now. He knew what they didn't. With Lady Lynnford's failing health, his mother had asked him to hold the secret close. He certainly had no plans to shout it to the world. He wasn't quite certain how he felt about Lynnford being his father.

A part of him felt a sort of betrayal because he'd not known. But truly, what difference would it have made? Lynnford had served as his guardian, had been there for so many occasions. He'd taught him to hunt pheasant, to fish, to ride.

He'd been his mother's lover. She'd given Stephen leave to tell Westcliffe and Ainsley, but he wasn't quite ready for that. What good would come of them knowing?

He continually circled back to that. Not all truths needed to be known by everyone. Some didn't need to be known at all.

John's crying intruded on his thoughts. The boy was angry about something, wailing so loudly that Stephen wondered if he'd get any sleep at all tonight. Setting his drink aside, he wandered from his bedchamber to the nursery. Jeanette was pacing, bouncing John. The boy's face was a mottled red.

Jeanette turned, her disconcertedness obvious. "I'm sorry, sir. He won't stop crying. I know he's not hungry. It's only been an hour since I fed him. He's not wet. I don't know why he's carrying on so. Shall I send for a physician?"

John was wailing as though his heart was breaking.

"No," Stephen said quietly. "Let me give it a go."

Jeanette couldn't hide her startlement at his offer. "Are you sure, sir?" she asked as Stephen took the bawling babe from her.

He'd hoped for immediate silence. Instead he got a rise in crescendo. His son was furious. "You're not happy with me at the moment, are you, lad? I'm not quite happy with myself, either."

Jostling John slightly, he studied Jeanette for a moment. "Did you know the truth about the boy's mother?" he finally asked.

"Yes, sir. I know that Lady Lyons is his mother."

Stephen gave her a wry twist of his lips. "In Paris, did you know about Fancy?"

Jeanette shook her head. "No. Lady Lyons sought me out after the lady had left. When I met her, it was only her and John, and the babe was so hungry. She had tried dribbling milk into his mouth but he'd have none of it. I don't think she'd slept in two days. She'd told me"—she gazed down at the floor—"that her . . . milk had dried up." She lifted her eyes to Stephen. "I did not know she had not given birth to John until she told me a few nights ago."

Stephen nodded. "Thank you for that."

He turned—

"Sir?"

He glanced back, waited while Jeanette wrung her hands. "I know it is not my place . . . but the boy is hers. It does not matter from which womb he came."

Stephen did little more than nod as he left the room. He wondered if Mercy had inspired such devotion and loyalty in Scutari.

He carried John to his bedchamber and laid him on the bed. He tucked a pillow beside him and lavender wafted up. John paused mid-yell, his eyes wide and blinking.

"That's what you were missing, isn't it? That's the reason I haven't gone to bed yet. Because she's still here."

He nudged his finger against the boy's hand and it fisted around his finger. Stephen caressed John's soft hair with his other hand. "You don't give a damn that she didn't give birth to you, do you?"

John's eyes closed, popped open.

"Did she steal you? That's the question. Did she always plan to use you? Why wasn't she honest with me from the beginning?"

He'd get no answers from John. The infant had drifted off to sleep.

Stephen pressed his lips to the boy's head. "I miss her, too, lad," he whispered. "I miss her, too."

Chapter 25

Unfortunately, we are unable to visit at your residence. However, I thought it would interest you to know that John's nursemaid will be taking him through Hyde Park at 2:00.

My son has lost all shred of decency," the duchess said as she strolled into the gallery where Mercy was having her portrait painted by Leo.

She'd told Leo countless times that she was not in the mood to pose, but he'd insisted.

"What else do you have to do with your time?" he'd asked.

But time wasn't the issue. She had far too much of it to fill with regrets and longing for what might have been. She'd told him honestly, "It will be a portrait of a woman whose heart is breaking."

He didn't seem to care, and quite honestly, neither did she any longer. So here she sat, gazing out on the dreary day while he stood behind his easel. She'd written three letters to Stephen trying to explain everything, but words on paper seemed so inadequate and she'd torn each one up before she'd completely finished it. Stephen had told her that he loved her, so what did it matter if it appeared she'd tricked him into marriage? At the base of it all was her love for him and for John. But as she'd feared, the foundation was not enough to weather the secret when it was uncovered.

Why hadn't she simply told him the truth when Fancy had shown up in their lives? In allowing her fears to rule her good sense, she'd lost exactly what she'd feared she would: John and Stephen.

She was so accustomed to snuggling against Stephen through the night that she'd hardly slept since leaving Roseglenn. She'd slept in his arms in Scutari, after she'd been brutalized, when her mind, body, and spirit had been shattered. She'd never thought to want a man to touch her again, but he'd been different. One of London's most notorious gentlemen had made no untoward advances. He'd provided her with a safe harbor from the storm. Now she felt as though he'd tossed her back onto the choppy seas—but he'd somehow managed to give her the knowledge to stay afloat. She'd not succumb to the loneliness or her fears. She would survive this banishment. She would emerge from it stronger, until nothing could ever hurt her again.

"I asked him to send John 'round for a visit with his grandmother"—the duchess continued, and Mercy perked up, straightened, her vows quickly forgotten at the thought of seeing John—"and he refused my request."

Mercy slumped back down and gazed outside. The past three days had been interminable. She needed to find a purpose in her life. Perhaps she'd contact Miss Nightingale. Surely, she could recommend her to a hospital in London. If Mercy were near, there was always a chance that she might see John.

"However," the duchess continued mysteriously, "the boy will be in Hyde Park at two with his nursemaid."

Mercy sat up again, hope once more beating wildly in her chest. "Only his nursemaid?"

"Apparently."

"Will you excuse me, Leo? I must prepare to go to the park."

She didn't wait for his permission, because it didn't matter what he said. Nothing was going to prevent her from getting to the park to see John.

She sat on a bench alone. She'd arrived an hour early just in case the time in the letter had been a mistake or circumstances changed and required an earlier arrival at the park. She didn't want to walk about because she feared that she and Jeanette would be like two ships passing in the night. Better to sit in one place and simply wait.

But dear Lord, the moments ticked by so slowly that she thought she might go insane. She also had to admit that as much as she longed to see John, she also wished she could catch a glimpse of Stephen. She wondered how he fared. She knew she should care nothing at all about him, but the heart was fickle and forgiving. It made excuses for his no longer trusting her, no longer wanting her. She *had* deceived him, and while it had all been with the best of intentions, it had led her down a wayward road.

She thought about writing her father, but she was fairly certain that he would be convinced that her true actions were as egregious as her implied behavior had been. While she could claim that she'd never lied, neither had she been completely honest.

No one stopped to speak with her, for which she was immensely grateful. She didn't wish to be distracted from her purpose. She quickly scanned every person walking by, searching, searching, searching—

And then she spotted Jeanette and the black perambulator. Joy surged through her with such intensity as to bring her to her feet. Waving frantically to catch the nursemaid's attention, she hurried forward, dodging around elegant couples. When she finally reached Jeanette, she gave her a warm hug.

"Whatever are you doing here?" Jeanette asked, clearly dumbfounded. "I wasn't able to get a message to you."

"Sir Stephen sent word to his mother that you would be in the park with John." Reaching into the basket, she lifted out her son, hugged him tightly, held him up to inspect him, then held him close once more. With him nestled against her shoulder, she swayed back and forth, inhaling his sweet fragrance. "Oh, my dear, dear sweet boy. Mummy has missed you so terribly much."

"He misses you as well," Jeanette reassured her. "Sleeps with his father or not at all."

"Truly?" Mercy asked. "Sir Stephen allows him to sleep in his bed?"

She couldn't imagine that the man who had paid so little attention to John in the beginning was now providing a haven for him in his bedchamber. Was it because of his feelings toward the boy's real mother?

"He does. And it is the strangest thing. He'll not let anyone wash the bed linens."

"Why ever not?"

"He doesn't confide in the servants, of course, but

I think it is because he's not yet ready to lose your fragrance."

Was he missing her then? If so, then why not come to visit with her?

"Is he well? Sir Stephen?"

Jeanette glanced around guardedly as though she feared someone might overhear her. "He's turned into something of an ogre. The only time he isn't grumbling is when he's with John."

"He should not be taking his anger at me out on others."

"He doesn't. It's just that it's abundantly clear that he isn't content."

She felt the now-familiar prickle of guilt. If only she'd trusted him. "I did him a disservice."

"You defend his sending you away?"

"I understand his anger. He thought he had given me John." She touched the curls on his head. "And what of . . . the other? Is she living there now?"

"No. She arrived for dinner last night. Sir Stephen brought her to the nursery, but she merely eyed John as though he were an odd creature she'd never seen before. She didn't hold him. She looked terrified of him, if you want to know the truth."

"How can anyone be frightened of my boy?" Mercy asked, kissing his head. "Jeanette, how long do you have in the park?"

"Only an hour."

Smiling with joy, Mercy said, "It is an hour more than I ever thought to have again. Come along, I brought a blanket. It's over by the bench. We shall simply sit and visit for a while. I want to know everything John's done since I last saw him."

And if she could find the strength she would not inquire further about his father, although Lord help her, she was desperate for news of him.

Sitting astride his horse on a small tree-covered rise, Stephen watched Mercy smiling and carrying on with his son. She appeared so joyously happy, so excited, so full of life. He thought he even heard her laughter on the breeze, although surely he was too far away for such a gift. She sat on a blanket with Jeanette, but it was obvious that all her attention was focused on John.

People stopped to talk with her, to smile, to share in her joy.

How different she was from Fancy.

Fancy had come to visit the evening before. John had cried whenever she'd tried to hold him. She quickly gave up trying. He didn't blame her. It would take some time for the boy to get used to her.

He tried not to compare her to Mercy, but he couldn't see his wife giving up as easily as Fancy had. She'd have cooed and cajoled and won him over. No matter how long it took.

When Jeanette had finally taken John away, Stephen and Fancy had gone in to dinner. It had been a ghastly affair. He'd asked her to tell him about her time in the East. He'd not revealed that his own memories were lacking. He'd simply indicated that he wanted to know what she'd been doing when he was no longer near the hospital, when he was back at the battlefield.

Complaining a lot, it appeared. Floors had to be scrubbed. Shirts were sewn so the men would have something to wear other than their bloody clothes. Bandages were rolled. Their living quarters were small and crowded, a dozen women sleeping in one cramped room. The food was not up to snuff. Comforts were few. It was horrendous.

Mercy had never complained about her own discomforts. She had been more concerned with the discomfort of the men, and harbored guilt because she'd been unable to eradicate their suffering completely. She still dreamed of them, of what she considered her failings.

Who held her now when the nightmares came? Leo, perhaps. The man was devoted to Stephen's mother, but he had an artist's gentle soul. Surely, he would hear her cries; he'd not leave her alone to face her demons.

Not as her bastard of a husband had done. No matter how justified he felt in his anger, the guilt ate at him.

Stephen had never intended to ever allow her to see John again. He was loath to admit it but he'd brought Jeanette all the way into London to stroll through the park for an hour when other parks were nearer to his residence for one reason and one reason alone: he wanted to see Mercy, even if only from a distance. He'd known if he sent a missive to his interfering mother alerting her to John's visit, she'd share the news with Mercy, and damnation, but he'd needed to see her smile in order to erase the painful memory of her parting. He, who abhorred the loss of memories, wanted to forget the moment when she'd strode out of his life with such dignity and strength and poise. Dear God, not even a queen could have been so regal.

Yet gazing on her now only served to add more remorse to the tragedy of her being sent away. He damned his pride to perdition, because it wouldn't allow him to invite her back into his life.

Tugging on the reins, he turned his horse about and began to gallop away. He'd seen enough. He'd seen too much. His foolish pride prevented him from going in the other direction, in going toward Mercy, in greeting her, in talking with her. He sought to punish her and all he accomplished with this silly farce today was to punish himself.

And Leo, it seemed, was intent on punishing him as well, damn the man. When Stephen returned home, he discovered a small package waiting for him on his desk. Inside was a miniature of Mercy—

And damn it all if she didn't look like a woman whose heart had shattered. With his finger, he touched the face rendered in oils. It was a poor substitute for her warm skin.

Unfortunately, he no longer knew where to place the blame for this hideous life he now lived. Fancy, for following him to the East and getting herself with child? Mercy, for pretending she was the child's mother? Himself, for allowing her deception to cut him to the core?

"My man had no luck in Paris," Ainsley said. "He was unable to confirm whether the child was stolen or abandoned. Apparently, Fancy and Mercy were most discreet."

Stephen stood at the window in the library. It seemed of late all he did was gaze out windows, as though he would spy Mercy strolling past, introducing John to the world around him. No joy greeted his days.

Fancy had visited again, but she had no interest in John. Instead she spoke of clothing styles and the up-coming Season and all the balls they would have to attend. And the theater. And dinners. They would be the talk of the town, she assured him.

Ah, yes, in the midst of scandal once more. Surrounded by speculation and gossip. Why did she crave what he abhorred?

He pulled the miniature of Mercy from his pocket where he always kept it now. He thought of the dinners he'd shared with her, the lively conversations, the quiet moments. He thought of waking up in the morning with her nestled in his arms. He reminisced about their lovemaking. Always different. Always breathtaking. Always touching—on so many levels. She caressed his body, embraced his soul, reached deep within his heart. When he was with her, it was almost as though the past no longer mattered.

"I did have a bit of luck, though," Ainsley said now.

Stephen tried to give the appearance that he had a care for whatever it was his brother was blabbering about, but he was once again lost in the memories of Mercy. The way she could look at him with a slight tilting of her head, a mischievousness in her whiskey eyes that spoke of her being both a lady and a vixen. Innocent yet knowledgeable. Sweet and yet tart. Demure and yet daring.

Fancy had become as skilled as he in the art of seduction, and yet he'd not even bothered to kiss her since she'd been re-introduced into his life. He knew of a time when he'd barely been able to keep his hands off her. But he had no desire at all to marry her, even if she was John's mother.

"I discovered a sergeant who served under you. Gent named Mathers. Name mean anything?"

"Mathers?" Stephen rolled the name around in

his head, hoping it would latch on to some shred of memory. Tall or short? Fat or thin? He couldn't envision the man. He could draw up nothing from the dark recesses of his mind. "No."

"He'll be at the White Stallion tonight if you want to buy him a pint."

Stephen glanced over his shoulder at Ainsley. "And what would be the point in that?"

"To begin filling in the holes of your memory."

Business was brisk and the crowds boisterous at the White Stallion, but Stephen managed to locate an empty table in a far corner. He thought he should be excited at the prospect of talking with someone who had fought beside him. Hadn't he for months now wanted to know exactly what had happened, what he didn't remember?

Instead he wondered if there would be more surprises, things he wished he didn't know. Like the fact that Mercy was truly not John's mother.

Why had she never encouraged Stephen to seek the truth about his time in the Crimea? What did she truly know? Her parting words resounded through his head, made an icy shiver race up his back.

I have a wish for you, dear husband. I pray you never remember what happened in Scutari. For if you do, you will never forgive yourself.

What had happened? What had he done? Why could he not remember?

He'd hoped Fancy could shed some light on the matter, but she spoke only of her experiences there, of their time together. If she had a clue regarding precisely to what Mercy had been referring, Fancy was skilled at pretending she didn't. What the devil had happened over there?

Suddenly, a large, strapping fellow blocked his view of the establishment. His jacket was brown tweed, one of the arms pinned up as it was not needed. The man's long brown hair appeared a bit ragged, but it was obvious he'd recently shaved and his brown eyes were somber. They were the eyes of a man who'd seen a good deal more horror than most men. Stephen was taken aback by the kinship he felt with this stranger.

"Good to see you, Major," the man said in a voice that even when spoken low still boomed. "Or I s'pose I should say Sir Stephen. I saw in the *Times* where you got knighted. Well-deserved, sir."

Stephen almost asked, "Was it?" Instead, he took a chance and said, "Good to see you, too, Mathers. Join me."

The man took a chair and Stephen had the serving girl bring over a pint.

"I'm sorry to see you lost your arm," he said somberly, wondering if he should have known that.

Mathers shrugged. "Would have lost me life if not for you, sir. I swear you were a bloody heathen out on the battlefield. You were a sight to see. Gave no quarter. Then carrying me off the field under fire. Not just me. Others too, I hear, but that was after my time." He lifted the tankard. "Still, to the boys of the Light Brigade, sir."

Stephen tapped his mug against Mathers's. "To the Light Brigade."

They sat in silence for a few moments. It was obvious Mathers was lost in reflections. Stephen wanted to know the path his mind traveled. Perhaps he should tell him where he stood—with no memories at all. Here was a man who could tell him anything he wanted to know about his time in the Crimea.

"I don't remember you, Mathers."

The man rubbed his head. "Well, sir, I don't know what to say to that. I'd never considered myself an easy bloke to forget, what with my size and all."

"I was wounded, you see. You came back without your arm, and I came back without part of my mind."

"You mean, you don't remember nuthin'?"

"Nothing at all."

Mathers seemed to ponder that revelation. "I'd heard you took a cannonball to the head."

"Not sure if I'd still have my head if that was the case, but something happened."

"If you don't mind me saying so, sir, it might not feel like it, but it's a blessing. It was awful out there, sir. Awful. I hear there's nearly five thousand buried in the cemetery near the hospitals in Scutari."

"Five thousand," Stephen whispered. How had he forgotten something that had to have been horrendous? "They're expecting peace any day now."

"Yes, sir. I pray for it." He shook his head. "We were so bloody cocky when we marched off. Held our own, though, sir. But, God help us. What a price."

Again they fell into silence as though the words that needed to be said were too heavy. Finally, Stephen asked, "Tell me, Mathers, do you remember a nurse, a nurse named Mercy?"

Mathers shook his head. "Sorry, sir. Can't say as I do, but then I weren't nearly as familiar with the nurses as you were. I remember there was always at least one at your bedside."

"But I'm interested in one in particular. Mercy," Stephen insisted. "Mercy Dawson."

Mathers grinned. "Miss Dawson. Yes, sir. Remember her well. An angel she was. If I may say so, she worked as tirelessly as Miss Nightingale. Many a night I heard her praying over a lost soul. Shame what happened to her that bloody night. Can't believe she didn't leave straightaway, but she was there the next time I was wounded. Held my hand when they took my bloody arm."

Stephen felt an uneasiness that he couldn't explain. He didn't want to think about what Mathers had suffered. He was a big brute of a man who'd not welcome sympathy. But something else he'd mentioned had Stephen breaking out in a cold sweat. "What happened to her, Mathers?"

"She was attacked, sir. Fortunate for her that we got there when we did, you and me, although I'm a-betting she was a-wishing we'd gotten there before the first blackguard was finished with her and the second was queuing up."

Stephen's stomach roiled. Mathers couldn't be implying what Stephen thought he was. Mercy had told him that he'd arrived there in time. He'd saved her. Were they lining up to hit her? *No, you damned fool, they wouldn't line up for that. They'd only line up if what they were doing allowed only one man at a time—*

God, he thought he was going to be ill. He took another chance, praying that this time he wasn't wrong. "We gave them a sound beating, didn't we, Mathers?"

"We did, sir. Especially the first blighter. Thought you were going to kill him. Maybe you did. He didn't leave the field following the next battle. But then neither did the other two. I made damned sure one of them didn't. Either you or the Russians took care of the third. My money was always on you." He leaned back, blew out a quick breath. "Whew! I never before confessed to what I done. It's a bit of a relief to have it off my chest."

Mathers looked at him expectantly, as though he wanted a reciprocated confession.

"Sorry, man. As I said, I don't remember . . . any of it. But I've no doubt that what you did was the right thing to do. And I hope I had your courage to see justice done."

Mathers nodded and stared into his tankard. Then he tossed back what remained and ordered another.

After it arrived, Stephen asked, "What of Miss Whisenhunt? Did you know her?"

Mathers scratched his jaw. "Yeah, she was a real beauty, but she weren't as caring as Miss Dawson. It always seemed like she thought of everything as a chore. I know it was work, all of it, everything they did. None of it was fun. But Miss Dawson always made it seem as though she was glad to be able to do something to ease a man's suffering. Always smiling with a gentleness in her eyes that reminded a man of home, reminded him why he was fighting. I think many a soldier fell in love with her, sir. I wonder what happened to her."

"She had the misfortune of becoming my wife."

"Where the devil is she?"

Startled from her relaxing pose on the fainting couch, her bare feet in Leo's lap where they were receiving his devoted attention, his mother glared at Stephen standing in the doorway. "Good evening to you as well. I daresay you look like hell."

"Where is she?" he repeated, in no mood to suffer through her taunting.

She must have realized it because she answered quickly, "The blue bedchamber."

He rushed up the stairs, taking the steps two at a time, the length of his stride torturing his leg, but he ignored it. When he arrived at the correct bedchamber, he threw open the door with such force that it banged against the wall.

Mercy leaped up from the chair by the window where she'd been reading, the book falling to the floor with a soft thud. He could see her trembling in the white linen nightdress, her bare toes curling into the carpet. He saw the moment she regained her composure and straightened her backbone. She'd not be cowed by him. He couldn't see her being cowed by anyone.

He imagined some brute lifting her hem, spreading those sweet thighs—

"You lied to me about not lying to me." He took a step closer, and she held her ground. Brave, courageous Mercy. She'd been there to help the soldiers, to ease their suffering. If the men who'd attacked her weren't already dead, he'd tear them apart with his bare hands. He'd never felt so barbaric. Was this what he'd learned on the battlefield? "You told me I got there in time to stop them, in time to save you. I didn't."

She went as pale as snow and quivered as though she'd just been dunked in an icy river. Tears spilled onto her cheeks. Reaching behind her, she grabbed onto the back of the chair, needing something to support her. Any other woman who looked on the verge of collapse would have succumbed to her body's need. But not her. Somehow she found the strength to continue standing, just as she'd found the strength to return to the hospital, to care for the men. Courageous Mercy. His Mercy.

"Tell me you don't remember. Please, dear God, tell me you don't remember my shame and humiliation."

"I don't. Not a single second of what happened to you. But it was not your shame and humiliation, Mercy. It was theirs. For God's sake, why didn't you tell me?"

"Why would I? For the love of all that is holy, why would I want you to remember such an ugly, ugly . . ."

Tears rained down her face. She sank onto the chair and buried her face in her hands, her shoulders quaking with the force of her sobs. He wanted to touch her, to comfort her, but he'd sacrificed that right. He'd doubted her, and in so doing he'd doubted all that was virtuous. He'd hoped war had turned him into a better man, but it was her, everything he knew about her that called to him to be a finer person than he'd ever thought himself capable of being.

"If you hadn't held me afterward, touched me so tenderly, comforted me, I'm not sure I would have ever been able to stand the touch of another person." She lifted dew-filled eyes. "Nothing happened beyond that. Between you and I. A little touching, gentle caresses. On my face and my hands. Here." She touched just below her collarbone. "Where the first one tore at my bodice and gouged me. You kissed it. You murmured such sweet words. We only had until dawn. But you never left my side. You had Mathers find us a room. You washed . . . so tenderly where the brutish man had

been. I made a vow to myself that I would find a way
to repay you for your kindness."

"Kindness? Mercy, any man would have come to
your rescue—"

"Only any man didn't. You did. When Fancy told
me she was carrying your child, and she had to leave,
I went with her to ensure she was taken care of. When
she told me that she didn't want John, I could hardly
believe it. I told her I would take him. Then we saw
your name on the list of the dead. We argued over what
to do. John was all that remained of you. One morning
I awoke to discover Fancy was gone and John was still
there. I knew I had to bring him to your family. It was
all I ever intended. You must believe that."

His heart was shattering one word at a time. "I do,
Mercy. You don't have to say more."

"He was so like you. I fell in love with him a little
bit more each day. I couldn't bear the thought of leaving him. So I said I was his mother, because I thought
no one with any decency would separate a child from
his mother. When I learned you were alive, I feared if I
confessed to not being his mother, that you would find
fault with me and not want your son around a woman
who spouted lies. So I continued with the charade."

"It was no charade." He couldn't stop himself. He
cradled her cheek, cold and damp with her tears. "You
are his mother. Can you ever forgive me for doubting
you?"

She shook her head.

"Mercy, God, Mercy, I will do anything you ask of
me. I won't search for the memories anymore. I won't
worry about the past. I'll hoard every memory from

this moment on. They'll be enough if they include you."

"I was wrong to deceive you."

"You didn't. You are John's mother. I have no memory of our first night together, but I have no doubt, my dear, precious, courageous wife, that if I did remember it, I would discover that I had begun to fall in love with you that night."

Weeping, she fell into his lap. He held her close, rocking her, whispering sweet words of forgiveness and love. There was a familiarity to the moment that surprised him, as though he almost did remember holding her like this.

"Come home with me, Mercy. Come home to me and to John."

Against his shoulder, she nodded. Lifting her into his arms, he carried her from the room.

His mother was waiting expectantly at the bottom of the stairs. He wasn't surprised. He was astonished that she hadn't been standing in the bedchamber doorway listening.

"Where are you going?" she asked.

He tightened his hold on Mercy. "To make memories."

Everything seemed so familiar, so welcoming as Stephen escorted her into the residence. He'd held her close in the carriage as though he were afraid that if he released her for even a second, she'd disappear from his life forever. He'd kissed her and murmured how much he loved her, how he would ensure that she never regretted being married to him.

He made her feel special again, made her glad for every step she'd traveled along the path that had led her to him.

Upstairs they went to the nursery. After giving Mercy a few minutes to hold John close, breathe in his fragrance, and then tuck him back into bed, Stephen led her to the bedchamber. He made short work of removing her clothes and his. They tumbled onto the bed.

With reverence, he trailed his fingers over her body—slowly, provocatively. She skimmed her hands up his arms, over his chest.

"Don't think about it," she ordered softly.

He lifted his gaze to hers.

"That night. So long ago," she said.

"I can't think about what I don't remember."

But somehow he'd learned about it, and although he didn't have the memory, he now had the knowledge. He brushed his lips over her throat.

"I love you, Mercy," he whispered. "It almost killed me to send you away."

"Then why did you?"

"Stubborn pride. But more than that." He threaded his fingers through her hair, his palm cupping her cheek. "From the moment I woke up in that damned hospital, I've felt lost. Until you came into my life. You provided me with an anchor, and when I learned the truth, I felt as though I was once again floundering. It's not an excuse for my behavior. But rather an explanation for it."

"And now."

"I feel as though I've finally come home." He took her mouth gently, but with an urgency that spoke of desire loosely leashed. He would release it soon and they'd become lost in the heat and the passion, the familiarity of each other.

His touch was different this time. Or perhaps it

was only the way she perceived it. No secrets lay between them. Whatever memories were lost to him didn't matter. The two of them existed now, within this moment. Just as he'd said as he'd carried her out of his mother's residence, they would make new memories. She would give him so many that he'd never remember them all. Thousands upon thousands until neither of them thought about the past two years, until neither of them ever again spoke of Scutari. Or dreamed of it.

They took their time, caressing and stroking, as though each wanted to memorize every detail of the other, reaffirm the familiar, make note of the newly discovered. It always amazed her that somehow she always learned something new about him. A scar that had been overlooked, a spot on his side that was ticklish, an area that was more sensitive. They would have years of this. Learning, savoring, cherishing.

But she didn't want to think about the future. She wanted to concentrate on this single moment, the beauty of it as he joined his body to hers.

"Home," he whispered near her ear. "With you, I'm always home."

He began to rock against her, slowly at first and then more quickly. Her body reacted swiftly and strongly to the rhythm. They touched, they kissed. His mouth latched on to the peak of her breast, and he suckled. Pleasure tore through her in undulating waves, carrying her higher and higher. . .

To heights never before reached.

"Oh, God," she moaned, pressing him closer, digging her fingers into his shoulders.

"I love you, Mercy," he rasped, his breath harsh, labored.

Opening her eyes, she held his and saw the truth of his words. Not that she'd doubted, but here was more evidence, the love he felt for her reflected so clearly in the blue of his gaze.

"I love you, Stephen. I have for so long."

"Love me longer."

"I'll love you into eternity."

"You're the only one, the only one I've ever loved."

Groaning low, he dipped his head and pressed a kiss to the tiny scar on her collarbone that remained from that long ago night. If it had not already healed, she thought the press of his lips might have had the power to heal it. It was as though everywhere he touched, she felt renewed. Tonight was a cleansing, a ridding of lies, deceit, and mistrust. She'd always thought that when they were together they were as one. Only now did she realize that a thin barrier had existed between them, placed there by her fears of discovery. But now he knew the truth, all of it, and here he was. Whispering words that touched her deeply. Taking possession of her with a fierceness that claimed her as his and announced he was hers.

Raising himself above her, he slid into her, glided out, his movements deliberate, with purpose, lifting her awareness, spiking her pleasure until it climbed—

"Oh, my dear God!" She arched back, then curled around him, holding him near, pressing against him as his rhythm quickened.

He cried out her name as his body jerked and spasmed. He never loosened his hold on her gaze.

Triumph washed over his face, but it wasn't that of a victor. Rather it was that of a man who had conquered himself. As he lowered himself and buried his face in the curve of her throat, she circled her arms and legs around him, holding him tightly and dearly.

For the first time since she'd left Scutari, she felt as though she, too, had finally come home.

Chapter 26

Iwant to know everything, every moment I spent with you that I can no longer recall."

They were lying in bed, completely unclothed, she on her back, he raised up on an elbow, skimming his fingers over her continuously as though he couldn't bear the thought of even one second of not touching her.

Lowering his head, he pressed a kiss to the swell of her breast. "Tell me, Mercy."

And so she did.

Of how she'd first seen him sitting against a wall awaiting medical treatment. Of assisting with the surgery. The hours she'd sat by his side when fever raged. The talks of England they'd had while he was recovering. The nights when he'd gone out for some fresh air. When she had spotted him leaning against the building. The nights they'd taken a stroll, even though she knew she'd be suspected of notorious behavior, knew that if she were caught Miss N would return her to England.

"Why risk it?" he asked.

"Because like all women, I never could resist you."

He skimmed his knuckles along her cheek. "Never compare yourself to all women. You are nothing at all like any woman I've ever known."

They were quiet for several moments while she gathered her courage to tell the tale and he gathered the strength to hear it. Finally, she told him about the night of the attack. The horror of it. The wonder of it.

"You ordered Sergeant Mathers to find us a room. He did. It was only you and me in there. You laid me on the bed, examined me so carefully, so gently." She brushed her fingers through his hair at his temples. "You washed me. Then you held me, told me you cared for me. You gathered my tears with kisses. You made me believe that everything would be all right. That I could survive it. And so I did."

He cradled her cheek, held her gaze. "I love you so much. I don't know what the devil possessed me to send you away."

His mouth covered hers and once again they became a tangle of limbs, touching, exploring, pleasuring.

Tonight the lovemaking was different, more intense, more . . . free. No secrets. Only honesty between them.

When he filled her, she welcomed him gladly. They moved in a sinuous motion, the passion building, the fire burning. She had no doubt that he was hers, now and forever. Nothing, nothing at all would ever take him from her again.

When pleasure eclipsed all else, it was celebrated with him calling out her name.

Mercy, Mercy, *Mercy*.

The joyous jubilation swept away the last of her nightmares. As she nestled against him to fall asleep, she knew they'd never return.

In the hallway of the terraced residence Stephen waited to be received. It was nearly noon. He'd planned to arrive earlier, but his vixen of a wife had kept him in bed longer than he'd expected. Not that he was complaining. Once this business was over with, he planned to spend each morning in bed as late as his wife desired.

Glancing up at the sound of footfalls, he watched as Fancy descended the stairs, a provocative smile greeting him. She was still a fancy bit of work. He remembered a time when that smile had taken him to the edge of passion. He felt nothing for her now. Nothing at all.

"Good morning, darling," she cooed as she approached him with movements designed to entice.

She placed a hand on his chest and before she could get nearer, he extended the envelope between them. Her smile changed into one of anticipation and her eyes glowed. "What's this?"

"Four thousand pounds." He'd had to borrow it from Ainsley. "I believe that's the price you quoted my wife for her silence."

Confusion marred her features. She stepped back without taking his offering. "Why—"

"I made a mistake," he said flatly. "I mistook you for John's mother."

"I gave birth to him."

"That does not make you his mother. Mercy claimed that honor, and so she will keep him and me. This is simply a payment for your services. The only payment you'll ever receive from us. Do with it what you will. But do not bother us again."

She snatched the envelope from him. "I shall need more. Four thousand a year. Otherwise, I shall tell everyone the truth of your son's birth."

He smiled. "No, you won't. It would lessen your value. Make it more difficult to acquire a benefactor.

Men favor women who know how to prevent by-blows."

"I've discovered this is not the life I want." Once again she placed her hand on his chest. She looked up at him with a plea in her eyes. "Not every man is you. It is *you* whom I desire."

"I am taken."

"You'll grow bored with her."

"No, I won't. And if you do tell the world that you are my son's mother—so be it. I do not intend for him to grow up not knowing the truth. However, be prepared to face my wrath as well as my mother's."

She paled with the force of the second threat.

"Yes," he said quietly. "She can assure that London never opens its door to you again."

She crushed the envelope to her chest. "Another four thousand and I'll be silent."

"You're getting only what I just gave you. Go see Westcliffe. He'll help you invest it. Perhaps with his help you'll become a lady of leisure."

He turned to leave—

"Stephen, you will be back. And I will be waiting."

He glanced back at her. "I love Mercy. That will never change. Wait if you wish, but it will be in vain."

He strode from the residence and down the steps to the waiting carriage. Once inside, he kissed his wife passionately as the carriage took off. When he finally drew back, she asked, "Did it go well?"

"She'll not bother us."

"What do we do now?"

"Go see Leo and arrange to have a family portrait painted."

Her beautiful smile still had the power to take his breath away. He suspected it always would.

Epilogue

June 26, 1857
Hyde Park

It was called the Victoria Cross, each one cast from the bronze taken from a captured Russian cannon.

Standing in the park with Stephen's family, Mercy watched as Queen Victoria presented the symbol of valor to sixty-two soldiers, one of which was Mercy's much-beloved husband.

She recognized some of the faces, the names of the others who were honored. She had no fears that today's ceremony would bring forth the nightmares. She'd not had one in more than a year. What an incredible year it had been.

Fancy was no longer a part of their lives, although Mercy had heard through the duchess, who kept up with such things, that the girl was now enjoying her fifth benefactor.

Because Roseglenn was not part of Ainsley's entailment, Stephen had purchased it from him. The sheep were gone. He was raising horses. Lynnford would often come by to offer his advice. Some days their relationship was more strained than others. Mercy had not been surprised to discover he was Stephen's father. Stephen was slowly reconciling his feelings about it.

And in a few more months, John would have a brother or a sister.

With the ceremony finished, she watched as her husband strode toward her in his scarlet uniform. He was as handsome now as he'd been the first time she'd ever laid eyes on him.

Releasing John's hand, she laughed as he rushed headlong to his father. Stephen scooped him up and held him aloft, his laughter mingling with hers and John's. She'd never known such happiness.

Holding John tightly in one arm, he slipped the other around her and kissed her soundly.

While his heroics had been many, it was his carrying wounded men from the field of battle while under heavy enemy fire that had earned him this particular recognition.

Leaning back, she fingered the medal that was pinned to his jacket. "I'm so proud of you."

"I'm not certain I deserve it. I don't remember—"

She touched her fingers to his lips. "It doesn't matter. They remember," she said, indicating the other soldiers on the field.

He set down John, unpinned his medal from his jacket and pinned it to the bodice of her dress. "We'll share it," he told her, "because you're the one who truly deserves it."

Before she could protest, he took her into his arms and kissed her deeply while the world looked on. With his reputation, no one even raised an eyebrow. But Mercy knew the kiss symbolized much more. It was a celebration of their life, their love.

Next month, don't miss these exciting new love stories only from Avon Books

Wedding of the Season by Laura Lee Guhrke
Lady Beatrix Danbury always knew she'd marry William Mallory. So when he left England for the chance of a lifetime mere days before their wedding, Beatrix was heartbroken. Six years later, she's finally forgotten the wretch and is poised to make a splendid new match. Then William suddenly returns, and all the old feelings come rushing back…but is it too late?

Whisper Falls by Toni Blake
Following a failed career as an interior designer, Tessa Sheridan is forced to return home to make ends meet. A sexy bad boy neighbor who makes her feel weak and breathless is the last thing she needs…

Eternal Prey by Nina Bangs
Seeking vengeance for his brother's murder, Utah plans to vanquish all of his immortal enemies. Now that the beast within him is unleashed, he won't stop until every vampire is destroyed. But when he meets their beautiful, bewitching and mortal leader, Lia, they fall into a love that could prove dangerous for the both of them…

Sin and Surrender by Julia Latham
Paul Hilliard wants nothing to do with the League of the Blade—the secret, elite organization that raised him. But when he's offered a mission to save king and country, he can't refuse. Paul just never imagined his greatest challenge would be Juliana, the stunning warrior assigned as his partner for this task…

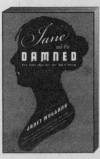

At Avon Books, we know your passion for romance—once you finish one of our novels, you find yourself wanting more.

May we tempt you with . . .

- **Excerpts** from our upcoming releases.

- Entertaining **extras**, including authors' personal photo albums and book lists.

- Behind-the-scenes **scoop** on your favorite characters and series.

- **Sweepstakes** for the chance to win free books, romantic getaways, and other fun prizes.

- Writing **tips** from our authors and editors.

- **Blog** with our authors and find out why they love to write romance.

- **Exclusive content** that's not contained within the pages of our novels.

Join us at
www.avonbooks.com